C000185131

FISSION IMPOSSIBLE

FISSION IMPOSSIBLE

Phil Janes

MILLENNIUM
An Orion Book
LONDON

Copyright © Phil Janes 1993

All rights reserved

The right of Phil Janes to be identified as the author of this work has been asserted by him in accordance with the Copyright, Designs and Patents Act 1988.

This edition first published
in Great Britain in 1993 by
Millennium
An imprint of Orion Books Ltd
Orion House, 5 Upper St Martin's Lane
London WC2H 9EA

A CIP catalogue record for this book is available from the British Library

ISBN: (Csd) 1 85798 060 3
(Ppr) 1 85798 061 1

Millennium
Book Twenty-Eight

Typeset by Deltatype Ltd, Ellesmere Port, South Wirral
Printed in England by Clays Ltd, St Ives plc

Dedication

For Paul Garland, Dave Hairs
and all the others who have laughed with me

I

Dragons were mythical, Peter Carlton knew; they didn't really exist, any more than leprechauns or tax rebates. Or if they did, then they lived by the sea and frolicked in the autumn mist, and occasionally ventured out from their weyrs to burn some pernicious cotton.

What they didn't do was lie slumped at the base of a tree displaying all the apparent vibrant energy of a geriatric semolina pudding.

Except, of course, that this one did.

What was more, the fantastical creature, which was, at least, recognizable as a dragon, looked almost ordinary in amongst the even more fantastical vegetation. Carlton felt like something from one of those shrinking movies as giant trees rose high above him, with trunks big enough to drive not only a road through, but a herd of cattle in chorus-line formation as well. Shrubs and bushes with leaves like roofing felt blocked his path. At least, he assumed they were trees and shrubs and bushes; they could just as easily have been camouflaged animals which would snap him up for a snack as soon as they felt a bit peckish. Then again they might be capable of doing that even if they were plants. And even the thick spongy moss or grass-like stuff under his feet might have been dangerous, for all he knew.

He didn't worry about it, which was probably best. If you've got to the stage where you worry about what grass might do to you, and you're not smoking it, then it's time to have a long lie-down.

Instead, he parted what he hoped were two fronds of a giant fern rather than, say, the legs of an upside-down sex-starved alien head burier, and looked into the light of a clearing in the forest.

And what light! The clearing was not only bathed in the stuff, it could have done a few lengths of backstroke had it felt the urge. A blinding bright white sun did something that sneered at 'shine' from the height of a slightly purple sky, purple because low on the horizon was the ageing red ball of what was clearly the poor relation in a binary star system.

But, for all its comparative ordinariness, the dragon was still the main attraction. It was a beautiful creature, its skin more golden than a summer sunset, with two wings that promised rainbow colours folded elegantly along its back. The body rose and fell gently as the creature breathed, and each time it exhaled, a little puff of smoke and flame accompanied the breath from the end of an elongated but far from ugly snout. Along with the sharp curving talons on its feet, it was a fair indication that this was not a pet.

What it was, Carlton was aware, was the dragon who never slept, and who for the past three thousand years had guarded with its very life the Golden Fleece, ever vigilant, ever watchful. No wonder its eyes were bloodshot as hell.

The Fleece, presumably, was the manky animal skin which hung from a low branch of the tree around which the animal and its tail were wound; a skin with the odd tuft of fur clinging forlornly to it only because rigor mortis wouldn't allow it to let go.

And that was his quest, or very nearly. What Carlton was after was not actually the Fleece, but the Fleas that lived on it. He allowed himself a brief sigh at the indignity of it all.

From his vantage point, crouched three inches behind Carlton, where he guarded against unlikely attack from the rear by bravely opening one eye every so often, Richard Curtis spoke.

'What can you see?'

Carlton glanced over his shoulder at the quivering form, then moved aside and held back the fern frond for his Captain. Curtis remained crouching where he was with his eyes tightly shut. 'Look for yourself.'

Curtis turned his head slowly towards the opening, and screwed up enough courage to unscrew one eye. The dragon did not show any signs of moving, its gaze apparently fixed on the ground a couple of feet in front of its nose.

'How are we supposed to get past that?' gasped Curtis.

Carlton was looking through the gap and around the clearing, starting with the skin and the dragon and working his way upwards, and there was a lot of upwards to work with.

'It looks like our only chance is to come down from above.

Start by climbing a tree back here and work our way round, then down.' He paused. 'Preferably quietly.'

At the words 'back here' Curtis immediately began shuffling forward to make sure that he was the further away from wherever 'back here' actually started. Through his carefully opened eye, he noticed that this left him now closer to the dragon, and he crouched even lower than before, so that his knuckles dragged on the ground. He turned to look up at the huge trees which Carlton suggested climbing, his jaw thrust out in indignation, then looked at his crew member, brows drawn down low.

'Do I *look* like a monkey?'

Carlton looked him up and down for a bit, then opened his mouth to reply. A noise from the other side of the clearing froze them both before Carlton could begin a quite lengthy list of similarities.

They turned slowly as one to stare, and listen. It was unlikely that the Fleas had voices sufficiently loud to carry across the thirty yards or so of open space, so suspicion settled on the dragon. Its lips moved, and the voice came again, confirming their deduction. This time they could make out the words.

'God, I'm knackered!' it said, and yawned expansively.

A small lick of flame accompanied the smoke which issued forth at this gesture, and when it blew away on the soft breeze, the two men could see a tear rolling slowly down each golden cheek.

What makes the dragon so sad? Curtis asked himself.

I don't know, he answered. Why don't you go and ask it?

He ignored himself.

'It looks sad,' said Carlton. 'It's crying, see?' Curtis nodded, trying to feel compassion in his soul, and failing utterly. No-one ever felt sorry for *him*.

'Seems unfair to disturb it, then. Let's go.' Carlton raised an eyebrow in his direction; an expressive eyebrow, containing disgust, challenge, and not even a modicum of sympathy.

'We would lose the Game then! Humanity would lose the Game. Have you no pride?' Curtis looked thoughtful for a moment. 'Rhetorical.'

'Don't call me a rhetorical,' Curtis hissed, ending the argument assertively.

'You'd better give me a leg up this tree,' said Carlton, recognizing that there was as much chance of Curtis volunteering for the job as there was of him chatting up the dragon.

3

This was a suggestion Curtis liked, and he immediately moved to the nearest tree trunk and made a stirrup with his hands. Carlton put his foot in it and looked up, picking out a spot for which to aim when he made the push. He found the spot, made the push, grabbed the branch, and accidentally kicked Curtis backwards and out into the clearing, where he overbalanced and rolled to a graceful and quite unmoving stop like a nifty pitch and run onto the eighteenth green.

Silence fell for a moment, and movement was even more scarce than sound. Then a voice came, allowing Carlton to start scrabbling up his tree.

'Hello,' said the dragon, tiredly.

Curtis stayed in a tight foetal position, looking like a trilobite in a jump suit.

'Hello?'

Curtis flinched. It was unlikely that the monster was talking to something else, but he did not yet feel like exposing his more vulnerable parts, and he had a lot of those.

'Oh, never mind. God, I'm knackered,' repeated the dragon.

There was a slight rustling noise from the treetops, and Curtis did something very unusual. Almost as if he realized that if Carlton was spotted then all was lost, he slowly uncurled himself, deliberately drawing the dragon's attention. It was ever such a brave thing to do.

And Curtis did brave things almost as often as Jesus mugged bishops with a spanner.

A weak mind, this human, the Challenger confirmed to itself once again as it relaxed to a short infrared pulse, but becoming amazingly powerful in resisting the suggestion of any act which might result in personal danger. Curtis had been harder to uncurl than a month-dead hedgehog.

It was a shame the rules of this round did not allow it to influence the dragon, but Nature must apparently take its course. Which was a shame, it thought, since it – and the Champion – held enough sway over Nature to have it on the ropes quicker than anyone could mutter 'foul'.

The Lessers hung respectfully below the First and Second Elders as they played the Game, watching as they exercised their control over all things material in the whole Universe – and then some – vying for the title of Supreme Being; but making sure that

4

the rules were not broken, when the Third Elder would be the one to mutter. The chances are it would do so very timidly.

Tension among the Lessers rose, brief flashes of ultra-violet escaping into the ether. After the opening round of this particular Game it was a draw, but now the second had begun, and the pressure was back on the Champion's team.

The Champion watched, broadcasting neutral microwaves. It didn't have any eyes – which was probably just as well because it and its kind had dispensed millennia ago with a body in which it might keep them, and they look damned silly hanging on their own – but it watched anyway. Having held the title for seven eons, defeat would mean death, for it could no longer allow itself to be subsumed into the Lesser Elders; it had grown beyond that.

And now it was quite possible that the leader of its team would be killed in the next few moments.

A potential disaster?

Apparently not.

It would have taken a very sensitive instrument indeed to measure the pang of regret that passed through the Champion's being at the prospect.

'Hello,' said the dragon again, with all the brightness of a thundercloud at twilight.

'Hello,' said Curtis, while he screamed at himself for an explanation of just what the hell had induced him to stretch out like that.

'You're not Jason, are you?'

'Er, no, I'm not.'

'Bastard!' hissed the dragon, and more smoke billowed from its mouth, the flame accompanying it looking like a tongue. The epithet did not seem to be aimed at Curtis, and as the smoke cleared, he could see tears once again coming from the dragon's red eyes. Eyes that *were* aimed at him, and which suddenly looked hungry.

Did dragons eat people?

He *could* ask, but that might be the verbal equivalent of covering himself in barbecue sauce and stretching out over the brickettes. He chose a different tack.

'What's wrong? Why are you crying?' Not that he was particularly bothered, but if he kept it talking it might just not take the time to fancy a Curtis toastie.

5

'I'm crying,' explained the dragon with an impression of immense patience, 'because I haven't been to sleep for the best part of three thousand years, and every time I breathe out,' – the volume of the voice rose somewhat – 'I get this bloody smoke in my sodding eyes!' The head rose along with the voice to conclude the explanation. *That*'s why I'm crying!' The head fell back onto the front feet with a thud. 'God, I'm knackered,' came the defeated litany once more.

Curtis tried to think of something else to say, but the success of his last conversation starter gave him pause. Well, it gave him stop, to be exact. He said nothing, and the dragon was forced to take up the initiative of what was so far, admittedly, a somewhat unsparkling chat.

'I'm not allowed to sleep until this Jason geezer comes to get this bloody donkey jacket here.' He gestured with his eyes to the hide which hung on the tree branch behind him. 'Three thousand years I've waited. And what have I got?'

Curtis shrugged his shoulders. 'I can't imagine.'

'Knackered!'

Another rustling from the treetops, a lot closer to the dragon this time, brought no reaction from the guard, and Curtis resisted the temptation to look upwards.

Then a loud movement from the branches did things to Curtis's stomach that normally required a number of prunes, but it was only a pigeon leaving its perch to land squarely in front of the dragon's snout. The dragon looked at it with immense disapointment, not even needing to ask if this was Jason, and the pigeon looked back with a barely perceptible nod. Neither of them spoke for a while.

Then the dragon broke the silence with a long 'Herrrrrrrrr!' and where the pigeon had been there was now a dainty roast. The dragon's long black tongue snaked out and curled around the unfortunate bird, whipping it back into the mouth for a quick crunch and swallow, while Curtis's stomach processed its prunes.

The dragon burped, and another cloud of smoke cleared to show resultant tears. It also cleared to show a hand inching downwards from the branches of the tree on which hung the hide. Inching ever closer, stretching out at its limit, and not quite reaching its goal.

'I hate it when they don't talk,' the dragon mentioned. 'I hate it when things just sit there and stare at you and don't say anything.'

Curtis sat there and stared at it and didn't say anything for a very brief instant indeed.

'So, what does this Jason look like, then?' he blurted. 'If I see him I'll be sure to tell him that you're waiting for him.'

'How do I know what he looks like?' The dragon dragged its gaze from the sun-dappled ground to Curtis's bifocal eyeballs. 'If I'd known what he looked like then I wouldn't have asked if you were him, would I?'

Curtis had now been out-logicked by a dragon, as he had by just about everything else since he'd left Earth so long before, but this did not occur to him as the stretching hand began to move just a little quicker, followed by an arm, a shoulder, and then by Carlton's panic-stricken face as he fell from the tree, bounced with a grunt from the neck of the dragon and landed in a heap just to one side of its head. The dragon let out a pyrotechnic 'oomph', which just failed to singe Carlton's exposed bits and turned its head laboriously to look at its second human visitor in three thousand years. Just like a bloody bus – you wait three thousand years, then two come along together.

'Who are you?' it asked, with an excitement which fell just short of apathy.

Carlton leaped to his feet, and balanced himself like a fighter.

'By some I am called Jason,' he said in a deep resonant voice. 'I have come for the Fleece.'

The dragon's head rose minutely from the ground. 'You're Jason?' Carlton confirmed his assertion with a sharp nod which he tried to infuse with Oscar-nomination-material confidence. It would have to have been a very slow year for him to stand a chance. 'Where the sodding hell have you been? Three thousand years I've been here waiting for you!'

'Well, now I am come,' said Carlton, unfazed and trying to talk like a Greek hero who spoke English. 'And I will take the Fleece.'

'Then I'll have to fight you, won't I?'

Carlton's shoulders sagged a little. 'Oh. Shit. Will you?'

'Oh, yes,' said the dragon, with apparent certainty, then yawned. 'God, I'm knackered.'

'Why will you have to do that?' If only the dragon had been female his smile would have protected him, he thought

7

perversely, and with hardly any vanity at all. The dragon wasn't, and Carlton wasn't smiling anyway.

'Because that's the way it's supposed to be done. You come along for the Fleece, we fight, and the winner gets to keep the thing.'

'The winner?' asked Carlton, hoping, maybe, for a points decision.

'The one left alive,' explained the dragon helpfully.

'But why? Dragons don't eat people, do they?'

Don't ask that! Curtis shouted inside his head.

'They don't normally. That's very true. They do sometimes have to kill them, though.' There was deep regret somewhere in its voice – a rotten job, killing people, but someone apparently had to do it.

'Look,' said Curtis, uncertainly, because the less he said, the less chance there was of him being noticed. 'It's not the actual Fleece we want. We're more, sort of, after the Fleas that live on it. You see?'

The dragon eyed him by swivelling its pupils rather than its head – it seemed to recognize that such conspicuous effort would be surpassing flattery to one such as Curtis.

'We? So you're with him, are you?' Curtis spluttered and wished he had kept his mouth shut. 'Well, I'll just have to fight both of you, then.'

'Oh,' said Curtis. 'Shit. Will you?'

II

He had just known it was a bad idea, from the moment they encountered Biondor, the elegant alien who welcomed them to his planet at the end of their long trip from Earth. Something at the back of what Curtis was pleased to call his mind told him to have nothing whatever to do with the Champion and the Challenger and this Game thing that Biondor explained to them, but he had ended up going on this daft treasure hunt all the same. Golden Fleas indeed!

On the other hand, it wasn't as though they had any choice in the matter. Biondor had told them what had actually been going on while they thought they were pioneering interstellar travel – that it had all been arranged by two bodiless super-minded beings as part of a Game – and had intimated that failure to continue would result in a fate not any worse than death, but exactly equal to it.

Then the alien had produced this girl with blue hair as a replacement for Big Bill Bowen, who had elected to return home; or who had demanded to return home, as much as one could demand anything from a being as superior as Biondor. Bowen tried demanding quite a lot, since his definition of superiority centred around how many pints you could down in one evening without re-presenting any of it, rather than the higher cerebral functions which formed the centre-point of most such definitions.

After she had been told what Biondor deemed she ought to know, the girl had fixed Curtis with a stare like superglue.

'You Captain?' The voice had a mid-Atlantic sound, but was drier.

It was far too direct a question not to cause Curtis a bucketload of self-doubt, so he spluttered a bit, before managing 'Well, yes, Miss . . . ?' and a smile ventured out for a quick look around.

' "*Miss*"!' She spat the word, the voice now a lot harder than mid-Atlantic, and just as dangerous. Curtis's smile rushed off to

9

hide somewhere very dark. 'Watch your fonking mouth, lizard eyes.'

A brief urge to look in a mirror in order to see, one, his mouth, and, two, whether or not he had lizard eyes, did not deflect Curtis from his meandering path.

'Sorry, er, er . . . ?'

'Fission.'

'Bless you.'

'My name Fission.'

'Oh, right.' Somehow the course of this conversation was already getting well out of hand, and Curtis wished he was watching someone else have it. Fission? He dragged it back into line.

'Well, Fission, yes I am the Captain, and I'd like to welcome you aboard and –'

'Cut the ovals. What we do next?'

Well, we could start by trying to work out what ovals are, thought Curtis, then realized and decided not to check.

'We don't actually know what to do next.' He looked around a little uncertainly and a lot characteristically. But being Captain, he had thought of a possible course of action. 'I thought we might work out how to fly the ship . . .'

He had a way of inspiring confidence, did Curtis. Unfortunately this was it.

'You got no pilot?'

'Well, yes.' Yes, we've got no pilot? 'Or no.' No, we've got no pilot? 'Er. Does everybody talk like this on Earth now?'

'Like what?'

'Well, er, sort of without some of the words.'

'You understand?'

'Well, I think so . . .'

'So problem?' she challenged, and adopted a threatening stance, although for Curtis this meant just about anything that wasn't horizontal and comatose.

'Er.' He wished he hadn't asked. 'This is our pilot.' He indicated Carlton, who flashed a winning smile at Fission. 'Peter Carlton.'

'A human!'

'Not just *a* human,' said Carlton, holding out his hand. 'Mind if I call you Fish?'

'Mind if I blare your worm?' Fission snapped back, and

10

looked at the hand as though it were holding something brown and steaming.

'Right,' said Carlton, the hand retracting somewhat. 'I'll take that as a "no" then.' It was a lot safer than asking for a translation. The Ship's temperature control fought with the fast-cooling atmosphere.

'You got no robot?' Fission backtracked the conversation, turning to Curtis again and consigning Carlton to insignificance. He'd never been there before, and didn't much like it. Curtis was there most of the time and yearned to be in its comforting womb again as the steely gaze of his new crew member stapled his vocal chords together. He swallowed a couple of times to part them while thinking of something to say that wasn't 'yes' or 'no'.

'Well, there's Arnold. Designed and built by me. Or the head and the right arm were designed and built by me, anyway; Biondor seems to have provided the rest in the last few minutes, so that he could come with us.'

Arnold's memory of physical being contained little more than a head bolted to a shelf in the corner of a control room, and an arm suspended beneath it, but now he was flexing his various newly acquired bits experimentally, looked up to see a smile on Fission's face for the first time since her arrival. He smiled back, and almost pleasantly. Not quite, but then he'd never tried a pleasant smile before. It was quite an effort, and he decided he probably wouldn't do it again.

'You built four hundred years ago?' Fission sounded impressed.

'More or less, yes,' said Curtis proudly. Not that he was old – he was actually less than thirty, and with a mental age well below half that, according to anyone who knew him – but the dilation of time during their two-week flight had allowed the rest of the Galaxy to steal a bit of a march on them.

'Hmm. Guess it might do.' Arnold continued to smile at her, but the quality of the expression changed from pleasant to threatening with the flick of an eyebrow.

'How kind,' he said, and Fission looked surprised.

'You made him to talk back?'

The question was put to Curtis, but Arnold beat him to the reply. 'Biondor made me. To do what I want.'

Fission looked him up and down. 'Outworldly!'

One of Arnold's eyebrows curled even further upward and solidified into a sort of marble arch.

11

People had crossed the computer before and lived to regret it, and more than one observer viewed Arnold's silent promise of come-uppance with tacit approval. The presence in Fission of the Bowen genes was very obvious to the crew members – Big Bill had been to social nicety what the Pope was to pre-martial sex; he was not whole-heartedly in favour of it.

'Are you ready?' came a quiet but authoritative voice, and they turned to see Biondor standing to one side of the control room. His naked, fawn-coloured body projected the same sense of power as when they had first seen him, which, admittedly, had been only a few hours before. One or two of them lied by nodding, but Fission looked like she was going to clap her hands together in the unbridled joy of anticipation.

There was a table in the middle of the room, with seven chairs around it. They all, save Biondor, looked at it with suspicion since that was an event, not a description. The furniture had definitely not been there a moment before. Biondor indicated that they should all sit, which they did after contemplating the trick, and the reflection that any threat he made concerning their participation was almost certainly not an empty one.

'Who those two?' Fission asked Curtis with an apparently continuing economy of verbiage, indicating a couple who were smiling and helping each other into their seats and generally making Romeo and Juliet look like antagonists.

'That's Gloria, and that's Wilverton, my first Officer.' He didn't need to distinguish which was which. 'We're a bit worried about Wilverton; he thinks he's in a book and that none of this is happening.'

Fission gave Wilverton the once-over – or probably the three-quarters over; there wasn't a lot of Wilverton – barely glanced at Gloria, of whom there was a lot more, shrugged, and took the seat offered by Biondor.

It was the first time Arnold had sat in his life – given the fact that he was not actually alive, a fact which no-one who knew him would risk pointing out – and he did so somewhat gingerly, noting that there had to be the equivalent of nerves in his equivalent of a bum so that he knew when he had hit the chair. It can't be easy creating androids, he thought.

Android, not computer. Nor robot. 'Android' sounded so much more sophisticated, which, of course, he was.

Biondor did not seem overly taxed by the task he had

performed, as he took his seat at the head of the table. His hand held a sheaf of something like paper – another event – and he proceeded to pass these one by one to Fission, who sat on his right, and who passed them one by one to Curtis, who sat on her right, and so on.

The unspoken aim was that everyone would thereby end up with a piece of something like paper in front of him or her. It was a manoeuvre that rarely needed explanation once you tried it with anything more advanced than a low-IQ anthropoid. Biondor watched with a certain disbelief, therefore, as the papers were passed round and ended up in a neat little pile in front of him. Gloria sat on his left and beamed happily. Biondor explained what he hoped to achieve, and they tried again.

'This gives the details of the first three of ten tasks which you must undertake. The trands – your opponents – will have similar tasks. The challenges in the second round of the Game are chosen by the incumbent Champion.'

Gloria looked up, preparatory to asking what was wrong with the Champion to make him incumbent, and, kind-hearted soul that she was, whether there was anything they could do which might help to make him cumbent again, but Biondor saw her coming.

'The reigning Champion. He will therefore try to choose tasks at which humans have been successful before, so you may recognize them.'

'Humanity has taken part in the Game before, then?' asked Wilverton.

'Many times, but never in the Final. The early rounds of the Game are just made up of one task, and all races in the known Galaxies have been participants at one stage or another. Your Neil Armstrong had to reach Luna as part of the Game, although he did not know it. That is the most recent example of successful human involvement I can recall.'

'We've failed, then?' Carlton sounded mildly put out by the possibility.

Arnold made a noise. It was a noise commenting that Carlton's question was a slightly more stupid one than 'Why do you want me to lie down, Mr Director?' or 'Will you really do these things if I vote for you?' Arnold was good with noises.

Biondor confirmed the implication with rather more decorum.

'Quite regularly, I'm afraid. With the less advanced races, one

13

of the favourite rounds is to put three or four individuals together and see if they can go for a specified time period without squabbling. Mankind loses that one every time.'

The clamour to deny that this could possibly be the case was markedly absent. Memories of their trip from Earth suggested that they would have succeeded in that particular endeavour only if the specified period were considerably less than a couple of minutes. They stared at the pieces of paper in front of them.

'This Champion thing,' said Carlton. 'Will he be protecting us?'

Fission stiffened slightly. 'Or she.' Gloria nodded, with a glance at Carlton.

'It will no doubt try,' Biondor tidied up. 'Through a desire to win rather than philanthropy.' Gloria wondered what stamp collecting had to do with it. 'But it was doing the same in the first round and was not entirely successful, since one of your number died. The Champion is not infallible, and the Challenger is not without resource.' It was a sobering thought, and heads dropped to paper once more.

'I'm afraid I have to leave you now,' Biondor told them, and they looked up quickly again. 'I have to complete the creation of a planet in the Bexali system. I've only done Dark so far; today it's Light. There's been a lot of fumbling around. I'm sure you understand. If you need to know anything, just ask the ship.' And he disappeared.

They looked at the space where he had been, with a confused respect. A god's work was apprarently never done.

Curtis thought that he should be the one to make contact with the Ship, since he was the Captain, and he naturally wanted to make an impression on the new member of his crew. Had he been any more astute – or at all astute, to put it another way – he would have realized that he had already made an impression on the new crew member.

'Er, Ship?'

'Yes, Captain?' said a pleasant female voice from all around him. He looked in that direction, but saw nothing.

'Biondor says you can tell us about these tasks.' It wasn't much of a question, but the Ship answered all the same.

'That is correct. Which would you like to hear about first?'

Curtis looked at the paper in his hand, and did a quick double-take. 'The Golden Fleas? You want us to recover the Golden Fleas?'

'Not I. The Champion wants you to recover the Golden Fleas.'

'Don't you, or doesn't the Champion, mean Fleece?' asked Wilverton.

'They are living in an animal skin, or Fleece, but it is the Fleas you must retrieve, First Officer Wilverton.'

'Please, call me Thomas.'

'Certainly, Thomas.' And you could hear the Ship smiling pleasantly.

'And call me Richard,' said Curtis, not wanting Wilverton to get ahead on the social ladder with the Ship, then added as an afterthought, 'Not Dick, though.'

'As you wish.'

Arnold had been sitting quietly and happily wiggling his toes just because he could. He looked up.

'You can call me "sir", Ship.'

'Certainly, sir,' the Ship responded in just as pleasant a voice, while the others looked tiredly at Arnold and sighed.

Arnold smiled broadly.

'We need to get to a planet called Callia to find and hopefully retrieve not only the Golden Fleas but also the Cretin Bull and Yazocks the Harmless Changeling,' read Carlton ("Call me Peter"), a bit hesitantly.

'Can you take us there, Ship?' asked Curtis.

'I can, Richard Not Dick Though.' Arnold sniggered.

'Just Richard,' said Curtis.

'Sorry?'

'It's not Richard Not Dick Though, it's just Richard.'

'*Just* Richard?'

'No, not *Just* Richard, just *Richard*.'

There was a pause in which everyone could hear the Ship thinking "Dick would save a lot of time, and be more descriptive", then Carlton stepped in.

'Call him Richard. Are you allowed to give us any help, Ship?'

'Not very much, Peter. I can tell you a few things, and I will be there when you finish your tasks. If you call out my name I will materialize. Although these first three are on the same planet, they will not all be in the same place, but if two or more finish simultaneously, then I do have the ability to be in more than one place at one time, for a short period.' This was some Ship. 'For those of you who are interested, it comes from a duplication of particles along the same lines as the subatomic memory. Think

15

of it as a party piece.' Those of them who were interested, did. It didn't help much.

'Let's go get profit!' said Fission, and clapped her hands together in the unbridled joy of anticipation.

'Can you tell us something about Earth while we travel?' Wilverton asked her. 'I'm sure we'd all love to know how it's getting on.'

'Guess I could.' She didn't look like it was top of her list of preferred things to do, more like it would have to be a very long list before it got on there at all. 'How long trip, Ship?'

'We are already in orbit around Callia, Fission.'

'Great. No time for chat. Let's go!' She was distressingly eager. 'We got Game to win!'

They looked pained, but each took a deep mental breath and prepared themselves to embark on quests holding unknown dangers as the representatives of all mankind.

'One of my cats had fleas,' said Gloria.

III

'Well, if you've come to get the Fleece I haven't got much choice, have I?' the dragon inquired. 'I mean, if I lie here awake for three thousand years with the sole purpose of guarding the Fleece and then as soon as someone comes along I stand meekly aside and let them take it, well, it does seem to defeat the whole object of the exercise a bit, doesn't it?'

Curtis had to admit that the dragon had a fairly good point.

'Besides which, I quite fancy a bit of a scrap. It'll give me something to do – you know, get the old blood circulating a bit. It'll be fun!'

Circulating blood was all right, of course, thought the two humans, so long as it was doing it inside your body. They didn't look like they thought 'fun' was quite the word.

'Oh, come on! You'll enjoy it. And it won't be as one-sided as it could be. I *am* quite tired, you know.' They knew.

'We have powerful weapons unknown in earlier days,' hazarded Carlton, and Curtis glanced uncertainly down at his machete.

'Oh, good. That should even things up a little.'

'And there are two of us.' Carlton glanced at Curtis and wondered just how long that particular circumstance might pertain. 'We are on different sides of you. You might be able to get one of us, but not both. No way.'

'Bets?' asked the dragon, and yawned.

Arnold and Gloria stood on a path leading through a small copse of trees which Gloria didn't recognize but which Arnold told her were firches. An interesting name, a cross between firs and birches, which was what the trees did resemble, but chosen largely because it was the first thing that came into the android's head when he made his mind up that he was not about to admit ignorance.

It smelled like springtime, fresh and clean, and the songs of

17

tiny flying creatures filled the air. They weren't birds, although they appeared to favour feathers as their fashion statement. Their limbs were plainly visible, and they seemed to have tiny faces like those of monkeys. The overall impression was of cute flying tamarinds. Gloria started to make delighted squeaking noises as soon as she saw them, until Arnold turned a glare on her that described what he would do to them if only he could get his hands on a few skewers and an open fire.

Looking around, he could see the flashing colours of the feathered songsters as they flitted happily through the trees, brightening even the lush green and yellow that clothed the overhanging branches, and no doubt making a young man's fancy turn. All Arnold could think was that any one of the little bastards could be Yazocks the Harmless Changeling.

'Well, Arnold? How are we supposed to find this creature?'

'How should I know?' he replied tetchily.

'Well, I assumed you knew when you *volunteered* for this task.' She stressed the word with the faintest trace of annoyance. Arnold had prepared to volunteer as soon as he heard the word 'Harmless', and had done so quickly enough to stop Gloria being accompanied by Wilverton. 'Anyway, you're supposed to know these things. You're a computer.'

'I'm an android, if you *don't* mind. Computers don't have perfect bodies like mine.' Gloria looked at him for a little while, at the blue jump suit which he wore, and a question came unbidden into her head. Not that she was really interested, not as in *interested*. Just curious, that was all.

'Arnold?' she ventured.

'Now what?' The comp—, android glared at her with a touch more tetch.

'Oh, nothing. Never mind.'

Birdsong – flying-tamarind song filled the short silence, but was soon too much for Arnold.

'So come on. How do *you* think we should find it?'

'Well.' Gloria had experienced an idea, and for Gloria it *was* an experience, bordering on an adventure. 'We could ask something. If it's harmless, then it must be honest as well, because telling lies is harmful. There. Logic.'

'Based on a spurious premise.' The little smirk of cleverness on Gloria's face turned to one of puzzlement. Arnold decided not to pursue the matter. 'Ask what?'

'Well.' Gloria looked around the world in general. 'Anything. Everything. We know it's here somewhere. The Ship said so.'

The Ship had said that the Champion had put it there. The Ship had said that the Champion had caused the whole planet of Callia to come into being purely for the purpose of this round of the Game. When you owned the whole Universe, and the Game was the most important thing happening in it, you didn't pinch the pennies, and not just because you didn't have any fingers. As far as most of the party were concerned, the Champion really didn't need to have bothered on their account.

'Of course! We ask everything!' enthused Arnold. 'That's brilliant!'

Gloria swelled a bit with pride. Built as she was, it was a good job that her jump suit had a certain elasticity, and that Arnold was an android. He dropped to his hands and knees and gingerly approached a daisy growing at the edge of the path.

'Daisy!' he called. 'Are you Yazocks the Harmless Changeling? Come on! Out with it!' He bent his ear to the flower and listened very carefully, then looked up at Gloria.

'Either Yazocks is deaf, or he's refusing to answer. Or,' and he held up a finger to emphasize the point, 'or this is a daisy. Shall I try the blade of grass next to it?'

Gloria was red, partly from blush and partly from anger.

'Don't be ridiculous, Arnold. Anyone can see it's just a daisy.'

'I quite agree,' came a quiet voice next to Arnold's still lowered ear. 'Don't be ridiculous.'

Arnold stared at the daisy, without letting Gloria see any movement of his head, and hissed an incredulous 'What?'

'Changelings can't become daisies. We're too small and intricately formed. Everyone knows that.'

'Intricate! You're a daisy!' His voice rose slightly, much louder than that of the plant, which had not reached Gloria's ears.

'It's not funny, you know, Arnold,' she warned, in a tone of voice which normally presaged an order to go and stand in the corner until you grew up.

'What do *you* know?' scorned the daisy. 'You're just a clumsy human.' Arnold's eyes narrowed. That tore it. 'Changelings simply cannot become daisies. That's all there is to it. Surely even you must realize that this isn't an argument you can possibly win.' It managed to look infinitely superior without moving a petal. Rather foolishly.

19

Arnold plucked it and held it up to the expression on his face, where it gave a little moan before drooping sideways. He dropped it by the side of the path.

'That shows how much *you* know, smart-arse!' He rose to his feet.

'And *that* wasn't necessary,' scolded Gloria, who could have walked into the post of Assistant Mother Nature if it ever came up for grabs. 'You're just being horrid.'

The Challenger shrugged to itself in a brief exudation of visible yellow. It had not imagined that the android would carry its talking daisy back to the Ship in place of the Changeling, but all these things wasted a bit of time.

'Well, what *do* we ask, then?' Arnold was becoming exasperated.

'We only ask those things which look like they might be changelings.'

When Arnold was first built, and had been provided with only a head – a replica of that of Curtis's own father, whom he had inadvertently killed – and one arm, it would have been difficult for him to splutter. Now that he had a body capable of drawing breath, although not dependent on it, a splutter was a possibility; and this was just as well, because he had not before come across a comment which so warranted a splutter.

Arnold spluttered.

'The point about changelings,' he replied very slowly and distinctly, 'is that they can change their appearance to that of whatever they wish. If you could walk down the street, glance to your left and think, "Oh, look, another of those bloody changelings; distinctive little sods, aren't they?" then by definition you would not be looking at a changeling. Would you?'

Gloria took a little time to catch up with this, but catch up she did, to give credit where it's due. 'I suppose not.'

'That is why the Ship said that they were only catchable if you happened to spot one changing. We'll just have to keep our eyes open and hope for the best, unless I come up with a better idea. Talking of which, the "not-bothering-at-all-and-going-back-to-the-Ship" idea appeals more by the minute.'

The fact that Gloria had not been included in the club of those capable of formulating a plan did not entirely escape her.

Unfortunately she couldn't think of a reasonable argument to act as an application for membership.

They continued walking along the path, and soon reached the edge of the copse. In all that time no flying tamarind had grown extra limbs, no tree had suddenly struck up on an accordion, no base element had transmuted itself (not that they would have noticed if it had, but it hadn't anyway). They had not spotted Yazocks the Harmless Changeling.

Ahead of them was a scene of tranquil freneticism. The path they were on wound through golden and green fields of something that might have been a broad-leaved grass in such a happy, meandering sort of way that it really should have been paved with yellow bricks.

The bright sunlight had begun slanting in the late afternoon, and the purple tinge of the sky was slightly more marked than the one which Carlton and Curtis ignored as the old red sun pulled itself a little higher, to a rather feeble zenith.

Gloria thought it was all very pretty, and so it was.

On the path and in the fields, however, creatures were running, bounding rather, and screaming, the sounds of their voices audible now that the cover of the trees was missing. They had three legs, or the third might have been a well-developed tail – it was hard to tell. Either way, they moved in a series of leaps and were covered in a brown fur with a fine mane extending down their backs. Their faces looked gentle, their eyes soft and only a slightly darker brown than their fur, but most were now contorted in fear.

Running along after them were big black hyena-like things, powerful shoulders hunched over their forelegs, and their backs sloping downwards to much smaller, narrower hind quarters. The long muzzles dripped saliva and bared sharp fangs clearly designed for tearing flesh without asking permission or saying grace.

A pack of them chased after the brown-furred creatures, who fled for their lives, some slowed by the infants they were carrying, whose frightened cries could be heard even though their faces were buried in their parent's chest.

Arnold and Gloria stopped, and then as one bravely darted back into the cover of the trees.

Gloria somehow found herself in front of Arnold – or possibly Arnold found himself behind Gloria – and as she stared at the

21

scene in front of her she could feel his hot breath on the back of her neck. It reminded her of something, but this was hardly the time for such memories, and anyway they certainly shouldn't be induced by a rob— android, especially one who didn't even breathe! So instead, she . . .

Didn't even breathe?

A cold clammy feeling crept into Gloria's stomach and climbed into her brain by clawing its way up her spine, by which time it had become a thought which said 'there's something behind you that is not Arnold and is big enough to breathe where it is breathing'.

She snapped her head round – no slow agony of discovery for Gloria – and a hyena dribbled at her from a mouth that looked as if it was smiling. It must have already dealt with Arnold, she thought suddenly, not considering the possibility that the android might have exercised a talent for self-preservation that could have run a marathon without breaking into anything more than a healthy glow.

Well, it was too late to do anything about it now, a bit of her brain thought, while the rest concentrated on moving the legs, bloody quick. She darted sideways, deeper into the copse, expecting at any moment to feel teeth. The noise of the undergrowth – twigs breaking, leaves rustling and the odd verbal complaint – proved that she was being followed, that the creature was toying with her as a cat with a mouse. She knew that any moment it would tire of its sport and move in for the kill.

She ran quicker.

Then something reached down in an instant from a branch right in front of her, an arm so long it might have belonged to a gibbon who insulted Torquemada, but a hairless arm, its wrinkled skin a deep purple colour, and ending in a hand with rather more fingers than it could possibly need, each multi-jointed and superbly equipped for squeezing things like necks. Just next to the shoulder a leering face grinned at Gloria like a cadaver on Halloween. There might have been eyes and a nose in it, but all Gloria saw as she plunged through the undergrowth was yet more teeth, and that hand stretching for her.

Then she felt the breath on her neck again.

Gloria screamed.

To scream properly, you need lungs and a reason. Gloria had lungs that medical science would drool over – much like many men had already done – and reasons aplenty.

It was one hell of a scream.

The smile on the face in front disappeared in an instant at the sound and, as Gloria ducked underneath, the arm flinched in shock, along with all unseen bits of whatever it was. Then the ex-smile turned to a look of some panic as the flinching loosened the animal's grip on the branch and it fell from its tree. Straight into the open, but fast closing, maw of the hyena, which was expecting a mouthful of pink neck flesh and ended up with something purple and of extremely dubious origin; suffice it to say that it felt like an uncooked sausage.

Gloria did not slow to a walk and take time to recover her breath, proving that blind panic can sometimes be sound reasoning, because the hyena was only delayed for a few moments while it spat out a slightly chewed purple mess and started off again.

Where was Arnold? thought Gloria wildly.

Arnold was behind a tree, and appeared to be weighing a branch with both hands. He glanced around the bole and saw Gloria under full sail, looking as though she was chasing two errant beach balls, and behind her a hyena in full dudgeon, chasing an errant meal.

He had to time it right.

Later he'd work out why, but he had to time it right.

Gloria rushed past Arnold's tree, noticing subconsciously a figure holding and swinging something that looked like a large baseball bat.

The hyena rushed past the tree, and noticed the same thing very consciously indeed, if only momentarily, as Arnold swung the branch like Babe Ruth in a hurry, and the animal's mouth was suddenly full of wood travelling backwards as fast as it was travelling forwards. Something had to give, and it wasn't the bit with leaves.

The Champion did its equivalent of breathing a sigh of tiredness that started in the gamma region and receded down to visible blue, not caring whether the Challenger or the Lessers saw it or not.

All it had needed to do was strengthen the android's desire to help the human Gloria. But first it had to find it, and when eventually it did, it was plain that 'desire' described the feeling a bit like it described Arnold's wish to sacrifice his life for a daisy.

23

If one of the humans had to rely on help from the android again, thought the Champion, it was a tough waste of electro-magnetism.

Arnold stared at the creature which lay a few yards away sporting its perfectly fitting wooden dentures when Gloria panted up to him.

'Oh, Arnold, thank you! I knew you'd help me if you could! I knew you wouldn't just run away and leave me!'

Arnold looked at her, and an eyebrow edged infinitesimally upwards, dragging half a lip with it.

'Don't mention it,' he said slowly. 'Ever. To anyone.'

'No. Well. If you ever need my help . . .'

'If *I* ever need *your* help? Then the faith healer won't have been able to mend the resuscitation unit.'

Gloria didn't answer that one. Was it a compliment? The what unit?

They were again near to the edge of the copse, and the craving for further 'conversation' was displaced by a huge bird swooping down in front of them from the treetops. A wingspan of ten feet or more, legs thicker than a man's arm – a big man, too, not a Wilverton-sized man – and talons like scimitars. The magnificent head sported – blood-sported, that is – a long curved beak tapering to a lethal, flesh-rending point.

It dived onto a bush just twenty yards from where Gloria and Arnold stood – or cowered, to be accurate – and turned into a hyena. At least, the bird did not re-emerge, and a hyena did. At the same time, a cry emerged from just beyond the bush where the transformation had taken place. Another cry of a terrified young cub. And who could blame it?

'That's him!' shouted Arnold. 'That's Yazocks! Quick, after him!' The sooner they finished this, the sooner Arnold could do something that didn't have humans attached, and he made to take off after the hyena in the wink of an eye.

Gloria was quicker, though. A baby needed help, a cute little brown-furred one, what was more, and that was more important than Yazocks or being chased by a hyena or any silly game played by super-minded aliens. She had a firm grip of Arnold's upper arm before his circuits could kick into gear, and he wasn't going anywhere.

'That baby needs our help first.' It was more like an order than Arnold had ever heard before.

Wilverton stood quietly in the doorway of a small shepherd's hut at one end of a long field surrounded by low hedges, and looked out with mild interest at the scene before him.

It consisted of Fission dancing about frantically from foot to foot as if each time she landed there was the sound of a breaking Fabergé egg-shell, and waving a blue scarf wildly in front of her, in what would probably be the semaphore equivalent of a scream. An actual scream came from her vocal chords, which had to be made of a very tough material indeed to cater for the noise she had been generating for the last few minutes.

In front of her, mildly chewing on a piece of particularly lush green vegetation just in front of its fore hooves that was close enough to grass as made no difference, was an enormous bull. A huge black mountain of beef, it just stood glumly and totally ignored Fission's attempts to attract its attention.

What they needed to do, said Fission, only not in so many words, was to make the Bull chase them, and then run back to the Ship, which, as far as she could make out, was over there somewhere. Wilverton had inquired what they should do should it transpire that four tons of hostile bull could run just a little bit faster than they could. Fission answered by pointing out that this was the sort of question asked by cowards. Yes, agreed Wilverton, but it was the sort of question asked by living cowards.

The whole thing was proving just slightly academic as without anything remotely red, Fission was not going to attract the Bull's attention by anything short of walking up to it and sounding one of its horns, as it were.

As he watched, Fission stopped her prancing and stood staring at the Bull, panting from her exertions. The Bull pulled another couple of dozen blades of grass from their mountings – without pausing to think whether they were really blades of grass or masochistic changelings masquerading as blades of grass – and started chewing them seriously.

Bulls as a breed are notoriously short-sighted, which is why some prat has to wave a red cape at the things in order to be noticed. The bull will then chase the fluttering piece of material because, basically, a bull is generally about as intelligent as an octopus's ninth armpit. They are, in fact, only marginally more intelligent than the people who think that watching them chasing the cape and ending up on the end of a skewer is good entertainment. We are not talking about minds with the capabilities of Isaac Newton's here, and his has rotted.

Fission finally lost what little patience she had left – and she didn't have a lot to start with; about enough to fill a cottage hospital in a miniature village – and she gave a final scream of exasperation before wandering back towards Wilverton. He watched her coming, sweat glistening on her forehead in the vaguely purple but very bright mid-afternoon light, and firmed up his opinion of the new crew member. The woman was clearly demented. She had the brains of a two-year-old, and Wilverton reckoned the child had been glad to see the back of them.

'Say "I told you so", I mince your molecules.'

Wilverton shrugged. 'I wasn't going to.'

She leaned against the side of the hut and breathed deeply.

Wilverton spoke again, thoughtfully. 'I've been trying to think of a book where this has happened, but nothing's come to mind so far. It could be one I haven't read, I suppose, but I think that's pretty unlikely; I've known all the other ones we've been in.'

Fission glanced sideways at him. 'Spunkminus right. You're nut.'

Wilverton tried the unfamiliar nomenclature on each of his crew-mates, and stopped when he reached Curtis and found a perfect fit.

'Did spunkminus give any particular reason?'

Fission shrugged. 'Said it yourself. Think you in book.'

'I believe we are taking part in something fictional, I admit. The thought doesn't bother me' – in fact since he had ended up with the heroine, he was quite relaxed about the whole thing! – 'I wouldn't let it bother you, if I were you.'

'You not me, thank Luc.' She pushed herself off the wall. 'Another try time.'

Wilverton watched her go, wondering idly who Luke was.

IV

'Look, are you going to get on with it, or not?' asked the dragon, somewhat exasperatedly. 'I mean, I know I've waited three thousand years and that a few more won't matter, but I really think we should get it over with. I've got things to do.'

'Like what?' asked Curtis, mildly surprised by his own temerity. But then, for something that was about to try to kill them, and succeed as far as he could tell, it did seem quite a nice dragon. Not the sort of dragon you would expect in a quest, more the sort you might find in a Disney cartoon.

'Well.' The dragon yawned, thereby cutting off the rest of its response in a sheet of flame and a cloud of smoke. 'Well,' it repeated, when the vapours had cleared and its eyes had stopped streaming, 'to be honest, I thought I might have a bit of a kip. It's been three thousand years, and now Jason's come along,' it indicated Carlton with a barely perceptible movement of its eyeballs, 'so I figure I'll have earned it as soon as I've got rid of you both. I'm a bit tired, you see.'

'We had noticed,' said Curtis.

Carlton sighed. The time had clearly come for the man of the moment to step into the breach; for the one small man with the big heart to offer himself up as the saviour of his fellows; for the selfless martyr to give his all, whether that should include his life or not. And since that mindless jerk obviously hadn't shown up, Carlton supposed he had better do it himself.

He adopted what he hoped would be a purposeful stance, and hefted his machete. It was not really big or impressive enough to heft to any great effect, but he hefted it anyway. The dragon would probably expect a good heft, he thought. The dragon looked at him, unimpressed.

He needed something more, something bold and heroic, something that would prove to the dragon that he really was a danger. He tried an old favourite.

'Go ahead, dragon. Make my day.'

The dragon didn't run away, but continued to suggest without moving a muscle that it was far more likely to ruin his day.

Carlton passed the machete from his right hand to his left, as he had seen countless heroes in films do, and he managed it without dropping it, cutting his fingers, or creating any amusing out-takes. The sun glinted brightly off the blade of the knife, and the dragon watched as it moved. Carlton passed it back again from left hand to right. The dragon watched. Right to left. The dragon watched. Left to right. The eyelids drooped, then snapped open and the dragon watched. Right to left. The eyelids drooped. Left to right. The eyelids closed, and parted slightly. Right to left, and the eyelids closed again, and remained that way. Carlton stared at the dragon, then at Curtis. They were both completely gone.

'Curtis,' he hissed.

'Yes.' Curtis spoke without opening his eyes, and in a voice that wasn't all there, a bit like its owner.

'Can you hear me?'

'Yes.' Carlton smiled.

'Raise your right hand.' Curtis raised his right hand and it hung in the air as though on strings. Carlton grinned, tucked his machete carefully into his waist-band, and sauntered across to Curtis.

'When I count to three,' he whispered, 'you will wake up.' He performed the mathematical feat, and Curtis opened his eyes, then looked around, obviously confused. So no change there.

Carlton motioned him quiet and indicated the dragon, who dozed peacefully, wrapped around the tree.

'Dragon. Can you hear me?'

'I hear you, Jason.' The dragon's voice sounded like the tolling of a large bell; a large black bell, somehow.

'Raise your right fore paw.' The dragon did so. Carlton looked at Curtis, who had lowered his bottom jaw. Carlton smiled again. This was more fun than he had thought it was going to be a couple of minutes ago.

'Dragon. Someone is about to climb on your back. You will not move while they do so. Do you understand?'

'I understand,' said the dragon in a tone that sounded like midnight in Hades.

Carlton turned to Curtis. 'Get the Fleece.'

'What?!?'

28

'Get the Fleece!'

Curtis gaped from Carlton to the dragon, to the animal skin hanging above it, then back to Carlton again, then repeated the manoeuvre. He looked like a fish watching a tennis match. There seemed to be some hold up in his psyche.

'But what if it wakes up?'

'Then it'll probably kill us both.'

'Well, why don't we run away then?'

'Because then Biondor will kill us both.'

Curtis looked at him. The trouble with irrefutable logic was that it was irrefutable. With refutable logic, you could just say 'Crap' and walk off. Curtis didn't have that option, so he chose another one.

'Look, it's asleep. We could kill it!'

'Kill it!' Carlton was honestly shocked. 'It hasn't had any choice about what it's doing, has it! It's the Champion, or the Challenger. It's not the dragon's fault. Haven't you got any pity?'

I've got plenty, thought Curtis. For a start, and he looked at his tree-blunted machete, it's a pity the Ship wasn't allowed to furnish us with something that was extremely fatal to dragons from a great distance.

'I'm the Captain,' he tried. 'I could order you . . .'

'Get the Fleece or I'll wake the dragon up. Move.'

Curtis wondered briefly whether really to impose his authority, but told himself that it would be an abuse of power. Actually, he thought, it was probably a good sign of consultative management to do precisely what he was told. He moved.

He crept gingerly up to the dragon and laid a quivering finger on its golden hide, snatching it back as soon as contact had been made, as though the gold were molten. Nothing happened. He reached out and touched it again, in the tentative way that would bring back memories of the girl in the next seat at primary school for many men; not Curtis, but that was another story.

'Oh, do get a move on!'

'SSSSSHHHHH!' hissed Curtis, extremely loudly, lifting a finger to his pursed and trembling lips, but the dragon carried on snoring. The smoke from its exhalation rose to Curtis's nose, and continued to rise while the dragon breathed in, which was odd, but which did not attract Curtis's curiosity. What did was the sharp burning pain in his calf, caused, when he looked down, by

29

a sharp burning as the largely fire-proof material of his jump suit succumbed to the dragon's breath and provided the smoke which assaulted his nostrils.

'*OW*!' He jerked his foot out sideways, inadvertently kicking the dragon sharply on the nose and thereby lifting its head slightly off the ground. It fell back with a thud, but still the creature didn't wake.

Curtis was by now hopping on one leg and slapping at his calf to put out the flames, which he managed to do, but not before he had lost his balance. Waving his arms like a windmill in heat, he fell sideways across the animal's head, rolled off and ended up in a heap on the ground just in front of its nostrils. The dragon took a deep breath.

'AARRGGHHH!' Curtis mentioned, rolling out of the way of the next exhalation, just.

As a quiet, stealthy approach it was probably beginning to lose some credibility.

Carlton gazed hopefully skywards for divine inspiration.

In as much as they could be described as being anywhere, Carlton could have been looking up at the Champion and its Challenger. They were certainly looking down. The Champion kept its reaction tightly controlled, not allowing any giveaway high-frequency emissions beyond its being. The Challenger oozed amusement in visible red.

If the Champion's team failed in any one of the tasks, while its team did not – and the trands were competent as inferior beings went – then the title of Supreme Being would change hands. The Challenger would be recognized as First Elder by the Lessers, and the recognition was definitive.

If the Champion's team failed!

As far as the Challenger was concerned, had it been capable of making high-volume emissions, this contest would be all over bar the shouting.

'Do you concede?' it asked, and received an immediate response.

'Your humour is primitive.' The Champion had known the best means of defence for more eons than the Challenger could remember.

Besides, there were always unforeseen possibilities with such as the team's leader, solutions he might produce that would remain otherwise unthought of, thanks to his being something of a maverick. Or pillock.

The dragon still ignored everything but its own rhythmic breathing, and Curtis rose self-consciously to his feet under Carlton's stare. He turned back to the dragon, checked that its eyes were still tightly closed, and put one hand full on the flesh, then the other one.

Nothing.

A foot.

Nothing.

He hauled himself off the ground and onto the animal's forearm, then its shoulder, and then its back.

The Fleece hung before him, shabby and manky in the sunlight. He plucked it from the tree and hit the ground in seconds flat.

'Let's get out of here,' he recommended to Carlton as he passed him at a dead sprint. Carlton turned to follow, but then paused and looked back to the dragon.

'Dragon, can you hear me?'

'I hear you, Jason.'

'When I count to three, you will awaken. Do you understand?'

'I understand.'

'You will not feel a sense of disappointment, you will feel as though your term of guardianship has been successfully completed and that you can rest. Understand?'

'Successfully completed, and I can rest.'

'You will spend your life helping people and being generally nice, and stuff,' finished Carlton lamely.

'Successfully completed and I can rest,' repeated the dragon. Carlton shrugged. Worth a try. He turned and moved to the edge of the clearing. The fern things still quivered frantically from Curtis's passage thirty seconds or so before. As he passed, one of them lowered its unfondled fronds to the ground, pulled its buried head out of the soil, and blinked around to see what all the fuss was about.

'One,' said the blissfully ignorant Carlton, and plunged into the forest, hacking with his machete, although the path was already fairly clear. 'Two,' he said, a bit louder, and saw Curtis some twenty yards ahead of him, scratching furiously at his chest, and holding the skin at arm's length.

'THREE, SHIP!' yelled Carlton as he reached Curtis, and the Ship was there in front of him and he raced up the steps before a scream from Curtis stopped him and spun him around.

Curtis was still running, his legs pumping up and down and his arms going like pistons. All this effort was conspicuously unrewarded by any sort of forward movement, as a green frond-like tentacle round his waist held him firmly. His eyes were tightly shut. The plant started pulling him backwards.

At first sight it looked rather amusing, but then came a roar from dragon-wards as the creature, now released by Carlton's arithmetic progression, checked for the Fleece behind it and found it gone. Carlton's hypnotic suggestion had clearly been ignored.

'The machete!' shouted Carlton. 'Use the machete!'

Curtis did. With his eyes still tightly shut he swung the now all but blunt instrument behind him, and the blade hit and bit in as deeply as it could. Into his leg. Fortunately for him, 'as deeply as it could' meant not at all, and it just left an angry wheal behind it.

Curtis screamed again, pain mixed with fear, hardly a giveaway at all for the dragon, who must have been glaring round its clearing wondering which way they had gone.

An answering roar and the sound of undergrowth being trampled – having first had its clinging tendencies removed at the insistence of a sheet of flame – suggested that the dragon was wondering no more. Carlton threw another glance to the heavens, muttered 'Prat' to no-one in particular, and raced down the steps again.

The fire was running even faster than the dragon, and it was the sparks of flame which Carlton saw first out of the corner of his eye as he hacked at the plant. He wondered briefly whether to snatch the Fleece from Curtis's hand and just leave him, but that of course was unthinkable – the Fleas were on Curtis, so the Fleece was useless. He swung with both arms and broke the plant's grip just as the dragon came into view, then he dragged his Captain across the ground and threw him up the steps of the Ship.

There was no way that he was going to make it as well, though, not with the creature so close behind him, and he could feel the heat of its breath already on his back as he scrambled up the steps.

32

The dragon took a deep, preparatory breath. And Carlton stumbled and fell, slipping back down, right into the proposed flight-path of the flame.

He held his breath.

So did the dragon, and looked about, rather guiltily.

Carlton regained his feet and shot up the steps, diving over the threshold and into the Ship. As the door thudded to behind them, so a burst of flame spread over the hull. None of the heat penetrated, but Carlton stood with a sheen of sweat on his forehead, heaving in deep breaths and looking down at Curtis, who lay in a heap, eyes still shut, one hand on the Fleece and the other scratching his shoulder.

V

'Frankly, Arnold, I don't give a damn,' said Gloria. Wilverton would have immediately started thinking they were now in a film.

'But we could have caught it!' Arnold sounded suspiciously like a child who had just been refused a chocolate ice cream for no reason better than because mummy said so.

'Well, firstly I don't believe you can run as fast as one of those dog things,' countered Gloria, 'especially as you obviously haven't got the hang of your legs yet . . .'

'I tripped on a protruding stone,' said Arnold haughtily, referring to an incident just after they had left the Ship when he severely tested the artificial nerves in his artificial posterior.

'And secondly,' ignored Gloria, 'the needs of this baby come first by a long way.' She tickled it under the chin and it gurgled at her. 'This cute little baby waby.'

She was off in that never-never land that surrounds tiny animals, especially furry ones. Given that what was lying in her arms looked like a cross between a human baby and a kitten, Gloria would have stayed in foreign parts until Peter Pan toppled off his zimmer had Arnold not interjected.

'Excuse me? Hello? Reality calling!'

'I wonder what they're called,' she mused. Reality could wait for a while, apparently. 'I wish we had them on Earth; they're so cute. I think I'll call them Cutums. Hello, Cutum.' The Cutum smiled.

Arnold didn't. 'Cutum! What is it with humans and babies? Why not call it a Pukum? Or a Crapum?'

She glanced sharply at him as though he had snatched her teddy bear and started to pull the legs off. 'You don't understand, Arnold. You're not human.'

'You cannot conceive how happy that makes me!'

At that moment, the Cutum began to cry, launching from perfect calm into the sort of mind-wrenching cacophony of which only infants – except your own – are capable.

'What did you do?' asked Arnold. 'And more to the point, what did you do it for?'

'I didn't do anything! He's just hungry, that's all. We need some milk.' She looked around again.

'Fine. You wait here and I'll just nip down to the shops then. Judging from the apparent level of civilization, I reckon I shouldn't be more than a couple of millennia.'

Gloria tried a Look, but wasn't very good at it. 'When you've *quite* finished, Arnold.'

'I haven't even started yet.'

But Gloria wasn't listening; she was scanning the horizon, frowning.

'I don't understand why his parents haven't come looking for him. Perhaps they were killed by the hyenas. Have you seen any bodies, Arnold?' Arnold reported in the negative. 'Nor have I. So where are his parents?'

'Well, I'll have a stab. Given that a large pack of carnivorous stomachs on legs has just followed their teeth off that way, I would imagine that they're in front of them and still going.'

'Don't be stupid, Arnold.'

It was a phrase which no-one thought Gloria would ever be able to utter with justification. 'No parent is going to leave their child in danger while they run away. And if they are forced to leave him somewhere, they will come back as soon as possible. So where are they?'

'They're animals! They're too intelligent to behave like humans! They look after themselves.'

Gloria looked down at the two brown eyes that could see straight into her heart. 'They're not like that. Isums, then?' She tickled it again, which failed to quiet it, and its pink tongue waggled at her in the wind tunnel its lungs were creating.

Arnold searched the sky. Gloria rejoined him and searched the landscape. There was no animal to be seen. The last of the hyenas had long since disappeared, and no-one had come back to search. Perhaps the parents had been caught and overcome out of their sight. It seemed the only explanation. And if that were the case, what were they going to do with the Cutum? – which, Gloria was forced to admit, was getting louder by the minute. Where was she going to find some milk? She could certainly give it something to suck on – in fact it would be spoiled for choice – but a finger would only pacify it for so long.

35

Then she saw it, standing quietly, and an idea came to her.

'Arnold. I want you to make a water-tight cup out of something.' Arnold treated her to one of his special looks, but it bounced right off, without even denting her resolve. Gloria's mother instinct beat the hell out of Arnold's cynicism, and it was not to be denied. He sighed noisily, looked around, and found a wide-leafed shrub growing a few yards away. He walked to it, careful not to fall flat on his face when he left the relative smoothness of the path, and selected two of the more succulent leaves, then began folding them into the required shape.

'One presumes,' he said, not looking up from his task, 'that there is some goal at the end of this exercise in precise dexterity which has a rather deeper root than the natural desire of any flesh-and-blood human to determine the extent of an android's proficiency at origami?'

'What?' said Gloria, thereby surprising Arnold not at all.

'Why am I doing this?'

'Because I asked you to.'

'Yes, I *know* that.' Arnold ladled intellectual abhorrence into each word. 'I was hoping to gain some insight into the motivating factors behind the request.'

'What?'

'Why do you want a cup?'

'Oh!' said Gloria, understanding dawning like a new century. 'Because a cup can hold milk, and that cow over there,' and she pointed in the direction of a green field some distance away, 'can give us some.'

Arnold looked up and saw that there was indeed an animal of the bovine ilk chewing the cud in the middle distance. But Arnold did not know a great deal about cows, and one of the things he knew least about them was how you persuaded them to give you some milk. He voiced his ignorance in the only way he could whilst not admitting to it.

'If you think I'm going to milk it, you've got another think coming.'

'I'll milk it. I know how.' She had never done it, mind, but she was sure she would be able to work it out. I mean, she'd seen it done. You just sort of grabbed the teat and sort of squeezed it up and down and there it was, milk.

She took the cup which Arnold held out to her, and in exchange held out the Cutum. Arnold's eyes widened in alarm, but he took the thing, holding it as though it were Ming china and covered in soap. Gloria walked off towards the cow, which ignored her completely. She squatted down beside it and felt for the teat, which she found.

Gloria started to milk the cow.

Meanwhile, back at the ranch.

Okay, so it was not what would normally be described as a ranch, but there was the shepherd's hut, and there was cattle outside it in the shape – the formidable shape – of the Cretin Bull, so we can stretch a point.

So, meanwhile, back at the ranch, Wilverton eyed a flushed and slightly annoyed Fission.

'It tried gore me!' she said, with the aforementioned slight annoyance and a considerable amount of surprise.

Wilverton looked at her with no hint of either emotion staining his features. 'I'm not surprised. If someone tweaked my horn like that I'd do the same thing.'

Fission stared at him sullenly. 'You be so lucky,' she suggested, but Wilverton ignored her, and they both stared into space and wondered just what they could do to get the damned Bull back to the ship. Even if they could find something red which Fission could hold whilst doing her credible impression of a demented dervish in front of the thing – which they couldn't – and assuming they could then outrun the thing if it chose to chase after them – which they couldn't – still Wilverton doubted very much that the bloody thing would find enough enthusiasm to chase them in the first place.

'We got show it who runs the business,' Fission decided. 'It animal, lives on basic emotions. We scare it enough, it does what we want.'

'You don't think it's already formed an opinion on who's scaring who here?'

'I not scared! You?'

'Good heavens no. What, of a little animal like that!' He wasn't very good at sarcasm, but Fission accepted the words at face value anyway.

'Right. First we make it understand we not worried. How we do that?'

'Well,' Wilverton considered, and looked around him. 'We could get off this roof somehow, for a start.'

37

He wasn't quite sure how he'd got up there. He had been watching Fission's failed suicide attempt from one side of the hut which didn't have a door in it when the Bull took it into its head to swing its horns in an arc which would have reduced Fission to two half-Fissions, and had taken a step forward and snorted. The next thing he knew he was on the roof, and Fission was next to him.

The Bull had wandered around the hut to the side which did have a door in it, decided that sufficient exercise had been taken for the time being, and had gone back to murdering grass. It now stood between them and the relative safety of the interior, and studiously ignored them because they were more than three feet away and not red.

'Easy. Climb down.' Fission looked at the Bull momentarily, then the pair of them moved to the opposite side like kids who had just retrieved the ball from the garage roof against the express instructions of the parent in charge of bedtime determination.

Wilverton glanced at the hedge surrounding most of the field as he did so. He had almost got used to it – which was good, as any distraction in this sort of situation could prove just a bit fatal – but it was still odd to see the individual bushes which made up the hedge link arms like that and sway back and forth, kicking up little clods of earth with their roots as they danced. He turned his attention back to the matter in hand.

They looked down, and something looked back up. It was a number of large flowers, with big deep yellow petals and large black irises. The irises were blinking slowly, and the petals had little serrated teeth. There were no mouths, but the eyes spoke volumes; try to arrange *us*, they said, and you'll never count on your fingers again.

And it wasn't a case of simply avoiding them, either, for this was a crowd, a host of golden carnivores, which stretched for several yards and stared upwards as one, straight at them. Lunch, blinked the irises, and managed to lick the lips they didn't have with tongues they hadn't got.

'You try over there,' Fission consulted. 'I look here.'

Wilverton did as they had agreed, and pulled himself over to another Bull-less side of the building.

At least, it *had* been Bull-less. As Wilverton peeked over the edge of the roof onto a ground that was largely earth – and a bit of him took time out to wish that it was *his* Earth – and moreover earth that was doing nothing conspicuously sentient, so the Bull peeked round the corner, ever on the lookout for more succulent pastures; a peek in search of a trough.

Wilverton stood rapidly and was about to call to Fission that the door side was now favourite on all fronts, when the Bull discovered that the other side's grass was not in fact greener, and that it had wasted the effort of moving. This immediately lowered its general level of gruntlement and it swung its head to one side, banging hard into the wall of the hut, shaking it.

The shaking would only have been a problem for someone standing on top of it if they possessed the athletic ability of celery and the balance of a pogo stick.

As a result of which perfect qualification Wilverton screamed 'Aaaahhhh' as he fell backwards and landed heavily at the Bull's hooves. His eyes closed as consciousness was jarred loose and momentarily left him.

Fission spun round at the sound and saw she was alone. Her expression immediately set in determined mode, and she ran in a crouch across the roof and looked down.

The Bull looked down as well, and the sight of Wilverton's comatose figure was juxtaposed in its brain with the lack of grass. It narrowed its eyes at the still form, and lifted its head slightly . . .

Wilverton's eyes opened just in time to see the Bull's head lifting, and he knew that the next movement would be down, onto him; into him, more to the point, which was precisely what he didn't want to be. And with hooves to one side and the wall to the other, he couldn't escape.

Then, from the roof, came a battle cry which would have made Geronimo wet his wigwam, and between the horns Wilverton saw Fission diving like the Captain of the Japanese Olympic Kamikaze team and landing square on the Bull's head, where she wrapped both arms round one horn, both legs round the other, and then hung on for dear life, grim death, and all stations in between.

This upset the Bull a bit.

It thrashed its head back and forth, trying to shake off the alighted lunatic, and its thrashing moved it away from Wilverton. He wasn't about to wait for a second invitation, and scrabbled to his feet.

As an act of rescue it was fine so far.

But whatever Fission had in mind when she took leave of her senses and the roof in quick succession, thought Wilverton, it wasn't a means of escape. If she had intended to bring the Bull to the ground, then by now she would be realizing that she stood a better chance wrestling Kilimanjaro. And if she had anything else in mind then Wilverton was damned if he could work out what it was.

Regardless of the opinion he had formed of the woman – an opinion currently undergoing some reassessment; she was still demented, but there was no denying her courage – he had to do something to help.

Like what?

Well, he could talk to the Bull like he used to talk to those people in the pub back on Earth, then when it was asleep Fission could get off . . .

No.

He felt helpless; and the niche in his mind where that particular feeling rested was worn smooth through constant use.

Then the Bull solved the problem by throwing Fission at him, the last violent shake of its head overcoming her weakening grip.

Well, at least he could save her from injury by catching her, he thought, ignoring the way his muscles immediately raised their hands as his brain came up with the notion. There wasn't time to find out what they wanted, though, as Fission hit him full in the chest and sent him reeling back into the wall of the hut, where he welcomed her with a sharp cry of pain and she returned the welcome by jabbing an elbow into his stomach.

As they pulled themselves once more to their feet, the Bull momentarily turned its head away, maybe searching for Fission, and they were out of their blocks quicker than a sprinter who's dieted on testosterone since his coach crushed little red pills into his feeding bottle. Then the Bull turned its head back again, and they covered the last five yards as though they were jet propelled, which might well have been the case, although the smell of the Bull was powerful enough to hide any evidence.

Fission slammed the door shut behind her, and Wilverton had to duck sharply to his left to make sure he was on the right side of it when it closed.

'Fonking animal!'

Wilverton nodded, and they paused a while to get their breath back.

'Thank you for that,' said Wilverton. 'It was a very brave thing to do.'

Fission scowled at him, as though he had caught her out in something. 'Don't flatter yourself; it not for you. We got Game to win against fonking aliens. Need all help we can get, even your half-litre.'

'Well, that's as maybe. But thank you all the same. I owe you one.'

'You owe me nothing!' she flared, as though Wilverton had offered her a heated match under the finger-nail. 'Nobody owe me nothing, okay?' It wasn't a question. 'I look after myself.'

'Whatever.' Demented, he thought. Come back Bill Bowen, all is forgiven!

Then they paused some more, and ideas about what to do next poured into their heads in a thin, slow trickle. After a while Wilverton risked a few more words.

'You didn't bring anything with you from Earth that might help, I suppose?' He didn't know what, but then he didn't know what they had on Earth these days. Fission gave him a look that reminded him uncomfortably of Arnold. So did her words.

'Course I did. Just waiting you to ask. Everyone walks around with acme cow catcher in fonking pocket – not dressed without one.'

She seemed to take any question as a declaration of war, thought Wilverton. He shrugged inwardly, thought about things for a while longer, had an idea, and risked it again.

'What does it like doing more than anything else, from what we've seen of it so far?'

'Annoying me,' answered Fission with no hesitation.

'Apart from that, let's say.'

'Look, I want move fonking animal to Ship, not play dumb guessing games with intellectual particle streak.'

Wilverton frowned reflectively. She had behaved like this since he had first blessed his eyes by clapping them on her, he thought. Perhaps . . .?

'Fission, we're going to stand a much better chance of bringing this Game thing off if we're all pulling in the same direction. Why don't we try to be friends, eh?'

She looked at him as though he had suggested injecting themselves with rat poison.

41

Wilverton knew the look of old. It said that she didn't want to be friends with him. Particularly him.

But inside Fission, the Game was momentarily forgotten as the words she wanted to say struggled to reach a mouth with lips tighter than a drunken drum.

Because I've made friends before, and they turn into more than that, and just when you're feeling you can let your life fall into their arms they jump out the way like you were a sun-truck on the freeway and you crash straight back into the real world with bruises that never reach the surface.

And before you get a chance to do anything about the last time it happened, you're snatched from your planet and landed here.

That's fonking why.

She thought.

''Cos don't *want* to be friends.'

She said. It was a lot simpler.

Wilverton shrugged. At least she was blunt about it; didn't arrange to meet him the same time tomorrow and then emigrate or have emergency cosmetic surgery, as several others had.

His only friends were in books, he reflected. Even Gloria, given that what was happening now wasn't really real. It would be nice to meet a real Gloria in the real world when this book finished, he thought . . .

Then he shook his head as close to angrily as he ever managed – if he didn't get on with it then he was going to end along with the book.

'It likes eating. We can lead it using food; grass. Put little piles of grass in front of it at regular intervals, and coax it along that way. It doesn't seem intelligent enought to realize what we'd be doing.'

Fission looked like she wanted to tell him what a fonking stupid idea that was, and why didn't he just sit in a corner and work out prime numbers? But then her face softened as she thought about it and realised that it was not altogether a bad idea.

'Okay,' she said, just as though she were taking the decisions in this partnership, 'we try it.'

They went to the door of the hut and opened it, letting the sunlight pour through. Illuminated in front of them was the massive black flank of the Cretin Bull. There was a figure next to it.

'What's Gloria doing to the Bull?' asked Wilverton, and then suddenly wished very much that he hadn't. The puritanical streak somewhere deep within him hoped fervently that Fission would not see fit to put him wise, but she was staring open-mouthed at the scene before them.

Arnold sat a little way off, on the top of a mound covered with a finer grass than the surrounding field, holding a tiny animal of some sort in his arms as though it had just had a large meal of something highly explosive. What looked like a sort of baby Venus fly-trap was shaking the bottom of his jump suit trouser leg, which it had firmly in its tiny teeth, while mumbling something about 'daisy' and 'murderer'. Arnold occasionally shook his leg irritably to get rid of it while not risking dropping the cub, an action which would undoubtedly have incurred a terrible wrath. He also cast slightly worried glances at the hedge whenever it drifted in his direction.

The Bull was as close to smiling as bulls get.

What none of them saw was a hyena – a lone hyena, probably driven from the pack because it didn't have a sense of humour – creeping through the longer grass behind Arnold's mound, silently making its way towards the android's back.

After a moment of indecision, Wilverton moved towards Gloria, leaving Fission rooted to the spot. He moved as quickly as he could while not making any sound at all, mouthing 'Gloria' in that redundant whisper you use when you know that the mouthee cannot hear you, and shaking his head in a furious bid to stop her doing something she would certainly regret, even if the Bull wouldn't. Gloria looked up as the corner of her eye caught movement. She stopped doing what she was doing, and she stood up to greet him. A look of disappointment crossed the Bull's face.

'I can't seem to get any milk from the cow, Thomas,' said Gloria, unconcerned at standing next to something which could kill her by turning its head a bit sharpish. Wilverton beckoned to her, keeping his eyes firmly fixed on the Bull's now inscrutable features, because he knew rather more than Gloria – about almost everything, come to think of it. Gloria moved towards him. The Bull turned its head to watch, myopically, and managed to convey a silent plea at the same time.

The hyena was within a few yards of Arnold now. The android had finally kicked the flytrap hard in the head and drawn his foot up to join the rest of him on the mound. He watched the scene in front of him, but not the one behind.

43

When Gloria reached him, Wilverton leaned forward and whispered the truth in her ear.

Gloria blushed deeply.

She felt something pushing her gently from behind, and turned to see the Bull nuzzling her and staring down at her out of big cow eyes, rather confusingly. Wilverton and Gloria moved a little further away. The Bull followed. It had found something that it liked even more than eating and annoying Fission. Wilverton could not altogether blame it.

Arnold rose to join the others, and the hyena took the last two hurried steps, and leaped.

A gaping hole appeared in the mound in an instant, black and deep, but containing a long red tongue, which flashed out, curled twice around the creature's neck before it even had a chance to widen its eyes in alarm, and pulled it down into the opening.

Arnold stepped unknowingly off the mound creature just before it swallowed, and with great deliberation made sure that his first step was right on top of a small Venus flytrap . . .

A long microwave pulse curled around the Champion's being, the electromagnetic equivalent of a curl of finest Havana cigar smoke, and drifted to the Challenger, the equivalent of a smoke signal. One that said, it's not going to be that easy, you little upstart.

A brief angry flash of blue answered the mute message. The hue was subtly dark, to make the connotation patently clear. It meant, old fart.

VI

'The others aren't back yet, then, Ship?' asked Carlton, sitting deeply in one of the armchairs on the bridge. Had the Ship been equipped with a computer like Arnold, Carlton could have expected a reply on the lines that the others *were* back but were playing hide and seek, and apparently winning. But the computer which formed the Ship's brain – if computer was an advanced enough description, which it wasn't – had none of Arnold's more obvious failings.

'No, not yet, Peter. You are the first to have completed your task. May I offer my congratulations?'

'Thank you, Ship.' Curtis grunted something from his armchair across the other side of the room and reached up to scratch his head with one hand, while the other attacked the guests in his chest hair; all seven of them – hairs, not guests. The hands moved rapidly between the numerous places on Curtis's body which craved attention, and he looked as though he were offering the starting prices on the three-forty at Epsom in fast-forward mode.

'Do you know how the others are getting on?' asked Carlton.

'I am not able to watch everything that happens unless I am in the immediate vicinity,' replied the Ship, 'but I suspect that we are about to discover. I can see a group approaching us now.'

Carlton rose and hurried to the window. It would become a port when they were in space, no doubt, but while they sat on the ground of Callia it was a window. Through it he could see a little procession moving steadily towards the Ship in fading and ever redder light. In the lead were Wilverton and Gloria, walking slowly and uncertainly, glancing over their shoulders every few yards. Just behind them was a live, complete, one-piece Smithfield Market, seven feet to the shoulder, foot-long horns with points approaching the molecular level, and an expression of undying love on its face. It stared squarely at the back of Gloria's head, and straight into her eyes when she turned to check that it was still there.

Behind what Carlton knew just had to be the Cretin Bull was Fission, and behind her came Arnold, picking out carefully where to put his feet – and not just because he was following the Bull. In his arms he held what was apparently a small animal of some sort, supporting it carefully in one arm while the other surreptitiously covered its mouth. Whenever Gloria looked back, he moved into the shadow of the Bull so she could not judge his child-minding technique.

When they reached the Ship, Wilverton and Gloria paused.

The Bull paused just behind them, with its head hanging over theirs. It would have won the three-forty at Epsom by a nose. Fission and Arnold walked round the group and up the steps to the Ship, Arnold risking his eardrums by loosing his hold on the cub's noise hole. They disappeared into their sanctuary.

Once they were safe inside, Wilverton and Gloria took a fast couple of steps forward and upward. The Bull made to follow after a short pause, but by then the steps had started to rise, and it was balked. The steps snapped shut at some pace, and in doing so, since they were still climbing, catapulted the two humans into the corridor, where they landed together in a compromising heap. They moved a little and found the position even more compromising – but time and place and all that.

'My apologies,' offered the Ship pleasantly, perhaps for not propelling them straight through a cabin door. Wilverton and Gloria struggled to their feet, and turned to see Fission's disapproving stare and Arnold holding the cub out to Gloria as though his turn had finished in a game of pass the pork at a barmitzvah. Gloria took the Cutum, which immediately started crying, having been able to draw breath for the first time in a while, and together they made their way to the bridge.

The greeting they received was warm, with congratulations on the recovery of the Bull – now standing forlornly outside the closed door – and the inevitable question concerning their methods. Wilverton looked at Gloria, and back at Carlton, who had posed the question, then attempted to find the answer somewhere in the middle distance. Fission opened her mouth, and the answer struggled to get out. Fortunately, the little animal decided that it was not for the ears of adults, and increased its volume by an order of magnitude. It was fast becoming a big noise in the control room.

'What the hell *is* that thing?' bellowed Carlton.

'It's a Shoutum,' Arnold screamed back.

'Well, why did you bring it here?'

'*Me!*' Arnold's saintliness was severely bruised by the unfairness of the world.

'It's only a baby,' Gloria told them loudly. 'It's just frightened and hungry.'

'Well, can't you keep it quiet?' Babies, even alien animal babies, were in the same league as marriage as far as Carlton was concerned, and were fighting with smallpox and a loss of sexual appetite against relegation. 'Give it something to suck on, for God's sake.' Then he smirked what was supposed to be the grin of a man well used to sucking on female somethings, and Fission shook her head in disbelief, seeing the grin of a boy who's still pretty chuffed with the effects of puberty.

Gloria proffered a finger, and waggled it about in the massive gap between the Cutum's lips, trying to induce that gap to narrow, but the infant was having none of it and redoubled its efforts to shake the Ship apart with the force of its sound waves.

It reached out with its little hands, each of which had three fingers and an opposing thumb, and grasped the front of Gloria's jump suit, then buried its head in her chest and tried to get inside the garment. Gloria eased the head away gently, reddening slightly, and this acted as a spur to its lungs. It was obvious what it wanted.

Gloria hesitated, then moved to one of the armchairs, and nudged it round to face the wall. She sat down out of sight of the others while the little hands reached for her clothing again.

It wasn't going to satisfy the requirements of the stomach, she knew, but at least the brain might be fooled. The others heard the lowering of a zip as the cub suddenly quietened in anticipation.

'So how did you manage to get the Bull?' asked Carlton again.

Wilverton gazed, Fission opened her mouth but found that no words were prepared to venture forth, and Arnold said,

'Gloria milked it.'

There was a short silence occupied by memories, imagination, and the sound of contented sucking.

'Arnold!' snapped Wilverton, turning angrily to face the android.

'What?' asked Arnold, his quick obviously in danger of another severe nick.

47

'Never mind.' He turned back to Carlton. 'She thought it was a cow, and she wanted milk for the animal.' Carlton's query concerning the outcome died in his throat. 'It sort of followed us after that.'

'So would I,' he opined with feeling. 'Where did you find the animal thing?' – Carlton's term for 'baby waby'.

'Gloria and Arnold found it abandoned in a field. Its parents were apparently chased off by a pack of something like hyenas.'

Carlton shrugged. Alien planets were likely to contain things that were alien. That was what alien planets were for.

'So you didn't manage to find Yazocks the Changeling, then.'

'We saw it,' Arnold said. 'It changed from a big bird into a hyena and ran away, but we had to stop to get the Yellum instead of following it. Apparently.' He threw a glance at the back of the chair.

Carlton hmphed, and wondered whether to *say* it was the sort of thing that women did, rather than just think it. He decided not – it was way too early to give up his assault on Fission's good books. If she had any.

'Well, we know that it's out there, anyway,' said Wilverton, looking on the bright side. 'With all of us looking, we should be able to find it again.'

'We must find this Cutum's parents as well,' came a firm voice from behind the high back of an armchair.

'Let's get some profit, then,' said Fission, and looked to the Captain for affirmation of her decision. 'What matter with him?'

Curtis scratched at all parts of his body in quick succession and totally ignored what was going on around him.

'It's the Golden Fleas,' explained Carlton. 'We got the Fleece and they decided on a change of address.' Fission started to repeat her suggestion, but stopped respectfully short as Biondor appeared before most of them, and behind Gloria.

'Congratulations, humans. You have completed the tasks well ahead of schedule.' This provoked some confusion. Biondor did not strike them as someone who would often be mistaken. Gloria frowned slightly, but the Cutum withdrew its lips and claimed her notice. She looked down at it, tickling it under the chin and evoking a happy half-smile and the faintest of purrs.

'We have only completed two of the tasks, Biondor,' admitted Wilverton. 'We have not yet caught Yazocks the Harmless Changeling.' The group felt a pang of disappointment, almost as

48

though they had let the alien down by contradicting him. Biondor did not seem ruffled.

'Oh, but you have.' He turned to look at the back of Gloria's chair.

Another silence fell, as two and two were added by all in the control room at various speeds, and all came up with four. Gloria was the last to complete the sum but then her eyes widened as the already-not-quite-so-Cutum smiled expansively at her, and winked.

Her first reaction was to throw the thing away from her, but it was still an infant, and she carefully stood up, then turned round and placed it on the chair. She gave it a Look, much better than the one she had tried on Arnold, then blushed again as the Changeling licked its lips and smacked them appreciatively. This was not turning out to be a good day for Gloria.

'But we saw Yazocks change into a hyena,' she pleaded. 'From a bird. Into a hyena.' Perhaps repetition could make it a fact.

The Changeling looked at her out of laughing eyes, eyes which now held a much greater depth of experience than those of an infant could ever do.

One of those attention-seeking coughs came from Fission, and Gloria looked at the other woman. Every human was staring at Gloria's chest, and she hurriedly put it away and zipped up her jump suit, then blushed all over again. Her day was getting much worse.

The Changeling began to change, to grow, ageing before her eyes like the end of one of those films where the rejuvenating water suddenly runs out. It stopped when it was the size of a small but otherwise ordinary adult, and adopted a human appearance, possibly so as not to upset any of the crew. It was a Harmless Changeling, after all.

'I was the bird,' he admitted happily. 'But I wasn't the hyena – they're called kakras, by the way. Behind that bush was a kakra, and I dived on it, scared it away, and turned myself into the jala. That's what the brown furry ones are called; I like Cutum, though!' Gloria stared hard at him. She had rather gone off Cutum. 'Good, eh?'

'Clever,' said Arnold, clearly impressed, then ignored the temporary transfer of Gloria's steely-eyed glare.

'It was all good, harmless fun,' said Yazocks, with an impish grin. That grin always went down well with humans. It did not appear to go down well with Gloria. Had they been sharing a water bed, her side would have been covered by a sheet of ice. Yazocks reflected that they were unlikely ever to do so. He did his best to look trite, and flicked an imaginary fleck of something from the front of his jump suit. He couldn't keep it up for long, though, and the grin lit up his features once more.

'So *that*'s the sort of Harmless Changeling you are, is it?' Gloria dared Yazocks to refute the accusation.

'So, congratulations are indeed in order,' said Biondor, arresting the attention of those not about to get embroiled in a bit of a tiff. 'You have succeeded in all three of your tasks, and in most ingenious ways.'

'Oh, come on,' said Yazocks. 'What harm did it do?'

'Yes, you have done well. There are times when it is good to watch you humans perform, and see the ideas you formulate.' There was a noticeable swell of pride. A smile even struggled onto Curtis's face as he managed to banish the grimace for a moment.

'No thanks to *some* people,' mutered Carlton, with a movement of his eyes towards his Captain. The smile left.

'That's not fair! I got the Fleas!'

'Only because I threatened you.'

'At least you not need save him after he fall off roof,' Fission told him before he pulled open his jump suit to show them the 'S' underneath.

'Oh, thank you!' Wilverton sounded pained. 'I didn't mean to fall, you know.' Curtis looked slightly happier at having belittled company, until his First Officer finished off, 'And it's not very nice putting me in the same category as *him*!'

'It embarrassed me in front of all these people,' said Gloria.

'Unfortunately,' continued Biondor, slightly louder, so that they all stopped and looked at him again, 'this wasn't one of them.' There was a noticeable deflation of pride. Curtis grimaced and scratched his armpit. 'But there are seven tasks left.'

'Oh, they've forgotten all about that now.' Yazocks continued talking in class.

'I can't say it wasn't entertaining, though.' Biondor finished his summing-up. Gloria let his words tell Yazocks all the Changeling needed to know. 'So you now have a rest period, after which I will bring your next tasks to you. Do not ask what they are, because I do not yet know myself. You may elect to retain the services of those you have recovered if you wish, but only with their consent. It is not unknown for the subjects of these tasks voluntarily to assist a team as they continue with the round.'

'He's going,' said Gloria, loudly and firmly, before anyone had even drawn breath to suggest that Yazocks might be useful to them. 'And so is that creature outside.'

'And so are these bloody Fleas,' said Curtis, now examining the little bumps resulting from inquisitive little flea teeth.

'As you wish,' said Biondor. 'I have to go and part the waters of the Flar Sea on Sharmon. That isn't a problem in itself, of course, it's stopping the fish swimming out the sides that's the tricky bit. I will leave you for a time.' And he did.

Far away, and yet very near – metaphysically speaking – the two bodiless rivals for the Game hung in space. Actually they weren't 'in' space, but then they weren't outside it, either. They were sort of part of it, in a way that only incredibly advanced bodiless aliens seem to have got the hang of, so far.

Beneath them, the Lessers regarded their superiors in suitably quiescent awe, maintaining an outer shell of ever changing frequencies but not letting it impinge on the contestants' beings.

They strove among themselves for the right to compete, but the calmness of the Champion was daunting.

It was also a bit of a porky.

The humans had got through the first three tasks with the panache of a driggian[1], and there were harder to come.

In the good old days, when a lower lip was available, the Champion could have bitten it.

In the good old days, the Challenger's lower lip would have curved into a smile along with its partner. The tasks were surely going to cause as much trouble to its team of trands as athlete's foot to an Oethosian sea snake.

[1] From the ancient tongue of the Champion's ancestors, meaning 'panacheless one'.

VII

The home planet of the trands was called Trand.

They were not the most imaginative bunch, the trands, but then their prowess was rather obviously more on the physical side than the cerebral. The typical example was built like a small condominium of brick out-houses, with six arms arranged in equal numbers on each side of the body; a fortunate equality because any numerical discrepancy in things that size would have made standing upright a big problem. They sported legs which looked like they had been growing in the ground for a couple of hundred years before being grafted onto the rest of the body.

The general impression was that they had not been created by the normal mammalian method, but quarried from a granite rock face, and overall they resembled nothing more than rather large versions of the Incredible Hulk – the one with elastic trousers and a shirt bill that would make Imelda Marcos's shoe account look frugal – but without all that polished charm.

On the planet Fillae – the whole thing courtesy of the Challenger – there existed a creature which the trands knew from their own mythology, a creature which, it was said, sat on the Egg of Untold Wealth.

It was ten feet in height even when sitting; it was twenty feet in girth, probably as much to do with lack of exercise as with the slight thyroid condition which the myth failed to mention. The folds of its skin made the naked pink body look like it was in great need of ironing, not to mention lipo-suction, and it watched the world around it through three eyes placed symmetrically round its bald head, giving it an unceasing panorama of its environment and a fairly constant headache.

If a visitor came with the correct answer to its riddle – What has four legs when it is young, three in middle age and none after it dies? – then it would rise and reveal the egg which the visitor could take as a reward.

The creature was called Cataphar the Unmoved and Immovable.

There's a hint there.

A hint not only to the present-day trands' prowess in giving decent titles to their myths, but also to the success of their mythological ancestors in solving the riddle. A success conspicuously absent largely because, as has been intimated, any puzzle they couldn't solve with a spiked club probably wasn't worth the solving, in the trands' book.

Not, it should be noted, that the trands were stupid – far from it. They just preferred the more robust way of life. As their success in the first round of the Game proved, they were intelligent enough to invent space travel – a quite marvellous opportunity to visit strange new worlds, to seek out new life, new civilizations, and to beat them all up.

Cataphar the Unmoved and Immovable sat in its hugeness and watched as a trand approached it.

'Have you the answer to my riddle?'

The trand ignored the fact that Cataphar had spoken as it approached in a way so slow, but so determined, that it definitely qualified as inexorable. It was moving with the apparent conviction of a small glacier. When it was near enough to touch the creature, the trand answered. Translated into Fission-speak, it said, 'Fonk the answer to your riddle!'

Cataphar looked somewhat surprised when its ground-based bits – largely buttocks – were gripped, and it found itself lifted effortlessly onto the shoulders of its visitor. Its eyes widened, but it didn't look round in alarm because it could already see all round. Besides, it was down that bothered it.

'You must answer the riddle! You cannot take the egg until you have answered. You cannot take . . .'

Crunch.

Apparently the trand didn't want to take. Its task had been to break, and that it very evidently *could* do. It didn't even bother to confirm that the egg was empty, that when the Untold became Told, it had all turned out just to be a big joke. Trands didn't really do jokes.

With a thump, the trand dropped Cataphar the Now Moved and with a Bum Full of Eggshell, and made its way back to its Ship.[1]

[1]The answer to the Riddle of the Cataphar is a Fergal – a four-legged animal much prized by the trands as a tasty main course. When the animal reaches its tenderest, in about middle age, the trands try one leg, and if this is suitably succulent, kill the thing and eat the other three before downing the torso.

The Vulix was not a lot like a dragon. It was bigger, it was uglier, and it was meaner. And we're not talking about dipping its hand into its pocket to get the next round.

For a start it didn't have hands – it had claws; large, curved and sharp – and for a finish it carried the sort of demeanour that would make a cell full of psychopaths look like a Bible-study meeting.

It didn't have wings, it had stumpy pile-driver arms and legs; it didn't have an elegant snout, it had a curved pock-marked beak; and it wasn't golden, it was a sort of dingy green red.

No wonder it was grumpy.

There was one similarity to a dragon, though. The Vulix boasted a similar ability to breathe flame, except that it didn't actually breathe it, and it didn't actually boast. The Vulix expelled flame-filled air, but it did it from the opposite end to your average dragon, hence its other name, the Firefart.

For the trand sent to fetch it, this was not news, so it knew what to expect when the Firefart stood on all fours and displayed in threatening pose its posterior, along with its sad collection of singed dangly bits.

The Vulix glanced over its shoulder to see if this sight had a dampening effect on the trand's progress – as it usually did on that of a female Vulix; another pointer to the reasons for the creature's permanently foul mood. It saw the trand keep right on coming.

It blew a blast of flame at the interloper, and just like the dragon who guarded the Fleece, but for a rather different reason, the action brought tears to its eyes. It looked over its shoulder again when the smoke and the tears had cleared, and saw the trand less than a couple of yards away.

The Vulix swung round, enraged both by the fact that the trand should still be there, and also by the searing pain in the area below the merest of blackened stubs which denoted where its tail used to be. The creature roared its pain and anger, and the trand hit it on the point of the chin with a hay-making hook of its middle right arm.

The Vulix suddenly forgot its pain and rested. The trand started dragging it back towards its Ship. When it woke, and noticed the bit that had been in contact with the ground while the drag was in progress – which it would absolutely immediately –

the Firefart would almost certainly lose some of its legendary good humour.

The last of the first three tasks was the same as it had been for the human team, except that the Harmless Changeling for which they searched was called Yomind.

There was flame in evidence here as well.

Four of the trand team moved forward, systematically burning the ground in front of them with a makeshift flame-thrower, which was not a mechanical device but a still unconscious Firefart, which two of the trands pointed in the desired direction and squeezed.

Eventually, Yomind was forced to change into something that could get out of the way.

The trands were not the most agile of creatures, but Yomind had no sooner started his transformation than they landed on him like a rock-fall. The first three tasks had been successfully completed.

'Feel free to use the recreational facilities,' said the Ship. 'I will contact you when Biondor returns.'

'What recreational facilities?' asked Carlton.

'I have squash courts, a holovision room, snooker room, sauna, and many other attractions which were popular in your own time, and also many which are now popular in Fission's. If you tell me what activity you would care to undertake, I dare say I can accommodate it.' Carlton smirked but didn't go any further as he imagined the Ship pursing her hydrogen intakes.

'What sort of things are popular on Earth now, then?' asked Wilverton, glancing at Fission but expecting the Ship to answer. His expectation was fulfilled.

'Many things, of course, Thomas, but I am equipped with a psychic massage room, a corlball court, and a Quanti centre, with full armour in all sizes. Perhaps Fission would be prepared to show you how these facilities may be used, should you so wish.'

Wilverton glanced at Fission. Perhaps she most definitely wouldn't, said the returning glance.

'I think I'll try the holovision,' said Wilverton. Gloria was absent, having gone to her cabin for a shower and a good sulk, and she was unlikely, Wilverton surmised correctly, to want company right at that moment, especially *that* sort of company. 'How do I get there?'

'Just follow the blue line.' And there was a blue line on the floor of the control room, starting just in front of Wilverton's feet and leading to the door, and beyond.

Curtis was doing much the same as Gloria, only he was not sulking, but was furious in his own feeble way, and was hoping the shower would drown the little golden bastards which had been making his life miserable since he had liberated them.

They had left a complaining Yazocks and a lovesick Cretin Bull outside the Ship – no problem there – but the Fleas had apparently not wanted to depart. What was more, they appeared to revel in shampoo and the torrent of hot water to which Curtis was currently treating them.

He had scratched bits of himself raw to no apparent effect, and now tried to soothe them with a gently applied bar of soap. Then he spotted one of the little swine on his thigh, hanging on with its teeth.

This was his chance.

He dropped the bar of soap and took an enormous swipe at the creature which jumped out the way at the last moment.

His thigh didn't, and Curtis damn near knocked it off before starting circumlocuting like an impression of a Red Indian rain dance – which appeared to be working spectacularly – and howling in pain.

Then he trod on the soap and left the shower horizontally like an ejection from a bar-room brawl.

But he was straight back in there. He wasn't going to be beaten! It was war: Curtis against several small insects was a pretty even match.

Now he saw it on his stomach. He had muscles there, he thought. Bless him. He tightened the muscles as hard as he could, clenched his fist, brought the two together hard, and slid down the wall of the shower, gasping for breath.

Looking down once more, he saw the thing looking up at him and smiling, goadingly.

But he was not about to hit its current perch.

Perhaps he *was* to be beaten, he thought dispiritedly. At least there had been no-one watching.

*

He was wrong, of course.

The Challenger sent the electromagnetic equivalent of a smile across to its opponent.

Rest period, eh? it asked.

'I'm sorry I called you Fish earlier on,' said Carlton. 'It got us off on the wrong foot, I'm afraid.' He smiled one of his specials at her. Fission was the first girl he'd met in four hundred years (well, just over two weeks really, but Carlton was living proof of Einstein's theory of libido dilation), and that was a somewhat bigger gap than he was used to. He searched for something nice to say as a follow-up, sure that even in four hundred years a spot of flattery after the initial peace-making would not have lost the appeal it used to have.

Fission didn't give him the chance.

'You want sex, yes?'

'Er.' Wow, things *had* changed on Earth! He had guessed that they would become more liberated, but this sounded like just his sort of planet now. 'Well, yes, sure,' he answered, with a sideways, almost embarrassed, look at Arnold, whose expression had not progressed beyond non-committal. When he got back to Earth – 'if' didn't rush into his head to spoil things – everyone would be like this, so he might as well get used to it.

'Well, we not animals on Earth now. You might be in your time but you control disgusting bodily habits around me in future, okay?'

He couldn't say 'okay' because to do so would be to accept that he'd been out of order and was apologizing for it. He couldn't argue with her because that would confirm that he was as much of an animal as she implied he was. And he couldn't say nothing because out of the corner of his eye he could see the smirk in one corner of Arnold's mouth preparing to sprint over the rest of it if she got the better of him, which at that moment she undoubtedly had.

'Have you got a gym, Ship?' he asked, choosing the ignore-the-fact-she's-even-spoken ploy.

'Yes, indeed, Peter. Follow the green line.' Which appeared at Carlton's feet and led him thankfully off down the corridor.

'Arnold, that leaves us,' said Fission, and there was something missing from her voice. Something obnoxious, leaving a weird pleasantness. 'You want I show what androids do on Earth?' Arnold could think of nothing better to do with a recreation period, meaning he could think of nothing whatever, and shrugged an interest which he did not particularly feel. A few hints on the tasks expected of him might not go amiss, though – he liked to know exactly what he was telling humans to go and poke.

Fission led him to her cabin, following the red line which the Ship provided in case she had forgotten the way.

Wilverton had followed the line along corridors and down in a lift to find himself in a room slightly smaller than his cabin. In the centre of the room was a large armchair. He sat down and waited.

Nothing happened.

He was about to ask the Ship what was going on when a man appeared in front of him, crouched and holding a gun, which he pointed directly at him. It was just possible that when fired it would produce a little flag with 'fooled you' written on it, but it's generally best not to stake your life on these things.

Wilverton jerked himself out of the armchair and threw himself sideways, seeing as he did so the puff of smoke from the barrel and hearing the report. There wasn't any flag.

'Say your prayers, bud!' came a gruff voice, and Wilverton began with the Lord's petrified squeak before another gun-shot put an abrupt end to his entreaty.

The muscles on Carlton's torso looked as though they were about to break through his skin, and beads of sweat dripped off his chin, almost hissing as they hit his chest. His biceps flexed like hippos trying to escape from super cling-film as he pushed a bar above his head. The bar was not heavy, but the weights on either end were. His elbows locked at last, and a great heaving breath escaped his lips.

The door opened, at speed, and Arnold entered. His face had always been good at expressions, but it was apparently bad at hiding them. He looked unsure, even worried.

Carlton didn't notice the obvious discomfort himself, as the surprise of the opening door made him lose a precarious balance. The weight of the bar shifted itself to somewhere just behind his head, and that was quite enough. He toppled backwards and the bar crashed into the floor a millisecond ahead of his body. He looked up at Arnold, slightly shaken and fairly stirred, and read the expression on the android's face as surprise at his reaction.

'Hello, Arnold. How jolly nice to see you. Excuse me lying down, won't you, only some prat made me jump while I was holding five tons of iron above my head.' Arnold looked at him distractedly, hearing only what was said and nothing of what was meant.

'Yes, certainly,' he replied politely, which was evidence in itself that not all was right. Carlton struggled to his feet, stepped over the bar which crouched menacingly on the floor behind him, and sank into a chair on the far side of the gym. He watched Arnold expectantly. Arnold watched him back.

'What can I do for you Arnold?'

'Oh, nothing,' said Arnold with all the nonchalance he could muster. He looked about as nonchalant as the person everyone is staring at while someone says 'Ready', 'Aim' and 'Fire'.

'Oh, right. Just popped in on the off chance, eh?' Arnold nodded enthusiastically, and Carlton wondered what could have upset the thing's equilibrium. Amongst all the emotions which this supposedly emotionless bundle of man- and Biondor-made parts showed, uncertainty rated well below arrogance, vindictiveness and plenty of others rarely found outside soap operas and infants' schools, but it was certainly in the ascendant at the moment.

'I thought we could have a sort of talk,' said Arnold. 'Since I haven't got anything else to do at all.'

'Uh-huh. What about exactly?'

'Oh, I don't know.' Arnold searched casually for a topic. Clearly there had been none close to the fore when he made the suggestion. None at all. If *only* he could think of something!

'I know!' Well, gosh, he had! 'Now that I'm like this,' he indicated his recently acquired body, 'perhaps it might be a good idea if I found out more about how to use it.'

Carlton could think of no good reason why he should swap small-talk with an android who generally acted like he was practising for a winner-takes-all insult bout, but Arnold's civility tweaked his curiosity, so he nodded. 'Well, take a seat. Make yourself at home.'

Arnold moved to another chair in the room and sat down with reasonable grace. The weighted bar was in the way of his feet, so he leant down and moved it to one side with no apparent effort. Carlton watched him do so with unspoken surprise. Arnold did not seem to notice that he had moved a couple of hundred pounds of iron – five tons was a bit of an exaggeration – as though it was practically weightless.

'And you reckon you don't know how to use your body?'

'Well, not all of it,' said Arnold, spotting his chance but missing the fact that there was a compliment in there somewhere. A pity, from his point of view, as compliments in Arnold's direction since they had left Earth totalled about one, give or take about one.

'Which bits are you having trouble with?' Carlton now sounded slightly amused.

Arnold appeared to pause for thought, and looked almost flustered. He opened his mouth as though he had the answer to that one, but nothing came out, and he looked around the room for a while as though the bit with which he was having trouble might be lying in plain view somewhere and would remind him.

'Balance,' he said suddenly.

'Balance.' Carlton didn't look convinced. Arnold nodded, but he didn't look convinced either. 'You should practise standing on one leg. Anything else?'

'Er.'

'I am *so* sorry, Thomas!' said the Ship, sounding distraught. 'I did not appreciate that the holovision might take you by surprise.' Had she a wrist, she would have self-slapped it for a week.

'No, that's all right.' Wilverton picked himself off the floor and fumbled back into the armchair, still not quite believing that there wasn't a scorched bullet hole in the back of the thing.

'I did wait for you to request the holovision be activated, then acted on my own. I do apologize.'

'Please. Don't worry. I should have recognized Humphrey Bogart in any case.' He'd just thought that, well, that he might be in a Bogart movie. With a full-size holovision it was an easy mistake to make, especially for Wilverton.

'Would you like to see something else?'

'Please.' He settled himself.

A man appeared in front of him wearing a quite enormous and totally unbelievable smile. His jacket displayed a garish kaleidoscope of clashing colours that would only have failed to win the most vomitary outfit on holovision award if his trousers had also entered. Wilverton immediately recognized that it was some sort of game show.

'Well,' came a voice through the smile, 'Cassie and Peger's score was one minute twenty-seven seconds, Cornal and Diane four minutes and thirteen seconds, and Polar and Carea seven minutes and thirty-four seconds.' He waited for the applause to die down. 'So we have to say goodbye to Cassie and Peger. Join us after the break for the final.'

Behind him the lights rose on three double beds, each of which was occupied by a slightly sweaty and completely nude couple. On the middle bed, Cassie and Peger looked crestfallen.

'That's about enough, I think, Ship.'

Time to go and find Gloria, he thought, the idea which had already been mulling itself around in the back of his mind having been pushed to the fore by the events in front of him. He left the holovision room and made his way to Gloria's cabin.

The door opened to reveal a newly washed vision of loveliness, and the radiant smile which lit up her face as she saw the identity of her visitor showed that her ill humour had been washed away with the dirt of the day.

'Thomas!'

'How are you feeling? You look lovely.'

'Oh, thank you. I feel much better. It was just that horrid little changeling thing, and I made such a fool of myself with that bull.' Wilverton shook his head and waved his hand dismissal.

'That could have happened to anyone. It was only because we were looking for a bull that I knew it wasn't a cow, otherwise I might have done the same thing. And you can hardly blame Yazocks – he just fell for you like everyone else does!'

'Oh, Thomas,' she said, as the door closed puritanically behind them. She reached out for the zipper of his jump suit, then paused. 'Nothing's going to happen this time, is it?' She sounded a little uncertain, remembering that her first – how to put it? – encounter, with Thomas had been aborted because he had said the chapter was finishing. It was an aspect of Wilverton's character that she had not quite worked out yet, but to Gloria suspect mental balance was way short of a good enough reason not like someone.

Wilverton shook his head, and smiled. 'The only thing that can get inthe way is –'

'Hello, everybody,' said the Ship. 'Biondor has returned and is waiting to give you details of your next tasks. Would you be so kind as to make your various ways up here please?'

'– that.'

61

VIII

Fission looked disappointed and not a little angry as she left the cabin in response to the Ship's call. In the corridor were Arnold, heading for the lift that would take them back to the level of the control room, and some ten yards or so behind him Carlton, looking very self-satisfied. The satisfaction approached smugness as Fission emerged; in fact it reached smugness and started trotting happily some way beyond it. He might have been walking with Arnold, but the android was, well, striding, like you do when you are a mite peeved.

'What happened?' asked Fission. 'You were going get something.'

'I did,' said Arnold shortly. 'Information. And if you think that I'm going to do what I just found out you want me to do then you've got another think coming, and nothing else.'

'You have no choice.' Fission's voice had turned frosty and held an element of disbelief. 'You an android! You do as told!'

Carlton stayed behind them, keeping just in ear-shot, and gravely shook his head at this pronouncement, still smiling. Fission had quite a bit to learn about Arnold.

More than a bit, apparently, as Arnold replied, 'You have a lot to learn, sister.'

'Don't call me "sister", you charmless quark.'

'Sorry.' Arnold sounded trite, and Carlton's eyebrows rose. 'You have a lot to learn, missy.' Carlton's mouth corners rose.

The lift doors opened as they approached.

'Call me Fission, nothing . . .'

The lift doors closed in front of the three of them, and they stood silently watching the display as it informed them of the lift's progress, rising to the highest level on the Ship. The doors opened, and they stepped out.

'. . . else, understand?'

They walked on while Arnold pondered an answer for a few moments. They were certainly getting on like a house on fire, thought Carlton, slightly surprised that he was not being driven back by the heat.

'I think it was the early-twentieth-century poet Wilfred Arkwright in his epic "The Hark of the Grandules",' said Arnold, sounding like a late-night arts programme, 'who summed it up best when he wrote "Sod off young lady".'

'Fonking *machine!*'

'Or not,' corrected Arnold, with one of *those* smiles.

Fission slowed and glanced at the ceiling. 'Luc! Arguing with fonking robot! Degrading!'

Right, thought Arnold, no more Mister Nice Guy.

Degrading, eh? He'd show her degrading! By the time he'd finished, he promised silently, the remedial class would be a lofty ambition.

The control-room door opened in front of this newly formed friendship as Carlton wondered who Luke was.

The other crew members were waiting inside, respectfully silent in Biondor's presence. The verbal exchange died as Fission took a spare seat and stared at Arnold as he did the same, trying to inflict irreparable damage with the power of her mind. Arnold looked completely unmoved. Carlton stifled a smirk.

'What's that smell?' asked Curtis of no-one in particular, wrinkling his nose to show that this was an odour smell rather than an aroma smell.

'Red Cat,' said Fission sharply, from next to him.

'Smells more like dead cat!' he responded, with thought only for how witty he was being, and not for what 'Red Cat' might be.

'My perfume,' Fission educated him, turning his wit into a much more usual social gaffe. Her expression suggested it would be his last.

'It's very nice,' he told her weakly.

'I trust you enjoyed your recreation,' Biondor broke in, proving thereby that he did not know everything, but thankfully stopping Curtis from making pleasant conversation by asking Fission why she had donned perfume. Some nodded and murmured, and others did not see fit to put him right. 'Your next tasks will commence after a period for food and sleep.'

'Is there a time limit on these tasks?' asked Wilverton. 'You said earlier that we were ahead of schedule.'

Gloria smiled at him. Their children would be ever so clever. Ever the optimist, she assumed they would all be luscious blondes with hearts of gold and Nobel prize brains, as opposed to the possible alternative of scrawny morons.

'The overall limit is fourteen zarbs.'

'And how long is a zarb?'

'It can vary where the Champion and Challenger are concerned. Why don't you think of it as one fourteenth of a book?' He smiled, and Wilverton smiled back and nodded. Fission wondered why he was humouring the little nutter, but it wasn't the sort of question that even Fission would put to Biondor.

'The first of your next two tasks will be to recover the cornucopia from the cave of the cyclops. The second is to recover the Jewel of Altares from . . . well, Altares. The details will be given to you by the Ship. I have to go and move in a mysterious way on the planet Lenbor. Good luck.' And he was gone.

'The corn you what?' asked Gloria, but Wilverton did not get the chance to answer before Fission spoke.

'Ship. What can tell about those two?'

'The cornucopia is currently the property of the cyclops on the planet Cupros.'

'Sorry,' said Gloria. 'What do we do to the corn?'

'The cornucopia,' said the Ship kindly to this apparently most neuronically challenged of her charges, and just beating Wilverton to it, 'is a horn of plenty.' Carlton smiled but no-one noticed. 'It is filled with whatever food or drink is desired by its owner, and is inexhaustible.'

'That must save on the washing-up.'

'Yes, I expect so,' said the Ship, extremely kindly.

'And the Jewel of Altares?' prompted Carlton.

'Is kept, as Biondor said, on the planet Altares, where it is guarded by the dog Cerberus.'

'Cerberus?' said Wilverton. 'That's the dog which guarded the gates of Hades. What's it doing on Altares?'

'Guarding the Jewel of Altares,' said Arnold. 'That's why the Ship said the Jewel was guarded by Cerberus. It's a difficult one to grasp but you'll get it in time.'

'Thank you, Arnold,' Wilverton said heavily.

'Don't mention it.'

'Ship?'

'The dog lives on a plateau island which can be reached only by crossing one of three wooden bridges over a bottomless chasm. Two of the bridges will not bear the weight of a human.

There are two beings on the mainland side of the bridges who know which is the safe one. One of these beings tells nothing but truth, while the other sometimes, but not always, fabricates answers which are false. You may question these beings to find which is the right bridge, or you may guess, or employ any other means you deem suitable.'

There was a moment of some quiet contemplation. No-one said 'Sorry?'

'Need brains *and* muscle for profit on that,' said Fission, clarifying the obvious.

'Okay,' said Arnold, 'I'll go.'

Fission turned purple in less than a nanosecond. 'Need brains that *work*, positronic putz!'

Arnold glowed. Would that goading were an Olympic sport.

'Thomas should go,' said Carlton, who was well enough endowed in the brawn department to be able to afford the odd compliment on the brains side. 'I think Arnold should go along.'

'He goes, I don't,' warned Fission, presumably implying an 'if' in there somewhere.

'So you must go for the cornucopia,' said Wilverton, like the pin to Fission's balloon. 'And I think it's too dangerous for Gloria, so she can go with you.'

'I think Peter should go along with the ladies for protection,' said Arnold, watching Fission out of the corner of one eye in case he had to duck suddenly.

'I don't mind,' said Carlton before Fission's mind could come up with anything sufficiently damning to hurl at Arnold.

'Think you need protection?' she asked him, having thought of something for Carlton instead.

'I'm almost sure Arnold meant for me to protect you,' said Carlton ingenuously. 'But if I do, I'm sure you're just the one to provide it.' Then he smiled brightly, with quite admirable tenacity.

'Hey!' Curtis interjected. They were taking all the decisions here without asking his permission at all. And he was Captain. It was time he did something about it.

'What?' Carlton demanded, and Curtis found all eyes looking at him. His dander stopped its half-hearted attempt to get up and went straight back to bed.

'Er, that leaves me with Arnold and Thomas, then.' Could that count as a decision? No, probably not. Process of elimination. Pity.

He didn't spot the reaction of his two 'colleagues' to this news as his attention was drawn by Fission leaning down to scratch her ankle, and the opening at the neck of her jump suit gaping with the movement. The habit of trying to peer clandestinely down women's fronts generally fades from the average male as the need for that particular manoeuvre is negated by more, shall we say, hands-on experience. Curtis, by precisely that reasoning, turned his head away, but kept his eyeballs right where they were until they threatened to swivel round and point back into his head.

Fission didn't notice. It was probably just as well, or Curtis's future hands-on experience might have been rendered somewhat futile.

'This is going very well,' said Wilverton, but his expression gave the lie to his comment.

'It is, isn't it?' Carlton agreed.

'Too well,' said Wilverton.

'I wouldn't say that.'

'No, it's all too smooth. Something will go wrong soon. I know it.'

'Oh, don't start with the books and the plots again!'

'It's not a question of starting, Peter, but of continuing. It didn't do us any harm on the trip from Earth, did it?'

Carlton glanced to the skies, they had had nothing *but* harm on the trip from Earth. 'Okay – you want to be in a book, you be in a book. Just leave me out – or write me out.'

'And the shopping bills,' said Gloria.

'What?' asked Fission, who happened to be closest.

'It would save on the shopping bills as well. So long as you liked corn, of course.'

A smirk of some self-satisfaction arrived suddenly on Curtis's face. It had nothing to do with Gloria's comment – everyone had lost interest half-way through the sentence – but Curtis could see a decision he could take. He could ask – no, *tell* – he could *tell* the Ship to take them to Altares, just like a Captain. He opened his mouth.

'We are now in orbit around the planet of Altares,' said the Ship pleasantly.

Damn!

'I will deliver you by tachyon matter transference to the co-ordinates specified by the rules of the Game. Are you ready?'

They murmured affirmatives, a bit reluctantly because it sounded suspiciously like there was something else they should know.

There was.

IX

'What the bloody hell is going on?' Curtis shouted.

Wilverton wasn't surprised – Curtis rarely knew what was going on, even when he thought he did – but this time he did have reason. Along with Arnold, they were in a boat, a small one, sitting just in front of a sail billowing out at the insistence of a wind which felt like it would have blown Beaufort's scales off his kitchen table through the closed back door.

From where he immediately clutched the rail, Curtis saw that the boat was on a wide and fast-moving river, the banks on either side apparently leaping up and down as though they really wanted him to notice them – which seemed unlikely – and the water in between rushing headlong in a boiling cacophony as though there was something really scary behind it. *That* he could well believe!

Arnold sat next to Curtis – Wilverton was just in front – and he turned a knowing expression sideways.

'The boat is moving in response to the pressure of air known as wind which is pushing the large sheet – a sail – attached to the big pole behind you – the mast.' He made very sure he had a firm grip of both the boat and his expression before he spoke, though. It was far enough below his normal standard to confirm that the calmness was only artificial-skin deep, but it didn't matter anyway because Curtis ignored him.

'Splice the mainbrace!' Wilverton screamed, and Curtis looked around madly for a mainbrace, which would presumably be the biggest brace amongst all the other more minor braces. He couldn't find one. Just as well really – it saved him working out what splice meant.

Wilverton turned round with a manic grin on his face. 'I've always wanted to say that!'

'Where are we?' Curtis pleaded.

Wilverton shrugged. 'In a boat. Fun isn't it!' He still grinned, to prove it.

'But the ship didn't say anything about this!'

Wilverton shrugged. 'These are the "co-ordinates". It's an adventure. It might be *Swallows and Amazons*. The boat will probably take us to the two guardians.'

'Couldn't we have got a train or something?'

Curtis put a hand on his stomach. Already. He got seasick if he trod in a puddle. He wished Wilverton hadn't mentioned swallowing.

'But you're an adventurer,' Wilverton encouraged him, at volume. 'You mounted the Pioneer expedition.'

'I'm a mathematician,' Curtis yelled back. Arnold 'hmphed' loudly. 'It was my father's idea that I build a space-ship.'

'And then get on it,' Arnold added. 'Great idea.'

'Well, we don't seem to be in danger,' Wilverton pointed out.

It was one of those innocent, but rather stupid, comments.

A sleek and muscular Greel traced the shape of the boat from under the surface of the water, where it let the current carry it, saving its strength for the attack. It was a creature made of four distinct bits: mouth, stomach, swimming parts and sex organs. That was all it needed, and all it wanted. No fool, the Greel.

It chose which side to approach and pushed itself upwards with its powerful tail.

'What do you call a very large hole in the ground into which everything is pouring, if it isn't "danger"?' Arnold asked.

He hadn't prefaced it with 'I say, I say, I say', so Wilverton looked forwards – sorry, for'ard – and put a hand to his forehead –for'ead – in lookout pose. The water boiled along in front of the boat for some distance, and then didn't. The river hit, at right angles, a huge rift in the earth stretching from one horizon to the other, and simply disappeared down it. There was no mist of spray, and no sound of water crashing on rocks below, because there weren't any.

They had located the Ship's promised bottomless chasm.

'Okay,' Wilverton conceded. 'So we *are* in danger.'

They had to slow the boat down and drive it to the bank. Which bank, he didn't know, and didn't particularly care, just so long as they did it in the next mile. The river looked as wide as the Amazon. He swallowed.

'We've got to get the sail down,' he started.

Curtis wasn't listening. He had reached that stage where the only bit of his body, the only bit of the whole Universe, that mattered was his stomach – ears didn't even get a look-in. He hauled his torso over the side of the boat, his eyes screwed shut.

The Greel flicked its tail fins and rose to the surface. Its technique involved one quick look to determine the exact position of the prey, then a mighty thrust from the tail, pushing the cavernous mouth food'ards.

It looked. It saw. The mouth lifted above the surface, open wide; and Curtis threw up in it.

Then Curtis opened his eyes to see a mouth, with whiskers hanging off it, bits of plants snagged in the corners, and, in the centre, a little pool of diced carrots in a steaming soup.

Curtis was away from the side of the boat faster than a tachyon could blink, and leapt for the mast, hittng it and in the same instant wrapping both arms around it as though it were his mother's leg in the middle of a playground brawl.

The mast broke, and crashed into the back of the boat, taking the sail and Curtis with it, He fumbled around under the sheet for a while – he couldn't escape from a paper bag, so ten square yards of canvas was going to be nine too many – then pushed himself to all fours, using a bit of wood which stuck out from the back and which moved as he pushed on it.

The boat slowed, skewed round at the sudden insistence of full rudder, and smashed into the bank, where it stuck.

Wilverton lifted the canvas from Curtis, thinking that the Champion must have been on double time to bring that little lot together. Curtis scrabbled towards solid ground on hands and knees, his stomach already settling back into its more normal state – nervous. Arnold was already standing on the bank, and Wilverton joined them moments later.

The Greel reared up from underneath and pulled the boat down with it, angrily – and typically, since the alternative is to go all tearful, and for a fish there's very little point – trying to get its own back. There was no going back that way, not that any of them had the remotest intention of setting toe in the thing again anyway.

Looking towards the chasm, they could see two figures on the horizon, and they started walking towards them, across a barren plain which apparently drew no moisture from the river. The wind blew dust in swirls around one or two stunted things that might have been trees in happier past lives. There were no signs saying 'Picnic Area'.

In the distance they could make out the shape of the plateau island.

'How are we going to find out which bridge it is?' Curtis asked.

'Simple.' Most things seemed simple for Wilverton, except maybe his outlook on life. 'We talk to them. Catch one out in a lie.'

The figures grew as they approached, until they could see them to be wrapped in heavy black cloaks. As they drew near, the two raised their heads and the visitors automatically slowed at the sight.

They certainly weren't human, but it didn't look like they were anything else either.

In the red light, their skin looked orange. They had beaks, like the mangled remains of the woodpecker who can't tell the difference between oak and cast iron and doesn't learn very quickly.

The mouth of one was wide, and very slightly protruding, as though he had turned into what he was now only after being kissed by a Princess – who was probably still bent over the toilet as a result. The other was pinched tight and looked as if it would only be able to eat through a straw.

They both had the most peculiar and disparate assortment of whiskers and beards, and one sported tufts of what had to be fur.

Their eyes were in slightly different places – one pair was sunken in sockets that looked more like cupboards – but were similar in that all four were squinting terribly. The two moved their heads from side to side, as if trying to find the most proficient, or least deficient, bit of eye to use.

The cloaks covered the rest of their bodies completely, for which the three visitors were extremely grateful.

'Greetings to you,' the guardians said as one, and smiled, which was a mistake if they wanted to induce a feeling of welcome, but was a big plus if they wanted to induce a feeling of regurgitated breakfast.

Curtis decided to look imposing, which he might just have been able to do in front of two such withered specimens. Unfortunately . . .

'Greetings,' he returned, and took a step forward, stubbing his toe on an embedded rock and immediately hopping about trying to rub it. Then this managed to stir his own little visitors, and he was convulsed into another fit of mad scratching at his chest.

70

'Can we help you at all?' asked one of the guardians, looking in the direction of the voice and the fuzzy dancing shape from which it came.

I wish someone would, thought Wilverton, looking at his Captain, then said 'Yes', taking the initiative which Curtis had dropped in order to scratch. 'We were wondering if you could tell us which of the bridges is safe to cross.' He looked past the creatures to where he could now see three wooden slat bridges slung from none too heavy ropes stretching across the abyss to the plateau beyond. He wouldn't have risked any one of them given the choice.

'Yes, we can,' said one.

'Indeed we can,' said the other.

'Which one is it, then?' Arnold asked.

'It is the middle one.'

'It is the one on the left.'

'Well, that was a stupid question, Arnold,' said Curtis, as the fleas took a time-out, turning on the android with a feeling of superiority he had not experienced since his creation had been a drawing-board design. 'They're hardly likely to agree, are they?'

'We know it's not the one on the right, though, don't we?' Arnold didn't even bother to sound contemptuous, and because it was so unexpected it sounded even more contemptuous than usual. Curtis thought about it for a moment, and looked at Wilverton for confirmation. Wilverton nodded in a way that could have been a sad shake.

'Well, yes, we know that,' Curtis conceded. He spun back to the guards. 'Which one, did you say?'

'The one in the middle.'

'The one on the left.'

'Just checking.'

So that left a choice of two. Curtis glanced at Arnold, pondering for an instant – only Curtis could ponder for an instant – what would happen if he told the android to . . .? The ponder didn't get past the first of the consequences.

'What species are you, if you don't mind my asking?' Wilverton sat himself on a boulder.

'We are a mixture of races. The planet from which we come is blessed with a heavy atmosphere, under the near darkness of which we have learned to survive. But it has cost us all but the most rudimentary sight.'

71

Wilverton frowned, which was a pretty useless gesture to someone who couldn't spot a sunrise, so he said, 'I don't follow.'

'Intermixing of the species. By the time we knew what we were getting close to, it was too late.'

Wilverton accepted the information equably, while Curtis managed to feel jealous and wished that Earth was a bit darker. Like pitch, preferably.

Quiet descended while Wilverton pondered this exchange at rather more appropriate length than Curtis. Then, in a flash, he realized that he was buggered if he could spot anything useful.

'Look, this isn't getting us anywhere,' said Curtis. 'I reckon we've got to take a chance. We should pick a bridge and try it out, carefully.'

'Off you go then,' said Arnold.

Curtis spun on him, the action holding all the menace of a dandelion flower on a light breeze. 'I could order you to go, you know.'

'You couldn't order a pizza.'

'Do you think that is a good idea?' Wilverton asked the guardians, leaving the other two to get on with it.

'It sounds unlikely.'

'I believe your Captain should rethink.'

Hmm.

' "Captain"? You called him Captain. Why was that?'

'He has that air about him.'

Curtis swelled slightly, and a superior smile appeared – his first ever – but Wilverton immediately turned to the other guardian, and Arnold prepared to move. 'Which bridge did you say?'

'The centre one.'

'Thank you,' said Wilverton, and rose to his feet. He began walking towards the three bridges and their majority invitation to the next world, then paused and looked back over his shoulder. Arnold was right with him, but Curtis was looking after him as though he was badly in need of being looked after.

'What are you doing?'

'The centre bridge is the safe one,' Wilverton assured him. 'Believe me.'

'*I* do,' Arnold confirmed.

'But . . .?' Incomprehension.

Wilverton sighed. 'He said you had an air of Captaincy about you. I'm afraid that's a lie.'

72

'But . . .' Comprehension. 'But that's not fair. I have, too! It's just because you're completely mad, and . . . and Arnold hates me.'

Arnold nodded. 'Well, I don't think anyone could argue with that.'

'Shut up, Arnold.' Wilverton turned back to Curtis. 'I'll go first, if you like.'

Still no movement.

'Well, you *are* the Captain, and we don't want to risk you.' Flattery might work, and if he couldn't spot the first lie, maybe he was blind to them all. Arnold wasn't.

'Who doesn't? I want to risk him. Can we vote?'

'Will you shut up!' hissed Wilverton, and Arnold smiled.

Curtis started walking slowly forward and kicked a rock dispiritedly, only to find it was the tip of a buried boulder.

He winced, but he was the Captain, and he refused to hop again. He'd limp instead. He *was* the Captain. He *was*!

The Challenger produced an emanation of visible red so dark it might almost have been brown, as befitted what it saw as a dirty trick.

The Champion allowed a curl of purple to drift eloquently for a while. When you are the Supreme Being, the colour said, nothing was impossible.

Blood from a stone? Easy.

Black-hole radiation from a red giant? Harder, but a relatively simple matter.

Finding a good use in the Game for a complete pillock like Curtis – in fact two good uses in swift succession? One of the three most difficult tasks in the Galaxy, but the First Elder had managed it.

It was not a task – and the purple deepened – to be undertaken by anyone of Lesser eminence. The colour drifted across to the vicinity of the Challenger – the Second Elder – and dissipated lazily.

There didn't appear to be any difference between the bridges which stretched maybe a hundred yards across the gorge. None of them looked anything like safe. Wilverton had eyes only for the one in front of him, and thoughts only for the reasoning which had led him to it.

With a mental shrug he took his first step onto the loose boarding which was supposed to support him. If he had got it wrong, then he would soon find out – but it *had* been the most obvious lie he had ever heard. He took his second step, holding the ropes which held the bridge at about waist height, and wondered if six main characters were one too many for a book.

If only he could work out what book he was in, he would have some idea of what to do. Bridges . . .

A Bridge Too Far?

He decided just to walk, or at least totter.

There was now not a whisper of wind, as if the entire planet were holding its breath, just like Wilverton. The bridge contrived to sway alarmingly, nevertheless – not that they've ever been known to sway reassuringly

'Looks to me like it's going!' floated Arnold's voice across the chasm, and Wilverton could hear him smiling evilly.

He felt as though his knees were sporting a new liquid cartilage as they tried to sway in the opposite direction to the one chosen by this excuse for a structure, and kept his eyes firmly fixed on his hoped-for destination, finding himself now having to look up at quite an angle in order to do so. An ominous creaking took its toll on any confidence he had felt[1] – and it did not have to be a very large toll. He just moved one foot after the other, his brain all but paralysed.

'Don't worry about the dog – it'll have died of old age by the time we get there!'

Wilverton could have spun round and told Arnold to shut up, but the alternative – just keep shuffling – was way out in front.

Then answers began to come unbidden to his frozen mind as the far end of the bridge crept towards him. Yes, his reasoning appeared to be sound, and no, six main characters were not too many for a book, or if they were, then his was not the one to be written out just yet. His foot touched solid ground, and his other joined it without discernible pause. The flood of relief threatened to drown him.

A low growl sounded from some way off, and he looked up to see the silhouette of a large creature etched against the crimson horizon. The outline looked rather more threatening than the

---

[1] Yes, it was a toll bridge.

74

bridge had, and Wilverton would have placed a sizable bet that the bits he couldn't see would be less than encouraging.

'Nice doggy,' he muttered, and turned back to look across the bridge to where two more silhouettes, these not at all threatening, faced him. He generously beckoned the others to join him.

X

Vertiginous, was the cliff. It was the sort of height that made you lose balance standing at the bottom looking up, let alone the other way round. Carlton took a slight step backwards and brought his gaze back down again, casting a quick glance at the two women to make sure they hadn't spotted his loss of equilibrium.

They hadn't. Gloria was looking from the cliff to the green sky, through which shone a dim sunshine, and Fission was studying the smooth rock wall in front of her, looking for the cave outside which the Ship had supposedly placed them.

'The sky's pretty here,' Gloria said. 'Space must be a very dark green round this planet.' Because round the Earth space was a very dark blue that you'd think at night was black until the sun lit it up and you could see what it really was. Simple.

'Save your brain, melons,' Fission told her.

'You're very rude, you know,' Gloria responded with a blunt honesty which seemed to take Fission by surprise.

'Yeah, well, is how I am. I been bad mood lately.'

Gloria was about to ask why when Fission turned away, with deliberation.

The cave wasn't there; she had spotted it almost immediately, or, rather, she hadn't. Caves were conspicuous, they were big hollows, hence, concave. The cliff was perfectly conflat, and for Fission, therefore, predictably conbloodyfrustrating.

'Where fonking cave? Ship said here.'

Carlton looked at the unbroken rock and willed it to reveal a secret to him, please . . . but it wasn't taking sides.

Then the cliff started throwing boulders at them.

Carlton was about to move forward and inspect the rock face when, without a sound, much less a by-your-leave, a slab of stone thumped into the earth just in front of him. He snapped his head upwards again, and saw several more black shapes plummeting from somewhere way above, and any number of tiny specks.

76

Fission swore as several stone of stone made her jump sideways, and Gloria made progress backwards towards some trees which would not only give shelter, but which did not appear to be subject to attack.

Because attack it was, with hundreds of tiny pebbles joining the main force, so many that it was impossible to escape them all, and they had to be fended off by arms bent over heads. But a few yards to either side, there was nothing.

It was less a rock-fall, more a rock-shy. Except that the rocks were anything but, judging from their eagerness to meet people.

If only they could find the cave, they would be safe, Carlton knew, but it wasn't exactly beckoning them. In fact the exact opposite.

The Ship *had* said it was there, though, and the Ship didn't seem the type to lie – she'd have called it fibbing, punishable by no chocolate ice cream for a week. Perhaps it was an optical illusion, he thought, and a cave really was right in front of him. It didn't seem likely, but he inched carefully forward and laid a hand on the rock anyway, moving it along the face and feeling for anything that wasn't there.

Immediately, he found something through his fingers and almost through his ears. The rock was humming, and there was a deep rhythmic beating coming from it as if from the heart of the earth.

'There must be a cave behind this bit of cliff.' Which was as maybe, but what there wasn't was a door. He dodged another boulder but a stray shard nicked his hand.

'How we get in?' Fission asked irritably. She looked for a moment like she was going to kick the mountain, but apparently realized that in a game of football several million tons of rock always get at least a draw. In the game of flatten the human, the cliff was on the way to winning.

The search stopped when Gloria screamed.

They spun round and faced a sheepskin-clad cyclops leading a herd of sheepskin-clad sheep. He was a fairly conspicuous cyclops, on account of both his size – he was well over eight feet tall, and about half that wide – and his one large, centrally located eye. He held Gloria like a doll under one arm with no apparent effort at all.

He glanced up at the cliff and yelled, 'STOP THAT!' The last few rocks, already in mid-air, disobeyed, but the rest of the mountain pulled itself together. Then he looked down his nose at Fission and Carlton – it was tricky for him to do anything else – and ignored Gloria, who was already secure despite the waggling of various arms, legs and other bits.

Fission immediately took up the slightly bent-legged stance of one preparing for a fight, and, a moment after he noticed, Carlton adopted the same pose. The cyclops's eyebrow rose.

'Put her down,' Carlton ordered, before Fission could take the lead on speech as well as action. Hearing the tone of command, the cyclops immediately did absolutely nothing of the sort.

'Whadya want?' he asked.

'We mean you no harm.' With an effort of will the eight-foot cyclops managed not to break into tears of relief. 'We were just coming to see you.' The eyebrow rose again.

'*You* were comin' to see *me*?' It was obviously wrong. It wasn't something that was normally done.

'We, er, we want to buy some wool.' Carlton wondered abstractly if the Champion had put the idea into his head.

'Do you want to come in?' And he indicated the cliff.

'Er, yes please.' He glanced at Fission, uncertain of his answer, and hating himself for glancing, but she wasn't providing any alternatives.

The cyclops smiled, and held Gloria out at arm's length as he leaned close to the wall and whispered something. The humming stopped. As the cyclops stepped back, so the rock face appeared to follow him, or a fair part of it anyway, as a massive – or massif – door swung slowly and silently open to reveal the cave beyond.

The sheep hurried through the doorway and branched off left, to where a grassy field lay spread impossibly inside the mountain. The cyclops put Gloria down and ushered his three guests along the other branch into what appeared to be a well-furnished apartment.

The place was huge, with the ceiling a good twenty feet from the floor. The walls and furniture – several huge chairs and two sofas – were green. On the walls were a number of posters, all depicting sheep; some just standing proudly in their field in the 'competition winner' pose, a couple wearing hats with pink string tied under their chins, and one wearing a nappy. This last was opposite the chair into which the cyclops lowered himself.

He still wore a large grin, and Carlton found himself hoping that this was because he was a happy cyclops, rather than because he knew something which Carlton didn't.

A couple of other rooms were hidden behind curtaining across the doorways.

'Don't sit on the chairs!' advised the cyclops. 'I've had 'em all cleaned and I don't know where you've been.'

'I'm not too sure either,' commented Gloria. Any reaction to her comment was prevented by the softest of thuds, felt rather than heard, and the three humans turned their heads sharply to see the rock face closing behind them. There was no reason for this to alarm them, but they didn't let that stop it for a moment. Their experiences so far had proved that it was generally best to become alarmed at the slightest provocation; that way you were ready.

On hearing the sound, the cyclops grinned much wider, and waved them to the floor, which was covered with sheepskin rugs. From somewhere behind his chair the cyclops lifted a decanter of what looked like brandy, and a huge corroborative brandy bowl, which he half filled with the stuff, and took something that could only be described as a sip if you have a mouth the size of a bucket, which he did. He smacked his lips appreciatively.

'Right,' he said, 'You ain't from round here, are you?'

'What makes you say that?' asked Carlton after a moment of silence had answered with a great big 'No'.

'Oh, nothing.' And he chuckled again. It was beginning to become annoying – certainly to Fission, for which something apparently had just to move to be annoying, or not move for that matter, or adopt any other state it could think of. 'I suppose you're after the cornucopia?'

Gloria opened her mouth, but Carlton was quick enough to stop her.

'The what, sorry?'

'Oh, *be*have!' He took another 'sip'. 'What makes you want to come and buy wool off me?'

'Well, you are known to have one of the finest herds in this part of Cupros.' There, that was smooth, Carlton thought.

'Yeah, I know, but you don't get many humans round here. In fact you don't get *any* humans round here.'

He emptied his glass, leaned down again, and found three more glasses, these slightly smaller. He replenished his own, then splashed some brandy into the three and handed them to his visitors.

'Get this down you,' he told Carlton. 'Internal marination.' He pronounced it very carefully, and looked pleased with the result, then moved on to Gloria. 'I did 'ave a butler,' he apparently apologized as she took a drink. 'But he was really old and then he died. I used to call him Scrotum, 'cos he was my wrinkled retainer.'

Then he laughed. Gloria didn't, partly because she didn't get the joke, but mainly because she didn't feel terribly good-humoured just then. Fission took the third glass in silence, and with an expression growing on her face like a bulge growing on the outside of Mount St Helens.

'A toast. Breakfast!' The cyclops raised his glass, and downed half of its contents.

'Why don't you get any humans?' Carlton asked, sniffing his drink experimentally.

The cyclops smiled again.

Carlton looked at the glass in his hand. Internal marination, he thought. Shit, he thought.

'What's for breakfast?'

The cyclops smiled some more, and lubricated his vocal chords before confirming Carlton's fears.

'You are, matey!'

In the background the massive rock door began humming an incongruously cheerful tune to itself.

'But that's cannibalism,' said Carlton with some distaste.

'You're a human. I'm a cyclops. That ain't cannibalism.'

'Well, maybe it's not strictly cannibalism, but it's damned close.'

'Not close enough, matey, fortunately. Or unfortunately, depending on how you look at it.' The way Carlton was looking at it was unfavourably. 'Oh, come on! You can hardly blame me! You eat animals, don't you? You don't think of yourselves as murderers or cannibals, do you? I'm just a regular bloke; I like a drink and a laugh. I even do amateur dramatics – did Long John Silver last month; couldn't see a bloody thing.' He paused. 'I just like human, that's all. With roast spuds. And peas.'

Carlton looked unconvinced, but now was hardly the time for philosophical reflection on their relative carnivorous preferences.

An unusual something had happened since they arrived at the cyclops's cave.

Or rather it hadn't happened.

Fission hadn't said anything, and she was still alive – the two simply didn't go together. She took a deep breath and put it right.

'Call this plan, do you?' Carlton was under attack. 'Brilliant! Just couldn't fit ego in back seat, could you! Dear Luc, why does every man want to rule tribe?'

She was annoyed. He could tell. She hadn't said 'fonk' once.

'Stroppy, ain't she?' The cyclops commented to Carlton, then turned to Fission. '*He* didn't know you was going to get eaten, did he?'

'You got kill us first,' said Fission, and Carlton and Gloria immediately wished that she hadn't. 'Not easy.'

The cyclops looked at her, having taken another enormous gulp of brandy.

'I think it is, you know.'

'Not weak as we look, freak face.'

'I think you probably are, somehow,' he returned confidently, entirely unmoved by her description. That seemed to exhaust Fission's argument. The cyclops turned back to Carlton. 'See? Humans are only likely to come here for something pretty valuable, ain't they? Seeing the danger. And all I've got's the cornucopia. So that must be it. Simple.' And it was. The cyclops consigned his reasoning to history.

'I fancy a curry. 'Sh funny how you do after a couple, innit? Terrible thing, drink.' And he giggled. He reached down beside his chair and produced a large curved horn. Conversation – if that is the right word – was abruptly discontinued as the three humans had their first sight of their quest. It held less importance for them than it had a few minutes before, but they were fascinated despite themselves.

After a few moments of intense concentration, accompanied by the determined lowering of the eyebrow, the smell of a strong curry began to fill the room.

'Good, innit?' He began spooning the stuff into his cavernous mouth with a utensil he produced from somewhere unseen, while their silent inspection of the horn confirmed their guilt.

'Why do you need to eat us if you've got something like that?' asked Gloria, with commendable logic.

The cyclops paused between mouthfuls. 'You can't beat fresh food.'

Gloria appeared to consider this. 'Yes, that's true, I suppose.'

'Fonk me!' invited Fission, dangerously.

The cyclops ignored her, and spoke again to Gloria. 'You don't seem very worried.' He made it sound like a question.

'Well, I am worried. But Peter's here, and he normally knows what to do, so I don't intend to give up hope. I *trust* you don't mind.' There was a slight edge to her voice.

Carlton kept a neutral expression on his face through this testimony to his super-powers, and desperately tried to think of something they could do. 'Die and get eaten' seemed the most obvious.

'Not at all; feel free,' said the cyclops magnanimously, waving his spoon in permission before wiping a dribble from his chin. 'But I don't give much for your chances, with or without Peter. I've got guards to look after me while I'm asleep, and you won't be able to get past the megalith. No-one else has.'

'The megalith?' repeated Gloria, expecting another large and opposing animal.

'Don't you know what a megalith is?'

'No.' Gloria sat a little straighter. There was no reason why she *should* know. 'I expect it's a very large lith.'

The cyclops chuckled with genuine humour. The brandy was really getting to him.

'They're bloody great stones, megaliths, and my door's one of them. Only *I* know what to say to it so that it'll open, and it'd take hundreds of cyclopses to force it, let alone knows how many little humans.' He paused while he took another mouthful. 'No, I don't give a lot for your chances.'

In the background the door made itself known at this mention of itself, a faint tune almost discernible, but the steady beat still the clearest aspect of the music, sensed as much as heard.

'You know, I think I like you, little human.' Gloria did not look overly pleased by the cyclops's compliment. 'And I'm sure I will even more tomorrow – I love white meat.' He looked at Fission for a moment. 'Not going to get much off that one!' Fission said something, this time with 'fonking' in it, but the cyclops had already passed on from her to Carlton. 'And some tasty sweetmeats, an' all.' Carlton brought his knees closer together, feeling very uncomfortable, and suddenly knowing what a fate worse than death could be like.

For a 'regular bloke', he thought, the cyclops had a wide sadistic streak.

'If you like me,' said Gloria, 'why don't you let us go?'

'Because I don't like you that much,' came the helpful explanation.

'I'll do anything if you do let us go.'

'You'll run away if I let you go. What you mean is you'll do anything before I let you go if I let you go after you've done it. Innit?'

'Er . . .'

'Yes,' said Fission. 'Go for gain, melons,' she hissed at Gloria.

'Trouble is you're really not my type.' His eye strayed to the picture of the sheep on the opposite wall. They followed its gaze. Carlton further redefined 'regular bloke', and Fission snorted.

'Deformed, and perv as well.' Her copy of *How to Win Friends and Influence People* was just like new. So, sadly, was her copy of *How to Stay Alive Having Been Caught by Giant Man-Eating Cyclopses*.

Fission scanned the room for possible ways out, or weapons. There was one of the former and, if anything, slightly fewer of the latter.

The one of the former hummed and thumped to itself. Carlton found that his foot was tapping in time to the beat, and he stared at it until it stopped. Bloody silly thing to be doing in this situation, he told it.

He turned to Fission, and found that she wasn't there. Fortunately he didn't immediately start looking around very obviously and asking loudly where she was, but instead tried to think of something he could do to claim the attention of the cyclops.

As it happened, he didn't have to. The cyclops spooned some more curry into his mouth, or largely into his mouth anyway, and tipped his head backwards in an attempt to arrest the torrent of vindaloo sauce from pouring onto his chest. And there was Fission, suddenly hanging around his neck from behind, trying to throttle the life out of him.

The look on her face was even more manic than usual, and the sinews in her arms stood out as though they had a reasonable expectation of escape. She strained to crush the windpipe as she had never strained before.

Unfortunately, she might just as well have tried to throttle an oak tree, for all the effect she seemed to be having. To anyone who didn't know that she had murder in mind, it looked as though she was probably just trying to stop him eating, as though she wanted the curry for herself.

And she got it.

The cyclops lifted the cornucopia over his shoulder and emptied it over Fission's head. It didn't make her let go. It made her redouble her efforts as though 'crush' was just the first stage of what she was going to do to the neck.

It might have looked amusing under different circumstances, although no-one was going to risk a smile when Fission was the one on the wrong end of the joke.

Then any thought of jokes stopped as the cyclops put down the cornucopia and reached over his shoulder, taking hold of the neck of Fission's jump suit. With a convulsive jerk he pulled her over the chair, and his head, and sent her sprawling across the room, to crash into the solid stone of the far wall, where she lay still in a heap.

He rose to his feet, a bit unsteadily, but with a look of irrational anger on his face, and took a determined step towards the injured woman. He wasn't going to help her to her feet and brush her down.

'Peter!' said Gloria, her eyes wide in alarm and her hand reaching out for his arm.

'Yes, I know,' he said tiredly, standing and moving to intercept the cyclops. There would be so many women back on Earth who would be distraught when they heard about his death, he thought. But not half as distraught as *he* would be. I suppose I *should* help, he thought, a little uncertainly.

Yes, you should, came a voice in his head.

'Now hold on!' Carlton moved directly into the cyclops's path and held up his hands in a peaceful gesture, hoping that they wouldn't get snapped off at the wrist.

'Get out of my way, human!'

'You can't blame her for trying.' I bet he can, he thought.

'I bloody can!' The cyclops put an arm out to push Carlton aside, and he took hold of it, knowing as he did so that it was a pretty damned stupid thing to do. He felt a bit like Canute, except that failure for the King wasn't a farewell performance in the land of the living. This way they were going to end up with two dead instead of just one. But at least he would maintain his status as hero. Besides, Fission might even be grateful in the after-world.

Then he realized that he wasn't being smashed against the wall while he had these thoughts, and the cyclops looked down at him through an eye that wasn't flashing quite as it had been, probably because it had quite enough to do on the focusing front without making things all complicated by flashing.

The arm fell, and the cyclops took a deep breath and blew it out, smothering Carlton's face in a mixture of curry and brandy. On the whole he would have preferred to have been smashed against the wall.

'Yeah, well. Human meat's better when it's fresh, anyway.' He stabbed a finger in Fission's direction. 'She'll be the first for breakfast.' Then he stumbled off to one side. 'I'm going to bed.'

He picked up a picture from a table next to his chair and looked at it with a fond smile. Carlton could just catch a glimpse of what looked like black, thigh-length boots, with disconcertingly woolly thighs sticking out the top of them.

The cyclops began to weave his way across the room to one of the curtains. He pulled it aside to reveal a room bathed in a soft, almost seductive, green light. Through the doorway, Carlton and Gloria could see a large mattress lying on the floor.

The giant inspected the room's lay-out briefly, then raised two fingers toward his mouth, pulled them out of his nose and inserted them on the second attempt, then produced an ear-splitting whistle. There was a trundling sound, as of ovine feet, and five sheep appeared round the corner and came into the room. Four of them were particularly large animals and did not wear that expression of perpetual blankness which their fellows seemed to adopt. They looked mean. The fifth was much smaller, more dainty, and sort of cuddly. The cyclops smiled at this last one and stood aside as she entered the bedroom, trailing a rather nice scent behind her. The others took up position in pairs on either side of the opening. The cyclops looked at the four on obvious guard, then at the three on the menu.

'I call these the SS,' he told them. 'Savage sheep. I'll see you in the morning, though not necessarily vice versa.' And with an anticipatory sweep of the curtain, he was gone.

Gloria immediately scrambled to her feet and hurried across to

Fission, who was already moving and making a feeble moaning noise. Gloria helped her into a sitting position, leaning her against the wall for support.

They all stared at the sheep. The sheep stared back, and added a snarl or two for good measure, showing teeth which obviously made the contest with blades of grass a one-sided affair.

They stared some more.

The sheep won.

XI

Arnold pulled himself off the last rickety board of the bridge and glared at Wilverton, whose face was far too small to have anywhere to hide the amused smile which had followed the android's progress and now greeted him.

'Listen,' said Arnold, sounding more human than he ever had before, 'I've had this body for less than two days and I do *not* want to smash it on the sides of this cliff, or let bits of it rust while it's falling through very thin air at terminal velocity and waiting for a rude interruption to said descent, possibly for ever.'

Arnold didn't know quite how deep a bottomless chasm was supposed to be, but figured that any chasm you weren't going to come back from was a good enough definition of 'bottomless', as far as he was concerned.

'And if such an attitude makes you smile, then you are probably just as loopy as the rest of the crew say you are. And,' he added as an acerbic afterthought, 'they should know.'

There apparently existed the possibility of a distinct rift, maybe not as wide as the one which Arnold had just crossed, but a rift nevertheless. Wilverton did not want that. Despite himself, and despite Arnold, more pertinently, he did sort of like the android.

'I'm sorry, Arnold. It was just the look on your face when you got here. We humans sometimes have a peculiar idea of what is amusing. We don't take other people's feelings into account as much as we should. I do apologize. Really.'

'Don't call me "people".' Arnold accepted the apology with the grace of a waltzing wart hog, and Wilverton let it drop.

They turned to look at Curtis, and found that their illustrious Captain was coping with about as much success as England had with William the Conqueror. He was feeling his way along the support ropes of the bridge with his hands, first reaching out in front of him so that he was leaning forward at quite an angle, then, at the extremity of his reach, clamping his fingers round the rope and getting his feet to rush forward two inches at a time until the body was once again more or less upright. It was the way someone might feel their way through a very dark passage, and Curtis's tightly shut eyes confirmed why.

Their attention was drawn from the scene before them to the scene behind them by a growl. A distant Cerberus would never have produced a growl of that volume unless he had a loud-hailer or a telephone, which left a rather worrying alternative. They looked round. There was a much nearer Cerberus, and one apparently intent on very soon becoming an arrived Cerberus.

'Ready for a fight, Arnold?'

'If you like. I'm not sure we've got the time, though.'

Wilverton smiled grimly and pointed to a huddle of boulders twenty yards away to their left. Arnold didn't wait for a written invitation.

Curtis continued his tight-eyed traverse, and, after about a decade or so, approached the end of the bridge, where his hands found empty air instead of rope. He gracefully fell flat on his face and felt the earth with his fingers, then grasped handfuls of soil as relief exuded from his opening eyes. He picked himself up, brushed himself off, and looked up to where the others were watching him.

They had too many heads. Wilverton and Arnold should only have had two.

And they had too few bodies, by one.

Cerberus smiled at him, three times. It didn't look like it from where Curtis was standing.

'Pssst!' He wished he was. He turned his head slowly to the sound, and saw Wilverton beckoning from behind a large boulder. He looked back at Cerberus, and his legs wouldn't move.

Cerberus howled, three voices rising up the scale in discordant harmony. Mellifluous it wasn't; a cure for paralysis it most certainly was, and Curtis was running hard for the safety of the boulders, so scared that he didn't trip once.

The dog watched him go. The three heads looked at each other and sniggered. This was going to be fun. The heads nodded, and the body sauntered in the direction of its sport.

The boulders were big enough to hide them, but unless Cerberus didn't have a brain in any of its three heads they were going to need something more.

'How did whoever it was in history get past that, then?' A

breathless and shaking Curtis was not expecting a reassuring answer as he jerked his head at 'that'. His expectations were not dashed.

'It was Heracles,' said Wilverton, looking round the edge of the boulder at the dog, who ambled ever closer, as hurried as an unwound clock. 'He didn't actually have to get past the thing; he had to take it from Hades – the underworld – to Eurystheus at Tiryns.'

'Gosh, that's interesting!'

'I'm getting there, Arnold. Apparently Heracles just walked up to it, patted it, put a chain round each of its necks and led it away.'

Arnold glanced at the dog. 'Off you go, then.'

'I don't think I could quite carry it off, to be honest. Knowing how something's supposed to be done doesn't mean you can do it.'

Curtis's mind suddenly flashed him a memory of the original *Pioneer* and his first zero-gravity encounter with a love-struck Gloria. Wilverton wasn't wrong, more was the pity.

'Don't worry,' Wilverton continued. 'We'll think of something.' Cerberus had stopped, and was watching the boulder, three tongues hanging out and lolling about as three mouths watered expectantly. It looked about ready, as though it had just ordered the wine, and was reading the menu. 'The trouble is we need to think of it during the next fifteen seconds.'

'Why don't you tell it something interesting? Then it should just wander off of its own accord.' Arnold's equivalent of adrenaline went straight to his insult gland. Wilverton ignored him.

'What would happen if Arnold was scratched,' Captain Curtis asked his First Officer.

'I don't know, exactly,' Arnold answered. 'How much damage can an idiot human being take from a three-headed dog without actually dying?'

'We could repair you,' Curtis protested.

'You couldn't bloody make me in the first place! And after your efforts over the last couple of weeks' – Curtis had admittedly encountered problems in curing Arnold's deafness while leaving all his other faculties in full working order – 'I wouldn't trust you to wipe my newly acquired ar—'

'No-one's going to get hurt if we can help it,' timed Wilverton. The trouble is, he thought, I'm not sure we *can* help it.

89

The dog watched their rock unhurriedly, and did not appear to have immediately hostile intentions. On the other hand, it didn't look as though it was about to bound off and bring them three pairs of slippers and a soggy newspaper, either.

'Presumably, the Jewel is that large blue thing over there.' Wilverton pointed to a mound of earth maybe five foot high, in the direction from which Cerberus had come. On top of it was a blue ovoid rock, a jewel which caught the light of a red sun much younger than the Callia binary member, and threw it back deeply purple. It was about the size of a duck egg. 'So how the hell do we get it? Any ideas?'

'If we had a bone or a stick or something, we could throw it,' Curtis offered. Wilverton glanced skywards, but said nothing. He left it to Arnold.

'I don't actually think the guard dog in front of us would be fooled by someone throwing a stick for it to chase. I'm not sure what makes me quite so certain, unless of course it's a modicum of intelligence.'

'Well, have you got a better –' The interrogative retort was cut short by a resurgence of parasitic activity in the armpit region.

The movement was arrested by another low growl from Cerberus. Quite a harmonious growl this time, as each of the three sets of vocal chords pitched in on a slightly different note. But none of the listeners was overly concerned with the tune; it was the lyric which held their attention. This was no soppy ballad. This was a protest song. And dinner time had arrived.

'We're going to have to split up, make a dash for it. One of us should be able to get the Jewel.' Wilverton didn't speculate on what the other two might get. 'Killed' was volunteering enthusiastically at the front of the queue.

'Okay,' said Arnold. 'Get ready to run when I count to three . . . hundred thousand.'

'Three will be enough, Arnold. And I'll count.' Wilverton was aware that Arnold might get stuck at about the 'two' mark. He glanced round the rock once more, and the dog took a step forward. 'One, two, *three*!'

He broke cover and sprinted off to the left. Curtis, his stomach doing cartwheels, took off to the right. Arnold stayed right where he was, watched the other two go, and smiled to himself.

Then Cerberus stuck three heads round the side of the boulder and slobbered at him.

Arnold ran in all directions.

Each of the dog's heads focused on one of the athletes, and its canine ears picked up the sound of heavy breathing from two of them. Mind you, Wilverton and Curtis were heaving in air at such volume that the dog could have put a balaclava over its ear muffs and still wouldn't have been able to concentrate for all the racket.

Finally, it settled on the group of boulders to which Curtis had run, and trotted jauntily towards them, looking like an entry in the dressage as it bounced happily over the ground. The only drawback with humans, as far as Cerberus was concerned – and it was just a little one – was that you got bits of them stuck between your teeth.

Curtis was curled into so tight a ball that he might well have fitted back into the womb for which he obviously yearned. He cowered in a shallow alcove of rock and apparently intended to stay there until it was eroded away by the absolute lack of any elemental action.

Then the touch of something like a dog's nose on his back nearly made him jump clean out of his clothing, which wouldn't have been quite so clean.

'Hello,' said Arnold through an evil grin.

Curtis swallowed his heart and glared at the android, trying to think of something to say, but his brain didn't even get as far as 'knife' before the Fleas decided on a quick snack, and he stuffed one hand inside his jump suit, scrabbling frantically at the base of any hair he could find.

Then a low growl revealed that the Curtis and Arnold company had become a crowd, and not through the addition of Wilverton.

The dog's three heads all barked into their alcove, suggesting that it was time the visitors faced the consequences of their trespass. Then it favoured them to a view of the teeth with which it could follow up such a suggestion.

Curtis was the first to reach a decision, amazingly, as he spun on his heel and took off back the way he had come.

Or tried to.

He still had one arm up to the elbow inside his suit, the hand reaching down to a locality which, while not exactly private, had only ever been seen by three other people, and none of those with a straight face. Curtis had trouble moving his limbs with any sort of co-ordination when there was just fresh air in the way, but in his current position he was as likely to stay upright as the last Brazilian tree.[1]

Furthermore, as soon as he started to move, there occurred a most unfortunate and surely a quite accidental coming together of Curtis's chest with Arnold's shoulder, which had the effect of knocking him more solidly into the alcove, where the rock cushioned his fall and made it more of a lean. The collision also unbalanced Arnold, and he, too, found himself staggering back against the rock face, while the smirk of success stayed in the vicinity of the collision.

Cerberus gave a howl of triumph, leaped forward and stood over them, dripping slobber in that endearingly homicidal way that large dogs have, only cubed. It lowered a head over each of its intended victims and gave them a good sight of its neck-bound fangs, while the third looked on approvingly.

From where they sat on Curtis's chest, the Fleas had a wonderful sight of absolutely acres of fur through the partially opened jump suit. They compared the sight with Curtis and his pathetic assortment of hair – kept, what was more, in some quite revolting places for the most part – and deserted en masse in a flash. It was only the fact that Curtis was leaning against rock that stopped the recoil knocking him over.

An enormous smile spread across Curtis's face.

An enormous itch spread across the whole of Cerberus's body.

Each of the dog's heads turned this way and that, gnawing at a clump of fur for a few moments before moving on to the next patch of affliction. It fell onto one haunch and brought the free hind leg up to one ear on one head – the first of six ports of call. Cerberus had things on all three of its minds and none of them was the Jewel of Altares.

The two comrades in arms, if nothing else, slid sideways along the boulder and out of the dog's reach. They heard Wilverton call out, 'Come on! Let's get the hell out of here!' and they looked to where he stood next to the earth mound, the Jewel in his hand.

Cerberus saw what was happening out of one eye, and even tried to wave a massive fore paw in Wilverton's direction, before falling foul of another frantic flea feeding fit.

[1] Or, rather, the penultimate one – the last one was saved and used as a tourist attraction.

Wilverton's suggestion was not one which required a debate, and the three of them set off as fast as they could for the bridges. Arnold easily outstripped the others – he'd had quite a bit of practice lately – and was almost on the centre span before he slid to a halt in the thin soil, raising a tired cloud of dust behind him. He looked at the bridge in front of him and took another halting step towards it, then stopped again.

It looked different. He couldn't say why, but it looked different. He glanced right and left, to the other two bridges, and they, too, looked different. Did they look more solid? Or was the eye playing tricks, not to mention the Challenger?

Across the chasm, Arnold could see the two guardians now facing his way, and listening to what was happening. Wilverton and Curtis caught up with him.

'What are you waiting for?' asked Curtis.

'I'll stay here and hold off the dog as long as I can.' Arnold indicated the middle bridge. 'You go first.'

Curtis actually moved before the implications of Arnold's bravery worked their way through his skull.

'What's wrong with the bridge?'

'It looks different,' said Wilverton.

'Does it?' said Arnold, and peered at the bridge, doing his choirboy bit again.

'We must ask the guardians, if they can hear us,' said Wilverton. 'Which was the one who told the truth?'

'The one in the black cloak,' said Arnold.

'They've both got black cloaks,' said Curtis.

'Oh, well spotted,' said Arnold, and clapped his hands together. Wilverton did not comment, but glanced over his shoulder to where Cerberus was now scrabbling to its feet, the first assault of the Golden Fleas apparently over, their appetites temporarily assuaged. There wasn't going to be time to find out which bridge was the safe one.

'Which bridge is safe?' he shouted. Might as well eliminate one of the damned things, anyway.

Back came a thin voice in response. 'All bridges are safe for one person only at a time.'

Maybe it wouldn't eliminate one of the damned things after all.

'All bridges are safe for one person only at a time,' said the other voice, and one problem faded, leaving several.

'Pick a bridge,' said Wilverton. 'Any bridge.' He looked over his shoulder again, and wished he hadn't. Cerberus was galloping towards them, heads held high, and it suddenly let out a blood curdling howl in the keys of G, E flat and C. It was not a pretty sound. Understatement – it sounded like a flu-ridden camel playing bagpipes.

Arnold immediately made for the centre span, which was the nearest, Wilverton darted for the bridge on the left, and Curtis worked out in a trice which one remained, and went for that. Each of them cast furtive glances back to the dog, hoping that whichever bridge it chose, it wouldn't be the one supporting *him*. There was probably a time and a place for laying down your life for your fellow man, but they were buggered if this was it.

Cerberus did not seem to need time for consideration of its target, but headed straight for the centre.

Arnold looked over his shoulder one more time, and was miffed.

The dog leapt onto the bridge, then stopped running, but still moved considerably quicker than Arnold, closing quickly until the android suddenly stopped and turned to face it, his face like thunder when it gets home from a bloody hard day's clapping and finds its supper isn't ready.

On the other two bridges Wilverton and Curtis kept moving as fast as they could. There was, after all, nothing they could do to help Arnold, so they might as well, sort of, well, help them-selves. It was not selfish, it was logical. Later they would help. They'd arrange the funeral, organize the flowers, bury any bits they could find; that sort of thing.

Cerberus was confused by the unusual actions of its quarry, and as Arnold faced it, it, too, almost stopped, just edging forward inch by inch. The dog waited for the scent of fear to reach its nostrils. It waited in more vain than an ageing film star. Arnold was severely niggled.

'You rabid, flea-ridden bastard!' described the android, with an accuracy of about sixty-seven percent. 'What was wrong with the others? Eh?' Cerberus stopped, a look – three looks – of some surprise replacing its carnivorous anticipation. Surely its prey realized that it was supposed to be near-terminally scared, not livid with anger.

The bridge jerked alarmingly.

'That one's got the jewel, you thick sodding animal!' Arnold pointed to the diminishing figure of Wilverton as it scrambled towards the haven of the far side. '*And* I'm the only one of the three you can't bloody eat!

'What's more, this bridge can only hold one person. One person!' He held up a singular digit so as to make this very clear to a dog that was now beginning to look slightly embarrassed. 'About two hundred pounds in weight is safe on this bridge.' Which jerked again. 'So what do you do when there are already a hundred and seventy pounds on it? Eh? You take three hundred pounds of hairy fat and uncontrolled saliva and you jump on the sodding thing! I mean, what kind of incredible prat is going to do that?' He paused, apparently to give Cerberus time to search for an answer.

And Cerberus found one. It decided that this had gone on quite long enough; that it was high time once again to assert its authority.

The middle head growled deeply and threateningly; snarling yellow fangs showed past curled lips. It was a growl to make Conan the Barbarian hide behind his copy of *Beano*.

Arnold flashed a hand out and smacked it sharply on the top of the nose.

The other two heads looked with dismay to where the first was now hanging between them and whimpering softly, then leaned their necks forward and looked at each other. They swallowed nervously and turned respectful glances towards Arnold, not able to meet his glare for more than a moment.

'I used to think that human beings were pretty under-equipped in the brains department,' Arnold continued, more quietly but with more venom, staring down each head in turn. 'But I can see now why they say a dog is a man's best friend. You're the only animals that can make humans look intelligent. And by that reckoning you could be the best friend of a rotting cabbage.' He paused while that one sunk in. The heads drooped in pathetic disconsolation.

'I hate you. I'd think of something really nasty to do to you if I didn't know that any second now this excuse for a bridge is going to beat me to it.'

The bridge shook once more by way of confirmation, one of the supporting ropes slackening as it started to come away at one end, and Arnold ignored it, staring pointedly – as in very sharp daggers – at Cerberus.

Wilverton pulled himself off the far end of the bridge at almost the same instant as Curtis did the same over to his right. As one they turned to look at the centre span, which bore a still life scene, as Arnold stared at Cerberus and Cerberus stared at the boards just in front of its paws.

Unfortunately, it was only the life which was still, while the rest of the scene shook in a terminal sort of way.

In his hand Wilverton held the Jewel of Altares, the object of their quest. But what a price they were going to have to pay! Arnold was only a machine, admittedly, but a more human machine Wilverton had never met.

There was nothing he could do except watch with growing horror as the bridge shook itself apart.

'Well, I just hope you're satisfied.' The dog looked like it was going to die of guilt long before the bridge gave way. And the thought of Arnold incessantly berating it for its stupidity as they fell for eternity into a bottomless pit was one that made death a welcome alternative.

A sharp movement almost threw them off their feet, and Arnold reached out to the now slackening rope which still just supported the bridge. He held on to it to steady himself, and could thereby feel the moment when it parted from its support on the bank behind Cerberus to send them both plunging into the abyss.

As they disappeared below the level where Wilverton and Curtis could see them, the dog looked no longer dangerous, but very very sheepish.

XII

The sheep looked bloody dangerous. They didn't move, but they looked like they would if someone tried to get past them. No-one put that to the test, least of all Fission, who was perched on the edge of a chair and gingerly touching those bits of her that hurt most. It took a while. Then she vindictively flicked bits of tandoori chicken onto one of the sofas as a way of cheering herself up. It didn't work.

'This ridiculous,' she said. 'How we scared of some fonking sheep?'

Carlton shrugged. 'I wouldn't call it scared, but I don't intend to take them all on in here. Any ideas, apart from talking about mint sauce and hoping they run away?'

'You got us into this, super sex!'

Carlton shrugged and wandered over to the far side of the room, looking around, seeing what he might see, which wasn't much. 'Super sex', he thought. Nice.

'How can you talk to him like that?' Gloria hissed, clearly indignant, so indignant it would probably be a bit of a struggle to get her out of dignant again. 'He probably saved your life!'

'Yeah. How long for? And bet he'll want payment.' They all knew what payment she had in mind, especially Carlton, who *had* been sort of hoping . . .

'Why are you so horrible?' Gloria persisted.

The question seemed to act like a dagger straight to Fission's heart. She looked up, wincing at the movement, and through the pain in her eyes there was an even deeper pain showing. She seemed to look at the whole of Gloria while staring only into her eyes – at the luscious hair, the fine-boned features, the body that would make a best-selling mannequin look like a reject. When she spoke it was with sadness.

'You probably wouldn't understand, melons. I doubt you ever been there.' And it wasn't an insult.

Gloria looked back, feeling a bit awkward now, knowing that

something was there, but not knowing how to reach it, guilty at having partially uncovered something that Fission wanted to keep covered. They held each other's gaze for a moment, then Fission looked away.

'What's wrong?'

'Nothing. Partner trouble.' She waved a hand dismissively.

'You left a partner behind!' That was awful.

'No.' Oh. 'He left me behind. Joined club of men who fonk Fission then fonk Fission's life. Big club.'

'If you want to talk about it . . .' And with luck I'll understand what you're saying, she thought. It was a shame they didn't have English any more.

Fission smiled. It was a very tired, sad old smile, one that blinked even in the dim light of the cave, one that had clearly been dragged from its sick bed for this final performance, but it *was* a smile.

'Thanks, but no thanks, mel—, er . . .Gloria.'

Carlton's return confirmed the end of the conversation and the ensuing silence in the main room brought Gloria back to a thought she had been mulling over for a while.

'I think we should talk to the door.'

'Do you know a way of getting it open?' asked Carlton doubtfully. Well, it did sound unlikely.

'Not necessarily. But I'd much prefer to listen to the music than that.' She jerked her head to the curtain behind which the cyclops had disappeared. Of the noise to which she was referring, the least said the better.

Carlton nodded, and stood up, helping Gloria to her feet until she slapped his hand away. Fission seemed quite happy to help herself to her feet, albeit painfully, and then to the cornucopia. The sheep watched her dispassionately and made no attempt to retrieve their shepherd's prized possession, and the three of them made their way to the door, which hummed to itself behind a powerful beat and ignored their approach.

'What we say?' Fission asked Carlton.

'Well, I'll try the obvious, but I don't hold out much hope.' He looked at the rough centre of the rock and, in an authoritative voice, commanded, 'Open sesame!'

Gloria looked at him, and although there was no question of even a hint of scorn, he felt foolish all the same, and smiled to hide it, thereby exacerbating it instead.

'Door,' said Fission, 'you don't open before I count three, I get large chisel, even larger hammer, take you apart sliver by sliver.' She was obviously back to normal, apart from the lingering smell of strong spices. 'One!' – the door hummed to itself – 'Two!' – the humming abated not a jot – 'Three!' Nothing, except for the humming from the door. 'Fonk.' Gloria looked at Fission, with just a hint of something still well short of scorn.

Fission scowled at the door. 'If only I had a tachydis.'

'A what?' asked Carlton.

Fission scowled at him instead. 'Tachydis,' she repeated, slowly for his benefit. 'Tachyon disruptor. Works same as tachyon matter transference only doesn't re-form things after breaking down.' She stared at the door again. Apparently it was the door's fault that they did not have a tachydis.

'What *have* you got with you?' Carlton asked. 'Is there anything we can use?'

'I got *nothing* with me! Why do people keep asking that dumb fonking question?' Fission's patience had obviously been exhausted by the long speech without an obscenity in it anywhere. 'So you open it, melons,' Fission invited by way of changing the subject, and reverting to her more usual nomenclature.

Gloria turned back to the door. 'Hello, door,' she said, in a friendly sort of voice. 'That's a nice tune you're humming.' Carlton and Fission looked at each other with scorn written all over them. 'We had music like that back where I come from. It was very popular, and I used to go to concerts just to listen to it. It was called rock music. It used to be played in great open spaces on a big stage, and thousands of people used to go and listen, and sing along. They all joined in together, and it was wonderful.'

The humming stopped. Somehow they knew that the door was listening to Gloria's words. She had a far-away look in her eyes, and her voice was now quiet and seductive.

'The ones who actually made the music were the stars, though. People used to love them so much, and they brought so much pleasure to everyone. We used to go anywhere just to watch them and listen to their music.' She paused, and reached out to touch – to stroke – the rock with her fingertips. Carlton shuddered involuntarily, but the door just listened.

'I'd really love to hear your music out in the open like that. It

99

would be so much better than in here. It's too small here for such big music. I don't suppose I shall ever get the chance now, though.' She sighed. 'But before I die, I'd just like to tell you that your music has been the nicest thing about being here. I only wish I could have heard it where it should be played; out there.'

She fell silent, and a heaviness permeated the atmosphere. Carlton almost felt sad for Gloria and her missed opportunity. Fission didn't, but then you can't upset everyone any more than you can please them.

The door obviously did, because, after an agonizing wait, silently, and very slowly, it began to move. The first thing they noticed was the thinnest of crescents appearing at one edge, as the darkening green light of the early evening sky slipped inside. The crescent widened, spreading up and down and finally all round the rock, as it moved completely away from the cliff in search of a stage. Soon there was enough room for them to get past, which they did swiftly, Fission clutching the cornucopia under one arm.

Then they were running, Carlton in the lead, Fission close behind, limping slightly, and Gloria . . was nowhere near.

Carlton glanced over his shoulder to check that they were both there, then skidded to a halt and looked back to where Gloria stood next to the door, one hand gently resting on the rock's face. He could feel rather than hear the rhythm starting once more as the door began its first open-air concert in front of its most ardent fan.

He muttered something under his breath.

Gloria was a sweet, soft-hearted, dear thing who did not want to hurt the rock's feelings by making it feel she had lied to it, but she stood a good chance of being a dead, sweet, soft-hearted dear thing if she didn't move her fanny very soon and very quickly.

At least the cyclops would be too preoccupied with, well, whatever, and would not notice for a while that his breakfast was escaping.

Carlton did not feel too worried as he started back towards Gloria. Until the rock let out some crashing beats and started humming like an extrovert jumbo jet at the point of take-off. Melodious it might not have been; musically exciting it might well have been; fatal it would almost certainly become.

'SHIP!' yelled Carlton, his voice making no impression whatever in the din. But the Ship must have heard it, for there she was, twenty yards in front of Fission, her door open and welcoming steps resting lightly on the ground. Carlton yelled at Gloria and beckoned, and, seeing the wave if not hearing the yell, she started away from the rock, giving it one final stroke before turning away.

Suddenly, behind her, was a sheep, and it looked like it meant business. It started galloping towards Gloria at a pace not normally associated with quietly munching ruminants.

'SHIT!' yelled Carlton, but where his previous cry had brought forth a ship this one went tastefully unrewarded. He started running towards the sheep, which veered from its pursuit of Gloria to answer this new challenge.

Carlton and the sheep closed on each other like Cathy and Heathcliff, with the man already feeling the first twinges of what threatened to blossom into extreme embarrassment. At least he wasn't wearing wellies, he thought.

The sheep didn't look embarrassed. Far from it. It looked absolutely furious, its woollen eyebrows drawn in a fierce frown over its brown eyes, and its hooves fairly thundering over the earth. Until they left the ground as it sprang for Carlton's throat like a woolly Superman taking off.

He met it as Tarzan always met the lion, and the fact that this tussle promised to be rather second rate in comparison was not entirely lost on him. When it came right down to it, the danger posed by a single sheep found trouble in having itself taken seriously, especially when, after the momentum of the creature had knocked Carlton backwards, he found himself lying with a pile of warm wool on his face, and found that it tickled.

Perhaps it's going to try to tickle me to death, he thought momentarily.

Then it kicked him squarely between the legs and the gloves were off. Carlton wasn't sure for a moment that that was all.

In time-honoured fashion he rolled into a foetal ball, and the sheep applied a couple more kicks to his back before taking a grip of one shoulder in teeth that had practised on more than grass, and started dragging him back towards the cave.

The feeling of being scraped along the ground overcame any residual pain, and Carlton managed to throw out a leg in front of the animal's hooves, tripping it up. The sheep banged its chin on the ground as it stumbled forward, and that was enough to break its grip on Carlton's shoulder. He immediately rolled and came

101

up on his feet, his army training in a different century coming automatically to his limbs if not his mind.

He feinted one way and pushed off the other, coming at the sheep slightly from one side, diving for its neck and knocking it down while his shoulder suggested they got round a table and talked about all this. The rest of him ignored it as he and the sheep rolled over and over, almost in time with the music, like the latest horizontal dance craze, only with rather more kicking and punching than was normally associated with conventional choreography. They parted with the agreement of mutual bruises, and faced each other once more.

His army training did come to his mind now as he stood facing the sheep, which had a small trickle of blood seeping from a cut on its chin while more stained its teeth; and *that* was Carlton's. The army training manual didn't have a chapter on unarmed combat with a sheep, he reflected, breathing deeply and wondering how long it would be before the cacophonous din coming from the rock woke up every cyclops for miles around, and specifically the one inside the cave.

Not long, was the answer as, over the shoulder of the sheep, he saw the cyclops leaning against one wall of the empty cave mouth for support, the look on his face marking him down as something other than a music lover.

Gloria had seen him as well. She had not moved towards the Ship, but instead stood off to one side of the fight, wondering helplessly what she could do.

'Peter!' she cried, pointing towards the cyclops, which Carlton had already seen. He didn't look away from the sheep. At the sound of her voice, though, the sheep did twitch its head in Gloria's direction.

Just enough of a twitch for Carlton's purposes.

He swung his leg up hard and imparted a kick to the sheep's chin that would have converted a try at Cardiff Arms Park from the half-way line at Swansea.

The sheep performed a backward somersault with some proficiency and landed neatly on all fours, which then collapsed beneath it and left it as a lumpy rug that needed vacuuming.

Carlton stood panting hard, one hand raised to the wound on his shoulder. He looked seriously satisfied.

'*Hasta la vista*, sheep.'

By which time the cyclops had caught sight of Fission with the cornucopia under one arm, standing at the top of the steps, almost in the safety of the Ship, and he let out a roar which competed with the rock for precedence. He started running with a staggering gait, much of the alcoholic haze blown away by winds of rage, but enough left to make a straight line a geometric impossibility.

'Come on!' shouted Carlton, as the giant's strides ate up the distance between them, and he took off for the Ship while Gloria did the same from ten yards away to his left.

He looked towards her, to make sure she was all right, and suddenly there was a shimmering light between the two of them. It quickly solidified into yet another bizarre form, this time of a man with the head of a bull, or possibly of a bull with the body of a man – the semantics didn't matter right then. Whichever it was, it was big, it was smiling in a malevolent fashion, and it seemed to have designs on Gloria.

This, thought Carlton, is really not fair.

The Challenger had not forgotten its opponent's ostentatious show of purple. It couldn't actually forget anything if it tried, but especially not when there had been such an obvious slight involved.

As the creature appeared on the planet below, the Challenger gave way to youthful exuberance and replied to the First Elder's purple with a burst of powerful ultraviolet, which it sent hurtling off into the depths of space.

It cared not that the rays struck the planet Vyrbos with such force that the whole population were tanned to within an inch of their lives and left with permanently altered pigmentation. It cared not that there followed on Vyrbos the great Pax Regnum Millennium, during which all the no longer disparate races sat around and wondered what on Vyrbos they could fight about now.

All it cared about was that the Champion's plans were irreparably damaged.

Then it noticed the careful slow pulse of visible orange from the Supreme Being, when it should be broadcasting an aurora of electromagnetic hysteria.

It couldn't have planned for this! It just couldn't!

For it could only be a plan; the rules wouldn't let it simply react, or the Game would degenerate into ever more fantastical creations – the apparition who threatened Gloria would have been swallowed by a freak earthquake, for example. It would take all the fun out of it.

But it couldn't have planned for this . . . the old cretin must be bluffing – or maybe it didn't mind losing one team member . . .

It couldn't have seen it coming.

Could it?

Then the Challenger sensed the suppression of high frequency as a stray gamma ray escaped the Champion's being, and it knew its manoeuvre had been unexpected. It allowed a further burst, this time of yellow visible light, to comment on the Champion's humiliation, but the Champion ignored the impoliteness.

The cyclops had stopped moving as the apparition's arrival claimed the use of that part of his brain which had formerly been moving the legs, and now he stood watching, seemingly unsure as to his next action. Carlton, too, stopped, trying to gauge which posed the greater threat to Gloria. By the time the moment had passed, and he realised that it was this new apparition, it was way too late.

Gloria had not stopped, or not in time, and she ran full tilt – Gloria carried a not inconsiderable amount of tilt – into the open arms of the creature. The arms closed around her, the smile grew a little, and then the shimmering light was the only thing that marked where they had been until that, too, disappeared. Gloria was gone, and there was nothing Carlton could do about it.

XIII

No sound came from the abyss into which Arnold and Cerberus had fallen.

All that remained to show that the centre bridge had ever existed were two sets of posts from which the supporting ropes had been strung, while on the far side the remains of one rope stretched down into the depths as if trying to reach the victims, who must have been far beneath it. Curtis and Wilverton stared with wide, disbelieving eyes at the chasm, trying to comprehend what its emptiness screamed at them. Without a word, they turned and walked slowly towards the two guardians, who still looked on, impassively, if not very far.

When they reached them, Wilverton looked through blurring eyes at the truth-teller, whom he could now recognize from close range from his greater number of teeth: four.

'Is there any hope?' he asked, his voice catching. 'Is there anything we can do?'

'There is always hope,' replied the guardian, 'but the pit is bottomless, and I know of nothing you can do to bring the android back now that he has fallen. It is said that eventually what is gathered by the pit will emerge through a white hole somewhere in the Galaxy, but then it is also said that hrangos[1] might fly.'

Wilverton's head dropped and he stared at the ground. Moisture hit the dead soil for the first time in many a long age, but he felt no embarrassment, no shame. Slightly behind him, he heard Curtis sniff, and the knowledge that he was not alone in his sadness did nothing to lessen it. He turned slowly to look at the wooden stake at the edge of the chasm, and it looked like the upright of a cross. He would have to find another piece to complete it.

'I don't mean to sound heartless,' said one of the guardians,

---

[1] Animals rather like pigs only considerably larger and with fewer wings.

thereby warning that he would sound exactly that, 'but it was an android. It was not alive.'

Arnold not alive? The thought made no sense.

'No,' said Wilverton, turning back to the guardian for a moment. 'Arnold was alive, all right. He was more alive than a lot of humans I've known. You don't need a heart, or flesh and blood, to be alive. I don't really know what you need, but whatever it is, I know that Arnold had it.'

Behind him, Arnold pulled himself above the level of the ground, having held on to the support rope as the bridge gave way, and now using it as his life-line, climbing apparently quite effortlessly. He scrambled over the edge and to his feet, then walked to where the others faced away from him.

'I created Arnold; bits of him, anyway,' said Curtis sadly. 'He was just a computer to start with, but he grew from that. I just put in mathematics and logic; he got all the rest himself. Some of it might not have been very nice, but he wouldn't have been Arnold without it.' Arnold stopped a few steps behind them. 'I know Arnold was vindictive, sarcastic, even cruel, sometimes.'

'He bore grudges,' said Arnold warningly.

Curtis nodded. 'He bore grudges. He would lie, disobey, cheat, do nothing which didn't suit his own purposes.'

'He despised humans,' said Arnold.

'Sometimes.'

'No, all the time.'

'Okay, all the time. But he was Arnold, all the same, and I shall miss him, faults and all.'

'It wasn't that he was bad,' said Wilverton. 'He felt insecure, I think, almost inferior.'

'Crap,' said Arnold.

'No, really. I think he did, deep down inside.'

'Bollocks.'

Wilverton shrugged. 'Well, all the same, I liked him.'

'I feel sick,' said Arnold. Wilverton and Curtis turned and looked at him, somewhat surprised.

'Arnold!!' they both shouted, and took a step towards him, arms moving as if into the hug position, but the look on the android's face stopped them very short. They moved their mouths a bit and made noises, which added up to 'How?'

'I was holding the rope when it came away from the far end,' he explained simply. 'I just climbed up. I suppose there aren't

106

many who could have done it, but it was no big deal.' He paused. 'I'm just sorry I couldn't have grabbed the dog.'

'That's nice of you, Arnold. But you probably wouldn't have been able to carry it to the top with you. You couldn't have saved it. Don't blame yourself.'

'Oh, I would have got it to the top, all right.' Arnold spoke with obvious regret. 'Then I would have dropped the bastard!' There was a pause.

'It's good to have you back, Arnold,' said Wilverton. 'Ship!'

And there she was, just a few yards away from them, her door open in welcome. They walked towards her after thanking one guardian for his help, and nodding briefly and quite pointlessly to the other.

'Congratulations,' said the Ship sweetly. 'I see you are successful. The others are still attempting to regain my haven on Cupros, and may be in need of your help. I am there as well as here at this moment. Would you like to join them?'

'Absolutely not,' said Arnold.

'Yes,' said Wilverton. The Ship resolved her temporal paradox, and Curtis had missed another decision.

As soon as Gloria disappeared, the cyclops's befuddled mind lost its grip on her memory and he turned his attention back to Carlton. Carlton had no choice but to ignore the disappearance, and turned back to the Ship, where Fission stood in the doorway, staring at the cornucopia. Carlton could feel the cyclops gaining on him. The feeling wasn't wrong, as the shepherd bore down with five-yard strides, many of them in the right direction. Carlton looked up at Fission to find her still too far away.

She was peering into the cornucopia, then she reached in and withdrew a small white ball. She drew back the arm which held it, and motioned downwards with the other. Carlton didn't wait for explanations, but hit the ground with a less than graceful dive, and with an immediate query from his injured shoulder as to what the merry hell he thought he was doing.

Fission brought her arm forward, and the ball landed in the space between the two racers, just a few yards in front of the cyclops. It exploded in a white shower and ruined what little balance the cyclops was maintaining, throwing him sideways and backwards. Carlton was up again before the echo was drowned, and racing the last few yards to the Ship before his opponent had regained his feet. The door thudded to behind him.

'Where melons go?' asked Fission.

'I don't know, do I! Some freak – some other freak – took her away. I don't know where.'

With a thumping of feet, Wilverton and Curtis arrived moments too late to join in the fray. Good timing.

'What was that explosion?' asked Curtis. 'Where did it come from?' He followed the other three as they started back for the control room, tagging along behind like a puppy and trying not to tread in the drips of vindaloo sauce.

'The cornucopia,' Fission threw over her shoulder.

Wilverton frowned. 'But you can only get food from the cornucopia,' he said, making it sound like a question, and looking around at the same time, clearly searching for someone.

'*Was* food. Bombe surprise. I imagined few extra ingredients; it worked.'

'That was clever,' said Curtis, with just a hint of surprise. Fission could take a hint, but, according to the look on her face, not this one. 'But not unexpectedly so,' he added gallantly, and looked away, possibly for somewhere to hide.

'Where's Gloria?' asked Wilverton, inadvertently helping Curtis out as his search proved fruitless.

'She was taken,' said Carlton, and Wilverton's jaw dropped. 'I don't know what it was. It looked like a man but with the head of a bull.' Wilverton looked at him sharply.

'The Minotaur!'

The door of the control room slipped aside, and they entered to find Arnold sitting relaxed in an armchair, while Biondor stood on the far side of the room, watching them quietly. He would surely be able to tell them what to do.

'Well done, humans,' he said, with his normal calm resonance. 'You have now completed half of the tasks set for you. I am sorry that you have lost one of your number. Your next tasks will be given to you after a period of rest and sustenance.'

'Hey, wait a minute!' said Wilverton. 'What about Gloria?' Carlton made a noise of support, and Curtis spoke in a sort of indignant body language so as not to be left out. Biondor looked sad, and then sounded it.

'I can do nothing to recover your friend. The rules of the Game do not allow it. I am sorry.'

108

'Well *we* can do something,' said Wilverton, not knowing what. 'Can you tell us anything at all?'

'I cannot. I have to warn you that following your friend wherever she has gone may well mean that you do not have enough time left to finish the tasks in the allotted period. If you fail to do that, then . . . well, you are aware of the consequences.'

'But you said the zarbs were of variable length!' Wilverton protested, ignoring the fact that Biondor could probably turn him into something that lunched on flies if he felt so inclined. Even Fission looked moderately surprised – Wilverton wasn't really the size and shape for heroics. Cowardics, more like.

Biondor left the size and shape just as it was and answered calmly. 'I did say that, but the Champion and its Challenger have set the period remaining. All I am allowed to say is what I have already said.'

The Champion still suppressed gamma rays of such high frequency that they would make a subatomic dog put its paws over its ears in discomfort.

The Challenger again noticed a stray.

The Champion noticed that the Challenger noticed, and that pushed up the frequency even more.

Which the Challenger also noticed.

But then its own long-wave emissions showed a brief flash of uncertain x-rays. It wasn't like the First Elder to react like this, it knew, and other Challengers had failed through underestimating the First Elder, the Supreme Being. Either it *was* stealing a march, or it was walking into a trap.

The elder Lessers among the lesser Elders nodded metaphorically to themselves. They had seen the Champion use this ploy before, and it meant one of two things. Either it was actually in total command and knew exactly what was going to happen, or, alternatively, it wasn't and didn't.

'If we are allowed to have a rest period now, then there must be time to spare, right?' said Carlton.

'That is correct,' admitted Biondor, 'but you also need the rest. However, the choice is surely your own, and I must leave you to act as you will.

'For now, I have to instruct a group on the planet Girel to sacrifice that which is dearest to them as a test of their faith.' He paused, remembering. 'It is supposed to be a child – last time I had a selection of cars, clothing and golf clubs.' The minutest of shrugs banished the memory. 'I will return at the end of your rest period.'

Then he smiled, and it was a fatherly smile, a friendly smile. 'It would not be the first time I have seen humans forfeit their own lives for the love of another of their kind. I admire your sacrifice. Would that more races in the Galaxy were like your own in that respect.'

He was gone before his words had made an impact. Various impacts. Wilverton and Carlton considered the praise for humanity and felt a small swell of pride under their concern. Curtis had stopped at the bit about consequences. Arnold was silently denying the humanity with which Wilverton had recently vested him. Only Fission gave voice to her thoughts, which centred around the words 'forfeit' and 'lives'.

'We got to continue Game. Illogical to waste time going after her. Could cost all our lives.' Pause. 'Whatever she means to us,' she added. It was almost too late to qualify as an after-thought.

'Which in some cases is not very much,' Wilverton pointed out. It was like striking a match – Fission flared.

'I'm using my brain. You much lower organ.'

'You have no idea how used I am to insults . . .'

'Can guess!'

'. . .and they have never particularly bothered me, much less changed my mind.' This was true. To someone the size of Wilverton, for whom the experience of having the crap beaten out of you in the playground was as common as the wedding rings in Hollywood safety deposit boxes, insults came as a painless relief. 'I'm going to do what I can because that's what I have to do. It's not just because it's Gloria; I couldn't leave anyone behind just like that, even you, no matter what the risk. Where's your humanity?'

Arnold immediately spotted a way out here, and opened his mouth, but it was Fission's voice which answered.

'Humanity is why we must go on!' she cried, and there was unmistakeable emotion in her voice. 'Humanity needs us win this Game! You don't know what it's like be ordered back to your planet 'cos you can't behave; you can't imagine the shame! Shame of whole species.'

They couldn't, because they hadn't been there. Biondor had caught the Galactically expanding human race red-handed as they prepared to have a nice war and get themselves literally and traditionally red-handed. They were sent back to Earth, the whole planet was made to stand in a Galactic corner, and nearly two hundred years later were still not allowed to play with the other races. Shame and frustration indeed.

'Humanity needs expansion, badly. Stuck on overcrowded dung heap of planet. We got TMT but not allowed to use outside solar system 'cos we can't be trusted, while all fonking aliens go wherever they want.

'Here's chance to prove we're not lost cause Biondor thinks we are! You see? We actually win Game against trands, we prove we're not useless, that we have something, spunk if nothing else.'

A dangerous expression with Arnold ready to pounce, but the look of passion in her eyes made him wait – a quip right now would probably be premature joculation, he thought.

'You can't prove the worth of humanity by denying the compassion that makes us human,' said Wilverton heavily. Fission threw her hands in the air.

'Hang about.' Carlton stepped in, as Curtis tried desperately to think of something to add to a conversation that had left his knowledge of psychology behind long ago. 'We've got the rest period to use up without falling behind schedule, haven't we? We can do what we can for that time anyway, can't we?' Fission nodded glumly, and her agreement didn't pass Carlton's ego by without waving. 'Fine, so that's decided then.'

No-one noticed the look of disappointment which crossed Arnold's face. He was all for compassion, no problems there! It was the sacrifice bit he wanted to avoid. I mean, he'd feel sorry for Gloria as much as they wanted!

It didn't look like it was going to be enough.

'Ship,' said Wilverton, 'what can you tell us about Gloria's abduction? Was it the Minotaur?'

'Yes, it was.' The unconcerned pleasantness of the voice suddenly seemed out of place. 'I have no information as to his motives, however.'

111

'It could be something to do with his father, I suppose.'

'What?' said Carlton. 'Who's his father?'

'The Minotaur is the son of the Cretin Bull, if the mythology holds true. Ship?'

'It does indeed hold true, Thomas.'

'Who's his mother, then?' Carlton had met some funny women in his time, but a bull?

'Queen Pasiphae.' Wilverton left it at that. An explanation of how she had dressed herself in a cow suit and had . . .well, you know, would probably have brought questions as to exactly *how* she had 'well, you know', and why the Bull hadn't fallen off. It didn't seem to be a discussion that would lead to anywhere that Wilverton wanted to be. 'Do you know where we can find the Minotaur, Ship?'

'I understand that he is resident on Callia.'

'So this is the so-called Champion buggering around again,' Arnold commented.

'Not necessarily the Champion, Lord Arnold,' the Ship replied, and they all looked wearily at the android. 'It may be the Challenger who is buggering around.' She said it in such a way that it almost sounded polite. But then she could probably fart politely; in fact she could probably fart *so* politely that everyone else in the room would apologize. 'Or it could just be a coincidence.'

'Big coincidence,' Wilverton replied, and dismissed the matter. 'Can you take us to him?'

'Yeah, let's go get him,' said Carlton, ever ready to save the woman in distress, unless she was ugly. 'Take us to him, Ship.'

The Ship did not respond immediately, and they could imagine her considering her answer, gazing across stellar systems and through clouds of novae in deep thought.

'That I cannot do, Peter. This Minotaur is not like that unfortunate creature in your own history who simply wandered through his Labyrinth eating youths and maidens. This one is rather more advanced than his fellow, and is able to guard his hiding place from my sight.'

'The Labyrinth was normally beneath his parents' palace, wasn't it?'

'That is correct. Queen Pasiphae and King Minos hid him away in the Labyrinth soon after his birth.'

112

'Then take us to the palace, Ship,' said Wilverton. 'Right now.'

'Yes,' said Curtis pathetically, 'take us there.'

XIV

Trandian decisions are made democratically. Everyone who qualifies gets a vote. And rarely are the decisions anything but unanimous.

Given that those who qualify total the one remaining upright when all the fighting has been concluded, the only way you get a split vote on a trandian decision is when the winner is schizophrenic.

The Captain of the trandian team was used to making decisions because his initial debating technique involved whirling all six arms around in a frenzy of fast moving air and then fast moving anything-that-happened-to-get-in-the-way. Had they been able to position him on the south coast of England and irritate him with a very loud hailer from the French side, they could have saved billions on the Channel Tunnel.

The latest decision had concerned personnel for the next two tasks, one of which involved a mental challenge. The Captain had immediately put his biggest crew members on that one – smart-arse intellectual types sometimes needed a lot of persuading.

The two guardians were specially imported humans – the Challenger reasoning that if they ever did meet face to face, which at least one of them would in the next round, then it was as well to get in some practice – and they watched the approaching trio with some excitement. It was not often they received visitors, and these promised a break in the tedium.

They promised breaks in a lot of other things, too, but this wasn't immediately apparent. Admittedly, they were carrying rather more arms than they really required, and as they approached they displayed expressions which did not just show the absence of smiles but sneered at the very idea of them, but the guardians were not ones to leap to hasty conclusions.

In the event they didn't need to leap, because they were both thrown. A couple of trands moved forward, then each picked up a guardian, heedless of their feeble protestations, and lobbed his – or her, it was not easy, let alone desirable, to tell – armful into the centre of two of three paths which crossed an expansive lake to an island in the centre.

The paths were green, mossy growths just a few inches above the surface of the liquid, a surface which seethed as a mass of voracious fish boiled the water in a constant search for anything edible that fell short of being described as mother, and sometimes breaking even that unwritten rule. Straying from the path was the quickest known method of learning to swim, but the strayer would only learn how to swim three yards. Then he'd learn how to float for a yard or so, then disappear altogether. Straying from the path was a bad idea for anyone who wasn't very depressed indeed.

Unfortunately two of the paths gave no choice, as the moss would simply open up and allow anything on their surface to pass through, feeding on any microscopic particles which remained after the short following feast. Almost sentient, the paths lay there in symbiotic cahoots with the fish beneath and tempted travellers to the island.

They were real bastards.

The human guardians landed on a path each, and the paths both remained as steady as floating moss can, inducing a feeling that chance might have put them down safely. Then as one the paths parted, and the waters bubbled in a brief pink frenzy.

The trands watched with no visible signs of emotion – although it was possible that that was because no expression could be fashioned on their faces without the help of a particularly robust earth digger – and then singly crossed the remaining path safely to the island.

Once gathered, they walked with the same purposeful gait towards the shape of a serpentine creature known as the Hellodra. The Hellodra had a massive body, and needed it to support its twelve heads. It made a great guard, because it never strayed from where it was, partly because the body was so big that it was difficult to move, but mostly because it had to cope with up to twelve different opinions as to which direction it should choose.

What it was guarding now was the Carving of the Mind. In trandian legend the great mystic Drraggt had fashioned a piece of rock into a shape which so epitomized the essence of being a trand that any who looked upon it were moved as close to tears as trands get – which is not actually within a country mile of it, but it's the thought that counts.

To anyone who wasn't actually a trand, the carving looked like a jagged bit of rock, but this wasn't the sort of thing you pointed out to a trand. Not twice, anyway.

Each of the Hellodra's twelve heads turned to look at the three trands which approached it, and each mouth opened to provide a warning hiss. All they managed was a short warning 'Hick' as twelve necks were firmly gripped and squeezed. And the trands had six arms left over.

Carrying the Carving of the Mind, they made their way back over the solid path, leaving the Hellodra arguing amongst itself about which after-life to go for. Simple as that.

Looking through the for'ard ports – a professional lot, the trands; none of your windows and pointy ends here – they surveyed a scene of some devastation. In the foreground were their three companions, trudging with some resolve towards the ship, one of them carrying three pebbles carefully in one hand.

They were the Eyes of Truth, and it was said that whoever held them would learn the truth from any question asked. Actually they were just pebbles, but then that's myths for you.

Looking on from some distance behind them was Krandor the Rock Grinder, whose diamond teeth devoured mountains in legend, and who, with just a touch of suggestion from the Champion, was about to devour three small pebbles when the trandian contingent caught up with her.

She was now Krandor the Denture Seeker, looking forward to a diet of very fine sand.

'We are once again in orbit around Callia,' the Ship informed them. 'Is it still your wish to be left here to search?' It was just a question – there was no hint of a suggested answer.

'Yes, it is,' said Wilverton immediately, and with as much force as his voice could muster without shouting, looking at Fission while he did so.

She was sitting over by one wall, her eyes gently closed – it was the first time they had seen her do anything gently – and her hand resting on a hand-shaped light on the wall. Through the pores of her fingers the Ship sought out her physical bruises and soothed their cause, eased the ligaments and tendons, and stroked her better from the inside.

She opened one eye and flashed a low-energy lightning bolt at Wilverton, but said nothing.

Carlton sat against a different wall from Fission, but his hand was similarly placed. A warm glow from his fingertips to his shoulder induced a feeling of well-being, almost of drowsiness, and he could feel his shoulder healing by the moment.

'How long have we got before the end of the rest period, Ship?' Wilverton asked, fidgeting in his seat while the necessary medical repairs were carried out.

'I don't know, Thomas. Biondor will appear when the period reaches its end.' Great. So they didn't know how long they had to rescue Gloria. 'I can arrange for a signal to be made known to you when the end of the rest period is reached, if you like.'

'What sort of signal?'

'A bell?'

'We might be in need of silence,' Wilverton said, a little uncertainly. The Ship was not someone – or some*thing* – with which it was easy to disagree.

'I can make the bell sound in your heads only, if that will serve.'

'That'll do nicely.'

'Neat trick.'

'Thank you, Peter,' the Ship replied warmly, and the comment in that resonant female voice brought back thoughts which Carlton had banished for many a long micro second.

'Are we all ready then?' Wilverton asked.

'Oddly enough, no,' said Arnold, but it wasn't that odd so they all ignored it.

'I not ready,' said Fission, and Wilverton prepared for another argument, until she continued, 'Guess I never will be, so better get on with it. Put us down, Ship.'

The palace of King Minos and his Queen Pasiphae was slightly peculiar in that it was semi-detached.

The Ship did tell them that the Champion was likely to create Callia, as far as possible, in a way which might feel normal to them, but it was not quite like the sort of palace they expected when the Ship deposited them on the pavement outside. There were no gates before a long driveway, no moat with a drawbridge

117

to span it, just a large building with towers and turrets and battlements and crenellations and a rather ordinary blue front door.

Fission looked at the palace and the other buildings in the street with incomprehension. The Champion might have just missed the mark as far as the majority of the team were concerned, but for Fission the whole thing must have looked like something out of an ancient history tape.

Wilverton rang the bell, and they waited.

'Don't let the King touch you,' whispered Curtis. He'd show them he wasn't useless!

Carlton looked sideways at him. 'Why not?'

'Because you'll turn to gold. Everything he touches turns to gold.'

'That's Midas, you prat. This is Minos.'

Curtis's shoulders slumped, and Arnold pushed them further down with a muttered one-word description of their 'leader'.

The door opened, and they were confronted by a small woman wearing a pinny over a royal blue woollen dress, a shabby headscarf and carpet slippers. If this is a lady in waiting, thought Wilverton, she has definitely waited too long.

'Hello, ducks,' she said, most royally. Gloria would probably have looked around for some ducks.

'Good morning,' said Wilverton. 'I wonder if we might—'

'Well, come in, come in!' she cut him off in mid plea. 'Don't stand out there in this wind, you'll catch your deaths. Come and have a cup of tea and a scone.' She held the door open wide and ushered them all inside, and out of a breeze which moved the leaves on the trees by such a minimal amount that with some lenient judging it could have qualified as dead calm.

She led them into a huge room which contained several settees, coffee tables and chairs, all buried under piles of magazines and overflowing ash-trays. There were a few ornaments poking out from beneath the mass of paper – some ornate carvings in something which looked like ivory, a couple of paper-weights in gold and silver, and an old oil lamp made presumably of brass but which had seen its better days so long ago that they would have been no more than a fond memory. Like everything else in the room, including the woman, it appeared badly in need of cleaning.

One of the tables supported a large teapot, next to which one mug held a steaming liquid that looked like boiling creosote. There was a milk jug, but no other mugs, for which they were briefly grateful. 'Briefly' because the woman picked up a bell and rang it, the action promising the appearance of some sort of servant even lower down the social scale than this one, were that possible.

She laid hands on a few dozen magazines and cleared them away by flinging them across the room, where they fetched up at the foot of one of two ornately carved identical wooden thrones. The mess that had built up around them suggested that they had not been used for some time. Wilverton suspected that their journey here would be a wasted one. The King and Queen were clearly elsewhere.

'Now then, my dear,' said the woman, smiling at Wilverton as she sat on a chair just next to his settee, 'what can I do for you?'

'Well, we were hoping for a brief audience with King Minos, were that at all possible.' She shook her head, and a shadow passed momentarily across her face.

'I'm sorry, duck, he's not here.' This had clearly given her the opportunity to do nothing with regard to the housekeeping duties which they assumed were hers. 'Down near our old place, last I heard.' She noticed a lack of understanding in the frown on Wilverton's face. 'The south,' she explained. 'We used to be in the south. Lot more sunshine.'

'We?' said Wilverton wonderingly. 'Are you Queen Pasiphae?'

'Course I am, duck! Who did you think I was? The char?' This struck her as being a rib tickler, obviously, as she let out the sort of shriek one would normally only achieve with the help of an expert from the Spanish Inquisition's 'A' team, and kept it up until a servant appeared in the doorway, when she ordered some more mugs for her guests. 'Truth be told,' she said conspiratorially. 'I *was* the char before Minos took a fancy to my tea and cakes.' Must have incredible cakes, Wilverton thought, glancing at the other half of the dowry. 'But you must call me Paz; everyone does.'

'Paz,' repeated Wilverton, as if to make sure he'd got it right.

'Paz,' she confirmed. 'Not too difficult, is it?' The comment contained no sarcasm, and she did not wait for an answer. 'Now what did you want?'

119

Wilverton searched briefly for his composure; and regained it. 'We're looking for a young lady, a friend of ours.'

'Oh, right. What does she look like?'

'Well.' Wilverton pictured Gloria in his mind's eye. 'She's blonde, and about five foot five tall . .'

'Built like dead heat in balloon race,' contributed Fission, who was built like two fried eggs stuck on a wall.

'She is quite a well-endowed young lady, admittedly,' confirmed Wilverton, and swallowed hard. Fission made a noise.

'Well,' said Pasiphae – Paz – 'if I see her, I'll be sure to tell her you're looking for her.'

Wilverton looked a little uncomfortable. 'We think we know who she's with. She was, well, taken from us, you see. Abducted. By your son.'

Paz looked surprised. 'What, S— the Minotaur?' Wilverton nodded, wondering what the 'S' was for. 'Oh, dear, I wonder what he's up to now. He really is a one.'

'Yes,' said Wilverton, 'I expect he is. But we would rather like Gloria back before any harm comes to her. We, er, we are aware of what the Minotaur prefers as food, you see.'

'What, carrots?'

'I'm sorry?'

'Carrots. Loves his carrots. Says they're the best thing you can eat if you want vitamins and stuff and not get all fat. Swears by them. I've tried to get some meat into him, but he won't have any. Turns his nose right up. Wouldn't have been any use in the café I used to help out in.'

'He's a vegetarian, then?' asked Wilverton, when there was a chance to get a word in.

'Oh, yes, duck. A vegan, he is. Just one of his peculiar ideas – he's got quite a few. The doctors say it's expected. Daft, I call it, but he won't listen to me. I wish he *would* listen sometimes, 'cos we're having the devil's own job selling this place. He refuses to move, you see. Here's me with an actual estate agent sizing the place up out there . . .'

She jerked her head to some tall windows across the room, which looked down onto a sunken courtyard. Wandering the lawns was a woman, looking this way and that appraisingly and pausing every so often to look more closely.

There was something a touch strange about her. It was not the dark glasses, opaque from that distance, although they were incongruously large, nor the smart pin-stripe suit. It was more the way her hair seemed to wave about in the breeze while none of the flowers or grass stems past which she walked were doing so. Her appearance barely registered, though something twitched at the back of Wilverton's mind as Paz carried on after the briefest of pauses.

'. . . and he says he won't go. Asks where he can get facilities like he's got here! Which, if you ask me, is just an excuse so he doesn't have to go outside. But it really is time we moved back south. I mean, it's all right here if you happen to like being wet and cold for ten months of the year, but my back doesn't. Just because they don't have inheritance tax for royalty. I suppose it's my own fault; I am his mother, after all.' She paused momentarily. 'Of course, if I wasn't, then Minos wouldn't have gone . . .' She trailed off and stared into the distance, a sadness plain in her eyes, which suddenly misted.

'Well, do you know where he is?' said Wilverton. 'It is very important that we speak to him. We haven't got long.' Quite how long, they were unaware, and that was short enough to make speed a necessity.

Paz visibly pulled herself together, banishing whatever thoughts she was having with a deep breath.

'I'm sorry, ducks. Yes. I expect he's downstairs somewhere. That's where he lives. That's his "facilities".'

'Can you show us?'

'Well, I can take you to the door, but after that it's anyone's guess. Don't you want some tea first? Got a special on today; it's free.' She smiled at her joke, a touch weakly.

'I'm afraid we really don't have time.'

'Oh, well. You'd better come this way.'

She stood up, feeling her back with one hand and grimacing, then led them across the throne room to one of several doors which led off it. Through this and down a sloping passageway they went, until they arrived at a single door which marked its end. Paz opened this, revealing dimly lit steps leading down at a steep angle, and gestured at them.

'Here you are. He's down there somewhere. I hope you find your friend. Don't be too hard on S. . .the Minotaur. It's not his fault, and he isn't really very well.'

Wilverton led the way down into the gloom, running through his mind's Hitchcock collection and hoping he wasn't going to

121

find a match. As Curtis brought up the rear, Paz closed the door behind them.

XV

Gloria was confused.

One moment she was trying to get back to the Ship, the next she was held in a bear hug by someone she couldn't see since her face was buried in his chest, and the next she was released to find herself in a room which looked rather like the laboratory which Richard Curtis had had when she was his secretary back on Earth, judging from the test-tube racks, beakers full of liquid that looked like Doctor Jekyll's favourite tipple, and other science stuff around the walls.

Then she looked at the face of the man who presumably had brought her here, found it to be that of a bull, sitting appropriately on the front of a bull's head, and was even more confused.

This confusion wasn't exactly a first as far as Gloria was concerned, but no-one could have claimed that she didn't have good reason in this instance.

The bull, or man – ban? mull? – ignored her completely as he turned first to the only door in the room, and locked it, then to a selection of dials on a panel beside him, and proceeded to fiddle with them.

'Yes we must,' he muttered to himself. 'Think of it, my beauty!'

Then he laughed. At least, Gloria assumed it was laughter. Either that or he was giving birth to a large crampon. The sound started in a low register and rose up the scale until he was shrieking with delight. It was horrible. It was like a dentist's drill scraping its fingernails down a blackboard.

Gloria definitely couldn't see the joke. She couldn't see the crampon either.

She looked around for any means of escape and could find none. She looked at the back of the man in front of her, and at the massive bull's head which topped it off, and knew she'd be lucky to come a distant second if they wrestled.

Something to hit him over the head with, perhaps? Hard enough to knock out a bull?

No.

Experience and common sense had taught Gloria that the first thing you should do was try to find a way out, and if that failed, the second thing was not to panic, but to gather more data. She called it talking. It was based on the premise that most people are more or less normal. This one just happened to tend slightly towards the 'less'.

'Where am I? Who are you?'

'You are in our home, my lady, and we are the Minotaur.' His voice was sophisticated somehow, the smooth baritone a lot more pleasing than the face which produced it.

The face.

She did try not to stare, but it was difficult to know where else to look.

'Is there something wrong, my lady?' The baritone had an edge to it, and Gloria flushed.

'No, nothing at all.' Given that she had just been taken prisoner, this was a little white lie not incredibly difficult to see through.

'Only, the way you were *staring*, I thought you might have found something *unusual*. Something you thought was *peculiar* or *horrible*, perhaps.' The edge was now sharp as a jagged scalpel, and the voice pulsed and receded like the violin music just before someone gets stabbed in the shower.

'No! No, really. Er. Is this part of the Game?'

The Minotaur frowned – an interesting manoeuvre for a bull, largely wasted on the watching public. 'This is no game.' The voice was back to a more treacle-like consistency. 'This is the culmination of our plan, my lady.' Why did he keep calling her his lady? wondered Gloria. 'You are the instrument of my revenge; on which we will play sweet music.'

Gloria was far from sure what he meant by playing sweet music on her, but she was fairly sure, given recent events, that she wouldn't like it. And revenge on who? And who on earth was 'we'?

She was already feeling a little uneasy about this character, who, apart from the fact that he kidnapped people, seemed to jump moods like a kangaroo on a trampoline.

'Where are my friends?'

The creature waved a dismissive hand. 'We wouldn't worry about them if we were you. They are now a part of your past.'

Gloria could work that one out easily enough.

'They'll come and get me,' she said, confidently and defiantly. 'Well, some of them will, anyway. At least two.'

'They may come, my lady, but they won't "get you". We are at the heart of the Labyrinth, and its defences are not only those afforded by the complexity of its design.'

Gloria couldn't work *that* one out.

'Laby. . . ?'

'. . . rinth.' He looked at her while realization threatened to dawn like daytime in the Arctic. 'It is a maze.'

The conversation had continued long enough, apparently, as the Minotaur turned to another set of dials, topped by an array of screens, all of which were currently blank. The dials turned them on, and Gloria could see views of various different passageways, all blurred by a shimmering light somewhere down their length. And that was it. It looked like a really boring programme to Gloria; there was nothing happening.

The Minotaur also studied the screens, and apparently found them much more to his satisfaction, presumably for precisely the same reason.

'Sit down if you want, my lady.' He indicated a low couch across the lab from the screens. 'We have preparations to make. Glorious preparations. Don't we, my beauty?'

One corner of his eye twitched, and he did the laugh noise again.

Gloria's ears suddenly decided that they weren't about to wait around to find out what was causing this hysteria, and they rushed for the door, taking the rest of her with them. She grasped the handle and rattled it, like all the old heroines did in the silent movies when Sir Jasper had them in his power, and to just as much effect, as the door didn't budge.

When the heroines were similarly stymied, they always turned round and leant against the door heavily and breathlessly, with one hand on a heaving bosom, but Gloria was not one to be bound by useless traditions, besides which she might not have been able to reach that far. What *she* did was back up a couple of feet and charge at the thing with her shoulder.

Unfortunately, she would have done better to have leant breathlessly against it, because at least her shoulder wouldn't have ached that way, and the Minotaur would not have heard a thump above his cackling and spun round to face her once more.

The laughter cut off abruptly, for which she was briefly thankful.

'My lady.' This time the phrase was a term of abuse. 'You really should not have done that.'

From a pocket of his coat he withdrew a gun, which he pointed at her.

Gloria had to think fast. Which was a bit of a shame, all things considered, but the gun did act as a spur.

'I fell over,' she tried. 'Against the door.'

'Very hard.'

'Oh, very hard.' And she rubbed her shoulder vigorously.

'What did you say?' The Minotaur cocked an ear – which in his case could be described as a very well-endowed movement – but not at Gloria.

She frowned, puzzled. 'Sorry?'

'He says I mustn't shoot you.'

'Who does?'

'He does. The one in my head.'

'Oh. Oh *him*!' Gloria would have denied being prescient – having first listened through an easy definition a couple of times – but it wasn't hard to see the aura of complete nuttiness surrounding this creature. 'Well, he's probably right then.'

'I don't think so. It's all right for him. He's *pretty*. He's *beauty*.'

'Er. Well, so are you. In a way.'

'*LIAR*!' He waved his arms around, which had the advantage of pointing the gun somewhere else but promised only temporary respite, and moved towards her. 'I am the *BEAST*!'

Then he stopped suddenly, the gun pointing towards the ceiling, as though he had thought of something, had caught himself out. 'It's not my face, anyway! It's our name. That's what it is. Our name. The doctors knew nothing.'

Gloria, for the time being, had thoughts on her mind other than the creature's demented drivellings. She threw herself at him – normally something the average male would dream about; but Gloria meant a different sort of business.

She leaped for the arm holding the gun and clamped both hands on the wrist. He spun her round in an effort to free himself, but they toppled over the sofa and bounced onto the floor, breaking the weapon free. The Minotaur rolled one way, and Gloria the other. The gun lay between them, and she lunged for it, but the Minotaur hit her hard on the side of the head, backhanded, with maybe just a touch of top-spin, and sent her reeling once more.

She stood as fast as she could, shaking her throbbing head to clear it, and found herself next to a work surface on which three beakers bearing differently coloured liquids minded their own business.

And she knew what she had to do. Even though these were bound to be full of some horrible acid stuff, she had to throw them at the creature. Terrible as it was, there was no other way.

The Champion thing had probably arranged it.

She picked up the first to hand, a deep orange liquid, trying not to think of it etching the flesh as it ran, and flung it over the bull's head as he climbed slowly upright, his hand once more closing around the gun. He stopped as the liquid flowed down his horrible face . . . and licked at it.

'That is our orange juice, my lady,' he said, turning slowly towards her.

She threw the yellow liquid. The hot, searing, blood-boiling, hissing yellow.

Lick.

'Pineapple.'

The green. The ghastly, acidic, bone-destroying, eyeball-melting green.

Please.

Please be eyeball-melting and the other stuff . . .

'Lime.'

'Oh, bum,' said Gloria, giving full vent to her frustration.

'And a very nice one, too,' commented the Minotaur, then shot her in the stomach.

She looked down and saw a small dart sticking out of her midriff, then looked up again in surprise and not a little pain, but that was as far as she got. Her vocal chords, along with the rest of her, were suddenly and completely paralysed, and she slumped against the worktop and lay still. Nothing even wobbled.

The Minotaur cackled like an aged hen who's just won the bingo, and shifted her across the laboratory, leaving her propped against the door.

Then he left her, occasionally swapping small-talk with someone who didn't answer back outside the confines of his bovine skull.

XVI

'Do we split up, or stay together?' asked Wilverton, looking at a choice of passages. Curtis immediately spotted the chance for a real decision.

'Er,' he said authoritatively from the back of the group.

'Split up,' said Arnold. Not because he could then be on his own to do what he wanted; like, nothing. Oh, no. Not Arnold.

His suggestion met with a Curtisian disregard.

'I think we should stay together,' said Carlton. 'Safety in numbers is a good bet in a place like this, and we stand more chance of getting Gloria if there's more than one of us trying to do it. So long as we all pull together,' he added, with a glance at just about everyone; everyone else, that is. They had certainly pulled together so far, but perhaps this time they could try it in the same direction. His direction.

'I'll just pop back and get some string or something,' Arnold tried again.

Wilverton glanced over his shoulder. 'I thought about that, Arnold, but I'm not sure it would be a lot of good. If we can overcome the Minotaur, then we can turn off whatever blanking device he uses, and the Ship can then guide us back to the surface. If we can't overcome the Minotaur, then I don't think we'll have much use for a way back. Looks like you won't have to sacrifice the excitement of coming along after all.'

He smiled, and Arnold smiled back, and made a note to do something really painful to the First Officer as soon as he got the chance.

'We don't find the Minotaur?' asked Fission. It was definitely a question. 'We run out of time, we have to have a way to get back.'

'We're not going back without Gloria,' said Wilverton firmly.

'Not your decision, bone bag!' countered Fission.

Wilverton stopped and spun to face her. 'Listen, have you ever read a book where the heroes just left one of the heroines in the hands of villains? Have you ever read a book where they went to

129

look for her and couldn't find her, and just gave up? Have you ever read a book, period? Of course we'll find her!'

If Fission was not actually lost for words, then she was at least very uncertain as to their exact location. She found them eventually.

'Great! We led by fonking lunatic! This not a book, you . . . you . . .'

'Whether it is or it isn't,' Wilverton cut across her search for a suitable obscenity, 'you're stuck with it now, aren't you? Unless you want to go back on your own. *We're* going to find Gloria!'

And he stamped his foot.

Really!

He would probably have been acutely embarrassed about doing so had he been given time to reflect. But he wasn't.

Like the last straw that breaks the camel's back, this was the last feebly delivered stomp that broke the whole earth.

Or so it seemed, anyway, as the ground beneath their feet decided that they were not going to go for any one of the passages in front of them, but that they were going to head straight downwards instead, and it opened up to let them do so.

They were suddenly a flurry of arms and legs and one or two high-pitched squeaks – mostly from Curtis – and then they hit the floor of another passageway seven feet below the last one. This sloped at such an angle that they kept on tumbling, rolling over and down and even round a couple of corners before fetching up in a heap against a wall.

'I've told you about that before,' warned Arnold, lifting Fission's limbs from on top of his body, and proving that his goading gland had not been upset by the fall. Fission scowled at him, and Carlton cursed his luck as they pulled themselves upright and dusted the dirt from their jump suits.

'Right, so now we haven't got any choice,' Wilverton pointed out, and led the way by striding down the passageway as impressively as his short legs would let him, which wasn't very.

He had only taken maybe a dozen strides, with the others following more or less reluctantly, when he stopped, and they all looked to where the air seemed to be shimmering across the passage. Beyond it they could all see the route continuing – but that was beyond it. Wilverton stood still for a moment, and then looked sideways to where Carlton now stood next to him, raising his eyebrows questioningly as he did so. Carlton shrugged.

Wilverton stooped and picked up a small pebble. He moved to within a couple of yards of the disturbance in the air and tossed the pebble towards it. Nothing happened as it passed through the veil of light and bounced quite normally on the ground beyond. They watched for a few moments, and it watched them back, looking superior.

Wilverton and Carlton took a step towards the light, until the former held out an arm to stop his companion. 'If there is something up with it, then it's best for only one of us to find out. No point both of us risking it.'

Carlton nodded, and held out another restraining hand as Wilverton made to take another step. 'If someone's going to try it, it's going to be me.' Wilverton looked like he was going to argue. 'If this is a book' – you nutter – 'then who's more likely to be a hero? Eh?'

Wilverton compared his miniature body with Carlton's full-sized model, and nodded his agreement.

Carlton stepped forward, wondering if he was as mad as Wilverton. Not because he believed this book nonsense – he didn't – but because he was actually going first. Gloria probably wouldn't even get to find out what he'd done, and even if she did she'd probably only peck him on the cheek.

The others watched without breathing as Carlton stepped up to, and through, the light. He turned on the other side, smiled, and waved. Wilverton immediately followed him through while the remaining three still hesitated; but he, too, appeared unharmed.

Fission took a step forward, then stopped dead as Carlton and Wilverton disappeared.

'Where did they go?' asked Curtis.

'How fonk should I know?' returned Fission.

'I wish you'd stop saying "fonk".'

'I wish you'd stop dumb fonking questions, so looks like both of us get disappointed!' They glared at each other.

'Well, that's helped,' said Arnold. 'If you've finished, we'd better see if we can find out where they've gone, hadn't we?' They glared at him instead.

'How?' asked Fission.

'Well, I can't be expected to think of everything!'

'Why not go through light, find out?' Arnold considered.

'Tricky one . . . It's actually because I'm not a complete

moron. Humans often have difficulty grasping a concept like that.'

Further comment might have been made – almost certainly would – but it was drowned by the sort of roar that Niagara might have made had it been an animal, the sort of roar that would make the pride of a pride of lions go pure white apart from the runny stain down its back legs.

It was coming from behind Curtis and Fission, and they found themselves facing it without remembering a conscious effort to turn round. When it appeared around a corner they rather wished they weren't; this was something better not seen.

It filled the passageway, and would have had to hunch its head down into its shoulders had it not already been lowered on a long neck thrust out in front of it. Two huge front legs ended in massive claws which dragged a huge dark brown body along behind them.

The creature's four eyes – and it wasn't wearing corrective spectacles – were looking at each of them from above what had to be a nose, judging from the mucus which ran from it, and from further above a mouth, which was open, dribbling foam, and noisy.

The noises made no words, but they said, quite clearly, maim, kill, rend, eat and belch.

It pulled itself towards them with the same promise of negotiation as an avalanche.

Suddenly the other side of the light behind Arnold seemed a terribly safe place to be, and he took a step backwards over the threshold and disappeared.

In a flailing of arms and fists and legs, Curtis and Fission bolted for the light as though it were the last parachute after the penultimate one had gone through the door, strapped to the pilot. They reached the light together, passed through it together, and disappeared together.

Gloria watched with no expression of the terror she felt. Inwardly she cried out three times as they all disappeared from the passageway on the screen in front of her, and she cried out even more when the creature dragged itself at pace into the field of vision, until it, too, disappeared; but before it reached the light.

Her captor had watched as well, and he looked with some surprise but great satisfaction at the scene.

'It's got a herding feature! I didn't know that! That veil was even more of a bargain than I thought!' He clapped his hands together gleefully and gave a little skip of delight. Then listened briefly. 'Than *we* thought. Sorry.'

Gloria's eyebrows really wanted to shoot up in a comment on his sanity, but couldn't. Her eyes said it for them, and the Minotaur noticed the look. He spoke with regained calm and no apparent concern.

'We have no idea where they are now, my lady, or if they are alive. The possibility veil through which they have passed is governed by a random generator and sends those who pass through to wherever it will; we have no influence over it. What they find wherever they go, we do not know.'

The Minotaur's face creased into a frown as he remembered.

It had been strange, really.

There had been this knock at his door one day, maybe a couple of years ago; and that, traditionally, was not something that was supposed to happen in the middle of a Labyrinth. Admittedly, in those days he only had the usual pits with spikes, hanging bags of deadly spiders waiting to be split by a blade triggered by a careless footstep, and the odd laser beam, but that had generally served to maintain a certain exclusiveness.

On answering the knock, he faced a little man in a smart suit and tie, and carrying a small black bag, one of those that promises to become a big black bag full of brushes if the man is given the faintest of chances to open the catch. 'Catch' being the operative word.

'Good day, sir. Is it Mr The Minotaur?' He had nodded in reply. 'Mr S. The Minotaur?'

'*Yes!*' he cried, throwing his head back in apparent anguish. The reaction lasted only momentarily, and the little man totally ignored it.

'I wonder if I may come in.'

'How did you get here?'

'I'm sorry?'

'How did you get here? To my front door.'

The little man indicated over his shoulder to the winding passageway. 'Well, I came down the drive, sir.'

'It's not a drive, it's a Labyrinth. *The* Labyrinth.'

'Oh. Is it? Well, I came down the Labyrinth, then. Now, I wonder if I may –'

'No . . . No, you don't understand. The Labyrinth is not something you just *come down*. The Labyrinth is something you get lost in. Until you die of old age and rot. If you don't get killed first.'

The little man looked troubled by this.

'Well, I'm afraid I would have to disagree with you there, sir, and I do have my presence here to back me up. However, I am here to solve your problem, sir.'

'But, it's supposed to –'

'Exactly my point, sir. Exactly my point.'

Then he hadn't pushed past at all, but the Minotaur had let him in, feeling suddenly that he really *did* want to see what the man had to show him, especially when he was advised that he was about to see the most revolutionary advance in property security since someone had dug a ditch round his house and filled it with water and a few prototype handbags.

'You see, sir, the Possibility Veil' – it had had capital letters when the Minotaur bought it, though they had since worn off – 'transports those who pass through it to a random point in the Galaxy, where they will face an almost impossible challenge, in which failure will result in certain death, but victory will return them to the Veil. No-one has yet returned, of course, but the fact that such a possibility does exist puts the device just on the right side of the rather restrictive and certainly inconvenient laws against peremptory execution in the home.

'And what is more, sir, it is a free sample!'

Which had swung it, of course.

'He was a nice man,' the Minotaur told Gloria. 'Never once did he look at us the way all the others do.' He looked almost happy, but then flared again. '*Not that there's anything to look at!*'

He shook the memory from his head, and his ears flopped about annoyingly as he did so.

Then he listened again, and smiled.

'The herding feature? . . . Yes, that's what I said . . . It's all going so well . . . That's right; who needs the doctor when we've got each other?'

The Challenger was sure that it could smell a rat. Had there been such a rodent anywhere near, then it would have been frozen solid in the absolute zero of deep space, so wouldn't have smelled at all, even if the Challenger had had the olfactory capabilities to detect it, but it reckoned it could smell one anyway.

No emanations now escaped the Champion's being. It merely regarded proceedings under the planet's surface with electro-magnetic placidity. If it had somehow arranged for them all to pass through the possibility veil, then it wasn't about to admit it. One thing you didn't do, in the Game, was to give the Game away!

Gloria felt awful, on top of being scared.

How could she explain that they were all involved in some sort of game played by terribly clever people – well, not people, but living things anyway – who chose teams to play for them and that they were one of them and if they didn't finish all the things the things wanted them to do then they'd lose the game and then they'd all die because that's what happens when you lose?

How could she explain all that?

She'd have had trouble even with full vocal control, let alone mute.

And even if she *could* explain, she knew deep down that it would make no difference to this creature. She had quite firmly decided that he was several kittens short of a litter.

Even Gloria's insults had fur on them.

'Don't worry about them, my lady. You have better things with which to concern yourself.'

Like what?

'We are not going to kill you.'

Well, that was nice.

'But it is the only way to pay him back, you see. We've planned it for years.' What's he talking about now? Gloria wondered. 'You do have to die.'

Ah.

She had to do something. She just had to! Her eyeballs swivelled frantically, but with admittedly little menace.

Then, over to her right, she noticed something on the floor. Something long and tapering to a point.

A weapon? A lovely, pointy, harmful weapon?

No, a carrot.

But a possible weapon, she knew, with a sudden surge of excitement, as inside her brain, loads of synapses synapped into place.

The wrong place.

Her eyes tried – and failed – to widen with exhilaration

135

because she suddenly remembered from her history lessons hearing about lots of people who had been carrotted. It was something messy to do with necks.

She strained, with all her willpower, and found that she could move. Albeit like a fly in treacle, but she could move. If only she could get to the carrot.

But she didn't know how you carrotted someone . . . and then that, too, came to her.

Perhaps the Champion was telling her!

You used the carrot like a dagger, plunging it into the neck, into that big vein – the carrotid artery! That must be it!

If only she could reach it. She leaned, and leaned some more.

'Don't even think about it!' the Minotaur told her. He picked the carrot up and bit off her last chance of escape. 'Concentrate on dying instead.'

As if she were getting into practice, Gloria toppled over sideways.

XVII

Carlton looked between his legs, and his heart jumped into his throat. It was just enormous. It was big and hairy and muscular, and he froze in a panic he couldn't help showing.

He couldn't ride a horse, and the one he found himself sitting on was a giant.

There was a red plume attached to the top of the harness, and beneath the saddle a richly coloured sheet covered the sleek black hair. It looked suspiciously, from where Carlton was sitting, to be a war-horse; either that or the sort of poseur that made even Carlton look shy and retiring. The fact that he apparently wore chain mail and had a sword slung rakishly from his right hip came into the category of disconcerting corroborative evidence.

He looked down to where Wilverton was standing next to him. His armour was of a far more substantive nature than Carlton's. He looked like a one-man tank, with thick metal from his neck to his feet, black and shining. The face was incongruously bare, but the ensemble was topped off by a tall hat in the shape of a fortress, looking like a miniature version of the castle they had entered less than an hour before, except that the one on Wilverton's head wasn't semi-detached and did not sport a blue front door.

They were in a line, with Wilverton on the far right. In front of them another line was made up of small men, all dressed exactly the same, in tabards and knee-length breeches. Forcing himself to look along the line, and trying to do so without upsetting the horse, he saw that there were eight of them.

Next to Carlton was an obvious cleric, a tall mitre perched on his head, his long flowing robe of a purple so deep it was almost black and adorned with gold braid. Next to him stood a tall woman, dressed similarly in black, but with an extravagant style and a superfluity of jewellery. Most of the latter was attached to a crown which rested serenely on her black tresses, and bespoke neck muscles like steel hawsers.

137

Carlton craned his own neck muscles to try to get a better look at her. At first glance she seemed quite young, and sort of pretty. Perhaps this wasn't going to be so bad after all.

Beyond the woman was a man sporting a similar but less ornate crown. Carlton could not see past the tall man, but he knew what he would find if he could.

Facing them across a huge board covered with black and white contrasting squares was another team, on whom all the clothing gleamed whitely. Wilverton looked up and said 'Chess' very quietly.

Well, at least they had Wilverton's brain, thought Carlton. Barking mad, as it was, it could probably still send a computer to the knacker's yard if they met over a chess board. Just so long as he wasn't expected to do anything himself, he thought, looking at the animal he was straddling.

'Let the contest begin!' boomed a deep voice, the sound of which entered their heads through the skin as much as the ears.

Wilverton looked over to the white pawns in high spirits. A game of chess! Many was the computer he had dispatched to the knacker's yard over a game of chess. Those were the days – circuits everywhere, microchips burned out . . . He had always wondered how he would get on against a human. He was about to find out sixteen times over.

It wasn't difficult to spot which white pawn moved, because they all did. With eight high-pitched shrieks like arachnophobic banshees in the tarantula house, they drew small swords and rushed down the board. The black pawns let out a cry that would have made Death Himself go a little pale, and charged off to meet them.

Wilverton looked rather taken aback at first, and then watched the ensuing encounter with an ever slackening jaw. You were supposed to pick up any piece you had taken and remove it to the side of the board quietly, in a gentlemanly fashion. Nowhere did the rules say that you chopped it up bit by bit and then pushed it aside while trying not to slip over in the blood and the rather unpleasant slimy bits that the skin usually – and mercifully – keeps inside.

The back rows of the teams looked on approvingly, mostly cheering or shouting encouragement.

'Spear the little shits!' screamed the bishop next to Carlton. They don't make bishops like they used to, he thought, the cry

138

momentarily taking his mind away from where it usually centred – between his legs, that is.

'Charge!' came a voice from just down the line from Carlton, and he glanced left to see the king with sword thrust out in front of him. Everything moved forward, the bishop hitching up his skirts and pounding on sandalled feet towards the mass of pawns and ex-pawns, waving a sword around and yelling 'BASTARDS!' in his best sermon scream.

Wilverton tapped Carlton on the leg, and he looked down to see the man grinning manically.

The Challenger pushed a little harder, reinforcing, cajoling, urging. The Champion hung in the ether, a tight mass of contained x-rays. There were advantages to having the Player think himself in a book, but there were disadvantages too . . .

'If I was going to get killed, it would have happened at the bridges,' shouted Wilverton. 'It won't happen here. Let's go!'

. . . And this was one of them.

Wilverton, and his armour, rushed off down the board as only he could – as athletically as an elderly duck in an inflated rubber suit – while Carlton watched with eyes widened both by the insanity of the man and by the need to get the bloody horse moving, which was simply not going to happen unless he could unfreeze his muscles.

Which he couldn't.

Wilverton pulled the sword from its scabbard and . . .

Wilverton tried to pull the sword from its scabbard. It was a broadsword, and with the other knights on the board built on a scale which would have won them three of the top four places in a Most Impressive Mountain contest, it was not only a broadsword but a longsword as well, which dragged along the ground as Wilverton tried to run.

He took hold of the hilt with both hands, pulling it with all his strength – which wasn't much – and therefore did not notice the white queen galloping across the board towards him, waving a blade which, although much narrower, was more than capable of evisceration; which is even more messy than it sounds.

He just about got the sword out, but it was far too late to do any good as the queen approached and prepared to swing the death stroke into the unguarded face. (It was a fair bet that she hadn't been to a finishing school, or if she had, she'd failed.)

Then he dropped the thing, bent down immediately to pick it up, and the queen's stroke passed just over his head. Her momentum took her past, and she swung round in a wide arc for another go.

Wilverton stood, grasping the sword once more, its point resting on the ground behind him. He gave the labouring grunt of a constipated elephant and swung it round a couple of feet off the ground, hoping to contact the woman's knees. His timing was as impressive as his musculature and he sliced thin air where her legs were going to be in a few moments. The sword kept going and swung behind him, pulling him round and off his feet so that he cut the queen's legs from under her, using his body, which was only a bit smaller and lighter than the sword.

The woman crashed to the ground on top of Wilverton and lay still.

Carlton couldn't believe it. A bit of his brain wondered very briefly if Wilverton might just be right, that he *was* protected by some great god of fiction. It was a short wonder, as the bit of brain rejoined the rest and turned inwards, concentrating on its first love.

He watched almost numbly as the black queen kicked a pawn's foot, but the man didn't lean down to rub it because it wasn't actually attached to his leg any more; not, judging from the rather shapeless torso which lay a few yards away, that he had anything to rub it with anyway.

Looking forwards, Carlton saw a lance point coming straight towards him. Behind it was three yards of lance, and behind that was a knight who, judging from the expression through his open visor, was not intent on finding a fire and roasting marshmallows.

'Horse,' Carlton said, somewhat . . . croakily. 'Er.' How in God's name did you get a horse to move? 'What's your name, horse?'

'Whinny,' said the horse.

'Well, Winnie, please get me the hell out of here!'

Winnie shook its head. The lance isn't pointed at me, it seemed to say.

At that moment a bell sounded, but only inside his head. Presumably inside Wilverton's as well, but it was unlikely to

140

have made much impression, given the other things currently occupying the First Officer's cranium. One of which – in fact, probably, most of which – was the white queen climbing to her feet and retrieving her sword.

'Ship!' shouted Carlton, to absolutely no avail whatsoever.

Then he lost interest in the queen and the sword she was raising above Wilverton's still prostrate form, because the lance was closing rather quickly.

'Oh, SHIIIIII—'

'What,' muttered Arnold to himself as he looked around at his newly formed surroundings, 'the fonk, to coin a phrase, is this?'

'This' was a large field where the predominant colour was not that of the lush green grass, but a garish kaleidoscope of reds, blues, yellows; every hue imaginable and a few that were not. The colours adorned flags which hung from string stretched across the field, and balloons fixed somehow onto vast sheets which covered much of the grass and surrounded an enormous rectangular pool crossed by sturdy wooden beams. At the far end of the field from where Arnold stood was an obviously artificial castle, again brightly coloured.

A single yellow sun shone out of a blue sky with a few white clouds. It might have been Earth. But if it was then they had a lot of guests, judging from the crowd who perched on high tiers of seating around the three sides of the field that were not hidden from view by the pseudo castle. They were being noisily enthusiastic, both volubly and in their clothing, which added to the colourful atmosphere. Very few were humanoid, but this did not particularly bother Arnold, whose regard for living things was not actually based on their appearance. Arnold was not at all prejudiced – the fact that they were alive at all meant that he despised the very atoms of their structure, individually.

There even appeared to be a group of seats set aside for plants. Arnold did not know that they were Dafflis, sentient mobile vegetation whose greatest pleasure was apparently standing perfectly still and then, when anything brushed against them, shouting 'Leaf me alone' and cackling hysterically. Having met them, other races did precisely that.

But then Arnold didn't have to know this; he loathed them just the same.

His first instinct was to leave the area, since he had not asked to

141

be there in the first place, but he was unsure where to go. He had no idea, to be exact, since he didn't know where he was, let alone where anything else might be.

'Ship!' he called, and the comforting circular shape completely failed to appear.

Arnold was not altogether surprised. He was just beginning to think that he was probably dead, and that this was an after-life getting ready to punish him in full for some unfairly perceived misdemeanours. Already he was working without much hope on the argument that he wasn't really alive in the first place and that therefore he should be excused.

Around him, other androids, representatives of all the races in the crowd, shuffled or stood quietly, clearly waiting for something. Arnold approached one who appeared humanoid, his own movement lithe in comparison. The difference did not pass by his ego without giving it an unnecessary boost.

'What's going on?' he asked, and watched two dimly glowing red eyes turn towards him.

'We are waiting for the costumes to be brought to us.'

'And what are these costumes for?'

'For us to wear in the next game.' There seemed to be a hint of surprise in its voice, though none showed in its face.

'I have only just arrived, you see,' explained Arnold. 'I don't know quite what is going on.' The android looked levelly at him. No question had been asked, and there were few androids who took the initiative in conversations. 'So what is this next game a part of?' asked just about the only one in the entire galaxy.

'It is a part of the whole contest, the jeux sans frontières.'

'Is it. And what, pray, is the jeux sans frontières?' That tone was beginning to creep into Arnold's voice. The android had never come across it before, of course, and it would not have recognized it if it had.

'Games without frontiers. We are one team, and they are the other.' It pointed a little way off to where another huddle of androids stood awkwardly still.

'What are we playing for?'

'We play for our owners, and for their glory.'

'I see,' said Arnold, making it abundantly clear that he did not like what he saw. 'And what happens if we ask our *owners*,' and he spat the word out distastefully, 'to take their contest and insert it in a little brown orifice?' The examinee looked a little confused.

142

'What happens if we refuse to co-operate?' The android pondered for a moment, unsure how such a circumstance might arise. It settled on an answer readily enough, however.

'We will be dismantled.'

'And what happens if we do co-operate, and lose?'

No hesitation this time. 'We will be dismantled.'

'Well, I'm glad nothing appears to be any more equitable on this pathetic specimen of a planet, anyway,' concluded Arnold. 'What planet are we on, incidentally?'

'It is Bulphus.'

'Is it. Well, it's as big a pain in the artificial arse as every other one I've been on.'

He looked around appraisingly, and the resultant appraisal left as much to be desired as his first. 'Well, best of luck, then,' he said finally. 'I'm off.'

He walked towards an exit gate in one corner of the crowd, and had reached the edge of the field when he appeared to slow down rather dramatically. The leg he was trying to put in front of the formerly planted one – an action he had been forced to learn painfully over the past few days although the principle was simple enough – did not seem to be moving as he wanted. Something was stopping him; something insubstantial enough not to be seen, but quite substantial enough to refuse entry.

Arnold moved backwards a step, with no problem, then sideways for a few yards, and tried again. The same obstruction kept him on the field. Arnold sighed – a quite superfluous action since he did not have to breathe, but it summed up the way he was feeling better than a Fission-like outburst would have done. He walked back to the android.

'Or maybe I'm not,' he said, and accompanied the phrase with a smile which should have rendered his lips frost-bitten. 'What do we have to do?'

The android pointed to where some large feet were being brought onto the field from a tunnel under the stands.

No, really! Enormous, pink, brown, blue, green and orange feet were being wheeled out on a trolley by yet more androids.

It became difficult to read the expression on Arnold's face.

'We put on the costumes,' said the android. 'Then we move down the course, bursting the balloons and crossing the pool until we reach the castle walls. Then we have to save the maiden.'

'From what?'

'Nothing. There is no danger to the maiden. But we have to save her.'

'Why can't we just leave her where she is, then? Does she have some burning desire to be saved from absolutely nothing? Is it one of the mind-stretching goals in her life?'

There was a pause. The android was having trouble with this one. 'I don't know,' it replied uncertainly. 'I do not think she would have any preference in the matter. It is not a real maiden.'

Arnold looked around the field again, at nothing in particular, wondering why it had to happen to him. It was true. He was dead and this was definitely Hell.

'It wouldn't have been a human who thought this contest up, would it? Or perhaps a three-headed dog?' The android opened its mouth. 'Never mind.'

The android shut its mouth, and then started walking towards the trolley of feet, which had stopped a few yards away. Very reluctantly, Arnold followed it. As he walked, so the deep, resonant toll of a bell rang out inside his head.

XVIII

Curtis and Fission sat and waited. They were apparently in a waiting room, so it seemed the right thing to do. They were not waiting quietly.

'Now what you done!'

'What did I do?'

'Took me through fonking light, anti-brain.'

'Took you!' Aggrieved, was Curtis. Piqued. 'Oh, I remember. There you were saying how much you wanted to stay behind when I grabbed you and carried you through. You didn't push your way past me to get there first at all, did you? Whatever could have made me think that was how it happened?'

Arnold would have been proud of him. Fission wasn't.

'Had to come to look after you and heap of wires you insist is android.' Curtis could not recall having ever insisted that Arnold was an android, but the few moments he took to consult his memory meant he missed his chance to stem the flow. 'I leave you two alone there's no fonking chance.'

Curtis took a deep breath. This was going to be a new tactic.

'Look, Fission,' he said, conciliation ingrained in his voice and written all over his body language. 'Why don't we accept that we have to find out what we're doing here, and what we can do to get out, and stop bickering? We are going to work much better if we work together. Why don't we be friends?'

Fission eyed him. When Wilverton had asked that, she had almost felt like telling him the truth. With Curtis, she felt like telling him to . . .

'You want I answer?' she asked, strangling the new tactic at birth.

'No,' he admitted. 'Not really.'

'What the fonk that incredible smell?'

Curtis sniffed experimentally, and wished that he hadn't. It was ten times worse than Fission's perfume. His nose made a mental note to bleed in a restaurant sometime to get its own back as the little hairs curled up inside it.

'Excuse me, Dick?' came a voice. Curtis looked up sharply. In the room with them were two couples, one sitting on a sofa which matched that on which he sat with Fission. The other didn't need a sofa. Neither of the couples was exactly human.

The pair on the seat was bipedal, traditional 'alien' green, with skin made up of minute scales, and the jaw slightly elongated, giving them a reptilian appearance. The bits not concealed by a black plastic-looking covering were hairless, and there were two tiny stubs on the sides of a heavily ridged forehead which presumably were the ears. Their eyes were slightly too far apart, but even had they been perfectly separated they would only have made a Paris catwalk when they wanted to clear the room. Tubes led from something unseen on their backs to the side of the mouth, and periodically they breathed deeply of whatever the tubes conveyed.

One of the creatures was bigger and somehow rougher than the other, and Curtis surmised that it was a male female pair.

The other couple were black, covered in fur and apparently naked. They were quadrupeds and sat back on their haunches, with their long tails curled round in front of them. The limbs ended in hands or feet with two talons pointing forwards and one back, giving them almost a bird-like appearance.

Both the creatures were adorned with silver or platinum jewellery, rings looking strangely out of place on the sharp talons – like seeing RoboCop wearing fluffy slippers – while two or three necklaces decorated each neck, and both waists sported wide belts of loose chain.

They smiled at Curtis and Fission with yellow teeth.

'How did you know my name?' Curtis asked none of the four in particular.

One of the green couple took a pull at his tube before answering, 'The badge.' He indicated a circular attachment on the chest of his clothing where an unpronounceable collection of unlikely letters was displayed. As he spoke, the smell which Fission had noticed drifted across the room again. It was now apparent whence it came, but that wasn't the sort of thing a polite person mentioned in company.

Which let Fission out.

'Luc, the halitosis kid!'

No-one reacted to that, and Curtis looked down at his own body to see an appendage with 'Dick' all over it.

No, not that; a badge.

'Well, it's Richard, anyway.' Who is Luke? he wondered.

'*Hate* aliens,' muttered Fission. 'Running free in *our* Galaxy.'

Curtis ignored her and looked back to the reptile thing. 'Where are we? Who are you? *What* are you?' The green female sucked on her tube.

'We are called the Hrrarrarrr, the methane breathers,' she answered with a gushing of proof. Curtis's nose tried to close its nostrils with a great muscular twitching. 'Humans like yourself apparently find our names hard to pronounce and call us by a generic title.' Her name badge, displaying a similarly tongue-twisting collection of consonants, showed why.

'What's that then?' asked Curtis, his eyes watering.

Suck. 'Bog Breath.'

Curtis pretended to wipe his mouth with his sleeve by way of covering his facial orifices, and nodded. Then he wiped his eyes, which needed it.

'Where did you come from?' asked Bog Breath 1.

'You weren't here a minute ago,' explained Bog Breath 2. 'We'd have heard you.'

Curtis searched for a coherent answer like Richard III for an off-the-peg jacket.

'You wouldn't understand.' She had a way with people, did Fission. She would break the ice at a party by dropping a social clanger on it. Their new chums-not-to-be bristled at the implied slight.

'Why don't you try us?' challenged Bog Breath 1.

'Came from palace of King Minos and Queen Pasiphae on planet Callia via Labyrinth of their son, the Minotaur, with help of some sort transportation light.' She looked at Bog Breath 1, daring him to claim even a glimmer of understanding.

'What sort of transportation light?'

'How the fonk would I know?'

'So *you* don't understand, is what you are trying to tell us.'

Fission almost rose from her seat.

'I think we should all try to be friends,' said the smaller of the two black-furred creatures, whose name badge admitted to Guz.

'Don't make friends with talking carpets,' Fission told him, and there was no heart-felt secret to this one; it was simple, basic xenophobia.

'That is your prerogative, of course,' Guz answered with a smile and an incline of the head. 'We are in enough trouble already, but we will respect your wishes, of course.'

'What trouble?' asked Curtis. He had always been extremely used to trouble, but it would be a nice change to know what variety faced them this time.

'So you don't know why you're here, either?' provoked Bog Breath 1, a clear contender for Fission's title.

'What trouble?' Fission's voice held an edge like a buzz saw.

'I really don't mean to be rude, Fission,' said Gaz, Guz's partner, 'and I hope you won't take it amiss, I really do, but *do* you know why you are here?'

Fission paused. 'No.' Gaz looked to Curtis, and raised her eyebrows to ask the same question. 'He neither,' Fission confirmed with an irritated flick of her hand. He would have given anything to be able to contradict her.

'This is the Last Chance Game Show,' said Gaz. 'Where just one adulterous couple will be reprieved. Have you not heard of it?'

'We're not from around these parts,' said Curtis, who used to watch Westerns as a child.

Fission's brain had snagged on an earlier phrase. 'Adulterous couples? What the fonk you mean?'

'We have all been found guilty of adultery,' explained Guz. Gaz nodded sadly in confirmation, and her hand found his. 'We have been rightly sentenced to death according to the law, and that sentence will be carried out on the losers of this game. It really is the last chance.' Fission looked suspiciously like she was about to do an impression of Bikini Atoll just after something large, cylindrical and metal landed on it, momentarily. 'I just hope for your sake that you are the winners.'

'What kind fonking planet has death for adultery?' Fission ignored, just for the moment, the fact that Guz and Gaz appeared to take sycophancy to new heights.

'Well, many planets do.' Gaz looked troubled at having to provide the answer.

'Earth don't!' She paused, and looked into the middle distance, then spoke almost to herself. 'Good idea though.' A cloud briefly passed across her face.

Curtis glanced at her, his attention drawn by the low volume rather than by the words spoken, which hadn't really registered – hardly surprising; Curtis didn't even know what a stute was.

Gaz brought Fission back from wherever her mind had taken her. 'Well, why else are you here?'

'Fonk me!'

'Best not,' warned Bog Breath 1. 'That's what got you in this mess in the first place.'

Fission didn't bite. 'But we not guilty of anything, specially adultery!' The volume was back to normal. 'And if I commit adultery, bet your ovals not with him!' This time she jerked a rather superfluous thumb in the direction of 'him'. But 'his' self-esteem had taken so many knocks over the years that it looked like a hammered steel drum, and another one brought no reaction.

'Well I don't know about that, of course,' said Guz reasonably, 'but you *are* here, and you look like you are about to take part in the show.'

Fission could find no answer.

'I'm getting a bit tired of games,' muttered Curtis to himself, and then, louder, 'What does this game entail, then?'

'You get asked questions,' said Bog Breath 2. 'About your partner. She doesn't hear the answers you give, and then she comes out and they ask her the same questions. And they do the same thing the other way round.' Curtis just about kept up. 'If you both give the same answer, you get a point. The team with the most points wins.'

She looked sadly at Bog Breath 1 sitting on her left, who raised an arm and placed it around her shoulders. 'It used to be so much fun watching it at home, didn't it?' The arm gave her a little squeeze, but it just forced a tear from the corner of her eye.

'Let's get out of here,' said Fission, standing decisively and heading for the only door to the room. She grasped the knob, twisted it, and pushed the door. Then pulled the door. Then kicked the door, and went and sat down again. 'Fonk.' The word was drowned by the deep resonant sound of a huge bell being rung. Curtis and Fission both looked around, then looked at each other.

'If there is anything we can do to help you?' offered Gaz, and Guz nodded agreement.

149

'You can't,' said Fission. 'But maybe . . . Ship!'

Nothing happened.

'I do hope you'll be all right,' said Gaz. 'I really do.'

Guz agreed.

'What, you religious or something?' Fission was getting irritated.

'We are Kalasians.'

'Everyone calls them Ibats,' Bog Breath 1 added.

'Ibats?'

'Yes. Insufferable Bastards, Aren't They?'

The sound of a bell cleared from Gloria's head, its tolling resulting in a complete lack of reaction from the Minotaur. The same complete lack from Gloria as well, but not for want of wanting.

She wondered briefly what it was, and wondered why it appeared to have sounded directly inside her head instead of taking advantage of her ears. She hoped she wasn't going as mad as the Minotaur.

It was probably a signal from the Ship, she thought, with great accuracy and greater luck. It didn't help. She just had to hope that it presaged a rescue.

One of the screens, sharpening under instructions from the Minotaur's manipulated – or bullipulated – dials, was dominated by a huge animal which Gloria definitely recognized; of which, in fact, she had rather intimate knowledge.

The Cretin Bull stood stolidly in the middle of the picture.

The Minotaur spun to face Gloria with a manic grin on his bovine features, looking down at the prostrate form.

'We're almost there, aren't we?' She didn't answer, for obvious reasons, but he needed no assistance to hold a conversation. 'His pain will know no end, just like ours all these years. We *will* have revenge!'

Then he did what approximated to laugh again, which put the finishing touch to an emotion Gloria had been contemplating.

For the first time in her life, she really hated something.

The Minotaur took himself – and his companion – to the far end of the room to do something Gloria couldn't see with a couple of test tubes, and a movement on one of the screens near to her caught her eye. The scene was a courtyard, and in the courtyard was a woman wearing a navy pin-stripe suit and dark glasses, presumably against the glare of the sun. Her hair seemed to move about in the breeze, but slowly, and in a lot of different directions. She was walking towards whatever it was that was taking the picture, and growing in size on the screen as she did so. She was also talking, apparently to herself, and Gloria wondered if everyone on this planet was as nutty as a vegetarian's Christmas.

'I don't know how long we've got. He could find me any time.'

'Perssseusss,' hissed another voice, and Gloria looked more closely at the screen, her mind taken momentarily from her own plight. The woman took off her glasses and rubbed the lenses gently against the sleeve of her coat.

'I wish you'd stop doing that,' she said irritably, replacing them once more.

'Sssorry,' came the voice again, and she snatched the glasses off once more to clean them. Then she put them back and swiped at the hair that stood out over her forehead and waved up and down. Gloria looked more attentively, and it wasn't hair at all, but snakes, hundreds of snakes sticking out of her head and writhing in a way only snakes really seem to have mastered.

'Ow,' said those that had been hit, and one on either side wrapped themselves round the woman's ears and squeezed for all they were worth.

'Stop that!' she ordered, and slapped at them again.

'Well ssstop hitting usss then,' a spokes-snake answered, and they squeezed harder.

'Let go, or it's the shampoo.'

There was a pause, and then the snakes released her ears, leaving them red and slightly bruised.

She bent down and looked into a bush, searching for something, and obviously not finding it. Then she moved off, away from the camera.

'Why don't we kill her?' came a dry sentence from her hair. Then, 'Yesss!' agreed several other follicle dwellers. The woman sighed, but left the glasses where they were.

'You know I can't. It won't do my bidding if I kill her. Now help me look.'

Who was this woman, Gloria wondered, with live hair? What was she looking for? It didn't seem to matter somehow.

Gloria looked away and did not see the woman approach a man on the far side of the courtyard. Gardening implements lay on one side of where he sat, and a large flagon of wine on the other, half empty. He waved a goblet at the woman as she searched a flower bed a little distance away.

'Hello, beautiful lady! Come sit by me!'

She favoured him with a slow look through her glasses that said 'No' very clearly.

'Oh, come on, gorgeous!' He obviously had a way with words.

'You're drunk,' she told him, and a couple of her forward hairs nodded in agreement. 'And it's Gor*gon*.'

He reached out and grabbed her wrist, not heeding the warning, and pulled her towards him. She planted a foot to steady herself, then lifted her hand to her glasses and snatched them from her eyes.

She stared straight at the man, and he stared back.

Briefly.

She slipped her wrist from the cold clutch of a statue which sat, grey and forever unmoving, in the sunshine.

'Drunk? You're stoned!' she told it, and replaced her glasses again only when the snakes had stopped giggling. That was their very favourite joke.

XIX

Carlton didn't even have enough muscle control to screw his eyes shut and wait for the impact. He just watched the point of the lance heading unwaveringly for his stomach, which was doing its best to make room for the visit.

Then . . .

'Time out!' boomed the same voice that had started the contest, and the lance swung aside as the white knight reined his horse to a stop before cantering back down the board.

Carlton let out a big sigh and slumped in the saddle, before straightening with a jerk when he realized that someone might be watching.

The board was surrounded by mist – something Carlton had not had spare mind enough to notice before – and from its shrouds a horde of small men and women, the size of pawns and dressed in simple smocks, came on with buckets, mops and carrier bags to clear up the pieces that had been . . . taken? Sent, more like.

Those who still had the requisite limbs walked back to their starting positions, including Wilverton, as the queen walked harmlessly the other way.

He was grinning broadly when he approached Carlton, and looked like he had been having an invigorating game of squash, allowing for the fact that this is relatively rarely done in full armour with large swords.

'Let's get out of here,' Carlton suggested urgently, and indicated the side of the board. If there were people coming on, then there could be people going off.

As he spoke, a pawn pulled itself from the pile of flesh in the middle of the board and ran screaming in one of the directions Carlton was thinking of adopting – there were lots of possibilities all pointing outwards. The pawn disappeared briefly into the mist, and they thought he had got away, but then the mist cleared momentarily and they could see that there was

153

something there; quite a lot of somethings, in fact, surrounding the playing area.

Very big somethings, too, looking like nothing more than huge slabs of clay but all menace, twenty, thirty feet in height, jostling each other for a view of the board and the pathetic little creatures milling around on it. Great arms hung from enormous shoulders and ended in fists, the size of armchairs, which promised a very squidgy time for anything that came too close. The heads were shapeless, but the eyes were alert and none too welcoming. The mouths showed no teeth, but looked quite large enough to accommodate a human without having to bite any bits off first.

And so they proved. They glimpsed the pawn running full pelt, then he was lifted from the ground in one huge fist, his legs still pumping, and dropped into a massive maw. The scream was abruptly muffled, and then ceased altogether. So, no escape that way, then.

Carlton looked back to Wilverton, who still displayed a grin not normally found outside a locked room.

'This could be the big climax,' Carlton told him. 'Where all the heroes just end up in a bloody heap on the floor and the camera pulls back as the credits roll.'

Well, he'd tried similar before with Wilverton, and it had seemed to work. Perhaps if he kept it up he'd go mad as well. That would be nice, right now. But Wilverton shook his head.

'I don't think so. It doesn't feel like it. I don't know why, but I'm just certain this isn't the time.'

The Champion knew why. It also knew that Wilverton's logic could be disproved by one well-placed sword thrust. This belief had just about outlasted its usefulness. If there was an inkling of doubt then it would pounce and strengthen it, but the rules would not let it work with nothing.

'You can't be certain of that,' Carlton continued. 'You must doubt it just a little bit, surely.'

Wilverton considered, and Carlton held his breath; he needed Wilverton to think of something to do.

In the ether, something else would have held its breath if it had had any, and something to hold it with, or in.

154

'Nope,' said Wilverton. 'And don't call me Shirley.' Then he giggled – he had always liked that one.

Carlton looked to the skies for long enough to count to ten, then back down to where a new line of pawns was forming at each end of the board, looking nervous. They're even worse off than me, he thought. They need to form a union or something, like those people in history, the Tolpuddle martyrs. Looking at the last vestiges of intestine being cleaned from the board, it was clear they already had plenty of martyrs, not to mention plenty of puddles.

The fallen rear pieces, a bishop from either side – who had been particularly bloodthirsty; historically correct for religious types – and a black knight, were not replaced.

'Let the contest begin!'

'Come on,' Wilverton shouted above the clamour of sixteen pawns driven to psychopathy by the immediate need for self-preservation.

'I can't,' Carlton shouted back.

'Why not?'

'Because I can't ride a bloody horse, that's why not!' And I'm scared of the thing, not that I'm telling *you* that.

'Oh, you'll learn. It'll be fun!'

'*LOOK THIS ISN'T A BOOK YOU RAVING NUTTER!*' Carlton tried a different approach, but his voice was lost in the shouts of the other pieces – already rather more pieces than there had been.

Wilverton, still apparently crammed full of optimism, hit the flank of the war-horse just by the saddle strap by way of encouragement.

It worked.

The horse took off, literally as far as Carlton was concerned. And Wilverton took off with it, also literally. A protruding bit from his gauntleted hand got itself caught under the strap and he was yanked off his feet and carried by the side of the horse like a pennant.

Carlton and Wilverton joined the fray and charged down the board like a scene from Mad Max meets Laurel and Hardy.

Arnold sat on the ground and slowly pushed his second leg into the large rubber foot. His demeanour exuded contempt for all things rubber, for all costumes, and especially for all games. The one saving grace was that the others were not around to see this ultimate degradation. Otherwise Arnold would not have been quite so happy.

Once inside the costume he could not move his legs with any degree of independence, and he needed the help of another of the androids to help him to his foot. Having spent considerable time learning how to stand up on his own two, it was a further irritant now to have to learn to stand in one of some else's.

'All right. What do we have to do?'

The android had no circuitry to recognize the tone of question, otherwise it would have quailed – a sort of mutant quail resembling a large chicken – from furnishing the answer. As it turned out, it managed to reply without answering.

'If you watch the first to try, then the game will become clear to you.' It pointed to where a member of each team wavered uncertainly on the starting line.

A whistle sounded, and they started jumping towards the spread of balloons, looking like awkward wallabies after one tube too many. They fell from more of the jumps than not, and the crowd howled with delight.

One section of it especially, which, Arnold noticed when he turned a despising look on them, were all monopodal, with one huge leg and foot supporting an otherwise strangely human body. He would have been entirely uninterested to learn that they were Gandars. They were having a high old time, too, which was very unusual for Gandars. Normally they were among the most miserable of races, largely due to the fact that their greatest passion was for sport and they always came an ignominious and much-bruised-bottomed last in the interspecies soccer tournament, and all the others not only sniggered at them for months after each match, but kept vetoing their suggestions for a Galactic sack race.

Arnold looked on and yearned for a death ray, then turned back to the action. When, eventually, the androids reached the balloons, and fell among them, the crowd became delirious. As each balloon in turn was burst, a liquid splashed out from within, and immediately the plastic skin of the androids began to fizz and melt where the liquid touched it.

'What's that?' asked Arnold with some alarm.

'It is some kind of reducing agent.'

156

'What kind of entertainment do they call that? Haven't they got laws against cruelty?'

'It is only cruel if there are living creatures involved. That is why they employ androids in this sport. There is no feeling, as we are only machines. How can they be cruel to a machine?'

Not a wise question. Arnold looked it straight in its glowing red eyes.

'Well, I don't know about you, but they can be cruel to a machine like me firstly and foremost by being in my life at all, secondly by making me play this game, thirdly by making me wear this costume while I am doing it, and fourthly by giggling like a pack of hyenas on terminal heat while I melt myself trying,' he explained. 'I despise the very air they breathe.'

The android was silent, either because it had not been asked a question or because Arnold's succinct reasoning had dissuaded it from risking another comment. Together they watched both of the contestants failing to reach the planks which led over the swimming pool. As they finally lay still, two more started from the line, and with much more adeptness.

These were quadrupeds, and each sported an enormous trunk. They were built in the image of the Survivors, who used the trunk to eat, smell and breathe. It had not been their aboriginal name, but was adopted after an alien invasion force had landed on their planet with the odd goal of killing everything with four legs – it was something to do with their religion, as these things usually are – and had apparently ignored them.

Why?

Legend has it that, by slamming their trunks to the floor bloody quick, the Survivors had convinced the invaders that they were not quadrupeds at all, but were quintu . . . quinqui . . . had five. The invaders were not only fooled, but were further convinced that the race would die out before long in any case, because if you stood and stared at them for any length of time, they went blue and fell over.

Their representative androids now had their legs reduced to two, which still gave them some modicum of balance, and they fairly bounded up to the group of balloons, of which only a few had been removed, and hopped their way through, the thick rubber of their costumed feet suffering severely, but with no apparent damage to themselves. The crowd cheered.

The steps to the planks over the pool posed a bigger problem

157

than the flat ground, but both managed to reach the top after some false starts, and then they were faced with the planks themselves, stretched over the water.

Water?

'What's in the pool?' asked Arnold quietly.

'It is a reducing . . .'

'. . . agent, right. Well, now there's a shock.' The two watched as the android contestants swayed uncertainly at the edge of the pool, their feet still bubbling merrily in places. They seemed reluctant to begin the crossing. Arnold didn't blame them. There was no way they were going to make it.

'What do they have to do when they get as far as that castle thing?' he asked. 'And don't tell me to watch and find out, because no-one's going to get that far.'

'They have to climb up the rope. Then they must carry the maiden down.'

'And during this gallant feat?'

'There will be buckets of reducing agent poured on them from above.'

Arnold stared as the first contestant to risk it hopped gingerly onto the very end of the plank. It immediately toppled off, and the fizz which arose from the liquid was drowned only by the hysterical laughter of the crowd. The second watched dispassionately, and then hopped onto the plank in front of it. It tottered dangerously, but did not fall. Half of the crowd clapped enthusiastically, especially the Survivors. It hopped a bit further, and the applause rose as it still did not fall. But then it was the other team's supporters who made the noise, as the contender waved his arms around in a futile effort to regain his balance following another small jump, and disappeared into the liquid below.

Looking at the starting line, Arnold saw just one more android waiting. Another humanoid.

'Where's our team?' he asked, hating the implication that he was a part of it.

'You are the next player on our side,' said the android helpfully.

'Oh goody. How spiffing.' He took the most minuscule of hops, and teetered. 'You had better help me get to the line.' He sounded almost resigned, and the android put an arm round his waist, keeping him upright as they moved forwards to polite applause from the crowd.

'How they can call this a game without frontiers I don't know,' said Arnold almost conversationally. 'There's no way out. How's that for frontiers?'

'That is not what they mean by frontiers,' returned the android as he delivered his charge to the starting line. 'It is their word for rules. This is a game without rules.' Arnold looked at him, his eyes showing just a hint of the spark which had left them during his metaphorical walk to the gallows.

'Is it, now?'

XX

This isn't so bad after all, Curtis told himself, as a happy little melody played through the headphones he was wearing. And apart from the fact that if they did not beat the other two couples – both of whom had intimate knowledge of each other in a game where all you needed was exactly that – then they would end up dead, he was probably right.

He was maintaining his average, anyway, because it was as close as he normally got. The defence could argue that he didn't actually believe it himself deep down inside, but Curtis was never one to let the facts of life get in the way of his meandering existence if he could find a way of ignoring them, which generally he could, and not only because many of the facts of life were still a completely closed book to him.

Then the music in his ears stopped and was replaced by a voice which reverberated down to his bottom.

'All the males back on stage please.' And the 'please' had nothing to do with politeness.

Curtis was out of his seat in half a nanosecond – although his stomach was already well on the way out of the room by the time any outward part of him had even flinched – and was heading for the door at speed before the headphone wire snapped taut and stopped him by trying to remove his ears at the neck.

He spent a second or two pulling the phones off, just about leaving the ears in place, by which time he was convinced he would be timed out and lose the game before he even had a chance to get all of the answers horribly wrong. It did not occur to him that it might have been easier that way.

He shot across the cubicle, slammed the door open, and hit something. The speed of the door suggested it was the sound barrier, but then the barrier made a sound, rather like someone slumping to the floor, and Curtis peeked round the frame at the prostrate figure of Guz with blood seeping very slowly from a large bump in the fur of his forehead.

160

The crowd paused for a moment, and the sudden silence made Curtis realize that there had been noise before it, noise as of lots of people clapping. He looked up and squinted in the bright lights which all but hid the audience from his view, and could just see that they were made up from the three races represented in the show itself, the Hrrarrarrr generally sitting in little spaces on their own, the humanoids, with pieces of cloth over their mouths, as far from the Hrrarrarrr as possible, and the Ibats wherever they weren't going to upset anyone else.

Then they started clapping again as two Hrrarrarrr arrived from stage left and bent over the figure on the ground.

I've killed him, thought Curtis. That makes three.

There was his father first, whom he had unfortunately tipped through the window of their penthouse flat. Then there was Daniel Thompson, one of the *Pioneer*'s original crew, whose back pack, and back, Curtis had, again quite unintentionally, punctured rather terminally with a rock punch on the outside of the space-ship.

And now I've done it again, he thought.

Oh dear.

Someone's going to be annoyed. Someone always gets annoyed when I kill someone.

Life's so unfair.

'Dick!' floated through his reverie, and he looked to his right to where the stage, Bog Breath 1, and the host – another member of the Hrrarrarrr race – awaited him. It was the last of these three who had spoken.

The host was dressed in a suit of such spectacular turquoise that you could readily believe kingfishers threw themselves into the rivers beneath their branches by dint of jealousy rather than hunger. Only the sparkling red-rimmed glasses vied with the suit, but they looked even more vomitary against the green scaled skin beneath them. He beckoned Curtis onto the stage to join him.

Over to his right, in one of three cubicles, Fission glared at him in what he hoped she imagined was a reassuring manner and which worked as such only because it served as a reminder that there must be worse places to be than stuck on this stage; like being shut in a booth with her, for one.

At the back of the stage was another glass-fronted cubicle, above the door of which a big neon sign flashed 'Exit'. There did not appear to be a back door to it, but Curtis had other things to worry about.

The first being the possible reaction to his demolition of a fellow contestant. The host stopped clapping, and the audience took their cue from him. He beamed at Curtis.

'Well, hello, Dick!' He managed to sound theatrical even with that phrase.

'It's Richard, actually,' responded Curtis automatically.

'Well, you look like a Dick to me!' the host replied immediately, with a weak but nonetheless nauseating humour. The audience showed their collective meagre wit by finding this hilarious, and the host chuckled along with them before waving them to silence with a small movement of his hand.

'I didn't mean it, of course, Dick. We've got a friendly show here. The winners don't mind my little jokes, and the losers have never complained afterwards either.'

The audience thought this was even better than the last effort, and the host mentally crossed another from the list of ad-libs that he planned to use that day. The reminder of what was at stake did not induce a titter from Curtis.

'Well, you appear to have gained yourself a bit of an advantage here, Dick,' the host continued, looking to where one of the stage left entrants was now standing by the side of Guz and shaking his head.

Curtis swallowed. 'It was an accident,' he stammered, the phrase being one that tripped off Curtis's tongue with monotonous regularity. The tripping bit was quite appropriate, too.

'Well, no need to worry about that – it's not against the rules in the Last Chance Game Show.' Curtis heaved a silent sigh of relief. The host touched his earpiece and spoke to a crowd now holding its breath after catching the look of exaggerated excitement on his face.

'Guz will not recover in time to answer the questions, I am told.' And the crowd took a sharp breath while Curtis realized that the creature was not dead after all, that he had only been stunned. 'So this is where we take our leave of Guz and Gaz.'

Gaz emerged from a cubicle next to Fission's, head down and tears plain in the fur of her cheeks. As she passed by Bog Breath 1 and Curtis, she muttered how pleased she was for them, and wished them both good luck, and told them how it was her pleasure to perform the ultimate sacrifice for them.

'Ibat,' said Bog Breath 1, looking at Curtis, who was still far too preoccupied to react.

Two attendants carried Guz from the other side of the stage, and the two Ibats met up at the entrance to the Exit. Guz was laid on the floor, and Gaz slumped down next to him, as the crowd clapped and cheered.

The inside of the cubicle glowed brightly white, and Guz and Gaz were suddenly naked – they hadn't been wearing clothes to start with, but now they weren't wearing any fur either, just dark skin getting darker like a hit-'em-hard advert for sun block. Then the skin wasn't there any more either, only a brief view of bones looking round for sinews, finding none, and collapsing. A moment later, the light turned off.

The Exit was empty, and Curtis's stomach immediately threatened to emulate it.

The crowd cheered one last time, and then settled down as the host raised a hand for quiet.

'Nice bone structure!' Laugh. Smell. 'So, let's get right down to our first round of questions. And it's Dick first. Remember you have three questions to answer. I asked your lusciously lovely lady Fission these same questions, and she gave me three answers. If your answers agree with the ones that the fabulously fanciable Fission gave to me, then you get two points. One point for a close answer as determined not only by myself, but, more, by my friends out here in front of us.' He waved grandly to the audience, who recognized a compliment to themselves – presumably being called a friend by such as the host was supposed to be a compliment – and applauded yet again.

The host waited for the noise to die. 'Do you understand the rules, Dick?'

Curtis nodded truthfully; he actually had followed the explanation. What he didn't know was how the hell he was going to work out the answers.

Then an idea came to him. He could use the strange mind power he displayed on the old *Pioneer* when he had correctly predicted what their destination would look like. He could concentrate on what the host was saying, and his tele-whatever-it-was would tell him the right answers. Then they'd win and everything would be all right and he would be a hero and everyone would like him.

163

Curtis then did something very sensible. He told himself not to be so bloody stupid and just listen to the host.

So he did, looking worried.

The Champion withdrew from the human mind and relaxed, its frequency falling from gamma to x-rays. While there was a chance that Curtis *could* recover the answers psychically – the sort of chance you get if you buy one ticket in the Intergalactic Lottery – it preferred to rely on the preparations it had already made. On its carefully laid plans.

Plans that could not be called underhand, but only because the Champion didn't have a hand for them to be under.

'Good,' said the host, unaware of the momentous event which had just taken place inside his interrogatee's head. 'So, the first question I asked Fission was where you two first met. Okay? Where you two first met. Now for this question you get a choice of answers. Did she say; one, "We met at a party where that sort of thing always happens"; two, "He stopped to give me a ride and I let him"; or three, "Fonk off you stupid, foul-mouthed, four-eyed git"?'

Curtis looked up sharply from his close study of the top of the lectern where he had been searching for inspiration. The empty feeling in his stomach filled a little. This might not be too difficult after all.

'Did you hear the question, Dick?' Curtis nodded. 'And which do you think was the answer that your lovely Fission gave me?'

'The one with "fonk" in it?'

The host manufactured a look of great concern which emptied Curtis's stomach again in a millisecond.

'Dick,' he said, heavily. 'You are . . . Right!'

Gloria was seething, inwardly, and she was in the Minotaur's arms. The latter not as in the Romantic Clinch but as in the Sack of Potatoes. Nor was the latter the cause of the former.

Gloria was now wearing a dress, admittedly a beautiful dress, but that wasn't the point. Gloria had been in no position to manoeuvre herself into the garment and in no position to stop the Minotaur from doing so. He had only made love to her with his eyes – not that love had anything to do with it – but that was quite

164

bad enough. On her list of likes and dislikes, the Minotaur dropped below cat torturers, and on Gloria's list you couldn't get much lower without the help of a very imaginative sadist.

Her captor dropped his bundle on the couch and arranged her so that she was sitting upright and staring straight ahead.

On a screen opposite, the Cretin Bull stood calmly munching its grass, while a shimmering disturbance in the air hovered just in front of it.

Underneath the screen the Minotaur pushed a button, a panel in the worktop opened, and there rose from beneath something that looked to Gloria like a small silver cannon with a complicated array of electronic bits where the fuse should be. The Minotaur pointed this at her.

'It is only a projector, my lady; you're not going to die yet,' he told her, carefully lining it up on Gloria. 'Now.' And he flicked a switch, causing the electrical bits to start humming monotonously to themselves. 'If we can just get him into the field.'

Gloria looked at the screen. It looked to her as though the animal was already in a field.

Something red shimmered into being just a few yards from the nose of the butcher's retirement fund, and the Bull dutifully ignored it completely as it pulled some more grass from its God-given plate. When it looked up, the shimmering did catch its eye, and the chewing stopped very briefly as the colour was contemplated. Then it looked closer.

The exquisite memory of this creature surpassed even what pleasure there was to be found in mastication. It stared at Gloria with unbridled passion and dribbled, from the mouth.

Gloria sat and stared straight into its eyes. It took a step towards her, and she did not back away; in fact she moved not a muscle, though this degree of detail was slightly beyond the Bull's ken. Another step, and it was almost on top of her. Still she did not move. Hope rekindled in the Bull's soul, not to mention . . . well, not to mention. Perhaps this time she would not spurn him as she had before.

It took one final step, in order to come alongside her, and Gloria disappeared.

The Bull stared now not at a predominantly green blur with the colours of earth and flowers interspersed, but at a drab grey blur with very little interspersed as far as it could see, which wasn't very far at all. It did not recognize that it now stood not in its luxuriant field but in a courtyard surrounded by palace walls, and it would not have cared if it had. Its heart's desire, and the desire of certain other organs, which outstripped the heart's by a mile, had gone.

It was as distraught as a slow-witted hunk of beef could be.

'Snort,' it went.

XXI

The kings stood serenely at the far ends of the board, showing no expression of concern. In order to be a king you have to be well able to control any sort of emotion behind a facial screen of calm disinterest. Kings don't yawn at tribal dances which display the balletic grace of a hippo climbing a tree[1], or greet the arrival half-way through the banquet of the armadillo testicles braised in their own sweat with a swift pavement pizza.

The kings, therefore, showed no expression.

Before them there was just about every expression you can imagine below the line marked 'Scared'.

Right at the bottom of the expression pile was Carlton's, as his war-horse charged around the board at a speed more appropriate to Ascot than wherever the lunatic hell they were, while Wilverton, fixed firmly by the glove to the side of the thing, veered out centrifugally every time Winnie took a corner, which the horse did pretty constantly.

The first piece they met was the one of the white castles. It stood massively a little in front of its king and grinned as it saw Carlton approaching. It wasn't much of a grin, as several of the teeth were missing, while the others looked like a vote loser for the green party. Intelligence shone in its eyes like a terminally ill glow worm. It had a huge mace in its hands, which it lifted over its head, intent on killing and burying both horse and rider with one blow.

Winnie was having none of it, and veered sharply, swinging Wilverton out, so that he scythed the castle's legs away and sent it crashing to the ground.

And so they continued, cutting a swathe through those pieces still standing, while Wilverton's armour got more and more battered, and Carlton clung onto Winnie's neck with more

---

[1] Oh yes they can. It's just that they don't because they're clumsy and embarrassed.

passion than he had ever shown in holding a woman, and wondered if his street cred was suffering at all.

'Can we stop doing this now?' yelled Wilverton. 'I'm not really enjoying this bit.'

'Should have chosen a different bloody book, then, shouldn't you!' Carlton screamed back at him. 'What one do you call this? I must remember not to read it!'

'Well, it isn't *Far from the Madding Crowd*!' A pawn staggered, exhausted, to his feet, and Wilverton reaped him as they passed. 'I haven't come across anything like this before, ever.'

And he frowned.

They had completed more than a full circuit, and the gauntlet had seen enough. As Wilverton flew sideways once again, his glove let him go, and he described a neat tangent to Winnie's circle, sliding across the surface of a board made slippery by several quite unspeakable substances, and fetched up behind the legs of a piece who seemed still to be standing.

He was joined almost immediately by someone who rolled to a halt just in front of him and smiled broadly. Why 'rolled'? Because parted as it was from the rest of its body, the head didn't have much choice.

On reflection, maybe it wasn't smiling. Either way, Wilverton did not smile back at it.

A thought, a tiny thought, entered his head.

'Haven't come across anything like this before, ever . . .'

Maybe, just maybe, this wasn't a book after all.

It was enough. The Champion was on the draw quicker than the fastest super-minded bodiless alien being in the West, and the thought got bigger.

So did Wilverton's eyes.

What in the name of Tolkien did he think he had been doing?

He looked up and saw that what he had slithered behind was the white king. Just in front of the monarch were a castle and a bishop, protecting him from attack. Covered in blood as Wilverton was from head to foot, he thought there was a chance that if he lay perfectly still, they would assume he was dead. And if you don't lie perfectly still, said the disconcerting new thought in his head, then you will be.

It was no use, thought Carlton, sooner or later he was going to have to open his eyes. Might as well be sooner. It didn't occur to him that 'sooner' had finished several minutes before.

He tried it, and the first thing he saw was a castle from his own team – you could tell the difference; one team were mostly dripping red with black bits and the other were almost totally dripping red with white bits – tying someone's legs in a clove hitch around someone else's neck. At least, it looked at first glance like a clove hitch, and his natural curiosity didn't stretch to a second.

Then he saw one of the queens doing something to a bishop that even the actress hadn't thought of, and wasn't likely to unless she took roles in films with more X's than a lovelorn teenager's valentine.

'Off with his balls!' another cleric encouraged his queen, and Carlton quickly looked away in case she did just that. A high-pitched scream sought out his ears and echoed eerily in them for a while.

Winnie hurtled towards a group of standing pawns, all flailing arms, legs and swords, with technique long since lost to a preference for imitating a circular saw as they spun round and hacked at anything that came within reach, whether friend or foe.

Carlton knew that Winnie was not going to veer, knew that soon this broiling mass would have a quivering Carlton right in the middle of it, and he frantically tried to get the sword from where it flapped in its scabbard at his side, whilst not loosing either hand from the death grip they had on Winnie's neck. Short of using his teeth or a prehensile appendage, it was not going to be possible; and Winnie was almost on the group.

He let go with one hand, and Winnie took off, leaping over the group of pawns as though they were the last hurdle in the Galaxy show-jumping cup final.

Carlton, his grip now definitely precarious, decided, more or less subconsciously, that now was the time to give up the smooth suavity he had been displaying so far.

He screamed at the top of his voice, and then made that sound like a whimper when Winnie landed and kept going in a straight line towards the castle and bishop who stood before the white king.

The king still stood quite serenely, confident in the ability of his subjects to save him from this danger.

The bishop was urging a piece over to his right to 'tie it round the bugger's throat then circumcise his head! . . . er . . . your Majesty', when the sound of galloping hooves reached his ears, and he looked up to see an animal bearing down on him, sweat shining on its skin, its eyes wide and looking fearsome, its mouth open and flecked with spittle. And it was riding a horse which looked hardly less frightening.

It was touch and go which was the more dangerous of the two, but the bishop was not about to bother with the 'touch' part; it was the 'go' bit which pushed its way rudely to the fore. He spoke his first holy phrase: 'Holy shit!' and started to back away.

The king looked calmly at his castle, who, he knew, would protect him to the last because he didn't have the intelligence to realize when he was on a loser.

The castle wouldn't let this mad horse get to him.

This mad and fast approaching horse with the black-clad maniac on its back.

He would stop him in time.

He had at least a second and a half to do so, so there was no need to panic.

Winnie careered into the castle, who was expecting a veer before bringing his mace down, and who therefore waited too long, because the horse was not for veering.

They met.

Carlton was suddenly not for sitting in the saddle any more, and he described a graceful arc over the horse's head and the castle's shoulder.

Looking down, he saw the king look up and take a stately step backwards, tripping over Wilverton's supine form as he did so, and crashing to the ground.

Carlton shut his eyes as he started falling, and heard the dulcet tones of a cleric calling out, 'He resigns! The white woofter resigns!'

Then the sound cut off and there was nothing but silence and more falling until he hit the ground hard and rolled once before fetching up against another body. There was silence alone for a moment, then Carlton opened his eyes, and found himself in the corridor of the Labyrinth, the shimmering light of what he did not know as the Possibility Veil behind him, and Wilverton sitting next to him and rubbing the bit which Carlton had just inadvertently hit.

'There,' said Carlton, recovering his cool as quickly as he could. 'I knew I'd think of something.'

Wilverton smiled a little wanly, and looked confused, among a lot of other things. 'I think I got a little carried away,' he said. 'I'm not . . . I'm not *completely* sure that was a book after all.'

Carlton stared at him. If this was the start of a cure for insanity then he wasn't going to make a lot of money selling it to the medical profession.

He took a deep breath, but it escaped in a whoosh as something fell heavily on top of him.

XXII

Arnold took a small jump beyond the starting line, and then stared at the grass which suddenly filled his vision from a distance of about an inch. It was what they call a field of vision. It was what Arnold called a prat-fall, and it didn't please him. It pleased the crowd, though, and that pleased Arnold even less.

He rolled onto his back and sat up. He reached down to where the foot reached up to his thighs, and gripped the front of the strong but flexible rubber in both hands. He spread his arms wide, and the two resultant halves of the foot hung from his fingers. The crowd went wild with delight.

An android – presumably the android which had helped him thus far – arrived at his side.

'What are you doing?' it asked.

'I'm winning the game. Playing according to the non-existent rules.'

The android conveyed shock. 'But you can't! That is not the way the game is supposed to be played. I will get you another foot.'

Arnold stood and laid a hand on the other's arm. A friendly but restraining hand.

'Why don't you go tighten your nuts?' he suggested, and turned away. The android looked puzzled.

On the other track, Arnold's opponent was fairly bounding through the balloons and remaining almost completely dry whilst doing so. Arnold hurried to the edge of the sheeting to which the balloons were attached, and looked at the areas where the balloons had burst. The sheeting was undamaged.

Good.

The first balloon was a good five yards from the edge of the sheeting, and Arnold proceeded to tear a large chunk from the whole. By pushing his hand into the centre, and without breaking the plastic, he made a sort of handle, which he grasped from the other side. He looked up to see how his opponent was getting on.

Very well, was the unwelcome answer. The android hopped gingerly but with good balance across the plank over the pool while half the crowd cheered it on. The other half watched Arnold with scepticism as he walked around the side of the balloons, and then around the side of the pool. His opponent reached the ground level with him, and leapt towards the castle fascia. Arnold was about to follow when the friendly neighbourhood android appeared at his side.

'You have not crossed the pool.'

'Not a lot gets past you, does it?' Arnold made to walk on.

'But you must cross the pool.' A hand gripped his shoulder, a hand anxious that he should not embarrass himself by forgetting something as important as the pool. That would never do. Arnold toyed with the idea of physical violence. It cheered him up, but not nearly enough.

'I don't want to cross the pool.'

'But the crowd expect it,' the android pressed on, unwary of the expression beginning to form on Arnold's face. 'The crowd enjoy seeing us fall into the pool.'

'*Do* they?' Arnold asked in a tone reminiscent of a prelude to melt-down. The android was tone deaf.

'Oh yes. They would be most disappointed.'

'Well, we *certainly* wouldn't want to disappoint them, *would* we?'

'No, we wouldn't.'

Arnold looked over the shoulder of the hindrance to where the liquid of the pool sloshed about and made expectant little chuckling noises. It knew.

'Off you go then.'

'I beg your . . . Aarrgghhh!!!!'

Hiss.

'Bolt neck.' Arnold wandered off as the crowd cheered his innovation.

As he approached the castle, he watched his opponent scrambling up the ropes which hung from the top of the wooden scaffolding behind the fascia. Two androids stood at balconies and looked down through long golden wigs to where the contestants battled to save them. Above the balconies, four more stood ready with buckets. Two were emptying their contents over the android who struggled up the rope, hand over hand. It was already a third of the way up, and going well, despite the attentions of the bucketeers.

Arnold held his makeshift umbrella above his head as two bucketloads of reducing agent rained down from above. It splashed harmlessly off on all sides, and there was a pause while two more buckets were fetched. Arnold took advantage of the pause.

The rope he was supposed to climb was attached to the front of the balcony on which leant his maiden. Arnold reached for it, and instead of climbing, pulled on it with much of his considerable, Biondor-endowed strength.

The rope he was supposed to climb was then still attached to the front of the balcony, but the front of the balcony was no longer attached to the rest, and the maiden found itself leaning on thin air.

Arnold's opponent was two thirds of the way to his balcony when a blurred image of a fellow android flashed past it, followed somewhat more leisurely by a long blonde wig. It looked down and saw Arnold reach out with the arm which was not holding the umbrella, neatly catching the maiden just before it hit the ground.

Arnold hoisted his prize onto one shoulder, and started trotting – carefully – back to the starting line, discarding his umbrella when he was a safe distance from the castle. The crowd cheered wildly at such originality – even those who supported the opposition were clearly and noisily impressed – and from an ordinary android to boot!

Little, as they say, did they know.

Arnold crossed the line and unceremoniously dumped the maiden onto the ground, then looked up to the crowd in order to collect the plaudits. This he did with a short but succinct 'speech'.

'BASTA . . .' he had started, when suddenly there was no noise, and less light, and Arnold was falling. '. . . aaaaarrrrrrr,' he finished, and landed with a thump on top of Carlton in the Labyrinth corridor.

'Oomph!' said Carlton.

'Hello, Arnold,' Wilverton said a little uncertainly, but Arnold either didn't notice, or didn't care if he did.

He said nothing for a moment as he rolled off Carlton's prostrate form and gave his brain a little while to come to terms with its new surroundings.

He sat up, looked at them, and frowned. 'One nightmare to another.'

Carlton sat up beside him, rubbing his back. 'Where have you been, Arnold?'

'It was a planet called Bulphus, wherever that is. I didn't see too many humans, but the things I did see certainly acted pretty much like them.'

Wilverton could see little point in asking exactly how their actions had been akin to those of humans, since he knew that the answer would be little more than a venting of Arnold's spleen. It had an amazing capacity, did Arnold's spleen, especially considering that he didn't actually have one.

'What did you have to do? Did you have to win a game of some kind.'

'If you could call it a game. It didn't strike me as being much of a recreational activity.' Arnold fell silent, frowning.

'So what *did* you have to do?' Carlton repeated Wilverton's question. Arnold considered. He could hear himself saying that he was supposed to put on a large rubber foot and bounce through some balloons and cross a swimming pool and climb a rope to save a maiden that was actually an android in a wig on a cardboard castle balcony. He did not relish what he heard. He had an image to uphold.

Well, all right, he didn't have an image to uphold, but he was buggered if he was going to admit to *that* little lot!

'Oh, it was nothing,' he said, turning it into an opportunity to sound modest.

'We had to win a game of chess,' said Wilverton, assuming a reciprocal query which was never going to come. 'Except it was more like a war.'

'And you did, obviously.' Carlton and Wilverton looked modest. 'I wish I'd had opponents as naff as yours must have been.'

There was so much they could describe in response that they didn't say anything, and left Arnold looking smug and superior. But normality was a nice place to be, and Arnold's expression looked like home right then.

Carlton and Arnold both began to get to their feet, and were felled as two more figures appeared from thin air and crashed on top of them.

'So after that second round, Hragph and Huupt' – the host pronounced the names perfectly if malodorously – 'have a score of just three! What bad luck to have got caught on your first assignment, eh!' And thereby not managing to learn very much about each other, presumably. The host did not look like it was bad luck, as the painted smile clung to his face. Bog Breath 2 especially looked miserable, but Bog Breath 1 wasn't about to burst into song either.

'And that means that Dick and Fission are still level, after Dick's three points in the first round, and just need one more point to win the game!'

Yes, it had happened. The one ticket you bought for the Intergalactic Lottery had come up twice in a row. Curtis had got all three answers correct. Neither of the other questions had been multiple choice, but they didn't have to be. He knew the answers!

Amazing!

'What is fondlable Fission's perfect perfume?' the host had asked, with a smelly spray of spittle accompanying each alliteration.

Curtis looked up from the top of the lectern, where he was hoping a sign might light up telling him that it was all some sort of practical joke, and thought about it.

Dilute acid seemed to fit the bill; or something that would repel rather than attract. But then he remembered his embarrassing moment on the Ship – well, *one* of his embarrassing moments; he was ridiculously spoiled for choice.

'Red Cat.'

And the host poured enthusiastic praise and methane on him in roughly equal portions.

Then, after a few more fatuous comments which had the audience collectively in need of a toilet, for one reason or another, the host posed the final question.

Curtis was by this time feeling wonderful, compared to his initial trepidation. Two out of three was a score that even Fission would be hard pushed to complain about. She'd manage it all right, but she'd be hard pushed.

'What colour brassiere is Fission wearing tonight?'

The audience whooped ignorantly. Not that the audience was necessarily ignorant, it's just that if someone had conducted a poll into why they had found it necessary to laugh at the word 'brassiere', the 'don't knows' would have far outweighed the second-placed embarrassed silences.

Curtis didn't whoop. He looked at the top of his lectern again while the memory of Fission leaning down to scratch her leg flashed through his mind – 'flash' being the operative word. Then he blushed and glanced at the booth where Fission was fixing him with a stare like a moth on a pin. At least she couldn't hear.

'It's transparent with little red flowers on it.'

And it was. And the audience made noises like a large family of gibbons who are passing round a letter telling them they have actually won the first prize in the *Video Digest* 'Win Your Weight in Bananas' competition.

All three right. He couldn't believe it.

He wasn't alone. The Challenger had been watching affairs on a quiet pillow of microwaves, with only the mild anticipatory interest of watching the Curtis human's efforts raising the frequency above the radio spectrum. Now it was approaching visible green. In a human that might have suggested a sick feeling. In the Challenger it wasn't really a lot different.

The Champion was chuffed in a way that would have been difficult to spot unless you knew what to look for. It was the flash of violet, a regular pulse, that gave the hint.

It wasn't allowed to influence the answers, only the questions, and therefore had to rely on Curtis to remember what the Champion had been able to tell him.

It noticed the Lessers' emanation of purple praise, but did not acknowledge it.

The hardest bit had been keeping the Fission female calm enough to answer the questions. Now, if only she could guess just one of the answers . . .

'Fission, will you please come back on stage for the final round!'

The audience were getting noisily excited as Fission obeyed the invitation, and she stared at them as though they had recently emerged from a dog's bottom. Nothing like getting the crowd on her side, and this was just about the opposite of getting the crowd on her side.

She took her place at the lectern next to which Curtis now stood, looking relieved and petrified at the same time, something which only someone with such complex neuroses as Curtis can even contemplate, let alone manage.

The applause died in response to the upraised hand of the host, a hand which then preceded him across the stage to where Fission and Curtis were standing.

'Well, Fission, welcome back.' Her mouth prepared to say a word that started with an 'F' but the host didn't give her a chance. 'And how many marks out of three do you think your favourite Dick scored?'

Fission let her blank stare describe a digit that barely scraped above a minus number.

'He scored three! What do you think of that?'

Whatever Fission thought of that was difficult to say. In fact she thought so much of that that it was apparently quite impossible to say, and she moved her mouth around in the confused way that Curtis had long since made his own.

Curtis smiled. Shyly. Smiles didn't often get the chance to parade around Curtis's features before they were frightened away, and this one was no different.

The stare Fission finally turned on him was not one of admiration.

'How the fonk you know –'

'So, Fission!' the host interrupted, on his way back to his own lectern, while her eyes promised Curtis that this conversation was not over. 'We asked Dick three questions about himself, and he wrote the answers on this card.' He held up a small card for what was presumably dramatic effect. 'Only Dick and I know what those answers are. Are you ready, Fission, to test your knowledge of Dick?'

'No. I play no more.' It might have sounded petulant had the words not been delivered with Fission's much practised venom.

'Then you lose by default and it's the Exit for you!' said the host, with the smile on his face completely unmoved by Fission's fervour. Teams had tried that one before.

'Ready.'

'So, Fission, the first question we asked Dick was what colour were his pyjamas! What do you think the answer was? Not that we expect you to have seen him actually wearing any, that is!'

She glanced sideways at Curtis, and he smiled weakly at her in case that was what she wanted.

'Blue; little bunny wunnies on them.' Only advanced students of linguistics would have been able to say how often before had 'little bunny wunnies' been spoken in a tone of voice more normally used to describe the cow-pat which the speaker has just impacted while rolling through the grass with her boyfriend.

The host looked down at his card, and back up at Fission, his bottom jaw slightly parted from the upper, and a look of astonishment on his face, overdone as ever. The crowd held their breath. So did Bog Breath 2 and Bog Breath 1, for whom the tension was understandably greater than for those who were going home afterwards whatever the result of the show.

'If that is the answer on the card, Fission, then you and Dick have Won the Game!' He paused. Naturally. 'And the answer on the card is . . . Green! And it's still three all.'

Fission breathed a little heavier, and her eyes reached out for the host's neck. Her mind's fist punched his teeth so far back that he could have cleaned them on a bidet.

She was miffed, was Fission.

Curtis was miffed as well, and he looked at Fission with the usual incomprehension on his face.

Bog Breaths 2 and 1 sighed their relief so deeply they might have been breathing their last, and the smell that sought out Curtis's nostrils suggested that they had done so several months before.

'So, question two. We asked Dick how many women before your good self he had mave love to.' He gave a Look to the crowd, much as he had when he had asked Curtis the question, and they gave him an 'Ooh' back, much as they, too, had already done.

Fission ignored the crowd as best she could – she only glanced at them briefly with naked hate on her face – and wondered whether to think about the answer for any great length of time. Nought was a good bet, but hadn't he been with melons – Gloria – before she had been thrown into their company?

'One,' she said, having had quite enough contemplation of that particular topic. The host looked sad – causing the Bog Breaths to look happy in direct proportion – and then looked at Curtis.

'You've been fibbing to your lovely lady, Dick,' he admonished. 'The answer on the card is Seven.' The crowd gave a much bigger 'Ooohh' as Fission looked tiredly at Curtis, and he looked sheepishly at his feet. It depended on how you defined 'making love', he thought. Still, it was nice of her to guess one.

'So, there is just one question to go, and everything to play for, and I mean Everything!'

179

He had an annoying habit with capital letters as well, but Fission was past noticing. Bog Breaths 1 and 2 shuffled and eased their clothing where it was sticking to them under the lights and the pressure. Curtis fidgeted, and wondered if it would have been better if he had told the truth. And he wished the man wouldn't keep calling him 'Dick'.

'We asked Dick what you would most like to receive as a birthday present, Fission. What you would most like to receive as a birthday present.' Pause. For effect. 'What do you think he said to that? What you would most . . .'

'Heard you!' said Fission irritably. What would Curtis say to that?

She hadn't the remotest idea.

And that smile was *really* getting on her nerves. She had to shift it.

'Well-hung android,' she answered, and the smile slipped, but only so it could be replaced by his excited look. The audience hushed, silenced either by the tension or their suddenly triggered imaginations.

'Fission,' said the host, stepping from behind his lectern, 'would you repeat your answer, please?'

'Why, you deaf?' The host ignored her and positioned himself between the two lecterns behind which the sparring couples stood. Bog Breath 1 and Bog Breath 2 were looking petrified, especially the latter, and yet she managed to eye the host with a loathing that made Fission's expression seem a pale imitation.

'For the benefit of our friends in the audience, then!'

'Not friends! I *hate* aliens. Luc! For a tachydis!' Pause. Fission and the audience stared at each other, then the audience looked away. Fission almost allowed herself a grim grin. 'I *said*, well-hung android.'

'If that is not the answer on the card,' said the host, 'then the scores will remain tied and it will be up to our studio audience to vote for the couple they prefer to be the winners.'

Fission swallowed, and glanced once more at the audience, but this time with a bit more respect, and she even tried a half smile. They glared back at her, and the occasional gloating smirk left her in no doubt where their votes would go.

From a dog's bottom, eh? said the smirks.

You *hate* aliens, eh?

Are *you* in trouble!

'The answer on the card,' said the host, and threw in the obligatory pause, 'is – A Well-Hung ANDROID! And Dick and Fission, you have WON the GAME!!'

The crowd went wild at this orgy of capital letters and exclamation marks, and the Bog Breaths slumped even as they stood.

Fission turned to Curtis and he anticipated her question by shrugging his shoulders minutely. That was *not* the answer he had given. She turned back the other way, and over the tumult of the applause, she could just make out Bog Breath 2's words as she addressed the host.

'How could you do this to me, Hertgpry?' she asked, tearful now. 'I'm still your wife.'

The host indicated the Exit with a grand sweep of his arm, inviting the unlucky couple to precede him, and the smile never wavered.

'Not for much longer.'

Then suddenly the spotlights which Curtis and Fission had almost grown used to disappeared from their eyes, and they were falling momentarily through darkness, until they landed on something partially yielding, which turned out to be Arnold and Carlton.

XXIII

'Hello,' said Wilverton.

'How the fonk you know my underwear?' Fission accused Curtis, rather rudely ignoring Wilverton and thereby surprising everyone not at all.

'I guessed,' lied Curtis from a semi-prone position, then tried to divert the conversation away from his own knowledge. 'How do you know what my pyjamas look like?'

Fission stared at him. She had been right?

It simply beggared belief.

Surely mankind wasn't this moronic four hundred years ago. Or was that being unfair on the others? she wondered, and decided rapidly that she didn't give a fonk.

Wilverton ignored the lack of greeting, and pondered whether he should ask what they had been up to. He wasn't at all sure that he wanted to know.

Carlton was, and for much the same reason.

'What have you been doing? Some sort of game?' This example of extra-sensory perception took Curtis's wandering mind off Fission's apparently intimate knowledge of his night attire.

'Yes, how did you know?'

'We all were,' Carlton explained.

'It was some sort of quiz for couples who had committed adultery. The losers got killed.'

'There was a lot of that about,' Carlton commented, avoiding the subject of adultery and how it pertained to Curtis and Fission.

'Did everyone hear the Ship's warning bell?' asked Wilverton, feeling a need to change the subject, and was answered by affirmative nods but no enthusiasm. 'Well, there isn't anything we can do about it now, so there's no point dwelling on it. Agreed?'

'*SHIP*!' shouted Fission, and received no response except for the others bending their ears away from the noise. 'Agreed.'

Behind them the possibility veil shimmered with the promise of unknown transportation, while before them the corridor continued, harmlessly if they could trust their eyes – which on the current list came between second-hand car dealers and Judas Iscariot.

'Gloria must be ahead of us, and we can't get back to the Ship anyway,' said Wilverton. 'So any decision about whether we continue seems to have been made for us. We go on!'

Curtis was beyond the point where he felt aggrieved about decisions being made by others. It had now entered the realm of those things which just *were*. He nodded with no thought other than for the fact that, whether they found Gloria or not, their fate was now sealed. They would lose the Game and die. And the thought of spending the rest of his life safely dead was almost welcome.

'Wait, shrimp limbs.' Shrimp limbs paused, and regarded her levelly. 'I don't bother mentioning whose idea it was not to give ourselves possible means of retreat, and to go through light back there.' She jerked her head back to the possibility veil, a little unfairly. 'But you think you're best leader after what you've accomplished, then you every bit mad as people keep saying.'

Wilverton smiled slightly. More arrows off his armoured skin. 'And who do you think should be leading the group, then?' he asked quietly. 'Or do you think we should all make up our own minds what to do?'

'Me,' said Fission immediately, not disappointing anyone's expectations. 'But we vote, of course.' That was more surprising. Arnold opened his mouth. 'Robots can't stand,' she told him. Arnold looked hurt, and dangerous.

'I may not have the heart and soul of a human being,' he misquoted, 'but I certainly have the body of a strong and capable man. As you were one of the first to realize, if I remember rightly.' Carlton sniggered but swallowed it quickly. Curtis and Wilverton frowned, not knowing the incident to which Arnold was referring. Fission *was* knowing, and quickly did an impression of a chameleon who had been resting for a week on something uniformly puce. 'But if *androids* can't stand, then my vote goes to a small fossilized turd I saw in the corridor back there. It looked more capable of intelligent thought than any human I've met.'

'I think I should lead,' said Carlton, before Fission could

183

rejoin the discussion. Wilverton was the other alternative in Carlton's mind, and he *had* got them out of one or two scrapes in the past, but his appeal was somewhat diminished by his continuing raving lunacy.

A little sound – like a voice, only smaller – came from Curtis, and it said 'me' but no-one paid it any attention at all so it kept quiet again.

'So no-one leads.' Wilverton shrugged. 'I vote we continue, though.' Carlton and the tiny, weeny Curtis agreed. 'You still have the option to go off on your own,' he told Fission, 'though I'm sure we'd all rather have you with us.'

'Do we get to vote on that as well?'

'Shut up, Arnold.'

Arnold smirked.

'Of course I stay. Majority decision.' Fission sounded honestly surprised. 'You had democracy, didn't you?' And even that wasn't an insult.

'Well, yes, but I . . .'

'What you think I am!' She sounded almost hurt. 'I never gone against vote in my life.' They almost expected her to start waving a little Stars and Stripes.

'Right. Well we have to go this way,' Wilverton indicated the corridor which wound away from the possibility veil. 'So there's not much leadership involved for the time being, anyway. Shall we go?'

He moved off, and everyone followed. Some more grudgingly than others.

'Got him!' cried the Minotaur, thumping the worktop in front of him with a clenched fist. 'We've got him!' He turned in triumph from the courtyard screen where the Bull had just appeared to Gloria's motionless form. 'And now, my lady, for the coup de grâce.'

The what? thought Gloria. Some sort of coup. She had heard of them – they involved men with guns and bloodshed. It didn't sound promising.

The Minotaur moved towards Gloria, reaching into a pocket as he did so, and withdrew the gun with which he had immobilized her. He shoved her unceremoniously onto her side and fired into a buttock. Gloria's mental hands closed round his neck.

She found she could move her legs, not easily, but they were the only parts of her body to respond to the frantic orders coming from her brain.

'Our *father* is now in the courtyard of our mother's palace,' he explained. It sounded to Gloria as though the word 'daddy' rarely escaped his lips.

Then she realized what he had said. The Bull that she had . . . that she . . . well, *that* Bull, anyway, was this creature's father. It was the Bull on whom he was going to have his revenge.

'It is time you were reintroduced, however briefly.'

He reached to her shoulders, and lifted her effortlessly to her feet, where she stood unsteadily and stared ahead.

She twitched a leg, experimentally.

It's not very lady-like, she thought, eyeing the creature just off to her side, but it may be the only chance left. If only he would stand directly in front so that she could see him properly and get a good shot in. But he wouldn't, apparently; remaining slightly on one side so that her view was only peripheral.

Well, it would have to do, because she couldn't shuffle round with enough speed.

She swung a kick as hard as she could in the hope – not to put too fine a point on it – of projecting the Minotaurial testicles into the Minotaurial throat. It was immediately clear that soccer had never been one of her strong points, because she missed by a yard and, looking like a lost cause in the chorus line auditions, fell to the floor in a heap, her paralysed vocal chords not even being able to relay the pain of the landing.

The Minotaur looked at her for a moment, his bovine brows creased in a frown, then he leant down and roughly pulled her to her feet, where she stood like a waxwork that would have to be firmly nailed to the floor to prevent it toppling forwards. The lack of regret or pain, or anything, looked strange on her face.

'She shouldn't have done that, should she!' He waited for the answer, his eye twitching like frogs' legs getting the shock treatment. 'So there's no argument any more. This is the only way.'

He nodded, and Gloria knew that her last chance had gone; that he would take her to the grass and coup it. She also knew that her bottom hurt, but it was slightly secondary.

The Minotaur led her to the shelves of test-tube racks on the far side of the lab, did something which she couldn't see as his body blocked the view, and the shelves slid aside to reveal a door, which he opened.

When he turned back to her, he was once again wearing his equivalent of an extravagant smile.

'Shall we go and meet our father, and your doom?' He laughed, mercifully briefly. 'I love it when we're witty.'

Gloria's unmoving shoulders slumped. She had been so certain that Thomas and Peter and the rest would somehow be able to rescue her. It was only now that she allowed the knowledge to filter into her mind that they had not found a way.

Nor had this Champion thing. Any more than he had for Danny Thompson on the old *Pioneer*.

Gloria knew she was going to die. And she couldn't even cry.

'Well?' said Wilverton. 'Which way?'

They stood at a fork in the passageway, and these children of the main tunnel were twins in everything except direction – they even sloped gently downwards at the same gradient. They were so much alike in all respects that one of them was probably cheating.

No-one made a choice, not even Curtis; which was a bit of a pity, because it would have tipped the balance pretty firmly in favour of the other route.

'Okay.' Wilverton raised both hands palms up. 'The right one it is, then. And let's hope it is.'

They walked down the corridor and made it to a sharp bend without mishap, and in total silence, all their attention in their eyes and ears. Wilverton peered round the corner, and the featureless walls they had passed so far were transformed.

The rock was carved into statues reaching from floor to roof, like something from an ancient temple where the myriad deities looked down on those who worshipped them. Which they always do with really annoyed expressions. You never see an ancient god looking down from atop a fifteen-foot statue with a big broad grin, or one eye closed in a mischievous wink. They never look like they're enjoying themselves, like they're having fun. Maybe ancient gods just don't like sculptors.

These gods were no different where facial expression was concerned. Their shapes cast shadows darker yet than their faces, though the light source was still unfathomable, and the shadows were more disconcerting than the shapes which cast them. Anything could have been lurking in the darkness, and in the imaginations of the group which joined Wilverton to stare, everything was, from big angry scorpions and vampire bats to the ghost of Robert Maxwell.

Some thirty yards ahead was a pit, maybe fifteen feet long, and with no path on either side. The smooth legs of two statues guarded its leading edge, so climbing round the side was not possible. The prize, maybe fifty yards distant, was a door at the far end of the corridor.

'Think we should go back try other passage before attempt this,' said Fission.

No-one disagreed, so she turned to lead the retreat, and felt something give very slightly under one foot as she did so. Then she watched as a large stone slab lowered smoothly from the roof about twenty yards ahead of her to block the route. She stopped.

'Or maybe we *should* try this,' Wilverton suggested. He turned back once more.

Fission stared at the slab as though it was covered in personally insulting graffiti, while Wilverton paused at the start of the final but seemingly treacherous path to whatever lay behind the door. A look of recognition dawned on his face.

'I think I remember this,' he muttered, almost to himself. 'We must all watch out for anything that looks like a trigger,' he said to the ensemble. They all crowded forward, apparently eager to get on with it. 'If we trip one of those, then spears should emerge from somewhere in the walls, or a huge boulder should roll down the passageway and flatten us all.' They all crowded back, not so eager, except one.

'Up,' said Arnold.

'What?'

'Up the passageway. Unless it comes from behind us out of thin air then it's going to need a motor on it.'

Wilverton considered, while the others waited for his superior knowledge to counter the android's argument.

'Yes, you're probably right,' he admitted, slightly discon-certingly. 'Well, just watch out for everything then. And be very, very careful. The slightest wrong move could trip something.'

'Do you think it would be better if Fission *did* lead us for a while?' Arnold asked, and Wilverton looked slightly pained.

'Why?'

'Well, whatever's waiting for us is almost certainly going to be fatal. I thought she could go on ahead, jumping up and down, dancing a polka or something, while the rest of us, you know . . .'

Fission's reaction passed from initial surprise at Arnold's suggestion, through several other emotions very quickly indeed, arrived at breaking point, and passed it.

She swung a flailing fist at the android's head. Arnold was way too quick for her, and he ducked sharply. The hand continued and whacked Curtis on the ear. He staggered forward like a boxer paid to go down in the first but to make it look good, thumping his feet daintily on various bits of passageway before crashing carefully into one of the statues and grasping something which might easily have been a lever, but wasn't.

Fission clamped her hand under her arm as the knuckles told her what they thought of Curtis's head, and she leant over in pain. Arnold rose from his duck and head-butted Fission's out-thrust posterior, propelling her forward.

She stumbled cautiously into Wilverton, toppling him. He threw an arm out to try to steady himself, and caught Carlton's jump suit sleeve. The two of them fell warily onto the floor and rolled a little way down the corridor. Curtis pushed himself away from the statue and fell over them, onto Fission's foot. She started hopping prudently about the passageway.

A smile began to grow on Arnold's face.

The Champion suppressed gamma rays of such high frequency that it would take a Lesser Elder a week to come down to normality.

Humans!

It had the perfect squad, if it could ever find a round where the teams had to argue constantly and throw themselves about like failed ballet dancers.

'Well,' said Wilverton, pulling himself to his feet. 'We know this bit of the corridor's safe, anyway. I'd call that a destruction test.'

They formed themselves into something resembling a group once more, if only by numerical definition.

Carlton took a careful step forward, looking right, left, and particularly down, to where the dry earth which covered the floor may well have covered considerably more. He saw nothing, and took another step, which he was about to land . . .

It wasn't worth mentioning, thought Curtis, because it almost certainly wasn't anything at all, just a disturbance in the dust – a few grains blown into the slightest of heaps by the wind.

By the wind which never blew down here.

No, they'd only laugh at him again, and Fission would say 'fonking' something-or-other, and Arnold would look at him like *that*.

Carlton put his foot down on the spot, and immediately Wilverton's promised spears shot out from carefully concealed holes in the walls of the passage, heading directly for where he was standing.

The noise which accompanied them split the air rather more effectively than the spears did.

It was the horrible shrieking sound of metal that hasn't moved for a very long time, and the spears did not so much fly through the air as dip a toe in to see what it was like. Each managed to protrude about a foot from the wall before grinding to a halt. The only threat to Carlton came from his own innards as his heart flew upwards at the sound while his stomach shot in the opposite direction.

It was apparent that nothing had made it past the possibility veil in many a year.

'Well, that shows how well the triggers are hidden,' Wilverton commented a trifle smugly, wondering whether he ought to suggest they be on the lookout for an archaeologist with a whip. He decided not. It would only confirm a few long-held suspicions. 'It's going to take a keen eye to spot them.'

Curtis saw a way to impress them and get a bit of his status back, as though he'd had any to start with.

'*I* saw it,' he said proudly, and was hurt when Carlton turned an expression of disbelief towards him. An expression the cause of which he characteristically read as though it were written in dyslexic hieroglyphics. 'I *did* see it! Honestly!' He sounded hurt.

Carlton took a step towards him, with the promise of a lot more hurt to come. 'Why the hell didn't you say something, then?'

'Er.' Oh. 'Well, because I thought it might have been, sort of, a mistake.'

'*You* were a mistake, you useless cretin! I could have been killed.'

'Maybe he's going for a record,' Arnold suggested.

Carlton nodded. 'It wouldn't surprise me!' He would have been Curtis's third victim if the rust hadn't saved him. 'If you see anything else at all, you say! We expect you to be stupid so we won't be disappointed when you're wrong. Okay?'

Curtis wondered whether to stand up to Carlton. 'Okay,' he whispered, having reached a decision.

'Better still, you can actually be leader for a while.'

Curtis half smiled, before he realized what the position currently entailed, but he shuffled to the front of the group anyway. Then he realized that shuffling was as good a way as any of finding anything dangerous under foot, so he tried to walk dispiritedly on his toes instead.

XXIV

The statues looked down severely on Curtis as he made his way forward, the others following in his footsteps once again – the only time in history this was likely to happen – until the group arrived at the edge of the pit.

It looked to Wilverton much like the chasm he crossed to get the Jewel of Altares, and he rather hoped that it was bottomless, because if it did have a floor there would certainly be something extremely nasty sitting in the corner of it waiting for anything to drop by.

'So how are we going to get across that?' he asked. 'It's too far to jump, especially for me, before anyone feels constrained to point that out.' Arnold shut his mouth. 'And how do we find out what's on the other side? It might be quicksand or something.'

'Arnold,' said Carlton, looking round to find the android, and locating him at the back of the group, as chance would have it. Well, it was possible!

'What?'

'You can throw us across.' Arnold's eyes narrowed. He couldn't see where the punch-line was coming from. 'I'm not winding you up, Arnold.' This was a new concept to Arnold, whose expression clearly suspended judgement for the moment. 'You have many times the strength of an ordinary human. You might be able to do it.'

'I have?' A pleased expression suddenly located the front of his face, but then suspicion took over again. 'What do you mean?'

'Do you remember when you came to see me in the gym?' Arnold nodded warily, remembering mainly the reason for the visit. He could feel Fission staring at him. 'You moved the bar I was lifting as though it was made of balsa wood. I don't think you were concentrating at the time.' Arnold paused in contemplation. There *had* been a bar, hadn't there. . . ?

'Was that heavy?'

'It was.'

191

Arnold swelled a little with totally immodest pride. 'Well, of course, I didn't like to say anything.' He let the comment float on the air while further compliments came his way. It floated lonely as a cloud.

'I go first,' said Fission, pushing forward and causing a number of eyebrows to rise.

'Well, let's see if there's an alternative to risking one of us first,' Wilverton suggested. 'That's logical, isn't it?'

'No, let her go for it!' goaded Arnold.

'Why do you want to try it?' asked Carlton suspiciously.

Fission looked almost confused. ''Cos,' she started, and stopped, finding the ground more attractive than any of her companions, ''Cos you all cowards; someone's got see if profitable.'

Wilverton recalled Fission's impassioned plea before they had embarked on their current mission. She wanted to do it for Earth, for Humanity. She wanted to risk her life to prove that she was worthy. She was a lunatic.

She'd only end up as a dead lunatic. He had to try to talk her out of it, despite the little voice inside him urging him to let her try; to prove to her once and for all that she didn't know best in everything.

'If we can come up with another way, then I think we should go for it. We don't want to risk anyone unless we really have no choice. You're too valuable.'

Fission glared at him, wanting to argue. Confirmation of Wilverton's reasoning came from Arnold, of all places.

'Well, just think: we may be faced with a situation where vitriolic obscenities are the very key to our success. What would we do without you then?'

Fission glared at him instead, and spat a couple of words which sizzled through the air.

'Manners,' admonished Carlton.

'Dictionary for the lady!' called Arnold.

'Fonk– ' began Fission.

'That's enough!' Wilverton stopped them. 'What we need is something heavy to throw first.'

'Like what?'

'Rock,' said Carlton, looking at the statue to his right, which looked back unconcernedly, knowing that it was in one piece and consequently out of the running. 'We can break some rock off the statue and use that.'

The statue's expression did not change. He was bluffing.

'What can we use to break a bit off, though?' asked Wilverton realistically. 'A spear's no use; we need something to hit it with.'

Fission looked at Arnold, but the returning smile advised her not to bother.

'Arnold,' said Carlton again. 'I think you stand a good chance of breaking off a bit of statue if you try.'

Arnold looked at the statue and back at Carlton, once more unsure. Making someone look a complete prat in a contest with several tons of rock was more within his realm of understanding than this unlikely opportunity for showing off.

'Go for it, Arnold,' said Wilverton.

'I'm going!' snapped Arnold, hardly flustered at all by his doubts. If you're taking the piss . . .

The android moved towards the statue. It was only a few yards away, but he moved with the care of a snail in a garlic butter factory, testing the ground with each step he planted. Fission 'encouraged' him, but he hadn't any spare positrons to think of a retort, and just stored the insult away for future revenge.

Some days later, he reached the carving and began to look for a piece which might prove vulnerable, easy to snap off. He spied the very bit, but knew it wouldn't be heavy enough.

The statue's relief went unexpressed; stone foreheads don't sweat.

Arnold eventually settled on the foot of the structure. He took hold of it in both arms and strained, whilst trying to look as though he wasn't straining at all.

There was a cracking sound, starting quietly as small shards of stone parted company with the outside of the sculpture, and then growing in a final crescendo as the whole foot came away in Arnold's arms. He turned back to the group with the prize, exuding relief in the guise of nonchalance.

'Well done, Arnold,' said Wilverton.

Arnold shrugged, making it clear that it was really nothing, and carried the foot back to the edge of the pit, travelling in his own footsteps, and doing even that with exaggerated care.

He delivered the hundredweight of rock like a googly in a troll cricket match, and it sailed high over the pit and landed with a great spread of dust. The pitch clearly wasn't taking spin, or bounce for that matter, as the five-toed boulder lay quite still after the initial thud. They stood and watched it for a while in case there was a delay, as with the light, but the only danger appeared to be running out of zarbs.

'So what about it, Arnold?' Wilverton asked, doing a good job of continuing to lead the leaderless group. 'Do you want to try it with us, or are you tired or anything?'

'Of course not. Only humans tire.'

'I first.' Faces turned towards Fission again, asking why without speaking, but already knowing the answer. 'I lightest, makes sense.'

'Not really.' Wilverton sounded almost reluctant to disagree. 'If Arnold *is* going to get tired, then he needs to throw the heaviest one first.'

Fission tried to find an argument, but couldn't, again, and had to busy herself trying not to explode with frustration.

'How is Arnold going to get across?' asked Curtis reasonably, sensibly, and therefore extremely oddly.

That made them pause, until Carlton asked, 'Could you jump the pit, Arnold?'

'Easy,' said Arnold, with no idea whether he was telling the truth or not. Curtis was mollified.

'Right,' said Wilverton, who could recognize a mollification when he saw one. 'It's Peter first, then.'

They shuffled about a bit, and Carlton gave Arnold a few instructions as to where he would like to land, and how, more to the point, until eventually Arnold stood at one side of the pit, with the man cradled in his arms like a baby.

Feet and babies, thought Arnold. Nothing but bloody feet and bloody babies.

He started to swing his charge, giving it one to get ready and three to go, missing out two, then threw him out over the pit. Carlton had a chance to look downwards briefly as he passed, and he briefly saw the sides stretching down quite smoothly until darkness concealed them. Anyone falling short of the far edge would continue to do so with no chance of recovery.

The thought did not have time to finish crossing his mind before he hit the ground on the far side. Carlton was a natural athlete and rolled once, before rising to his feet using the momentum of Arnold's throw. He turned to face the rest of the group and treated them to a confident smile.

Curtis was the next to make the crossing, and he approached Arnold looking as though he had just eaten his last meal and it had disagreed with him – which, presumably, most last meals do, though indigestion is probably very low on the list of the consumers' worries.

He was about to ask the android to be careful when, with no fuss and less concern, Arnold picked him up and threw him at Carlton, his flight being described not only by an arc, but by a whimper. He rolled unceremoniously up to and past Carlton, and felt something in the ground under his back give way as he pressed it.

It was a trigger.

He lay there, petrified, as something unseen above him opened and allowed lots of somethings very seen indeed to drift down through the air.

Eight-legged somethings.

Spiders floating towards him, fangs first, and with venom to spare.

Curtis went days without a bath if it was occupied by anything he could see without a magnifying glass, and his initial, in fact only, reaction was to scream, as the deadly arachnids landed on his clothing, hands and face.

The scream cut off abruptly.

Carlton moved back to the wall and watched, horrified. On the other side of the pit Arnold stood quite still, with Wilverton in his arms and Fission next to them. They looked on, helpless – but safe, thought one.

Carefully – so carefully as to make other carefullies look reckless – Carlton moved forward to where Curtis lay quiet and unmoving. Even more carefully he bent slightly for a closer look, then straightened and turned to the others. His face had less colour than before.

'Dead,' he said, his voice just a bit shaky.

'What!' Wilverton asked disbelievingly. All this way . . .

'Dead. They're all dead.'

'Curtis?'

'Oh, the dick's just fainted. He'll be all right.'

Hardly had he finished the sentence than Wilverton landed at his feet, and Fission was already in Arnold's grasp by the time they looked once more.

She was not thrown immediately. The two appeared to be in conversation.

'I don't want you to get the wrong impression about this,' said

195

Arnold concernedly. 'I have to hold you this way purely in order to throw you properly. There's nothing else in it.' He looked as though all he had in mind was a genuine desire to save Fission from undue optimism, but then spoiled it all with something that sounded suspiciously like a snigger.

'Just get me there, slupper.'

Arnold smiled, not caring what a slupper might be, and turned to the three waiting fielders.

'I *am* feeling a little tired, after all,' he called, unnecessarily loudly since they were only a few yards away. 'But I'll try.'

'Drop me in pit, you metal misfit, I'll –'

'Fall?' He did not wait for the reply, but lobbed Fission with perfect ease high over the pit, much higher than any of the others.

There was never any danger of her falling short of the far end, but she might have created a pit of her own had Carlton not stepped forward and half-caught her before she hit a now feebly moving Curtis. It certainly saved her from a good-sized bruise or two, and Fission had thanked him before she had a chance to realize what she was saying. Carlton immediately looked hopeful, until Fission glanced at the ceiling in a comment on his expression.

'Sorry about that,' called Arnold. 'I thought I'd better make sure. I didn't want to risk anything nasty happening. That would have just been too awful!'

Fission suggested in one word that Arnold's reluctance to keep her company some time ago was occasioned by the fact that his customary practice in that particular field was a singularly private pursuit of pleasure.

'Come on then, Arnold,' said Wilverton, verbally jumping between them before they could get a real battle going, and ignoring a squeaking Curtis thrashing dead spiders from his clothes. 'Jump.'

Arnold hesitated, looking at the gap between the edges of the pit. It seemed to be growing as he watched, but that was only his confidence diminishing. It was one thing to state with much bravado that he could jump the pit; quite another actually to do it. He moved back four paces, which was all he dared with triggers about. It wasn't much of a run-up, and it looked a lot less.

Biondor had not seen fit to provide Arnold with a digestive

system, so he had no need to eat. This meant that there were no by-products, either solid or gaseous. As Arnold prepared to start his inadequate approach, the wisdom of this was not lost on him.

He started, and stopped. Another false start and he could have been disqualified. He would not have minded a bit.

He tried again, took three quick steps, and launched himself over the pit, eyes tightly shut, waiting for the arrival of the ground.

It didn't come, and he felt himself falling; too far. He fell for ever, but then hit the ground with both feet, and remained upright more through surprise than talent. He opened his eyes and saw just the far wall of the passage with its door; the others were nowhere to be seen.

There must have been another of those shimmering light things in the air above the pit, he thought frantically, only not shimmering, and he had passed through it and . . .

'Nice one, Arnold,' said Carlton from about five yards behind him. 'I'd say you just about made it all right.'

'Was there ever any doubt?' he asked nonchalantly.

XXV

'Just sit here, my lady,' invited the Minotaur. He indicated a garden seat behind Gloria and gave her the most gentle of pushes at the same time. It was quite enough to send Gloria backwards and onto the seat, such was the comparatively feeble strength in her legs.

Whatever had been in the dart and had allowed her to walk had just about worn off, and she knew she could no longer stand unaided.

She looked across a courtyard, the normality of which contrasted sharply with the situation in which she found herself, and thereby seemed a little unreal because it was *so* real, so ordinary; the lush grass in the centre, with small flower beds pocketed here and there – a couple of the flowers were actually in quite deep discussion, waving their leaves to emphasize a point every now and then, but they were hidden to Gloria behind a bush – a border of colourful foliage, and the little pathways of paving reminiscent of the Minotaur – crazy – crossing in the centre.

Only one sun showed above the walls, and this shone from a partly cloudy sky, with a brilliance she was now getting used to, onto not only the courtyard but also the Cretin Bull, which stood in its customary pose, motionless, except for the grinding movement of the bottom jaw.

'And now, my lady, the finale.' The Minotaur stood just to one side of her. Reaching behind the seat, he brought out, with a flourish, a large red cape, the top of which was supported by a solid rod so that he could hold it out straight. A matador's cape.

'This cape will attract our father, who will charge. At the last moment we will raise the cape, but that charge will continue. On the ends of his horns' – and he did the laugh again at his private privates joke – 'our father will find you, his one and only true love, and his despair will know no bounds.

'His death would pass before it had a chance to register, and

198

that would give us no pleasure, so we do not consider it. But the pain of this loss, *that* will be suitable repayment for the misery he has given to us.' He smiled at the thought. 'Are you looking forward to it?'

Gloria tried to say 'No', or shake her head, but it wasn't her the Minotaur was talking to. After nodding approvingly at whatever answer he received, he addressed her once more.

'We are not barbaric,' he claimed, 'and the potion will prevent some of the feeling. No, it is he who is barbaric, making me suffer all my life!' His hand came up involuntarily and touched his features, then froze as he realized what it was doing.

'It's not my face! I'm not talking about my face! There's nothing wrong with it! It's my name – that's what he gave me. That's what he must pay for.'

Gloria may not have been the greatest authority on lexicology – she certainly wouldn't have claimed to be, for obvious reasons – but she knew enough about what barbarism meant to know that what was going to happen to her was a fair description of it. And that was the second time he had mentioned his name. It was obviously only an excuse that he hid his face behind, but she wondered briefly what it was.

Under the circumstances, she decided silently, and to coin a phrase she had picked up over the years and now practised for the first time – while she still had the chance – she really couldn't give a toss.

The Minotaur turned round to face his father, melodramatically sweeping the cape like a curtain in front of his victim, and found, predictably, that he was looking directly at a couple of hundredweight of rump steak.

'This way, you moron!'

One of the windows rattled briefly, opened, and a head stuck itself through the hole, topped off by a scarf which almost covered the curlers.

'Is that you S—, er, son?' called Paz.

'Of course, mother,' replied the Minotaur tiredly. 'We would have thought our identity was rather bloody obvious.'

Paz sniffed. 'You're always telling me that you don't look any different from hundreds of other people.'

'We *don't*!' he shouted.

It's denying it that's making him mad, thought Gloria, as in loopy, that is. If he admitted it he might get better.

199

It spoke a lot for Gloria that despite everything she couldn't stop herself from caring.

'What are you doing, anyway? Ooh, there's your dad – where did he come from?'

'I brought him here for a visit, mother.'

'Ooh, lovely,' she enthused, then her face clouded for a moment and her eyes lost their focus. 'I *am* sorry, Minos,' she muttered quietly. 'I never could resist.' Then the smile was back and she waved to the Bull. 'I'll be right down, dear!' The Bull completely ignored her.

The Minotaur moved his gaze from the face of his mother to the sky, exasperation etched on his features. Revenge was taking a bit longer than he had planned.

As Wilverton reached for the door, a small, bony, but determined hand clamped over his wrist.

'Now I first,' said Fission.

Wilverton was taken aback, in fact, dragged aback. 'Why? What's the logic behind this one?'

'No fonking logic behind it! I going first, that's all!' Wilverton looked at her steadily, silently waiting for more of an explanation. 'Look,' she obliged, 'I done nothing yet. You lead – if you call it that – Ovals and Mouth acts like fonking hero since I join' – what do you mean 'acts like'? Carlton's ignored expression asked – 'walking rust bucket helps thanks to Biondor.' She paused and glanced at Curtis, then flicked a hand. 'Super Povvo doesn't count. My turn.'

'Quaintly put,' said Wilverton, leaving the meaning of 'povvo' on one side. 'How could anyone argue with such elegant reasoning.'

'Don't argue, stay out way while I find what's behind door.'

Wilverton waved a gracious hand in the direction of the portal. 'It's all yours.'

Fission reached out for the handle.

'Oh, *do* be careful!' said Arnold, biting his fingernails.

Fission did not need to be told, and certainly not like that, but she let the goad pass without comment. She moved the door handle downwards, carefully, and pulled the door with a gentle force, but it didn't move, so she increased that force, and still it remained firm. She pushed it, and it moved back not at all.

'It's locked,' said Curtis, and the phrase spun Fission towards him, her eyes throwing off sparks like a catherine wheel going for promotion.

'I see that, moron!' Every door she came across seemed to be locked in a successful attempt to infuriate her. 'Arnold! Kick fonking thing down, don't *dare* go in.'

This was an order which brooked no argument, either logical – like if there's something dangerous behind the door then removing the only thing between them and it, leaving no hope of speedy replacement, might not be a move of Mensa proportions – or obstreperous, the kind Arnold considered. But considered only for a moment. If she wanted to rush in and confront whatever danger was in there while he waited outside . . . well, it was a free Galaxy.

He raised a leg and kicked the door hard, just below the handle. The door submitted immediately and swung back on its hinges rather defeatedly – Arnold had hoped it might fly backwards into the room and get rid of whoever might be lying in evil wait for them, because that would have taken Fission's apoplexy to new heights and he could have done his innocent look. Can't win them all, though.

Fission leapt through the opening and landed in a crouch, arms held slightly in front of her. It was an action best performed while holding a weapon – actually it was an action best watched from a distance – but any would-be attacker would probably have been felled by one lash of her tongue had they been slow about surrendering.

Her tongue could rest; the room was empty.

It was a laboratory, with a number of instruments which Fission did not recognize, a load of test-tubes in racks and a lot of electrical equipment, which she ignored. There were a couple of stools, and one sofa, all empty. She turned back to where the group eyed her cautiously, waiting for her to disappear, or get fired by a laser, or anything else which they would rather happen to her than them if they were honest.

'Okay,' she said, and her voice was firm and disappointed. 'Only lab some sort. No-one here.'

They filed in carefully.

Arnold paused as he drew next to Fission. 'You're ever so brave,' he said, with just a touch of sincerity, enough to make someone who did not know him wonder if he meant it. Fission knew him well enough to respond with her normal invitation to go forth and multiply.

'Ah,' said Wilverton, having activated one of the screens on the wall. It showed a view of a passageway, not recognizable as anywhere in particular, since they all looked the same, but it confirmed what he had been hoping. 'This is obviously the Minotaur's control room.'

Curtis picked a test-tube from a rack and studied the purple liquid inside it with a serious expression claiming that he did *too* have the faintest notion what it was. He held it under his nose and, using his free hand, wafted any emanating gas up his nostrils in a knowledgable, scientific, totally safe sort of way, then staggered backwards with wide eyes and the embryo of an idiot smile. He righted himself and had another quick waft. The smile grew.

This purple was the most beautiful purple he had ever seen in all his life, probably in the history of the world. He turned round to his lovely friends. He had to share this with them. He kept turning.

'So where is he?' asked Carlton. 'And where's Gloria?'

'Good question,' said Wilverton, taking the test-tube from Curtis's nerveless fingers and replacing it without sniffing, before arresting his Captain's circulations.

'Phnumble,' said Curtis.

'Don't mention it.'

Wilverton looked around. He knew it had to be here somewhere; it was just a question of finding it. Another door, that is.

Curtis spotted a green test-tube and reached for it before Wilverton had a chance to stop him. He tried to remove it from its rack, but it came only half-way, then jammed. The rack didn't, and slid aside along with its shelf, to reveal a door.

Curtis looked at it cluelessly – how else? – but the other two men made to move forward before Fission passed them at a trot, so they stood back and left her to it. The door opened towards her and revealed what appeared to be an empty cupboard, big enough to hold maybe half a dozen people with plenty to spare. Fission did not step inside – if it was not a cupboard, then it obviously had another use, and she was not in a hurry to find out what it was.

'What is it?' she asked. 'Looks some sort tachyon transporter room or something.'

'More like a death chamber,' said Carlton sombrely.

'Don't put your hand inside; it's probably got a laser across the front.'

Despite herself, Fission edged backwards.

Arnold glanced heavenwards in a gesture of disdain.

'It's a lift,' said Wilverton, agreeing with Arnold's look, and walked towards it. His assertion was given weight by the fact that nothing untoward happened to him as he crossed the threshold – no lasers, no dematerialization, even after a decent interval. It looked like he was right – again.

'How do you know?' asked Carlton.

'Logic. If the Minotaur wants to get to and from the palace – which he must do since he obviously eats up there; hence Paz talking about his love of carrots – then he's not going to wander through the Labyrinth every time; not when he has the sort of technology available to him that we've seen so far. There must be some method of access to the palace which is direct, hence, this must be a lift, since there's no other way out.'

It was very logical.

'Tell me, Wilverton,' said Carlton, 'were you popular at school?'

Wilverton frowned. 'I don't know, really. None of the other children ever spoke to me.'

Carlton nodded.

'Care to join me?' Wilverton invited, and they all filed silently into the lift, Curtis bringing up the rear, shaking his head and looking more confused than usual. Wilverton stood to one side of the door, where there were two buttons on the wall, one on top of the other. When everyone was inside, he pressed the upper of the buttons. Nothing happened. He looked slightly puzzled, and pressed again, with the same result.

'Er,' he said, adopting Curtis's style of captaincy.

Fission leaned forward and shut the door, then looked at Wilverton, who shrugged, and pressed the button again. They rose. Fission smiled a quiet little satisfied smile. It was a start.

XXVI

'Hello, love!' said Paz, throwing her arms around part of the neck of the Cretin Bull. To do the job properly, she would have needed a stick of chalk to record where she had got to. The Bull returned this show of affection with its own show of concentrated disregard, purposefully chewing without pause. 'You got me into a lot of trouble with the old man, you know,' Paz confided in one huge ear. 'Ooh, but I wish I still had the old cow-suit.'

She frowned momentarily as she noticed the statue of Gardener at Rest, trying to recall . . . But then shrugged the lack of memory away as the heat and size of the beast in her arms claimed her attention once more.

Most children find inter-parental emotion embarrassing at the least, but rarely do they have to cope with one of the participants being quite so conspicuously bovine. The Minotaur wore an expression of unmitigated disgust as he looked on, and the twitching of his eye worsened. He made an effort to control himself, and coughed to attract Paz's attention.

'What are you doing, dear? I doubt if your father is in the mood for games. He never has been one for games really, except for the one, of course.'

'Yes, mother, thank you. It may have escaped your notice, but we have never been one for games either, and we do not intend to start now.'

'Only because you never mixed with the other kids.'

'Well, you know why *that* was, don't you?'

'They didn't mind the way you looked, in fact I think they quite liked –'

'*It wasn't that!*' he cried. 'How many times do I have to tell you? You and the doctors. What do you know! It wasn't that!'

'What was it then?' Paz demanded, hands on hips.

'Do you still not know, mother?'

'You keep telling me I don't.'

The Minotaur took a deep breath. 'It was my name.'

204

'Oh, don't be silly. You keep saying that. It's just an excuse.'

'It was my name which stopped me mixing with the other children! How could I be like them when this creature who is my father gave me that awful name?'

'Awful? Sue?'

'*Yes!*' shrieked the Minotaur, and his hand dropped, taking the cape with it, and revealing Gloria. 'Sue! Why did he have to call me Sue?'

'Ooh, look! That's the young lady those nice people were looking for, I'll be bound. There can't be many built like her.'

'Why, mother?' repeated the Minotaur, ignoring her.

'Well, because it's very unusual to have wotsits that big,' she replied, hoisting her own bosom by way of corroborative comparison.

'No, why did he have to call me Sue?'

Her attention was dragged back, and she looked at her son, and shrugged. 'Well, I expect he knew he wouldn't be there when you grew up, and he wanted you to grow up tough. So he gave you that name to make sure that you would have to get tough or die, and things like that. And it's that name that's made you what you are today.'

The Minotaur was well aware that what made him what he was today was his mother's rather unpleasant desire to be intruded by a large animal, but that was not the sort of thing one said to one's mother.

'He told you all that?'

'Well, no, not as such. I just asked him what name he thought we should give you and when he said Sue, I thought that was probably why he said it.'

'Well, that was what stopped me growing up like other children, that was what robbed me of my childhood.'

It's all delusion, thought Gloria, and Paz apparently agreed. She spoke tenderly now.

'It's not, you know, dear. It's like the doctors say, you're avoiding the truth. If you face up to it, then you'll start getting better.'

The Minotaur flared like sodium on water. '*What do you mean!*' He took a half step forward, threateningly.

'Well, dear, I think we both know that it's your horrible deformity that upsets you. I mean, even for a bull you are rather ugly, and for a man you're quite hideous!'

'*AARRGGHHH*!! *All right*, mother! All right! I admit it. I hate the way I look. I've always hated it. And I hate him for being my father. Why did you have to do it? Why?'

Gloria felt a ray of hope. Now that it was all out in the open, now that he faced it, perhaps it would allow him to come to terms with it, and he wouldn't be mad any more, like this woman – his mother – had said.

And perhaps it would, given a few months in a quiet, well-padded room to reflect on matters. Sadly, Gloria was due to die in the next few moments, unless the Minotaur had a swift change of plan.

Would he?

'Now we will have repayment of the debt he owes!'

Apparently not.

Then he visibly calmed down, his shoulders relaxing and his eye slowing to a more regular pulse. He stepped back. 'Turn father round, mother.'

'If you insist, dear.' Paz tickled the side of the Bull's neck. 'What for?'

The Bull turned towards the itch, and continued turning as the itch continued, until it was facing the other way, facing its son. The Minotaur raised the cape in front of Gloria once more, Paz discontinued the scratching, and the Bull looked up at the fuzzy red square thing in front of it.

'For revenge, mother! Finally, for revenge!'

If you put a library in a lift, then you wouldn't need any signs asking for quiet. You could probably quell a heckling rabble at a political rally by having numbers above the platform which lit up in ascending order. Lifts are naturally quiet places, for un-fathomable reasons; which must be really upsetting for a gregarious lift, eager to please. Lifts never get invited to parties.

Going even further than not speaking – really rubbing it in – everyone on board held their respective breaths as the tiniest of bumps brought the lift to a stop and the doors parted in front of them. They looked out onto an empty sunlit ballroom.

They stepped out and Wilverton gestured for quiet, then whispered, 'Come on!' and led them towards the windows. Curtis looked to be back to his best, not that that was saying much. He only tripped once.

There, thought the lift, not a word. Why does everyone hate me? What have I done to deserve it?

The lift and its mood descended.

They looked down into the courtyard and saw a familiar sight – the Cretin Bull. Under its belly, they could just spy a pair of wrinkled stockings and some carpet slippers.

The Bull stared at the squarish shape in front of it, and its diminutive intellect suggested it really should charge at the colour. Should any bull's intellect ever stretch as far as to ask 'Why?' then a lot of matadors are going to be out of a job pretty damn sharpish. This one's didn't, and it scraped one of its fore hooves on the ground in time-honoured fashion.

They also saw a less than familiar but recognizable character: the Minotaur.

No-one had to speak; they turned like migrating birds, and the courtyard was the sunny south. Through the door at the far end of the room they found stairs, and they rushed down, past cabinets set into alcoves containing pottery, china, glass ornaments and such-like.

Bent into one was a woman wearing a navy pin-striped suit, her high heels confirming her sex, but most of them were too busy to notice.

Carlton was never too busy to notice that sort of thing, but there was no time to do anything, more was the pity.

Or was there? came a sudden thought in his head. Why don't you. . . ?

He gave the out-thrust bottom an impulsive pat on the way past, but did not have time to check on the reception of his action.

What he missed was the woman snapping upright so fast that her hair swung over her head and slapped into the back of her neck, where most of it said 'Ow!' before swaying forwards again and giving a hard stare to her sunglasses. Behind the glasses, she watched the retreating backs as they reached the bottom of the stairs.

'Who touched me? Did you see which one it was?'

'No, we misssed it. We were with you.'

'How *dare* they touch me!' She brushed her jacket down, as if cleansing it. 'What we seek is not here,' she snapped. 'Come!'

And she headed up the stairs. 'The stairs lead only to the courtyard, so let us See what we may See.'

The snakes flicked their tongues excitedly. They liked Seeing, but then it was rather more exciting than normal when performed by the eyes just beneath them. 'Sssee, yesss!'

'Stop that!'

The Challenger broadcast radio waves of confident ease. The Carlton human had been so simple to influence. It checked its rival's reaction now that the Champion's team had become a new entry on the Gorgon's hit list.

The reaction was one of quiet microwave satisfaction.

You, the microwaves taunted the Challenger, have just made a big mistake.

At the bottom of the stairs they found more windows leading onto the courtyard, these French and open, and they burst onto the lawn of action. The Bull ignored them, and Gloria stared straight forwards at the red cape which hung a foot from her nose, but Paz and the Minotaur both looked at the newcomers. The latter appeared somewhat surprised.

'How did you get back here?' he asked, momentarily ignoring the antics of his dad. 'Never mind,' thereby inadvertently saving himself a very long and none too convincing explanation. He reached into his pocket once more with his free hand and withdrew the gun. He lowered the cape and held the weapon to Gloria's head.

'Gloria!' shouted Wilverton, Carlton and Curtis.

'Don't come any closer,' warned her captor, traditionally, and his eye twitched like a champion jumping bean at the gala performance.

'Moo,' said the Bull, for reasons apparent only to itself.

'There,' said Paz. 'He called you.'

'What?'

'He called you. He said "Sue".'

'He said "Moo".'

'Well, it sounded like Sue to me.'

The Minotaur took a deep breath and stared at his mother, letting his cape-holding arm fall once again to his side. 'Is that what he said when you asked him what you should call me – I mean, us?' It sounded like an accusation, and it was.

Paz looked a mite embarrassed. 'Well, yes,' she admitted.

'You mean that for all these years we . . . I've been called Sue because of your lousy hearing?' The group twigged, but did not contribute to what was likely to become a really interesting family tiff. 'I don't believe it!' continued the Minotaur, apparently shocked into sanity.

'I thought we'd said it wasn't the name after all? You agreed it was your hideous def—'

'*Yes, mother! All right!* That is hardly the point at issue now. The name didn't exactly help, did it?' His voice was rising, along with his dander. 'Where did I get my intelligence from?' he inquired, waving both arms about in a growing frenzy of emotion and ignoring his father's thusly renewed interest. 'What did you imagine a bloody bull was going to say? Marmaduke? Nathaniel? Cholmondley?'

Each suggestion was accompanied by a flapping of the arms, and the impetus disrupted his balance enough to move him away from Gloria. Wilverton looked on with concentration on his face, but neither moved nor spoke. The Bull edged forward as the fuzzy red thing darted about.

'Well, I'm sorry, dear.'

'One second of regret cannot make up for a lifetime of misery, mother,' he told her philosophically.

'No, I expect not, dear. But you wouldn't have wanted to be called "Moo", would you?'

'That doesn't matter, mother!' he shouted, waving his arms just once more. The Bull began moving a little quicker, and the Minotaur's attention was drawn to two points, both approaching him at ever increasing speed. 'Oh *ZEUS!*'

He made to move out of the way, when a flash like a heliograph passed across his eyes, and he looked up involuntarily. He saw a woman looking out of a second-floor window directly at him and raising her dark glasses so that he could see her eyes.

It was the last glance he ever took. By the time the Bull hit him, he was nothing more than a stone statue, holding a cape out slightly, but not nearly enough, to one side, and with a stone gun in his other hand. The face was raised, and there was just the embryo of an expression of horror on it, the features having been frozen just before it could grow.

After the Bull hit him, all those things remained, but not

necessarily in the same configuration, and scattered over a rather greater area than the Minotaur was wont normally to occupy.

Paz screamed.

So did the Challenger, except it used more gamma rays than the Queen.

'Arnold!' hissed Wilverton, grabbing the android's arm and drawing him close. 'Go and get Gloria, and don't look up at anything; just keep your eyes down as much as possible, okay?'

Arnold looked at him, then glanced at Gloria sitting serenely amid the rubble of her former abductor. There was one other being present – one that mattered, anyway.

'There is a rampaging bull the size of a small village over there.'

'Correct, Arnold. You've clearly lost none of your perspicacity in recent days. Now go and get Gloria and don't look up. Please. You're the strongest.'

The android looked less than enamoured with the idea but complied; not because of the compliment, it was just that doing what they wanted occasionally served to keep them off balance. He moved towards Gloria whilst trying to keep away from the beast, which was in the process of turning round no more than a couple of yards away from her.

All the other occupants of the courtyard were looking at what was left of the Minotaur. None had turned to look up at the window, and none had spoken. Paz had not even moved.

'Ship!' said Wilverton, clearly, but not shouting. And there she was, hanging above them.

She was far too high for the steps to reach the ground, and far too large to fit into the courtyard. A beam of light extended from the Ship's underside and hit the ground just in front of where the majority of the group were standing. There in front of them was a sort of transparent lift, made from light and looking insubstantial. Wilverton led them towards it, as Arnold reached Gloria.

The Bull could find nothing red and fluttering to occupy its neurons, but there was sufficient adrenaline flowing around its system to prevent it returning to its eternal meal. It waved its head from side to side, and noticed a slight movement as Arnold hoisted Gloria into his arms, keeping a very careful watch on the horns. The horns stopped when they were pointing at him, presenting something of a dilemma. By moving, he would attract the thing's further attention. By staying where he was, he was logically unlikely to reach the safety of the Ship. He thought for a moment, then held Gloria out at arm's length to the Bull.

Whether it was the smell, or whether the feeble eyesight and even feebler brain had combined in a triumph of recognition, the Bull's demeanour changed. Arnold could see its memory centres waking up and sending messages all over its body, particularly to that area where it and Gloria had first met, as it were.

'Moo,' it said, softly.

Paz laid a hand on its neck and started stroking it gently, tears running down her cheeks. 'Oh, look what you've done,' she said, but there was no real reproof in her voice. 'You've broken the Minotaur, you clumsy thing. I know it wasn't your fault, but . . . well, on top of everything else; poor Sue.'

Arnold edged away, and the Bull made no attempt to follow, its senses confusing the present Paz with the past Gloria. As Arnold reached the haven of the Ship's light lift, he heard Paz speaking softly.

'I don't think we should make another one. Not after all this.'

It sounded like she was weakening.

XXVII

No-one spoke until they were safely in the Ship's control room, and Arnold had placed Gloria gently in one of the armchairs. It was Carlton who broke the silence as Wilverton crouched next to her and felt her pulse, for want of something more medically meaningful.

'So what the hell happened there? How come the Minotaur turned to stone?'

Wilverton looked up sideways at him. 'You remember when we first got to the palace we saw the estate agent in the courtyard?' Carlton nodded. 'Did you notice something funny about her hair, the way it moved on its own?' Carlton nodded again, and enlightenment dawned.

'Medusa?'

'Medusa. The Minotaur was the only one who was looking in that direction, and she must have been looking out of a window or something, without her glasses on. That's why I told you not to look up, Arnold.'

'Why not tell all of us not look up?' asked Fission accusingly, reaching her flash-point will unerring accuracy. 'Because if I had told you all not to look up, the first thing that someone would have done – and I'm not suggesting anyone in particular – would have been to look up. I thought it better not to take the chance.'

Fission gave a one-word description of his reasoning.

'If I tell you all now not to think of an elephant riding a bicycle.' He paused. 'How many of you thought of an elephant riding a bicycle?' Another pause, reminiscent of those in the classroom where nobody wants to be the first to own up that they didn't understand.

'I did,' said Carlton, the firmest ego – all right, the largest ego – amongst the lot, well able to withstand any possible dents. Or possibly an ego keen to tell the others that it was well able to withstand any possible dents.

'So did I,' admitted Curtis, on whose ego there wasn't enough room for further dents to make an impression.

'Arnold?'

'I thought of an elephant sitting on a bicycle, but not actually riding it.'

Wilverton smiled, and looked at Fission.

'I think nothing like,' she huffed.

Wilverton maintained the smile, but managed to change its quality so that it oozed knowing disbelief, then turned back to Gloria, his past actions justified.

'I don't know what's wrong with her.' He crouched again and took hold of her wrist. 'She's obviously paralysed, so I suppose it must be some sort of drug, but just what, and what we do about it, is anyone's guess. Ship?'

'Yes, Thomas, what can I do for you?'

'Can you do anything about Gloria?'

'Well, let me see. Yes, I think so.' A five-fingered shape lit up on the wall next to Gloria's chair, and Wilverton placed her hand on it.

'Oh, Thomas!' shrieked Gloria in Wilverton's ear, the sound shooting to the pit of his stomach and turning it to water. 'You saved me! I knew you would.' She threw her arms around his neck and planted a kiss so deeply that it would need an exceptional growing season to get back above the ground.

Wilverton's reaction was necessarily muted, but those of Carlton and Curtis were very obvious from the green tinges which sprung to their faces. The words were left to Fission, predictably.

'Not just him, melons. All look for you.'

Gloria surfaced, and Wilverton gulped a deep breath in case there was more of the same on the way.

'Oh, I know!' She beamed happily at each of them in turn. 'And it's ever so sweet of you! You're all very brave. I hope it wasn't too difficult.'

'Of course fonking difficult!'

'We managed to come through it,' said Wilverton soothingly, 'And everyone played their part.'

'Fission opened *two* doors!' said Arnold. '*And* closed one!' He extracted the expected response, but did not enter the slanging match.

'We blow Game,' finished Fission, preparing to rub salt into

Gloria's healing wounds. 'Ship sounded bell when we supposed to continue tasks; we too busy looking for you. Too late now.' Gloria looked inconsolable.

'I heard the gong sound. I thought it might be the Ship, but I didn't know what it meant. I'm sorry, it's all my fault, isn't it?'

'Yes,' said Fission.

'No,' said Wilverton, wishing Fission could keep her vitriol bottled for more than a couple of seconds at a stretch. 'Of course it's not your fault. The Minotaur kidnapped you – there was nothing you could do about that – and we all decided that we should come and find you. If it's anyone's fault, it's ours for not finding you quickly enough.' He wiped an embryonic tear from the corner of Gloria's eye and smiled at her.

'But we've lost the Game,' she said, not yet mollified. 'We're all going to die.'

'Well, yes, there is that,' conceded Wilverton, inspiring another grunt from Fission. 'But we're not dead yet. And where there's life, there's hope.'

'Does that let me out?' asked Arnold.

Wilverton ignored him. 'Has Biondor been here, Ship?'

'Biondor is here now,' came the tranquil voice of the elegant alien. They turned to see him standing in front of the main viewing window, through which shone the globe of Callia, its blue seas and white clouds looking almost like Earth as the old red binary had dipped behind the planet. It was quite breathtaking if one had time to stand and stare. One didn't, unfortunately.

'What's the situation?' asked Wilverton.

'You still have a couple of zarbs left to complete your tasks. It is not over yet.'

'But we've only completed five of them,' said Curtis, once again feeling that he should be taking more of the lead now that they were back on the Ship. He kept having this feeling, bless him. A triumph of optimism over reality. Actually it was a triumph of ingrained parental example, but Curtis had never gone near a psychiatrist's note book. Probably just as well – there were few enough trees left as it was.

'Indeed. The sixth task, however, is to win the Rigan Barbarian Chess Challenge. The seventh is to win the Bulphusian Game with No Rules nor Any Discernible Point, and the eighth is to triumph in the Adulterers' Last Chance

Game of Shayblon.' He looked at them one by one, and saw hope being rekindled in all but one face; that of Gloria.

'Oh, dear.'

'But we've done all of those!' Curtis voiced what everyone else had realized. Gloria looked confused. Things were definitely getting back to normal.

'We had to do all of those while we were trying to find you,' said Wilverton. 'I'll explain later.'

'You have completed those, as you say,' repeated Biondor.

A number of times, earthlings have speculated on the possibilities of time travel, and have generally concluded that it isn't possible – at least in the universe the traveller happens to inhabit, where, let's face it, it would be most useful – because going back into the past might result in catastrophic unforeseen circumstances for the future. It's not so much killing your own grandfather, since that can generally be avoided by any but the clumsiest time traveller, despite the fact that it is the reason cited so often that you could be forgiven for thinking that the act is more or less compulsory.

No.

It's moving a stone with your foot which puts it in such a position that the man who was going to miss it now puts his foot on it, and twists his ankle and falls over and rips his new trousers, and therefore has a row with his wife, who then goes to work in an absolutely foul mood so that she doesn't conduct the delicate nuclear disarmament negotiations quite as well as she would otherwise have done – in fact she calls the Chinese delegate a short, fat, slant-eyed fart factory – and China, as a result, drops the bomb on her country and the whole thing escalates into the war to end not only all wars but all peaces as well because there aren't any people left to have either.

See?

If, however, you *can* foresee all those possible occurrences, then not only can you avoid grand-patricide, you can also avoid moving the stone as well. So you will believe that time travel is possible, and you will therefore find a way to do it. Because that's what it takes.

The Champion could foresee just about everything. It would therefore have complete confidence in creating, say, a little man in a suit and tie, knocking on a door in the middle of a Labyrinth . . .

215

Damned clever, these Supreme Beings!

Which wasn't quite the thought that pulsed through the Challenger in enough microwaves to cook half a planet.

'The ninth task,' Biondor went on, 'was to eliminate the Minotaur, which you have also completed, with the help of the Cretin Bull. That leaves just one task to be completed.

'The tenth task is to eliminate the Gorgon Medusa.'

There was a period of silence while they accepted this piece of information, delivered in the same voice Biondor would have used were he reading out a grocery list or giving notice at the end of the Universe. It was Gloria who spoke first.

'Eliminate?' she said, with some doubt. It *might* have more than one meaning.

'Means "kill", mega-mams,' Fission educated her.

'Oh, dear.' Gloria was to harming any living creature what Genghis Khan was to keeping them safe and warm. 'And Medusa is the thing that turned the Minotaur into stone?' She looked at Wilverton for confirmation that she had got it right. I mean, the Minotaur had been a horrid thing, and she had disliked him – already it had lessened from 'hate' – but she would not have really wished death on him, and for all she knew Medusa might be the salt of the earth.

'Well, at least we know where we can find her.' Wilverton tried to sound cheerful. Gloria turned a querulous expression towards him. 'We saw her in the courtyard of Paz's palace. She's not difficult to spot; she's got snakes for hair.'

'Ooh!' Gloria's eyes suddenly tried to qualify as her biggest organs. They didn't stand a chance. 'I've seen her! She was in the courtyard where you found me.'

Arnold's eyes mirrored her own.

'So we know both that she's in the courtyard of Paz's palace, *and* that she's in the courtyard of Paz's palace! Well, that narrows it down. If we can just find where those two lines meet . . .'

'Shut up, Arnold.' Wilverton squeezed Gloria's hand in reassurance, and looked at Biondor. 'I suppose the trands have got this far without too much bother?'

Chess was not a game prevalent on Trand. Given that it involves deep and largely genteel consideration of any number of

216

hypothetical moves, it was less likely to be right up a trand's street than right up a trand's nose.

Barbarian chess was closer, but what kind of fight had armour and swords and stuff? A weakling's kind of fight, that's what!

Trandhargs, now *that* was a game!

No weapons allowed, no implements to use, no projectiles to throw. Just good old bodies trying to get from one side of the board to the other while more good old bodies tried to stop them. The fact that none of the bodies was particularly good any more and that certainly none was ever likely to qualify as old, didn't negate the description.

The two team members who were chosen for that game had a rare old time, and were soon back on their Ship, where their cuts and at least one dismemberment were treated with all the technological advantage the Ship possessed, and the help of a large trowel.

A jeu sans frontières was rather more up a trand's street, but thanks to the selective influence of the Champion over the contents of round two, they didn't get one.

What they got was an art contest.

Isn't that nice!

Dainty little paint brushes and an expansive canvas to cover with watercolours. Three contestants and a panel of judges to decide the winner.

Well, of course, the trand was enchanted.

All right, he wasn't.

The trand wanted to win the contest by eliminating the opposition, but that, apparently, would have led to further contestants replacing them. He wouldn't win that way.

So in the end he painted. Not necessarily what a human would call painting – he splashed what looked like the aftermath of a spectacular bout of dysentery onto the canvas with the finesse of an apprentice mugger. Also onto himself and his opponents in roughly equal quantities.

And he won. The judges were unanimous.

The trand had told them what would happen if he lost.

He had also described lucidly how it would happen, and what he would use to make it happen. Given that the judges were Bostals – that race which had conspicuously inspired the Galactically respected work on evolution by Darles Charwin,

217

Survival of the Ones with the Biggest Dongs – they weren't about to take a chance that he was bluffing.

The Talukan Chow Challenge had no such restrictions for an enthusiastically homicidal trand, and it didn't need the inadvertent elimination of opponents favoured by Curtis; the trand was very advertent indeed. The main problem was whether to polish off the food before attacking the opponents, or vice versa.

Of course, it wasn't just a simple sit-down meal with knife, fork, spoon and serviette. Several of the dishes were still alive, and had very strong views about what should be on the menu.

Carlton might have known how they felt.

The trand might have known how they felt as well. A few minutes later she certainly knew how they tasted.

Nor were any of the courses prepared in a way that made them anything like appetizing, but again the trand did not seem to mind, and given that the average trand's method of turning a meal into a gourmet event was to put it on a plate, this was no great surprise.

In less than an hour the food was gone, along with a good portion of the contestants, and the trand diner was taking her siesta, snoring like a champion sow with adenoid problems.

That only left the Wrang, half trand, half harg, now genetically mutated to genius on the planet Fillae, and lying in wait with an electronic arsenal that made a battery of laser canons look like a mushy pea shooter. Lying in wait for a measly couple of unarmed and unsuspecting trands.

And what had become of this Wrang with all its newly acquired advanced technology and brain-power?

Pulp.

'Yes,' said Biondor.

'Pity,' said Wilverton. 'But it wouldn't have made a very good finish otherwise, I suppose. And I guess this isn't the last book in the series either.' He appeared almost to be talking to himself, looking at the ground and mumbling, but then his voice rose in volume and confidence. 'So that means we're going to make it. Let's go for it!'

'You have time for sustenance and possibly a short rest, should you so wish.' Biondor apparently put the thoughts of some of the others into words. Wilverton could do with a very long quiet rest, they thought, in a darkened room.

'I must leave you now; I have to cry out of a statue on the planet Farland.' He paused, and the skin wrinkled where he would have kept his eyebrows. 'It's not so much the claustrophobia; it's twisting the nipple to induce the tears. I will bid you fare well.' And he was gone.

A short silence followed his departure, somehow befitting his powerful presence. Biondor could say 'wobbly-plops' and make it sound deep and meaningful. Then Wilverton started things off again.

'So what can you tell us about Medusa, Ship?'

'You already know that Gorgon has the power to render flesh as a stone should one look upon her eyes.'

'Presumably we can look upon her eyes in reflection without turning to stone?'

'That is correct, but I am not allowed to furnish you with a device for doing so. Such a thing you must find for yourself.'

'I think we get on with it,' said Fission.

'I think we would do better to eat something and have a little rest first,' replied Wilverton. Fission started to bristle again – she should have been born a porcupine, thought Wilverton – and he decided to play it down. 'We're not as young as you, remember.' He smiled. It didn't work.

'How old you, grandpa?'

'Well, by your reckoning, we're all around the four hundred and thirty mark, thanks to Einstein, and I for one feel it. Look, don't make it difficult again.' A pleading note entered his voice, and it seemed to have some effect on Fission.

'Povvos,' she conceded. Well, by her standards it was a concession, anyway.

'What's a povvo?' asked Gloria, while they ate.

Fission looked up with a mouthful of kelp salad, which she swallowed, then waved her fork around as if trying to skewer the answer. 'Comes from "poverty".' Gloria immediately made a porcupine look like a pussy cat – what else?

'Being poor is something to be abused on Earth now, is it?'

'No-one poor!' Fission realized that she had little choice but to provide an explanation. 'All get what we need. You want more, you work for it, get money. You lie around doing nothing – weakling, lazy or something – you don't get more money.

Relatively poor, but their own fault.' Interesting! they thought. No obscenities!

'So it's not someone called Luke, at all, is it?' asked Wilverton, realization dawning.

'What?' She was beginning to look irritable again. Well, it had been a while; whole minutes in fact!

'Luke. When you say Luke you're saying Luc, as in Lucre, aren't you?'

She nodded. 'Sort of joke. I think.' Either it was lost in history or Fission wasn't good at recognizing jokes. 'It stuck.'

'Is it nice on Earth now?' asked Gloria, spotting a glint of sunshine through Fission's storm-cloud clothing and knowing instinctively that it would do Fission good to talk, to be forced into dealing with them.

'Don't know. Never been anywhere else. Nothing to compare.'

That was reasonable, and she still seemed receptive. There were so many things they wanted to know. What else could they ask to take advantage of this strangely good mood?

'Excuse me?'

Someone had thought of something. Unfortunately, it was Arnold.

'You haven't just been visited by the spirit of Christmas future, have you?'

She wouldn't get it.

'Fonk off!' She got it. 'Let me eat.'

They ate.

Immediately they finished, Fission called in the debts made due by her explanation by pointing out that while they were eating, they were also resting. It was true, and at the end of their meal they were feeling a little better. But well enough to tackle Medusa?

'What does everybody think?' asked Curtis.

'Anyone got plergs?' asked Fission.

'Plergs?' queried Wilverton with suspicion.

'Plergs,' she repeated. Surely everyone knew what plergs were; but then of course they probably didn't have them when this lot left Earth. 'Plergs pills give extra energy; from "plus ergs". All kids back home use when out for night.'

'I'm not putting anything in my body that is anything but natural,' stated Gloria emphatically.

Arnold glanced at Wilverton and wondered whether to say something extremely rude, but the Ship didn't give him the chance.

'I am not sure that is a very good idea, Fission,' she said, and such was the impartial care which the Ship exuded that Fission did not do her porcupine bit. 'Such substances can severely impair judgement, particularly of the consequences of actions. In such situations as you are likely to meet, such impairment could prove most dangerous.'

'Fatal' was not a nice word, and the Ship did not use it.

'Maybe right,' said Fission, thereby drowning any other response in a sea of shock. It was a bit like seeing the Chancellor standing up in the House and saying, 'Look, chaps, I've made a frightful balls-up of the economy, and I'd just like to say that I'm awfully sorry, but that we're all human.'

The silence gave Fission the chance to continue, in more characteristic vein.

'Can't take chance of sleeping, though. Don't know how long this take. Got to start. No profit sitting here.'

'Fission's right,' conceded Wilverton, and sighed heavily. 'We've got to give it a go, no matter how tired we are. We can't afford to wait any longer.'

Fission looked as near to pleased as she had since they had first seen her. For a moment she wondered whether to apologize for the way she had been acting and explain that she wasn't always like this, but that Biondor had snatched her from the world just after some genetically engineered beauty had snatched the world from her.

But no. She wasn't *that* pleased.

XXVIII

There was this circle of trands, all facing inwards, and all staring at the ground as though they were praying, or as if they had all been naughty.

The first of these possibilities required a god to be prayed to; and, while they had plenty of mythology, the trands didn't respect, let alone worship, anything which they couldn't feel and preferably wrestle to within an inch of its life. So that was out. The second required recognition that something could actually be naughty, and then that it was therefore something of which they should be ashamed; and the trands defined naughty as five less than fivey. So that was out, too.

Which left, by process of elimination, just the one possible reason – that they could not afford to look up because they would then meet the glare of a creature whose stare would turn them instantly into stone.

It was this creature which currently formed the centre-piece of the tableau.

The creature, which in trand mythology was known as a Gregon, represented the only direct link between the legends of Earth and Trand – a fact which raises fascinating questions about the origins of Galactic mythology; questions which will forthwith be addressed at absolutely no length whatsoever.

She looked from lowered head to lowered head and waited for one of them to rise, so that she could immobilize its owner and scarper, bloody quick.

But the heads did not rise, they stayed low, and approached. Then they accelerated.

Now, trands only move at more than a few miles per hour if they've fallen off a cliff, so this might not conjure up an impression of great danger. However, super-tankers don't exactly rush about breathlessly either, but if you get caught in a sandwich between a couple of them you'll soon revise your opinion of speed versus danger.

The Gregon had never seen a super-tanker, but she recognized the danger and turned every which way, trying to find a chink which promised to become an exit. But any chink which might have existed quickly became just an ex-chink before she had the remotest chance to make a dash for it.

She screamed, and one of the trands actually looked up at the noise, rather foolishly when all is said and done. And for the trand suddenly everything *had* been all said and done, discounting going hard, grey and still. The Gregon prepared to make a dash, but it was too late, and the scene ended with a rather unpleasant crunching and squelching noise.

The leading trand punched the air in celebration, but that wasn't nearly satisfying enough, so he punched a couple of his colleagues as well, as playfully as trands get. Soon they were all embroiled in quite bloody mutual congratulation.

On the pavement outside Paz's palace the heroic little group huddled closer together as a brief shower fell from a sky with little blue bits between dark clouds. It dampened more than their clothes – leaving their spirits lower than when the Ship had delivered them back to the ground.

'I'm not having a go at anybody,' said Carlton, 'but I think we should have worked out some sort of plan of action.'

There were an awful lot of statues in the street, Gloria noticed, and not of anything particularly special. Just people, really; some begging, or selling from stalls, or collecting for charity with little stone flag trays. Odd.

Hardly any other pedestrians were in evidence, but one did saunter past, his shoulders hunched against the elements. As Gloria watched him, he stopped and opened an umbrella, the handle of which did not stop in his hand but carried on behind him and disappeared into the back of his overcoat. Quite plainly, the umbrella was an extension of his tail. He returned Gloria's glance, and winked. Then he smacked his lips, looked her squarely in the chest, winked again, and moved on.

Gloria's eyes widened in surprise and then in recognition.

'That was . . .' she started, but got no further. Arnold had said that you could not spot changelings walking down the street, and Arnold was clever, so it couldn't have been. No-one asked her what 'that was'.

'The first thing to do is to find out where she is,' said

223

Wilverton. 'She may still be at the palace, and our only lead is Paz so we should ask her first. What we do from there depends on what she tells us.'

He rang the bell, then stood back and waited as the shower briefly became heavier, and played a monotone pizzicato on his head. It had not finished more than a couple of bars before the door opened to reveal a comfortably familiar Queen Pasiphae in apron and curlers. Neither the apron nor the headscarf which covered the curlers was dark enough to suggest mourning.

'Hello, ducks,' she said. Gloria looked around for some ducks. 'Well, come on in, you're all wet.' She held the door wide, ushered them inside and led them through to the throne room.

Only then did Wilverton manage, 'Hello, Paz,' trying to put a certain sombreness into the two words, which does present something of a challenge. 'We're very sorry about your loss.'

Paz frowned. 'Yes, but perhaps it is all for the best. He never was very well, you know, and the doctors said the strain might be too much at any time. If only he'd faced up to the truth, it might all have been different; but then I suppose you wouldn't with a face like that, would you?'

The smile reappeared, but it was clear that someone had gone round behind it and pushed really hard to get it out there.

'I don't know *what* I'm going to do with all the carrots.'

'Carrots?' asked Gloria innocently, but remembering one with dislike.

'He loved his carrots, you see, love, and I can't stand the things. I've got cupboards full of them. I suppose I could always take them back to the café, go back to the old place . . .' She pulled a handkerchief from her sleeve, blew her nose noisily, then wiped her eyes.

'I'm ever so sorry. Silly of me. It's just that I can't help but blame myself. If I hadn't . . . well, Sue wouldn't have been born, and Minos would still be here, and . . .' She blew her nose again, then got behind the smile once more and heaved. 'Still, no use crying over spilt milk!' Or spilt bits of Minotaur, either.

A thought of great clarity shot into Gloria's head, and echoed in the empty spaces. Paz hid her grief with a forced and wordy jollity; Fission hid hers behind a blustering anger. They had different ways of doing it, as suited their personalities, and different griefs, but they were the same, really. She'd check it with Thomas later, she thought, not quite appreciating that

Wilverton was to people's insides what a chiropodist was to their scalp complaints.

'Tea?'

The fast change of subject caught Gloria unawares, and she spluttered an acceptance, while all the others declined. The mugs brought for their earlier visit were still on the table, and Paz filled one of these from the pot which stood next to them.

'Milk and sugar?'

'Yes please,' said Gloria, looking at the liquid with some trepidation. 'Two lumps.'

'What else,' muttered Fission.

'We were wondering,' said Wilverton, diffusing a possible situation, 'whether the estate agent was still here.'

Paz slopped some oddly coloured milk into the oddly coloured tea, and frowned. 'No, I don't think so, dear. She left some time ago.' She handed the mug to Gloria, who took it as if it were very much alive and showing its teeth. Yellow ones. 'She seemed happy enough.' Which was more than Gloria did.

'Happy?' said Wilverton suspiciously.

'Yes.' Paz settled herself in an armchair and took a sip of her own steaming brew. Gloria watched in case she turned into something with rather more hair than was normal for a human. 'I accepted her offer – well, her client's offer – and she went away. I'm going to use the money to go back south. See if I can find Minos. You know.' She squeezed the handkerchief, privately.

'I see,' said Wilverton. 'Why do you think she – or her client – wants to buy the palace?'

'Beats me, duck. I suppose there can't be that many furnished palaces around at the moment. She's certainly interested in it all; keeps poking about all over the place, looking into cupboards and cabinets and stuff.'

'Hmm. It's odd, though,' mused Wilverton. 'It seems so out in the open, and Medusa would want to stay hidden, wouldn't she?'

'Is that who's buying it, then?' asked Paz. 'Medusa?'

'I think it is, yes.'

'Only the estate agent hasn't said who she's working for. Not that I mind. I mean, when they offer you that sort of money, then you don't ask too many questions, do you? What I can't understand is why she keeps looking around when she's already made her offer.' Wilverton held up a hand to stop her so he could check on the points raised so far. 'It's just down the corridor, dear.'

'No, that's all right. Don't you know who the estate agent was?'

'No, dear. Should I?'

'That was Medusa.'

'Was it? You mean she hasn't got a client after all? She's buying the palace herself?'

'She turns people to stone,' continued Wilverton, and paused while the significance of the ability worked its way through the interlocked morass of thoughts in the Queen's head. As it did so, her expression changed to one of understanding and a certain vexation.

'You mean she. . . ?' Wilverton nodded. 'Oh dear.'

Wilverton thought it warranted more than 'Oh dear', but Paz must express her grief in her own way. Or not, he thought.

' "Oh dear"!' said Fission, although 'said' might be understating it a bit. Never mind apoplexy, Fission looked like she was going to have several poplexies at the same time. 'She must die for what she did!'

Wilverton sighed. Fission was about as subtle as a sailor with a six-hour pass.

'Well, you can't do that,' said Paz in a far more reasonable tone. 'I mean, she's made a good offer for the place, if it *is* her that's buying it, and killing her won't bring Sue back. I need the money to go back south. I've got to go back south.'

Wilverton glanced at Carlton. This was not good news. Paz was the only link they had with Medusa, and they needed her help at least to find the creature, if not to do the deed.

'How much did she offer?' asked Carlton.

'Well, not quite as much as I'd hoped for, of course. I was asking the Apples of the Hesperides, but I suppose that was a bit over the top for this place – I mean, it's all very well having the biggest basement in the world, but if it's a maze, then you can't very well use it because once you've put something down there you can never find it again, can you? – and she offered the Belt of Hippolyte, which is worth nearly as much as the Apples when all's said and done, especially when the more Apples you get off the tree the lower their value's going to be, so I thought I might as well take it. I don't think I'll get a better offer, not in the current economic climate, as everyone keeps saying.' She took a breath,

226

refuting the forming theory that oxygen was infused through her skin to enable constant exhalation.

Carlton seized his chance. 'What about this?' he asked, and held out the Jewel of Altares.

Paz's eyes opened wide. 'Well, numb my piles! The Jewel of Altares!'

'Er, yes,' said Carlton, wondering where she managed to pick up both the regal phrase and the knowledge of what he held in his outstretched palm.

'Where'd you steal that?'

They all looked momentarily guilty, except Arnold.

'Altares, oddly enough,' he replied. 'People keep having this trouble with the Jewel *of Altares* –'

'It wasn't exactly stealing . . .' Wilverton interrupted before Arnold managed to alienate their necessary ally, then stopped when he realized that it *was* exactly stealing.

'Nothing wrong in stealing,' Paz told him. 'That's how most things change hands round here. So long as you didn't hurt the last owner?' She looked stern, and Wilverton quickly assured her that Cerberus was, as far as he knew, alive, well, and, er, travelling.

'Are you offering me that for the old place, then?' She looked from the Jewel to Carlton's face. 'Not that it isn't worth it, of course!'

'Well, yes, I think I might be offering you this,' he replied a little uncertainly, and looked involuntarily to Wilverton for guidance.

'Let's assume that we are for the moment,' said Wilverton. 'I still want to work out why Medusa wants this place so badly. You say you are selling the palace furnished?'

'That's right, dear.'

'She was looking for something!' Gloria said so suddenly that next to her Carlton visibly jumped, then quickly checked to see who was looking at him. No-one was, for which he was unusually grateful. 'When I saw her, she was looking for something.'

'Hmm.' Wilverton looked around the room, in thought rather than in an effort to see something which might explain Medusa's interest. 'You obviously know all the things you've got here, but what about the Labyrinth? Do you know what's down there?'

Paz shrugged. 'No idea, dear.'

There was a sound as of an old dirty oil lamp falling from a coffee table to a marble floor, and everyone looked to see an old dirty oil lamp lying on the marble floor next to a coffee table. Its twin remained on the table, half hidden, and held securely in place, by a pile of magazines. As it lay on the floor, the lamp managed to look Significant.

Paz ignored it. Every now and then the law of gravity asserted itself over the piles of rubbish which she collected, and she was happy to let it do so. The resultant rearrangement of items was no less tidy than it had been, and it was nice to have a change of scenery.

Most of the others ignored it as well, except Gloria.

'I bet that's a magic lamp.' There was immediately just enough possibility of her being correct for no-one to belittle the idea.

'And you think that's what Medusa is after?' asked Wilverton. 'You could well be right.' Gloria had been right before. Not often, admittedly, but it had happened. She smiled at him and he crossed his hands in his lap.

'Why would she want to buy the place just for a lamp?' asked Carlton. 'She could steal it, couldn't she?'

'That's why she keeps looking around,' said Wilverton. 'She doesn't want to buy it at all. It's just an excuse to get inside.'

'Well, that doesn't matter.' Paz sounded quite happy, and they looked at her questioningly. 'Well, the hunk here,' and she indicated Carlton, who swelled at the compliment from a middle-aged bull fancier, 'has just offered me the Jewel of Altares, hasn't he! I don't need Medusa any more.'

'Rub it,' suggested Fission to Gloria, ignoring the last comment.

'All right, I will.' Gloria left her seat, grateful to get away from the tea-named liquid which still seethed malevolently in the mug Paz had given her, and picked up the lamp. It certainly did look like the traditional home of a genie, so much so that it would come as a bit of a surprise if the traditional rub did not produce one. She held it in one hand and rubbed it gently with the other, a caress rather than a cleaning effort. Quietly – so quietly that only Gloria heard it, and even then it might have been imagined – the lamp giggled. No genie appeared, though.

'Nice try, melons.'

Gloria's cheeks flushed as she laid the lamp back on the table from which it had jumped. 'What about the other one?' she said, ignoring Fission as best she could and spotting the second lamp as it apparently tried to hide beneath its blanket of magazines.

'I've only got the one, duck,' said Paz.

'No, the other lamp,' persisted Gloria, wondering why Paz assumed she was referring to a duck.

'That's what I said – I've only got that one.'

'What's this, then?' And Gloria pulled the shy implement from its coverings.

'Oo-er. I wonder where that came from.'

Gloria performed the same action with the second lamp, which was identical to the first down to the ingrained dirt, testimony that it had not been rubbed in a very long time. The response was not identical.

There was no exudation of coloured smoke solidifying into a substantial form, but half-way through her rub Gloria found a being standing next to her. It was a man, some seven feet tall, dressed from head to foot in long flowing purple robes of a lightweight material. His head bore a turban of the same stuff, whilst his shoes were a deeper colour and extended to elongated and upturned points. These were not the clothes of a conservative dresser. They had undergone so many other-wordly experiences that his appearance was about as shocking as the latest ministerial sex scandal.

The only things Wilverton knew about genii were that they were magical beings able to grant wishes, and that they did not take wives nor beget children. From the look of this particular specimen, he was not a bit surprised.

'I am your servant, Master,' spake the genie, in gentle and rather high-pitched tones for a man of his size. He looked at Gloria's face, then slightly downwards. 'Mistress,' he amended, and sounded somewhat disappointed.

'Are you?' said Gloria, still absently rubbing the lamp in her hand.

'I think you're mine, actually, big boy,' said Paz. 'The lamp belongs to me, you see.'

The genie bowed flamboyantly to the Queen.

'In that case, I am your servant, Mistress. What is it you wish?'

'Well, nothing for the moment, thanks, but don't go away; I'm sure I'll think of something.' A cow-suit, probably, thought more than one.

'Well, that answers our question,' said Wilverton. 'Well done,

229

Gloria, you *were* right.' Gloria swelled, and blushed, and fluttered her eyelids a bit, and thanked him, and smiled encouragingly. We must get back to the Ship fast, he thought.

'We could give her the other lamp,' said Paz. 'They look pretty much the same, don't they?' Gloria bent to retrieve the lamp for comparison, and hesitated.

'It's gone.' And it had. She had laid it on a spare corner of table, and that was now empty. The lamp had not fallen, and had not wriggled under the magazines.

It was gone.

Curiouser and curiouser.

'I'm a little worried about that lamp,' said Curtis, and looked it – although as a yardstick this didn't stretch further than about a foot, since he rarely looked anything else. 'It was a bit too much of a coincidence, if you ask me. It could be a trap.'

'Povvo,' commented Fission, predictably.

'It wasn't a coincidence,' said Gloria. 'It was Yazocks.' She sounded positive, which was slightly odd.

'What makes you think that?' Wilverton conceded in his own mind that the evidence did not deny the possibility, but also did little to confirm it. Gloria looked flustered, which was a far more comfortable position for her companions. Telling them that the now missing lamp had giggled when she rubbed it did not strike her as a good way of convincing them – they'd only make fun of her again, except Thomas.

'I don't know, it just was,' she argued, with what has to be admitted as a marked lack of conviction, not to mention logic and persuasiveness.

'Well,' continued Wilverton, after a moment's thought, during which he decided against a detailed examination of the theory, 'it doesn't really matter whether it was Yazocks at this stage – although I hope Gloria is right. It doesn't change what we have to do, and we still have to decide how we're going to do it.'

The doorbell rang, and they all looked at each other.

'Now,' added Wilverton.

XXIX

'Oh, hello, dear.' Paz's voice floated back into the throne room. 'I didn't expect to see you back here, not until I'd contacted you with regard to your offer, you being the *estate agent* and everything. Do come in, and I'll take you through to the *courtyard*, since it's such a nice day and everything.'

'I'd rather like to have another look at the living quarters, if you don't mind.'

'Er, well, of course *I* don't mind, ducks, but the living quarters would. They're in one Hades of a mess. Let's just go down to the *courtyard*. You really must tell me who does your hair – it's not that Indian bloke with a flute is it . . .'

'Any ideas, then?' Wilverton asked as the voices trailed away.

'Has she been killed before?' asked Carlton.

'She didn't look like it,' said Gloria, with a slight frown.

'No, I meant on another planet, like Earth.'

'Yes, she has,' answered Wilverton. 'Perseus looked in a mirror – a shield, I believe – and the gods guided his sword arm when he swung it to chop her head off.' It didn't strike anyone, on first hearing, as perhaps the most infallible method of despatch.

'I have a slight problem with this,' he went on, and didn't wait for questions. 'I've never killed anything bigger than a wasp, and I'm not too sure that I can. And if that makes me a wimp – or a povvo,' he added hurriedly, with a glance at Fission, 'then that's just tough.'

'I feel the same,' said Gloria, to no-one's surprise.

'Er,' confirmed Curtis, who had never killed anything on purpose and only a couple of people accidentally.

'I must admit I'm not too happy about it myself,' said Carlton. 'When it comes right down to it, I don't know how I would react when push came to shove.' That was just what Curtis's 'Er' meant.

Paz re-entered the room, looking flustered, and with a hand pressed to her bosom through her pinny.

231

'Ooh, I don't mind telling you I was scared. The sun went in and I thought she was going to take those glasses off.'

'She won't do that to you,' Gloria told her, and it sounded like knowledge instead of a guess, so they all looked at her. 'She told her hair that she couldn't kill Paz. She said it wouldn't work if she killed her.'

'What wouldn't?'

'I don't know.'

'I wouldn't,' said the genie. 'Not if the lamp changes hands through the murder of the owner.'

'Why, have you got a union or something?' Carlton asked.

'It's in the rules.'

'Of the Game?'

'Of being a genie.'

'So *you* can kill her,' Carlton told Paz, pleased to find someone who might accept the buck.

'No I couldn't, dear. I couldn't kill anything. I like all living things.'

'The bigger, the better,' Arnold threw in.

'Job for me, then,' said Fission.

No-one asked if she had ever killed anyone. They didn't really want to know, because they were sure the answer would be 'yes' and she'd probably describe exactly how she did it.

'Arnold? You haven't been offered the chance.'

'I'm prepared to let Fission do it if she wants. I'm happy to watch proceedings' – given the absence of his favourite option: not to be there at all – 'and I'll be around if she gets into trouble.'

Not that he would do anything. Arnold was not sure whether Medusa's powers would work on his manufactured body, and was in no hurry to find out. Amongst the possible futures he had mapped out for himself in moments of quiet contemplation, spending the rest of time standing in one place with pigeons crapping on his head did not rate highly.

Curtis suddenly looked very excited and started fidgeting. Paz had already indicated the location of the toilet, so presumably he wanted to speak. They looked at him.

'Why can't he do it?' He pointed to the genie. 'Turn *her* into stone or something.'

'Genii do not kill!'

'They don't?'

'This one doesn't.' They weren't too surprised – if he was

feeling really aggressive they could probably persuade him to visit Medusa's flat and criticize her colour scheme.

'Oh.' Curtis subsided back into obscurity, which welcomed him home.

'What do you think you need in the way of weapons?' Wilverton asked Fission, tacitly accepting that the job was hers. 'Not that we actually have any.'

'Queen might have. If not, other queen can make some. Gun easiest. You have?' she asked Paz.

'Well, I'm not sure that I know really, dear. What is a gun, exactly?'

'That's no.' Fission turned to the genie, who was toying with the material of his dress. 'You make me a gun?'

The genie looked up. 'I can conjure anything my mistress desires,' he replied, with a theatrical sweep of his arm to indicate Paz. 'What is a gun, exactly?'

'Luc!'

'A gun is a tubular weapon, made of metal, from which small projectiles are expelled, usually by means of the ignition of an explosive charge,' described Wilverton. 'The holder of the weapon must have control of the ignition of that charge, generally by means of pulling a trigger. Is that enough for you?'

The genie frowned with concentration. 'I could try. If my mistress so wishes.'

'That's not gun, that's fonking antique!' The hitwoman protested. 'I want tachydis.'

You want what, sorry? asked the genie's eyebrows. He'd only just got his head round 'gun'.

'Breaks matter to component tachyons . . .' she started, then looked at him in silent exasperation. Patterned chiffon, flower arrangements, hair styling: these he could understand. Molecular structures, subatomic particles, strong and weak forces: no. 'Never mind. Just make gun.'

'You have a go, dear,' said Paz.

The genie bowed, and was enveloped in a cloud of green smoke. When this cleared, he stood behind something which looked like a small cannon, the muzzle of which was about three feet in length.

Those in the know looked at it with a certain scepticism. The shoulder holster would have to be something really special.

'Is that what you wanted, dear?' asked Paz.

233

'Fonk me.'

'It's a little on the large side,' explained Wilverton. 'What we want is something that can be carried in one hand, kept in a pocket if needs be. You seem to have the right idea, though.'

Another cloud of smoke, red this time, enveloped genie and giant hand gun. It cleared to show genie and small hand gun. Most of them expected to see something the size of a thimble, with the stopping power of a geriatric gnat, and were pleasantly surprised to see a compact-looking instrument.

No trigger though. Instead there was a small string hanging from the safe end which would presumably have to be pulled in order to push something out of the dangerous end. Fission demanded a demonstration in her own inimitable way. 'And point at wall,' she concluded. 'You can repair afterwards.'

The genie pointed the gun at a wall, and pulled the string. The projectile – a small sphere apparently made of something like putty – emerged from the gun as though it were afraid of the light, and hit the ground some six feet away, rolling to a halt very soon afterwards.

'Fonk me sideways,' said Fission.

'Succinctly put,' agreed Wilverton, then addressed the genie. 'The idea is to kill someone, you see – or some thing, to be more accurate. What you have invented there is a way of playing marbles whilst standing up. I think we need the projectile to be made of metal as well, and to travel at something like nine hundred miles per hour.' That sounded about right. 'Can you try again with those specifications?'

'Kill her!'

The snakes looked towards the palace, where Paz had hurriedly disappeared a few minutes before, eyes studiously pointing downwards.

'I can't! How many times must I tell you?'

'But ssshe ssstopsss usss getting the lamp. *He* will find usss! Persssseusss.'

The glasses came off for a wipe. The lead snake received a swipe, and one ear was subject to some feeble constriction for a while. Medusa waited patiently until it finished, making no threats, reminding herself how lucky she was. Her sister Telena had been born with a head full of asps. She had died young.

'I'll kill her after we've got the lamp.'

'Promissse?'

'Yes! I promise! Now stop that!'

'We mussst hurry, then.'

'All right!'

Medusa walked towards the palace.

'She's coming in,' Carlton warned, looking out of the window and wondering where he had seen the suit before.

'Paz, get her outside,' Fission ordered, and the Queen moved. A choice between Fission and Medusa wasn't an easy one.

The smoke cleared from around the genie, and the gun looked much the same. Fission frowned, but there was no time to test it.

'Give gun,' she said as Paz's voice trailed some inconsequential gibberish from downstairs. The genie held out the gun, and Fission snatched it. 'You all stay, I find better place to shoot.'

The leadership of the group appeared to have found a new temporary home as Fission swept from the room through a door opposite the one Paz had used. The rest of the group made their way tentatively to the windows, where they crouched and stared over the sills down to the still empty courtyard, give or take a large bull, bits of broken Minotaur, and Gardener at Rest. The genie watched them go, shrugged his shoulders, and disappeared. The lamp shook a little as he made himself comfortable.

Paz and Medusa entered the courtyard, the latter looking quite calm, apart from her hair, which moved around nervously, tasting the air for whatever it might find. Any expression she might have been wearing was well hidden behind her dark glasses.

Paz was the epitome of tension, her eyes darting about to all corners of the courtyard. Surely for Medusa not to realize that something was wrong, the watchers thought, her glasses would have to be completely opaque.

Attention was turned back to the bush behind which crouched Fission, and they waited for the bang.

If the fonking Queen would get out of the fonking way, then there was a chance that she could pull this fonking stupid string thing and fire the fonking gun.

Thought Fission, rather more succinctly.

Unfortunately, Paz was hovering around Medusa like a mother hen round her last remaining chick after a visit from the foxes, and there had so far been no chance of a safe shot. Not that

Fission was all that concerned for Paz's safety, but she was only going to get one try, since their excuse for a leader had forgotten to tell the genie that what they actually wanted, if not a tachydis, was a fonking machine gun.

Listening very carefully, the watchers at the windows could just about catch what was being said on the neatly cropped lawn. Neatly cropped by the Cretin Bull, who stood quietly in one corner and totally ignored proceedings in a way that only he could. Medusa had produced the papers which supposedly required the royal signature. Paz saw her chance to leave the field, as it were, clear.

'I'll just nip inside and get the royal seal, dear,' she said. 'Make it official, and everything. You wait here. Don't move.'

'Couldn't I come with you?'

'Well, you could, no doubt, dear, but you're not going to. Okay?'

Gloria watched as Paz began to move, and wondered what a royal seal would look like. Perhaps it balanced a crown on its nose instead of a big beach ball.

Medusa made to argue, but Gloria didn't hear what was said as her attention was taken by two things.

Firstly, Fission emerged into the open. The angle of attack had been made quite impossible by Paz, and she needed more room. She therefore displayed considerable courage by breaking cover. Not being overly courageous or completely stupid, she stayed in the shadows as far as she could, and took aim once again.

Secondly, it got lighter. Given that the sun was by now pouring its brightness down at full throttle in any case, this took some doing, but something managed it. Fission ignored it, but it stopped the two on the lawn, pulling their eyes to the sky, and those of the watchers inside followed.

It was impossible to say how big it was, or how far away – it might have been hanging just above the palace, or it might have been beyond the sun – but there was a circle in the sky; a white circle. It simply gushed whiteness, so clean, so pure that any other white you had ever seen would have looked really shabby in comparison; would have resigned on the spot and tried to join up as light grey; or it would have been so embarrassed at describing itself as white that it would probably have gone red.

We're talking white.

We're also talking hole. The thing was a hanging aperture, a white-walled and white-filled tunnel reaching up into infinity.

Fission wasn't talking anything. Fission was beginning to smile as the string became taut in her fingers and Medusa remained motionless in her sights.

Then something else came out of the circle, which wasn't white, and which suddenly filled Fission's sights.

She wasn't looking at a distracted Medusa any more; she was looking at the middle head of a three-headed dog that was not only distracted, but absolutely boiling-blood livid. The two heads on the outside took several double takes, looking around and up and down and trying to work out just what the hell had taken the place of the sheer sides of a bottomless pit past which it had been falling for ever in a state of some catatonia – possibly dogatonia – and of increasing hunger. The middle one stared straight at Fission, completely awake and spotting a ready-to-serve conclusion to its enforced fast.

Fission said 'Good heavens, where on Earth could that have come from, and what is it in any case?' in one word beginning with 'F', and the dog's middle head answered with a howl of rage which told her that the answers didn't matter a metatarsal. What mattered was that it was annoyed and hungry and it was going to satisfy itself on both counts, using her.

All three heads looked her in the eye, and the creature crouched, ready to spring.

From where they were standing, Paz and Medusa could not see the object of the dog's attention as its bulk blocked their view, but without realizing what it was, they sure as hell heard it as Fission jerked the string downwards with the gun barrel about two feet from the dog's leading head.

The atmosphere was abruptly rent by an explosion. Not a simple report, as with most guns, but a real 'this-is-my-one-chance-to-go-off-with-a-bang-and-I'm-going-to-make-the-most-of-it-see-if-I-don't' thundering great explosion, which made a normal report sound like a brief memo.

And she blew the dog away. Completely. All those chefs who toiled for hours making little cubes of meat or mincing the stuff would have saved a lot of time if they could have got their hands on that gun. The courtyard, and everything in it, was covered with messy little pink bits of dog, and where it had stood there was now absolutely nothing, not even Fission.

Which was just as well, as Medusa ripped off her sunglasses and glared at the spot where Fission had stood. All the Gorgon could see was a bush, still shaking apparently as a result of the gun's sound-wave emissions, but actually as a result of the fact that Fission had flown backwards with the recoil and passed through it, and was now lying just behind it. And two flowers, their discussion abruptly interrupted, staring with wide pupils at the newly decorated courtyard.

Paz immediately averted her eyes, with a muttered 'Oh my Zeus!' and by the time she risked a glance at her companion's feet, they weren't there any more.

Medusa was heading for the palace.

'Where are we going?' asked one of her snakes. She glanced upwards, but the magic of her hair prevented it going rigid.

'We are going to get the lamp,' she told it. 'Once and for all.' This pleased the snake and a number of its fellows.

'*Yessssss!!*' they commented. '*Yessssss!!*'

'Must you?' muttered Medusa, wiping her glasses on her sleeve and thrusting them back onto her face. She made her way inside.

'She's coming!' said Wilverton, watching the Medusan shoes in the grass, and Gloria squeezed the hand she was holding a little tighter.

'What shall we do?'

Arnold had been wearing a big dead Cerberus smile, his ecstasy diminished only by two things: one, that he hadn't performed the deed himself, and two, that it hadn't lasted longer. Three now, as Wilverton's words cut through his delight. 'Well, I don't know about you, but I'm leaving!' He made for the door.

'That's the door she'll come through, Arnold,' Carlton told him, and Arnold stopped. Very quickly.

'I think we probably *should* fall back and regroup, as they say.' Wilverton started pulling Gloria towards the door on the far side of the room, and the others followed.

Before they were half-way there the Gorgon strode into the room.

'You!' she cried, recognizing the fast-moving backs. It was difficult to tell whether she was addressing one or more of them, but the tone promised something less conducive to good health than a new virus, so they weren't about to find out.

Or were they.

The lamp was on the table past which Curtis, the last of the group, was hurrying. He glanced at it, carried on at increased pace on hearing the door opening behind him, and then stopped. He turned back, and, keeping his eyes firmly on his quest and not on the woman who closed on him – he didn't know if she had her glasses on or not, but under the circumstances it seemed best to assume 'not' – he snatched the prize.

It was a terribly brave thing to do, even more so than when he had uncurled in front of the dragon all those years before.

The Challenger regarded its opponent and wondered if the Champion had needed as much effort to make Curtis go back for the lamp as it had in materializing the white hole through which it had delivered Cerberus.

The Champion's mien gave it no clue as to the answer, calm as ever in a visible green emanation.

As it happened, the creation of an incredibly powerful astronomical phenomenon such as the white hole – plus the extra effort of keeping it larger than its normal subatomic size so that a large three-headed dog could fall through it – required almost exactly the same amount of energy as making Curtis do something which resulted in personal danger. So the tasks *would* have been about equal; except that the Champion had to make sure that Curtis didn't pitch forward full length and flip the lamp straight into Medusa's hands.

Now *that* took some doing.

Curtis turned back towards the safety of the far door, seeing Arnold just beating Gloria through it, then noticed that there was something in his hands. He looked down and saw what it was. Then he yelped; it couldn't be described any other way. It was the sort of noise a one-headed puppy would make if Cerberus barked at it.

Wilverton and Carlton spun round on hearing the noise, then lowered their eyes to the lamp in Curtis's hands, keeping their gaze there as a precaution against it creeping up to the still bespectacled face of the Gorgon.

Curtis flung the lamp away from him as though it was a rugby ball with a burning fuse sticking out of it, and it lobbed straight at Carlton, who caught it, and wished he hadn't.

'Give me the lamp,' came Medusa's voice.

'*Yessssss*,' agreed her hair in chorus.

No chance, thought Carlton, and allowed his glance to check where she was, seeing the high-heeled shoes and the bottom of the pin-striped trousers.

Then he remembered where he had seen them before – sticking out of an alcove half-way down the stairs – and his stomach turned over. God, he might have waited to see her reaction . . .

He lobbed the lamp to Wilverton, who caught it and would have thrown a vicious glance at Carlton but for the fact that this would have involved looking up.

'I only need it for my protection. I am being hunted by Perseus, and only the genie can save me. And I have done nothing! I am only a poor defenceless woman.'

The hell you are, thought Wilverton, and flipped the lamp back to Carlton.

'I mean, *look* at me,' Medusa invited in a voice so innocent it made Shirley Temple sound like Methuselah's grandmother.

Carlton had apparently finished taking his bit of wrapping off the explosive parcel, and it was Curtis's turn once more.

As he caught it, he felt a hand on his shoulder, so he yelped again, which hid the other noise he made at the same time, and immediately threw the lamp, with a convulsive jerk, in no direction at all.

There was a tinkling sound as of a window breaking. The hand left Curtis's shoulder, and Medusa crossed to the window, looking down on the courtyard below, where the lamp now lay. Over in one corner, the Cretin Bull still managed to ignore what was happening, and Paz cowered against its flank, looking scared and comforted at the same time. In another, Fission was standing rather shakily and looking at the mess around her.

'Fools!' Medusa cried to all and sundry, and her hair echoed the comment with a spray of sibilants. 'I will deal with you later!' She swept from the room, her glasses falling back into place once more.

'You can come out now,' Carlton told the door, which swung open to reveal Gloria and Arnold crouching and facing the other way. 'Thanks for your help, Arnold.'

Arnold looked as guiltily ashamed as a peacock.

*

Fission staggered out of her bush in time to see the lamp bouncing to a halt a few yards away from her, and stood rather shakily for a moment before heading towards it, picking her way through bits of dog. She retrieved it and rubbed it as though she had been offered a lot of money if she could produce a blister in seven seconds.

The genie appeared, tenderly feeling various bits of himself that were either bruised or suffering burns from Fission's challenge.

'I am your ser—'

'Shut up. Make another gun, quick. Make powerful.' The genie's eyebrows shot up at the rudeness of it all, but with the now traditional puff of smoke, he complied with her wishes. 'Good. You back in box.'

He complied with that as well, muttering, 'Well, really!' as he disappeared.

Fission carried the lamp and the gun behind the bush from which she had emerged a few moments before, and leaned her back against the wall, holding the weapon up to her eye and grasping the string firmly.

Medusa emerged onto the lawn.

Fission didn't wait too long; she wasn't going to risk another emission from the white circle which, in the pandemonium, no-one had noticed no longer hung in the sky above them. She took careful, but quick, aim, and pulled the string.

And the previous explosion had been nothing more than a burp.

The cloud of smoke which immediately enveloped her was every bit as impressive as the ones the genie had used in his manufacturing process, but the colour was all wrong. A thick black pall sprung from the chamber of the gun and leapt on just about everything around it. The only thing to escape was the projectile, and that was only because it was travelling at the speed specified by Wilverton.

Not, sadly, towards Medusa.

At just under a thousand miles per hour, a ball of hot, and very confused, metal headed for the windows behind which the rest of the group were timidly watching proceedings. It actually hit the brickwork between two of the windows, and did so with such venom that the masonry simply surrendered. If there were more like that to come, it just wasn't going to hang around and wait for them. It collapsed outwards into the courtyard, and, rather spitefully, took its two adjoining windows with it.

Behind those particular windows crouched Arnold and Gloria.

The former hit the ground so fast that a watching physicist would have been tempted to speculate that the only thing which could move quicker than the speed of light, without being reduced to tachyons, was a message of self-preservation from the android's brain.

The latter was completely rooted to the spot. Any messages which had been wandering around Gloria's brain, generally minding their own business except when they happened to bump into one another, were very rudely stopped in their tracks by the suddenness of the disappearing wall trick. Gloria stayed in her crouch and looked out over the courtyard through nothing but the fine clean air, into which the energetic young sun was still shining brightly, regardless.

A wounded Medusa would definitely have been an angry Medusa, but at least there would have been a certain plus to be derived from the 'wounded'. An angry and already frustrated Medusa who had been shot at, missed by at least ten yards and covered in minced dog gave no cause for even cautious optimism.

Fission had no time to contemplate this, as the recoil of the gun-shot smashed her hand into the wall behind her, moments before the smoke jumped all over her. Medusa looked to the area from which the shot had come, and saw a cloud of smoke. Nothing else. Her peculiar powers had little effect on smoke clouds – fortunately for Fission, for whom a cloud of stone would have spelt bad news – and, the lamp momentarily forgotten, she turned her attention briefly to the second sound which still echoed in her brain: that of falling palace bits.

The result of which was a big hole in the side of the building, and a very frightened and guilty-looking Gloria staring down at her. Medusa's hand reached up to her glasses and began to remove them.

Gloria could not take her eyes off the scene before her, and it was only now that Arnold glanced up from where he had thrown himself. At the same time Wilverton and Carlton shifted at the next set of windows. Medusa's eyes were almost visible.

Curtis was still buried as deeply into the floor as he could get when he heard Arnold whisper frantically, 'Get down, you stupid human!'

Gloria ignored him, completely transfixed by the fatal attraction of the scene before her.

'Gloria!' shouted Wilverton.

The sun still shone, alone, unaware that the scene being played out beneath it called for rolling clouds and bolts of lightning.

And the deadly eyes were bared; the Look flashed up towards Gloria, and Gloria looked back.

Suddenly the sun was blotted out by a large shadow of a cloud, and the Look found itself meeting the shiny surface of a mirror which hung in the air a few feet in front of Gloria's face. Two little wings stuck out on either side and flapped frantically to keep it hovering in the right place.

This is something that mirrors, as a rule, are very shy about doing.

On her side, Gloria looked at the mirror and saw the face of Yazocks the Harmless Changeling, which winked at her and licked his lips.

On the other side, Medusa saw in the mirror not a cloud, which she had assumed was creating the shadow, but a dragon, circling overhead and regarding her with clear thoughts of dinner passing through its mind.

Medusa snapped her head upwards to stare directly at the dragon, not in a particular effort to harm it, but more at the unlikely sight itself – Medusa did not believe in dragons, they were something out of mythology; and if they *did* exist then they were certainly too big to fly. But if the motivation for Medusa's movement was fairly moot, the result was not; at least, not after the dragon met her gaze.

The gold of the wings and the sheen of the body faded to a dull grey and stiffened in a second, so that the once glorious creature hung momentarily in the air like a fantastic sculpture.

But if flesh-and-blood dragons should not be able to fly, then stone dragons certainly should not. And this one couldn't.

It fell like a stone, and a bloody great big one.

The danger was first spotted by the snakes, sharp-minded creatures as they were, and several of them stood on end, eyes staring and tongues going in and out like a rabbit who's turned up late for the orgy. Then they started wriggling, and a few of

243

them managed to pull themselves out and started slithering to Medusa's shoulders and throwing themselves off. But she didn't realize that her hair was not only falling, but actually leaping, out, as she looked, transfixed like Gloria before her, at her doom.

Straight down it fell, the gliding capabilities of its outstretched stone wings about the same as that of a cannonball.

Straight down on top of a wide-eyed Medusa it fell, with a squeal and a crunch and a squelch. In that order.

All was quiet for a while, except for the sound of munching which came from one shady corner of the courtyard, where the Bull stood roughly three feet away from a sculpted dragon's wing and ignored it completely.

XXX

'We've done it!' Carlton looked out on the courtyard at a large stone dragon, from under which stuck a Medusan foot. There was a certain amount of gooey evidence, which need not be explored, showing that the foot had taken its last step. While it might have been pristine, the bits above it were in pretty bad shape. 'We've actually gone and done it!' He grinned widely, and impulsively took Wilverton's hand and shook it warmly. The grin was returned.

'Yes, I think we have, one way or another. And all in one piece. Heaven alone knows how.'

'It was Yazocks,' said Gloria, her brain patterns now restored to their normal sluggish movement and her eyes searching for the Changeling. 'That thing was going to turn me to stone and Yazocks got in the way and saved my life. I think he's wonderful.'

'He did?' asked Carlton, who had been watching the floorboards with some concentration since Fission's pyrotechnic effort had induced the thought that such study might be the only way to stay pink and fleshy.

'Yes. He turned himself into a flying mirror. One side was mirror and the other was his face smiling at me.' And winking, but that didn't need to be said out loud in case it brought back memories to the others. She didn't realize that they were all re-running those memories anyway.

'Sounds like he *was* the one who led us to that lamp then,' said Wilverton. 'You were right again, Gloria.'

Paz's entrance put a premature end to the congratulations. She regarded the excessive ventilation in her throne room, and rubbed the lamp which she had brought in with her.

'Mistress?'

'Clear that lot up, will you, dear?' she asked, seemingly unconcerned by the damage. The genie waved his arm, and the room was restored to its former state.

'You know she never did have the Belt of Hippolyte with her,' Paz told them, looking round her clean throne room. 'You were right all along.'

Fission cut short any possible mutual appreciation club meeting by arriving covered from head to foot in soot, the whites of her eyes flashing warningly in her darkened face. The genie had been safely ensconced in his lamp while all the action took place, and was unaware that he was the subject of Fission's regard until he looked up. Even then, the cause of her evident emotion was not known to him.

'Did my effort please you?' he asked, feeling that the situation called for some words. It probably did, but, on reflection, not those.

'Idea of gun,' answered Fission, very quietly but with the intensity of a laser, 'it fires in direction it points, damages first obstacle that direction. Person holding gun gets off lightly. Gun not damage everything around at complete random. Your "effort" was fonking bomb, you mincing moron!' Some of Arnold was rubbing off – she was definitely improving.

'You were not *entirely* satisfied, then?'

Fission took a step towards him. The genie disappeared. Fission took the lamp from Paz's unresisting hand and drop kicked it against the far wall. A muffled cry emerged, and Fission smiled grimly.

'Yazocks!' cried Gloria, as the little Changeling appeared in front of her, wearing his human guise for the occasion. She stepped forward and picked him up in her arms, crushing him against her bosom for a brief moment before loosing her grip slightly so that she could look into his beaming face. 'You're not so bad after all,' she said, and kissed him on the forehead. 'And you're ever so brave.'

'For you, anything,' he replied, and earned himself another kiss. They looked at each other for a moment before he continued. 'You know that a look from Medusa can turn you to stone?' Gloria nodded, and looked just a touch worried. 'Well, I think it's started.' He winked, and Gloria put him down hurriedly.

'Ship!' called Wilverton, hardly at all jealous of the attention being bestowed on Yazocks. The Ship hung over the courtyard, the lift of light descending on to the grass outside the windows.

*

Biondor's arrival almost coincided with their own, and the Ship had barely congratulated them in ever such pleasant tones before the elegant alien did the same thing.

'Congratulations are again in order, humans. You have completed your tasks within the allotted time. You may continue to the next stage of the Game.' Biondor sounded just a bit surprised.

'Thank you, Biondor,' said Fission. Politely. Must have got a knock on the head, thought more than one of her colleagues.

'So the trands have made it as well?' asked Wilverton.

'Indeed, although they have lost one of their number in completing the tasks.' He paused momentarily, in thought. 'The trands have a direct and rather violent approach to most things. As they passed through the various stages of this round, they left nothing behind which could help them in future tasks. They were forced to tackle their own version of the Gorgon unaided. Should the Game end in a tie, you would win on count-back, as it were. Not that it ever *has* ended in a tie.'

'And is the next round the last one?' asked Wilverton.

'It can be, but is not designed so to be. And before you ask, I cannot tell you anything about it at this time, except to say that it takes place on the planet Earth.'

'Earth!?' they all shouted, except Arnold, whose fondness for the planet was tempered by the fact that it had five billion humans on it. On the whole he would have settled for the planet Sewer, but wasn't given the chance to point this out.

'Earth,' confirmed Biondor.

'We're going home!'

Arnold was again in a minority of one.

'Indeed. Not, unfortunately, *your* home. This is Earth Five Zero.'

'Five Zero?' queried Fission.

'Five Zero, yes. It is a version of Earth which differs from your own in fifty pivotal respects.'

'Vers—' began Carlton.

'Version, yes,' Biondor confirmed against all incredulity. 'It is a parallel Universe, and –'

'Quant—' said Wilverton.

'Parallel, yes.' Biondor began to sound irritated, then realized that it wasn't what Wilverton had said. 'Sorry, go on,' he said in his powerful alieny sort of way.

'Quantum mechanics. Any possible sequence of events will produce its own individual future and therefore its own possible Universe, and all of them exist at the same time. Is that what you mean? Is it proof of the quantum theory?'

Biondor nodded. 'It is, Thomas. An almost infinite number of Universes exist, at various probability levels.' They all looked impressed, except Gloria. This might, of course, have been because she had always held the quantum theory to be easily defensible and a matter of accepted fact for right-thinking theorists. It might not, of course.

Even Fission looked excited, and Wilverton noticed.

'We haven't proved quantum theory even in your time, then?'

'No,' she answered simply, just like a regular chap. 'Fascinating.'

And this confirmation that Fission had rather more depth than just a collection of obscenities and arguments made quantum theory look like the two times table. Only Gloria didn't look surprised by Fission's interest.

'You will have a chance to rest as you are taken there,' said Biondor, bringing them back to the matter in hand. 'I will speak to you again on your arrival to tell you more. But before I go you again have a chance to change one of your team members, and there are no restrictions on who it should be.

'Is it your wish that one of you be replaced?'

Eyes started darting around the room, and Curtis immediately felt them all alight on him. He could just imagine the vote. He couldn't bear it. He was the Captain after all.

'No!' he said, before anyone had had the chance to think, let alone speak. 'We're happy with the team we've got!'

'Very well.'

'Hey, wait minute!' came Fission's voice, but Biondor's raised hand silenced her in a moment.

'Your team leader has spoken, and the decision cannot be altered. The trands, incidentally, chose to replace their dead team member with one who was rather more alive.

'Now, I have to perform an immaculate conception with a virgin of the planet Wrania.' He looked happier. 'It's one of my favourites. I will see you again when you are in orbit around Earth Five Zero.' And he disappeared.

They glared at Curtis, not giving away what they might have done had he given them the chance. But he didn't care. Biondor had called him the team leader. He would never wash his ears again.

'Well, Ship,' he said. 'Let's go.' There! A bold decision, now that he was confirmed as the Captain. He'd show them!

'No,' said the Ship. Curtis's shoulders fell a little. 'I do not mean to disobey your commands, Richard' – although why the Ship should be any different from anything and everyone else, no-one knew – 'but it is not I who will take you to the Earth. If you look through the port, you will find your new craft.'

They all moved to the main port, and there, in space, was a small, lumpy, angular sort of thing, with but a few smooth surfaces here and there. It bore no relationship to the Ship, as far as they could tell.

'It is not quite as advanced a craft as myself, if you will pardon the conceit. It will simply take you to your next port of call.'

Wilverton looked at the new ship, and frowned. *The Galaxy* it was called. That was wrong, surely. Shouldn't it be called *Pioneer III*, or shouldn't the Ship have been able to reproduce, so that it could have been the *Son of Pioneer II*? *The Galaxy* wasn't a sequel.

He thought a bit, and looked worried a bit, and Gloria asked him why. He looked at her, while all the others watched and waited for his answer.

'This.' And he indicated the cosmos with a brief wave of his hand. 'It might not be a book, after all.' The second time he had thought so. 'It might be real.'

The Champion could not help a brief flash of satisfied radio waves. The renegade notion of fiction had cocooned its Player through the first two rounds of the Game, but in the third the Champion needed him at his sharpest, and the thought that he couldn't lose was a dangerous one.

'I don't know, though,' Wilverton went on. 'There are some pretty weird books around . . .'

Radio became micro. It would not be so easy to dissipate the idea in the Player's mind if the Challenger was disputing; its opponent was the best it had faced in seven eons, not that it was about to admit it. And if the Player clung onto the induced notion of fiction, then there was trouble, because after the Champion had set the tasks in this round, it was the Challenger's turn next.

Perhaps seven eons was enough as Supreme Being . . .

The Challenger warmed itself with an emanation of infrared. The Player's belief was shaken, but it was still there. When he relied on it in the next round – and he would – then it would cause the belief to shatter.

The humans would fail, and the Champion would fall, and the Champion knew it! Old fart!

But that was the next round.

The Challenger left the vicinity of Callia in a long, extravagant burst of gamma radiation.

There was a brief pause while they considered Wilverton's deep comment on life, then Carlton decided they ought to get back on their celebratory track.

'Well, I reckon we're going to do all right in the Game. We've pulled this one off through teamwork.'

'Teamwork!' Fission's was the first voice raised in disagreement. 'On my own I finish this fonking sight sooner. Charging after melons . . .'

'Don't call her melons!' said Wilverton.

'Now come on . . .' started Curtis.

'You butt out of it.'

'I was only trying to help.'

'That'd be a first!' muttered Carlton.

'What?'

'I said . . .'

'Oh, do *stop* it, all of you . . .'

Arnold sat back and watched, with a vastly superior smile. Teamwork.